The Von

CW01657815

Valerie Rosenberg

The Von Veltheim File

Human & Rousseau
Cape Town Pretoria Johannesburg

For Gerald who gave me twenty-three years of space so that this book might be.

DRAMATIS PERSONAE

THE PROFESSIONALS

Franz von Veltheim – soldier of fortune and expert in coups d'état.
Charles Brown – his aide.

THE BOERS WHOSE LAND WAS SOWN WITH GOLD

Paul Kruger – President of the Boer Republic.
Tjaart Kruger – his son and Commandant in the Boer Secret Service.
Commandant-General Piet Joubert – President Kruger's election rival.
Hendrina Joubert – his wife and comrade in arms.
Jan Smuts – von Veltheim's original legal advisor, later State Attorney.

THE COUP BROKERS WHO CONSPIRED TO STEAL IT

Alfred Beit – German Anglophile mining magnate.
Oscar Beit – Beit's younger brother.
Barney Barnato – Whitechapel barrow boy turned Rand mining millionaire.
Woolf Joel – Barnato's nephew and anticoup negotiator.
Solly Joel – Woolf's younger brother excluded from the conspiracy.

THE WARMONGERS WHO STOPPED THEM

The banker to the bankers.
Erich Wernher – his reluctant recruit and Alfred Beit's partner.
Karl Braun – his agent. And double agent.

VON VELTHEIM'S WOMEN

Molly von Veltheim – his common-law wife.
Anne-Marie Mavrogordato – his beloved but bigamous wife.
Elise Caldecott – his ill-fated Johannesburg courier and casual paramour.

THE JOHANNESBURGERS

Harry Caldecott – Elise's father and Director of Barnatos'.
Harold Strange – Barnatos' company secretary and Woolf Joel's assassin.
Francis McDermott – deputy editor of the *Johannesburg Times.*
Alphonse Baruch – Barnato's stockbroker friend. And Kruger's.

THE LAW ENFORCERS

Robert Ferguson – Chief Detective of Johannesburg.
Von Harnach – arresting ZARP officer and ballistics expert.
Van Dyk – ZARP detective.
Coenraad Juta – Kruger's Secret Service undercover agent.

THE LEGAL ARENA

Landdrost van den Berg – presiding at the Johannesburg Landdrost's court.
Judge Morice – presiding at the Johannesburg Circuit Court trial.
Fritz Krause – Public Prosecutor at both.
De Villiers – his assistant.
Hal Smithers – von Veltheim's attorney.
Ex-State Attorney Herman Coster – von Veltheim's defence council.

AUTHOR'S NOTE

In 1896 when England's mining magnates failed to snatch the gold-rich Boer Republic for her, rather than go to war for it, they contracted Franz von Veltheim, professional in coups d'état.

Europe's arms dealers, enriched by a century of wars supplying opposing sides, needed to stop him. This is their story.

The conspiracy to abduct President Paul Kruger was real. The counterconspiracy that aborted it is the author's educated guess and the odd name has been modified accordingly.

For history you need a camera with two lenses – the telephoto and the kind of close-up with a fine, penetrating focus. You can forget the wide-angle lens: there is no angle wide enough.

We historical novelists have to be as interested in what might have happened as what did.

JOHN IRVING

THE PRIZE

FORT SANTA MARTA COLOMBIA – DECEMBER 1895

The temperature dropped just before the false dawn. Flat on his belly, a man inched through the dew-frosted grass to the bridge. He lay in its shadow, scanning the far bank, the freckled gunpowder scar around his right eye twitching. He could not make it stop.

At first he couldn't place the sensation. The Bulgarian winter campaign ten years before? He shivered at the memory of shrapnel ripping open his thigh. It was back – the marrow-chilling cold and the hot scalding pain. The smell of cordite and the slow seep of blood staining the snow a watery pink. He'd torn away the fabric of his breeches and stared in disbelief at the mess of blood, gristle and meat. The sickening proof that he was mortal. And when he'd turned his head sideways to retch he could see the town of Pirot burning through the sleet.

Fear? *Me*? He knew it returned to haunt other men. He'd heard them talk of it afterwards in the military hospital at Bucharest. Battle-weary soldiers invalided out.

Now in the chill dawn of another continent ten years later, forehead filming with sweat as he clenched his sphincter muscle, he suddenly knew that all those jokes weren't jokes at all. He wanted to soil himself. Vomit . . . Run . . . But most of all he wanted not to be laying the charges on the bridge across the Sierra Santa Marta gorge.

His comrade signalled in the distance. 'All right?'

But even as he managed a thumbs-up sign, the coppery taste of fear in his throat welled up from his gut like oil from a fault in the earth. And now there was a hollow chill in the sudden great void where his confidence used to be. Please God, only once more after this?

His fingers were stiffening; and he needed to control the gunpowder trickle between the sticks of dynamite he'd secured to the bridge. But his treacherous heart leapt like a frightened bird in his ribcage; and his disciplined mind had to rally the soldier in him trained to respond to commands.

Easy now, soldier.

Soldier's hands clenching and flexing.

Who's that?

Soldier freezing, alarm flooding his viscera.

The scrutiny of fierce watchful eyes.

Soldier feeling for the two emergency stick bombs attached to his belt.

Then, a parrot's strident squawk as it tosses its crested head.

Relief. Now a deep sawing breath to choke down the panic.

Now forcing himself to place one foot in front of the other, deliberately.

Creeping on, finishing the trail as he goes.

Touching a match to the powder trail.

Trail sputtering and fizzing.

Muffled footsteps? Closer. Sentry sauntering down the bank.

Soldier shrinking back into the fretwork shadow. Please, God ... not now. Fingers curling again around the stick bombs and listening to the sentry whistling as he urinates.

Sentry unhurriedly rebuttoning his fly. Looking around.

Soldier realising he's only a youth . . . wide-eyed, the whistle dying on lips that open to ...

Soldier choking down his revulsion, quickly doing what he has to do, and trying not to look too much.

Kepow! The explosion that cut off the cry sent the rag doll corpse cartwheeling as the bridge contorted, slewed sideways and clung drunkenly to the bank.

Only now the soldier felt as if his own insides were as shattered as the sentry's, as if they'd shared a common system like Siamese twins. Sick, he stared at the bridge, wishing he could make it unhappen. 'Die, damn you,' he commanded it through grated teeth.

Kee-pow! Obediently, the mutilated superstructure disintegrated in an avalanche of shattering timber, and crashed into the water below.

The report of Charlie's Webley shooting the lock off the arsenal door was a single thunderclap, and he hurled his device inside.

KEE-PO-OW! This time ten pounds of incendiary and cordite detonated in a deafening roar. The whole sky was alive with showering sparks, fragments of fort, and the raucous chorus of birds that squawked and flapped in its wake.

Together the two comrades crashed through the wild-banana fronds and pelted down the river bank to fling themselves flat. Minutes later, they were on their bellies, loosening their rowing boat from its moorings.

They waited, counting their pulse beats and breathing the mix of dank river smells and their sweat.

The sun's rind inched over the horizon.

Waiting.

A flight of heron rose in a hosanna.

Waiting.

Then, like an army of ants on cue, the new regime's advance guard crept out of the morning mist to occupy Fort Santa Marta at a running crouch.

Charlie saw the relief wash the face with the speckled scar. It had always reminded him of a swashbuckling buccaneer, but now he noted for the first time that the eyes were bruised and battle-weary. He lit his chief a cheroot. 'Lad couldn't be helped,' he said quietly.

Gratefully, the soldier drew the smoke into his lungs with a shuddery breath. 'Fortunes of war,' he agreed. But he didn't *feel* philosophical. He felt haunted by a beardless face, its mouth opened in an unfinished cry.

He thrust the image away and gripped Charlie's shoulder. Sandy-haired, speckle-eyed Charlie, the wildcat whose fingers could move with the delicacy of a lover's touch on the explosives he fashioned. But he also had something else. So the soldier poured two schnapps from his half-jack to toast the talent that gave his own vision practicality.

Charlie's face split in a grin. 'Viva the new Republic?'

'Rather the next one. Different country, longer odds . . . And my last.'

Charlie leaned closer, his light eyes narrowing to gun slits as they did in laughter or thought. 'It's that good, Count?'

Count Franz von Veltheim – alias the baron, alias Kurt, Kurtze, and a string of other names – sighed and grinned crookedly. 'Problem is, others want it, too.'

And he allowed his mind to respond yet again to the secret pull of that other country across the unquiet sea.

Halfway round the world in that same summer two mounted columns snaked across the wide empty Highveld, making purposefully for the Witwatersrand gold reef.

Not yet 8 o'clock, but in the midsummer heat Colonel Raleigh Grey could feel his uniform collar saw his sunburned neck like a rasp. The consummate British career officer, he wore that uniform immaculate, his boots brightly boned and his greying moustache waxed. But the lighter grooves that criss-crossed the tanned skin around his eyes looked as though they had been etched by years in the veld.

New Year's Day. God willing, we'll be in Johannesburg before the chimes die away, he thought hopefully. His British Bechuanaland Border Police had covered the hundred and fifty miles between the border in three days, but he had a premonition that God wasn't exactly willing.

He eyed Dr Jameson's Rhodesian column. The Cape Premier, Cecil Rhodes, had seconded the BBP to reinforce them; and in the chain of command he answered to Jameson, who answered to the mining magnates, who answered to God.

He glanced at Jameson - Administrator of Rhodesia. Interesting to watch you lead your rank and file, Dr Jim. All those fresh-faced titled guardsmen in their first khaki drills, virginal white puggarees around their felt smashers.

The BBP's legendary blue and white guinea-fowl speckled puggarees had been blooded in scores of border campaigns. His men looked what they were. Battle-hardened and sun-baked, fired in the kiln of bush war.

Together they numbered just under six hundred, all kitted out with new Lee-Metford magazine loaders and modern field artillery.

He watched Jameson canter up – perilously tilted panama half obscuring his cheery face, white dust coat flapping like the wings of a startled bird. 'I say . . . Good start to the New Year, what?' he panted.

'Stealing a country doesn't bother you, Dr Jim?' Grey enquired, straight-faced.

Jameson's eyebrow shot up in reproach. 'Rescuing, old chap,' he corrected him. '*Rescuing* Johannesburg's women and children from the oppressive Boer regime.'

'Hadn't thought of it that way,' Grey said truthfully. 'Silly of the Boers to fancy this's about gold.'

'Those ruffians?' A derisive snort. 'Ever seen what they use for an army?'

Grey thought of some of those bands of farmer-soldiers he'd encountered, and twisted in his saddle. Since last night he'd had this eerie feeling of being shadowed. Ghostly Boer commandos kept disappearing before they could engage them.

Near the western horn of the Witwatersrand the veld rolled away from a vlei rising in great ramparts like an ancient Greek amphitheatre. They reined in and Jameson squinted at his map. 'Old Queen Mining Company, it says.'

'Mention those ore-crushing tailings and earthworks?' Grey wanted to know.

Frowning, Jameson trained his binoculars on the old prospectors' cuttings. He blanched. 'Natural rifle pits, d'ye think?'

'A day's work. Probably with a couple of Boers apiece.' As Grey also traversed his binoculars along the ridge the skin over his cheekbones tightened. Abruptly he spun his colt and danced it back along the column to his field artillery and barked, 'Get those pom-poms out in front of that vlei!'

The fine red dust rose in billows, the column splaying open as eight two-man mounted crews trundled their automatic machine guns forward on chest-high wheels, and fanned out. Twenty paces to their rear the heavy-gun detachments advanced on horseback, trailing three Vickers Maxims, alternate guns wheeling left and right. They leapt from their mounts and, tossing their reins to their black grooms, broke up into five-man crews.

A horse suddenly whinnied and reared, eyes rolling and forelegs pawing the air in terror. All at once, the veld was swarming with nervous grooms struggling to hold whickering horses and grey-faced gun crews shoving artillery pieces. And above the cacophony Grey heard one of Jameson's pink-cheeked new arrivals sob, 'Oh, Nana!'

'Pom-poms aim!' he roared, 'Ready? Load one!'

Cartridge belts clicked.

No movement from the mine.

'Fire!'

Handles cranked, and they bit. The first fusillade blasted in repeated unnerving barks, spewing bullets in a solid jet, sounding like a row of Chinese firecrackers on Guy Fawkes night. Then all the pom-poms were shuddering and jerking and ripping and roaring, methodically sweeping back and forth until the whole amphitheatre rang with their mad cackle and bray.

One of the muzzles glowed orange like a demon blacksmith's forge, the steam from its coolant shrilling to a piercing squeal as it boiled, and then jammed.

'Cease fire!' Grey bellowed.

The instant hush seemed unearthly. The mine was as silent as the pyramids of Giza.

'You don't see them, but they're *there*,' Grey muttered uneasily. 'Like lion lying in wait.'

'Sweet Jesus,' Jameson whispered hoarsely.

Grey's eyes narrowed as he squinted at the mine's battery shed standing like a sentinel against the sky. He pirouetted his mount and cantered back to the twelve-pounders. 'See that misbegotten matchstick tower up on that ridge?' he bellowed. 'We're going to blast it to hell . . . so aim!'

The barrels swung and trained on the battery shed.

'Ready? Load one.'

Clank. Clickety. Clank.

'*Fire!*'

The guns roared, and across the vlei a sickly green cloud of lyddite and shrapnel and dust mushroomed as fragments of rock shattered and powdered the air. The heliograph winked back, signalling the range correction, and the layers adjusted the elevation.

The barrels shifted, and the muzzles gleamed dully in the noonday sun.

'Ready. Load two!'

Clank. Clickety. Clank.

'*Fire!*'

POW! The guns roared again. Grey's nostrils filled with the smell of cordite as the red and green mix of cloud grew denser, and the battery disintegrated in a shower of falling bricks.

All at once, from the mine, behind cuttings, between boulders, and beneath bits of overhang, a deadly protractor detonated. Right along the ridge a hundred-and-eighty degree arc of over three hundred rifles made an odd popping sound in the distance. But their murderous hail of bullets potted the British gun crews like clay pigeons before they could dive for cover. And along the pickets, startled troopers dropped as though they'd been scythed.

'Take cover!' Grey yelled. Hurtling out of his saddle in a flying tackle, he flung Jameson off his horse just as a sniper's bullet whistled past his cheek and exploded. It sent up a feather of chipped stone and dust from the spot where they'd stood. 'My God, what marksmen,' he whispered.

'Can't pin us down here.' Jameson's voice was ragged. 'Johannesburg's within reach.'

'Fraid not, Dr Jim.' Grey's eyes were riveted to the ramparts where the Boer sharpshooters lay under cover. 'Think your mining magnates need another way,' he croaked.

'Nou skiet julle!' Big Leendert Roux roared at his men stationed along the perimeter of the old Queen Mine. Down across the vlei he could see the English gun detachments disintegrate and the pickets blown away.

Two nights in the saddle had made him weary but at the gut tingle of battle the fatigue evaporated like morning mist in the sun. Big Leendert was Acting Commandant of the Lichtenberg district. It had taken him ten minutes after he'd heard about the English, Martini-Henry strapped to his saddle and bandolier over his barrel chest, to roar out of his yard.

All night he'd flogged his pony from farm to farm, mustering all able-bodied men whose land lay in his path. The first night he'd estimated there were more than a hundred – sometimes three generations from one family – thundering over the veld to cut Jameson off from Johannesburg.

Now there must be three hundred in a hundred-and-eighty degree arc along the ridge. Like himself, they lay, bellies hugging the ground, an assortment of hats pulled down over their faces, most of them bearded, and every one fierce-eyed. A ragtag lot of hunter-farmers, shod in home-cured velskoens, bandoliers slung over homespun shirts. And like himself, they could, with their old *voorlaaiers* and Martini-Henrys, bring down a man in one shot.

The *rooineks'* twelve-pounders roared again, blasting the wrecked battery from the ridge. Big Leendert flattened, disappearing in grass that one wouldn't have thought could hide a hare.

'*Goed.*' He nudged his fiery young veldkornet. 'Shrapnel fans out flat. Fired low, it sends up useless spurts of gravel. Higher . . .'

In reply, Grobbelaar gleefully sawed the air above their heads.

'So, what's the matter with you, man? Lie still.'

The sun hung not two Cape feet above the blue gums in the west, and the big guns had lapsed into a sullen silence when Big Leendert saw movement in the vlei. '*Allemagtig*! Are they *mad*?'

A bugle sang, sounding the advance, and the English pickets emerged from cover, formed up as though on a drill ground, and advanced with bayonets fixed.

Siting carefully down his muzzle onto the head of the first man to splash into the vlei, Big Leendert squeezed the trigger, and his Martini-Henry blasted. The trooper flung up his arms, pitching backwards, and a scarlet stain bloomed like a red poppy on his white puggaree. As he fell, his smasher tumbled off, and his blond hair shone gold in the setting sun.

Big Leendert caught his breath. 'Dear Lord, is it over some accursed yellow dust that we now kill children?' he whispered. But he aimed, squeezed again, and felt the recoil bite his shoulder. Another youth convulsed and, hugging himself with both arms as if to keep out the cold, toppled into the muddy water.

Right along the ridge Boer rifles whammed and boomed, and blasted and hawked, mowing the khakis down like teff. Still on they came, perhaps four hundred strong, singing some foolish song about God saving their gracious queen. Line upon line of them, they splashed through the vlei, calling to each other in their fashion to hold the line. And every one white-faced and trying not to show his fear.

Grimly, Big Leendert's men shot, emptying saddle after saddle. And everywhere horses bucked and plunged, and staggered and sprawled, and pitched their riders into the vlei.

Through his binoculars Big Leendert watched a trooper, crouched behind his dead horse and using his rump for cover, sight his Lee-Metford straight at Big Leendert's heart. The khaki's face was a chalk-white blob as he blasted away doggedly, fruitlessly chipping the rampart above Big Leendert's head. For a long time Big Leendert held his Martini-Henry aimed at the trooper's breast, but something stayed his hand.

Grobbelaar also could have shot him, but he slowly lowered his gun. 'They're all so young, Oom Leendert.'

'Too young and far from home to die so foolishly,' Big Leendert said shortly. He turned and bellowed over his shoulder, 'Hold your fire!'

The rampart grew quiet and Grobbelaar looked at him uncertainly.

'*Ja*, well, do we not all have sons?' he demanded hotly.

The sun was dipping below the horizon when the little English bugler sounded the retreat. Some *rooineks* in the vlei turned and galloped back, whilst others crawled away into the reeds, leaving their casualties littering the banks like laundry. It seemed to Big Leendert that a quarter of their number failed to return.

He buried his face in his great hairy farmer's hands. How many breech-birth calves have these killing hands delivered? When he looked up, he saw that Grobbelaar was watching him curiously.

'Would you take a truce flag down across the vlei so that they might fetch their dead?' Big Leendert asked gruffly. 'Their wounded may go under a white flag to Krugersdorp Hospital. See also if there's anything they need.'

Watching him go, Big Leendert fished in his pocket for his meerschaum pipe, and thoughtfully filled it. The Maxims had been harmless where his men lay today. But tomorrow he must drive the *donders* into an ambush and capture them fast. Lying on his belly, bloodshot eyes roving the vlei, he tamped down the tobacco with a toil-calloused thumb and lit up. It helped him to plan.

In his mind's eye he could see Farmer Brink's farm at Luipaardsvlei with great stretches of *ouklip* strewn in a horseshoe formation and with a tempting short cut to Johannesburg through the gap. A handful of sharpshooters posted at Doornkop kopje, and all he needed was a guide to lure the khakis there. Glancing over his shoulder, he could see beards of a dozen different shades. Better a youngster.

'Fixed up, Oom Leendert.' Grobbelaar dropped into a crouch beside him. 'Come.' He gripped Big Leendert's shoulder. 'You can do no more here.'

'*Luister*, man. The Lord and the land are on our side, not so?'

'Let us give thanks, although I've sometimes wondered since He sent the gold.'

'And are our commandos not good fighters?'

'The finest since Hannibal. An English journalist said it.'

'I don't know who is Hannibal, but where else can marksmen feed their families on springbok for four days on one bullet?'

'Come, Oom Leendert. You need rest.'

'I need an end to this waste. I also need a young *seuntjie* like that one.' He indicated with his pipe. 'One who knows English.'

The clear-complexioned lad with penetrating blue eyes thought that he was being summoned. He came at a running crouch and squatted in the grass. 'You wanted me, Oom? I mean, Commandant?'

'Oom will do. Do you know English?'

'*Ja*, Oom. My grandfather has a governess teach us in his Pretoria house.'

'His Pretoria house, *nogal*?'

'I was there on an errand for him when the commandos rode out. I'll go straight home to Wakkerstroom from here.'

'Your grandfather has a Pretoria house and farms in Wakkerstroom? Are you then Piet Joubert's grandson?'

The boy nodded uncomfortably.

'Hmmph. And how would our Commandant-General feel if I asked you to guide the English to Doornkop kopje tomorrow?'

'Happy I could be of use, Oom, I thi-ink.'

'*Goed*.' Big Leendert nodded. 'When you see him, greet him for me and tell him I voted for him last election.'

Grobbelaar stood watching the boy disappear into the dusk. 'You *really* voted for Joubert?'

'I voted for peace. Old Oom Paul's stubborn about dealing with the mining men's grievances, and Joubert knows how to talk with the English.'

'Paul Kruger says there's only one way to do that.' Grobbelaar patted his Martini-Henry. 'To the death.'

'I pray not. Because Jameson's just united the country behind Kruger, and Joubert'll never make President now.' Big Leendert knocked out his pipe. 'Only God can change that.'

'Or the devil,' Grobbelaar said softly.

1

EN ROUTE TO LONDON

Franz von Veltheim stacked the last of the £100 notes in the false bottom of his Gladstone. The Santa Marta coup in Colombia had been good to him, but being on a London-bound steamer again was better. Only this time the price had been the frosting in his dark hair and moustache, and those new lines that were making him a tad too distinguished for thirty-nine. And lately when he woke at two-thirty in the morning he thought about the bridge.

He was an uncommonly tall man with a world-weary air and a lumberjack's shoulders beneath the drape of his Jermyn Street suit. But sailors recognised the steadiness of hand and foot and claimed him for their own, as did soldiers for the plumb marksman's gaze. Then, of course, there was the casual indolence to his fighter's frame that caused some men to underestimate him, and the disarmingly boyish smile that confused men and women alike.

At the sound of the dinner gong von Veltheim locked his cabin and took the stairs to the dining saloon. Molly was already seated on the captain's right, laughing uproariously at something he'd said. It was an infectious laugh and he paused to study his common-law wife.

She was in her late twenties, but her corn-coloured hair set off her gilded décolletage even better than it had in Perth ten years ago. He knew that it made other men curious as to where it stopped. But he also knew how those aquamarine eyes that crinkled at the captain's jokes could narrow when she was scheming to manipulate him. And how those smiling lips could set when she failed.

Of late, between her incessant demands and his insatiable wanderlust their communication had been eroded to a series of exchanges that seemed to go, 'Why can't we?' or 'Why don't you? Why? . . . Why? . . . Why? . . .' Accusation and disillusionment.

Recrimination and despair. Now at last when they reached London he could afford to settle her in some seaside resort: he just didn't relish telling her.

'In the nick of time, Franz!' she called, laughing. 'We need a referee!' But his inner ear was attuned to her inner voice and it wouldn't have surprised him if she was saying to herself: Franz von Veltheim – explorer, sailor, mercenary and *bon vivant,* all your life. All that height doesn't hurt. That powder burn makes men comfortable, and women prefer a face with a past. Planning on leaving me, Franz? We'll see.

'Ah, Count . . .' Captain da Silva pulled out the chair on his left with a cordial smile. 'Perspective at last.'

'I surely hope so.' Courtney, the light-haired New Orleans industrialist, shifted his prosperous bulk in his chair. 'My first trip to England in two years, and if she's not at war before we reach Liverpool, my name's not Orville Courtney.'

Von Veltheim shot da Silva an enquiring look.

He held up the telegraph operator's note. 'It seems a Rhodesian column's just led a failed coup on the Boer Republic.'

Von Veltheim had discussed the Boers' Witwatersrand gold fields – treasure chest of the southern hemisphere – in low tones around campfires for almost ten years, and he could feel his heart quicken. 'Does it say who led them?' he asked casually.

'The Rhodesian Administrator,' Courtney grunted. 'Why, even as we speak, sir, the Boers must be asking their kinfolk in the Orange Free State for help.'

'Against *England*?'

'Sure as Trinity and twice as fast. Might as well go right on home and start splitting rails.'

Von Veltheim raised an eyebrow in a show of bewilderment. 'You did say "failed", Captain?'

'Failure doesn't count if he's a front for Cecil Rhodes,' Courtney argued.

Da Silva frowned. 'You're talking of the Cape Premier, sir.'

'Yes, sirree, and the most powerful figure in the British Empire. With those English politicians fixing to use President Kruger for clam chowder . . . You don't think this could be the biggest rumpus since Cousin Carrie lost her virtue?'

'You're right about the British, Mr Courtney; and the Captain's not wrong about Mr Rhodes,' von Veltheim reasoned. 'But if he and his colleague, Mr Beit, use eighty per cent of the world's diamonds to control fifty per cent of its gold . . . War's not even an option.' It was the grammar of peace and dinner-table intrigue, but a sense of mission had begun to throb like a drum in his head.

Courtney jammed a cheroot into his mouth. 'Then how'll they cover their investment?'

'Oh, a coup, certainly. If they find a professional,' von Veltheim smiled. And so innocently, no one could have guessed at the rendezvous the Colombian Chargé d'Affaires was right then arranging for him in London.

LONDON

'War? That's absurd.' It was with the weariness of the insomniac that Alfred Beit lowered himself into the barber's chair his valet had acquired for him at a local auction while he and Rhodes were waiting out Jameson's Raid at the Cape.

The rest of the dressing room at 26 Park Lane was furnished in English Georgian except for the few pieces he'd grown up with in Hamburg. His fox terrier, Jackie, now dozed on the same tapestry footstool on which he'd once sat at his mother's knee. On one wall a framed sepia panorama of his proposed residential township on the Johannesburg veld bore the name 'Sachsenwald' in Gothic lettering.

Alfred Beit was a short man, as powerful men often are, and just turned forty-four; but Groener could see why he was taken for ten years older. There was the greying fringe around his balding spot, the lower buttons of his waistcoat that refused to close, and the pouch eyes with the gaze so watery and unblinking, his mother affectionately called him *Fischaugen.*

'War,' Groener insisted. 'And not *if,* sir. *When.*' Neat in build and in manner, Beit found him the quintessential German version of the English 'gentlemen's gentleman', as he laid out the dailies he'd accumulated in his master's absence – the *Times*, the *Pall Mall Gazette*, *Der Spiegel* and the *Wiener Tagblatt.*

'Over the *Raid*? Quite absurd!' But he didn't sound convincing.

Groener wrung out a steaming towel and wrapped it soothingly around his master's face. 'Not with the Kaiser congratulating President Kruger, sir?' he reminded him, mixing the lather in the shaving mug with a badger-bristled brush. 'England's going to have to move smartly if she wants the Union Jack on Church Square.'

Carriage wheels clattered in the driveway, and Groener cocked his ear. 'That'll be Herr Wernher, sir. He left word last night he'd be by to pick you up for the office.'

Faithful Wernher. Sixteen years ago they'd been just a couple of German diamond agents in a corrugated-iron shack in Kimberley. Now Wernher Beit & Co controlled vast South African diamond and gold interests from London Wall Building. Still, it was a good half-hour's drive out of his way. Was London's mood that bad? Beit tossed the hot towel onto the marble washstand and awkwardly took the shaving brush from him. 'Then, you'll let cook know if he's breakfasted?'

His partner, Erich Wernher, was three-quarters of a foot taller than Beit, watched his weight, and still carried himself like the Prussian dragoon he'd once been in the occupying army of the Franco-Prussian War.

He swung the tall silk hat and chesterfield coat from his Berlin tailor onto the bentwood coat stand. 'Getting on a bit to go romping around Africa,' he chaffed Beit gently, 'with that bunch of old maids masquerading as bachelors? *Sûr tout* with our friend Rhodes?' When alone, he always addressed Beit in his silky Hesse-accented German with the odd French expression falling just as easily from his tongue. 'Married life's a lot safer, and not that bad.'

Beit lathered his face, thinking wistfully of Wernher's laughing family that made his house more of a home, whilst he tried forlornly to fill his own with his fox terrier and his art collection. Solitary things.

Wernher watched Beit's razor draw a passage of pink skin across the lathered cheek. 'I'm not interrupting you?'

Beit paused, his right cheek spread between finger and thumb. 'If London's full of snide remarks about "Herr Beit", I'd rather hear it from you.'

'Rhodes's Secret Society? *Merde!*' Wernher gave the *Pall Mall Gazette* a dismissive little shove. 'Does it matter what a bunch of Oxford graduates call you?'

'When they administer the Rhodes scholarships to Oxford and Cambridge for the empire? America? And even English-speaking Germans could be eligible?' Beit stropped his razor unnervingly in time to his rising inflection. 'In thirty years there'll be two thousand of them all over the globe equipped for world government.' He looked into the mirror to address his left cheek, but kept turning back to emphasise a point. 'You know it matters . . . Damn!' – he nicked his cheek, and a drop of blood trickled towards his chin – '. . . And how much Cecil needs us.'

'So long as it's anonymous?' With Beit's manicure scissors Wernher cut a neat strip of toilet paper to staunch the blood.

'He's reaching twenty years into the twentieth century, Erich.'

Wernher held out his hand for the razor. 'Then better let me, or you won't make it to next week.'

Beit surrendered it with a sheepish smile. 'For world peace, Erich?' he pleaded.

'For world peace,' Wernher echoed. 'And while we're about it . . .' – he squinted critically at Beit's reflection in the mirror – 'might as well prune that moustache.'

Wernher removed his jacket, and adjusted his expanders. Some novel ideas had recently begun reshaping his business philosophy, and now he was delighted to have a captive audience. 'Did you know Germany's also had a secret society? And for well over a century?'

Beit tried to shake his head.

'Careful now,' Wernher took his chin between forefinger and thumb and began to work. 'Probably where Rhodes's sanctimonious sidekicks got the idea in the first place. Adam Weisse's disciples might not have been academics, but can you imagine how many billions of Deutschmarks they turned over keeping Europe at war this century? That's why Rothschilds practically control the world's natural resources. Trade . . .' He trimmed a single whisker. 'Transport . . .' Another. 'Communication.' A third. '*Ca c'est logique*?

'It's diabolical!'

Wernher stepped back and admired his handiwork. 'Now for the other side. And think how all these wars ended with a shift of power? If a king misbehaved? . . . *Alors*!' He dropped the razor into the Frankenthal porcelain basin with a triumphant clang. 'And the war was decided by which way the financing went. Checking those debt positions would be interesting.' He backed out of the way of the mirror. 'So . . . You think it's good?'

'It's abominable.' And Beit didn't mean Wernher's handiwork.

Wernher eyed the trimmed moustache. '*Formidable!*' he pronounced. 'But it'll take getting used to. *De toute façon* . . . In a race between the British elitists and Europe's bankers, I know who I'd back . . .' – he dusted Beit's shoulder with the silver-backed clothes brush – 'They've just had more experience.'

Beit replaced the clothes brush as precisely among the gleaming array of scissors and silver-backed brushes and combs as though he had used a set square. 'So, Erich? How long have you been mixed up with "them"?'

'Long enough to let you cultivate the British, while I keep our options open in Europe. It's called insurance,' Wernher smiled. He slipped on his suit jacket, and looped an arm around Beit's shoulder. 'First let Jameson's dust settle,' he advised. 'Then quietly make another plan about the Rand.' He sniffed the air. 'Kippers?'

'And Kranzkuchen,' Beit confirmed. After a troubled night, he relied on one of his cook's hybrid Anglo-German breakfasts to set him up for the day.

Wernher swung his coat and hat off the coat stand. 'In fact, only last evening the Chargé d'Affaires was telling me how Colombia's indebted to a most useful fellow. It won't hurt to meet him.' And his cheek creased in a Machiavellian wink.

But Beit was suddenly assailed by his nightmare image of young guardsmen strewn, inert and flyblown, across the South African veld. He shook his head vigourously. 'Absolutely not, Erich.'

'Just in case, *mon ami*?'

And that was how Beit came to pour cognac in his study for Don Ramon Ciénaga, the patrician Colombian Chargé d'Affaires with the flair for diplomacy, and Franz von Veltheim, the specialist in coups d'état.

A comfortable room, von Veltheim observed. Pity the Adam fireplace and the butter-soft hide chairs, the Constables and Flemish oils all gave the impression of having been acquired with the same shrewdness as the most valuable share portfolio in the City, and not much else. The single personal touch was the fox terrier curled up in his basket.

Beit handed him a cognac. 'One is curious to know why,' he prodded.

Why? von Veltheim asked himself. To prove he was the best in his field? . . . His competence at soldiering or sailoring? . . . As a boy, he'd made a conscious decision to train himself to act bravely as an alternative to cowardice, and his antidote to his fear of failure had been teaching himself first to strike back. Then to strike first. But lately this had got confused with the memory of one bridge too many and a young sentry blown to smithereens. And now here was the seductive voice of a Pied Piper with a Hamburg accent asking, 'Why?'

'Because it's sound economic sense, and even better manpower sense,' he replied. 'Minimal casualties.'

He turned back to the tooled leather desk across which were spread a map of the Boer Republic, news cuttings of the *Crisis in the Transvaal*, and Melton Prior's artist's impressions for the *London Illustrated News*. 'Now there's a whole new brand of warfare. Camouflage. Hunting tactics. The Boers are masters of the ambush. They stalk the enemy from behind their cattle the way they hunt buffalo. And that's why Jameson failed . . . Because it *was* an invasion.' With a wooden pointer, he tapped the dot indicating Luipaardsvlei. 'The landscape fights on the other side.'

'Madonna!' Ciénaga's liquid Latin eyes fixed on the sketch of the ambush at Farmer Brink's sheep kraal. 'And his losses?'

'General Joubert says that gap where the Boers set up their ambush . . .' – von Veltheim touched it with his pointer – '. . . was held – not by fifty . . . Not even by a dozen. But by . . .' He held up five fingers. And then two.

'*Seven*!' Ciénaga hastily crossed himself. 'God help you.'

Beit thought of the empty sleeves and eye patches he'd seen when he'd visited the wounded. 'Sometimes I wonder whose side God's really on. We need reform. But war . . .' Words failed him and he gave a hopeless sigh. His fox terrier, Jackie, deserted his basket, cautiously rearranged himself at his master's feet and looked up at him with great worried eyes.

'Unless there should be a split from within?' von Veltheim said softly. 'I would strike for the heart . . . so.' He walked around the desk to where the tantalus stood and removed the brandy decanter and replaced it with the sherry. 'A small elite team for speed and mobility . . .'

And the level in the brandy snifters dwindled and was replenished several times while the talk ranged from tactics to strategy. From expansionism to the coup d'état as a tool for peace.

'As for Joubert?' Von Veltheim finally swept up the sherry decanter and, turning back to the map, placed it on the dot signifying Pretoria with a thump. They all stared at it. It sat there as bold and compelling as a spider in its web. 'Nobody'll know you're behind it. You've my word as a *Freiherr*.'

'Eccolo!' Ciénaga raised his glass.

Jackie raised his head from his master's boot, and Beit absently patted him until his stumpy tail drummed. 'I've lived away from South Africa quite a while; but Wernher, Rhodes and I have a fourth partner in the Kimberley diamond monopoly . . .' he said thoughtfully. 'Let me have a word with him. Barnato's always back and forth in his race for the Rand gold.'

'*Barney* Barnato?' Von Veltheim looked doubtful. 'But isn't he apolitical?'

'*Was.* Before his nephew, Solly Joel, got locked up for the Raid. In fact, by now he's probably right . . .' And Beit planted a plump forefinger on the map right next to where the sherry decanter sat.

2

Autumn comes to the southern latitudes as spring does to the northern ones. After the close summer heat the welcome breezes stir gently through the Pretoria poorte. But as Barney Barnato walked down from the carriage park to the covered market, requisitioned for the Jameson Raid treason trial, he suppressed a shiver. He knew that the highveld winters could be harsh.

The costermonger made rich through precious minerals and formidable through nerve, his ginger hair was brilliantined over the broad brainy forehead, and his shrewd blue eyes bright behind gleaming gold pince-nez. Johannesburgers affectionately doffed their hats. Pretorians, suspicious of these *uitlanders* Jameson was supposed to 'rescue', did not.

Pretoria's ripening from a hamlet to a dorp, and then not quite a city struck him as *opslag* – the growth of young grass after rain. Radiating from Church Square, her houses nestled among five valleys and her people were valley people. *Hardegat*, some said. Obstinate. This was one difference between Pretoria and his mining town in the veld thirty miles away. There were others.

Pretoria was forty-three years old: Johannesburg scarcely ten. The main streets in Pretoria had to be wide enough for a twelve-span ox-wagon to do a U-turn, and the blocks were long. In Johannesburg the blocks were short. Corner stands were prime real estate and the blocks were laid out with as many corners as possible. But the essential difference was that Pretoria still moved to the ancient rhythm of the veld, while Johannesburg throbbed to the tempo of the mining stamp battery.

'*Had* throbbed,' he corrected himself. 'The bloody place is in a state of siege. Solly, my boy, you and your Reformers are in deep trouble,' he told his nephew already inside under police escort. 'Jameson's letter says you lot *asked* him to come. Thank God we plea-bargained for your necks.'

A hemisphere away, from the porch of her new seaside villa Molly stared dumbly at the fine April rain sifting down on the sodden gardens of Weston-super-Mare.

Von Veltheim put down his teacup and pretended to be absorbed in the letter she had just passed him; but he saw with a guilty pang that her gilded good looks weren't proof against the reddened eyes and doleful mouth. 'I should never've let you leave your cavalry officer to take me on,' he said ruefully.

'Because I wear you down until you do things my way?' She tried her teasing smile that crinkled her eyes. 'Admit it's worth it?' she coaxed.

Worth it? Von Veltheim ached for them both. Dispiritedly, he picked at the stamp on the letter, and managed to ruin the Kaiser's moustache.

'We'll try Paris this time,' she insisted.

There it was again – that pretending that the stale relic of what they once had could still be revived at a price. Oh, Molly. Wearily, he stood and scowled at the rain.

Her smile twisted and became bitter. 'It's your von Veltheims again?'

The tears would be next if he didn't head her off. 'Molly, Molly . . .' And again the familiar lying reassurances slipping out so easily. And Molly probably recognising them as such again, and again pretending not to.

She stood and drew her shawl about her, face bleak. 'What did you want me to do?'

He slid the letter into his pocket. 'It's *the* big one this time.' The quivery edge to his voice told her that this, at least, was true. 'Charlie's in Germany and we still need our link. Can we count on you?' He cupped her chin in his hand and tried to fathom her expression.

Her smile was wintry and brittle. 'Always.'

He realised that word and her tears were the silken nooses with which she tried to bind him to her.

He folded her shawl more closely about her shoulders, but his hands moved as mechanically as a nurse's finishing a ward round before hurrying off duty. What happened to caresses? he wondered. 'We'll talk when I get back before I go south.' This time the false note of cheerfulness of a housemaster assuring the new intake of junior school boarders that the new term would be fun. What had happened to spontaneity? 'Things could be different then.' He wondered why he said that.

The old pattern of false promises and fake reassurances was a jaded play they were doomed to rehearse to infinity.

He brushed the top of her head with his lips. 'Bye, Molly.'

'Goodbye.' Low.

He walked down the path and turned at the gate. '*Auf Wiedersehen?*'

'*Auf Wiedersehen.*'

Von Veltheim strode off towards the station and turned the corner.

'*Damn* you, Franz! A seaside cottage and an allowance?' Molly hurled her teacup against the porch balustrade and it shattered. 'You'll be sorry! I swear it!'

The rain had stopped. An odd stillness lay over the peaceful holiday homes of Weston-super-Mare and a chill hung in the air.

Alphonse Baruch – pioneer member of the Johannesburg Stock Exchange, Barney Barnato's close friend and, incidently, President Kruger's – was balding faster than he was greying, had a walrus moustache, and gentle spaniel eyes that always shone with the joy of the deeply religious Jew who performed his devotions twice daily.

This day as he took his place next to Barnato in Pretoria's covered market hall the dark Semetic eyes were grave. He jerked his head at the flag behind the empty rostrum. Hand-sewn and faded, the *Vierkleur* had been rent and repaired so often its darning formed a tapestry. 'It's *hardegat* like the *Boerevolk*,' he muttered. 'They don't give in.'

They knew all the Johannesburgers – the prisoners' wives and fiancées in their cashmere travelling suits and Princess of Wales toques – subdued and conversing in low tones on irrelevant topics that led nowhere.

They didn't know the *Boerevolk* – the taciturn men in carefully mended *kisklere* and silent women in worn shawls and faded *kappies*, their faces etched with the harshness of the veld. And so Big Leendert Roux and his veldkornet, Grobbelaar, were just two more faces in the crowd.

At the prosecution table, the state attorney and his assistant had their heads together, but everybody looked up as the door opened. All eyes were on Judge Gregorowski as he mounted the rostrum. In accordance with Roman Dutch dress code he did not wear a wig as they did in the Old Bailey; and in his white-starched swallow-tailed collar and black robe he seemed more a harbinger of death than a man of law.

He cracked a joke with the bailiff, who reddened and scurried out; and a murmur of relief buzzed through the *uitlanders.*

Gregorowski hooded his eyes. 'Would any ladies wish to excuse themselves before sentence is pronounced?'

Barnato looked at Baruch, appalled.

The bailiff bustled in again and handed Gregorowski a scrap of black cloth. It slipped sideways on his head, making him look comical; but nobody laughed. He was saying something in Dutch, which few people understood. Except for the words, *hangen by die nek.*

Barnato hardly heard the *uitlander* women's stunned gasps, nor the despairing moan from the one two seats away who crumpled and collapsed in a dead faint. He was on his feet, dimly aware of Baruch, trying to steady his chair, teetering behind him before it crashed to the floor. 'You lot told them to plead guilty, and we make a plan. And you bloody *tricked* them! How much does it take, Gregorowski, for you to whore in the name of the law?'

Gregorowski gripped the rostrum. 'Sir! You are no gentleman.'

'And you're no bleeding judge!' Barnato's eyes swept the prosecution table. 'You call it justice, but it's revenge!'

From the corner of his eye he could see two ZARP constables moving towards him. Angrily, he strode to the nearest exit, and turned. 'Ten years ago Pretoria was farmland . . . *We* built your first decent buildings with small change. Oom Paul needs reminding.'

Baruch reached him and grabbed his sleeve. 'Don't fight with him, Barney,' he pleaded. 'Ask . . .'

'Not bloody likely!' he snorted. 'A mass meeting at the Johannesburg Stock Exchange tomorrow. And then if he can't see reason, I'll *show* him it's who's got the gold calls the shots.'

In the *Geheime Dienst* headquarters five minutes later the Chief Commissioner of Police hesitated. Usually the dissemination of information was by word of mouth with nothing trusted to writing; but this was an emergency.

He removed his confidential memo book from his safe, picked up his pen and began to write.

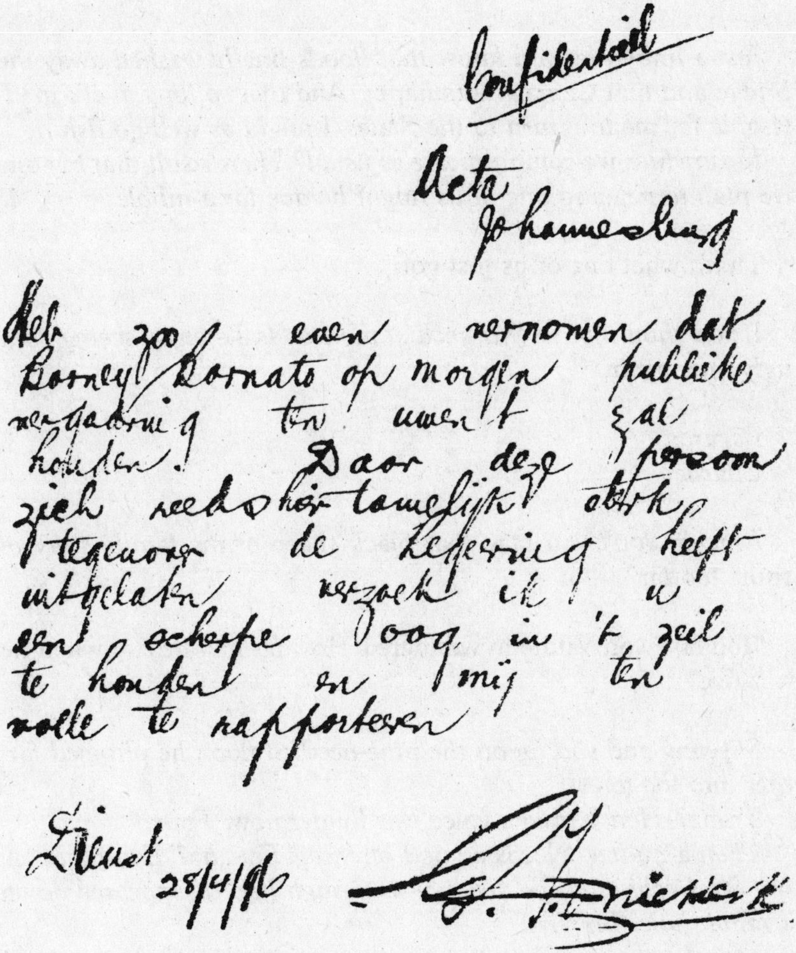

Confidentieël

Acta
Johannesburg

Heb zoo even vernomen dat Barney Barnato op morgen publieke vergadering ten uwent zal houden. Daar deze persoon zich reeds hier tamelijk sterk tegenover de Regeering heeft uitgelaten, verzoek ik u een scherpe oog in 't zeil te houden en mij ten volle te rapporteren

Dienst
28/4/96

Niekerk

Van Niekerk read the last sentence again aloud. 'Please keep him under surveillance and report to me.'

In his London hotel von Veltheim opened the letter with the damaged stamp. It was also marked 'confidential'.

Somewhere in Germany

April 1896
Dear Count,

Just a line to let you know that floods finally washed away the bridge and that Ciénaga was happy. And that so long as it's inadvisable for me to return to the States, I might as well go fishing.

Meanwhile, we communicate as usual? There's still that big one we plan to net, and one of us might be due for a nibble.

That's what one of us just got.

If you should be in this neck of the woods, I'd enjoy seeing your ugly mug again.

Regards,
Charlie

I mean, don't you take that black sheep of the family story of yours too far?

'Too far?' von Veltheim wondered. How far had he run when he was five?

Slipping and sliding on the pine-needled floor, he plunged farther into the forest.

'Franz?' Herr Kurtze's voice was louder now. 'Franz!'

Then a mutter, 'Needs a good birching. Fra-anz?' Exasperation, but diminishing in the distance as though he'd disappeared down a rabbit hole. 'Fra-anz!'

At last only the terror and his own rasping breath. Hours later, the grunt and yelp of police Dobermans that sent his heart slamming like a battering ram against his fragile ribcage. Please God, don't let them hear it.

'Here, I've got him,' another voice bellowed. The torch blinding him. Rough hands seizing him.

'Easy there. Poor little beggar's frozen . . .' A gentler tone this time. 'And scared half to death. Could do with a plate of good broth.'

Later. 'This is becoming a habit. Why, Franz?'

No answer.

'Herr Kurtze's like a father to you?

There was outrage in his childish treble and an ache in his child's breast. 'Stop saying that. I've GOT a father!'

How far had he run later when his legs were longer, and his voice had broken? When his parentage was no longer mentioned, and the space for the guardian's name at the Blanckenberg Gymnasium read: Thomas Kaufmann?

The principal's office: book shelves lined with a mix of dog-eared maths manuals next to a tooled leather set of Goethe. His gaze swivelled from the bookcase to the two men.

'A wayward lad, Herr Kaufmann,' the principal was explaining. 'He had the unmitigated gall to steal the gun from my study. Lucky it's only a powder burn . . .'

'You surely mean, lucky he didn't lose the eye?'

'I appeal to you, Herr Kaufmann . . . He belongs in a house of correction. But for the Freiherr's connections . . .'

'You're wise to remember them. The Countess von Bülow works with the Sisters of Charity.' Herr Kaufmann had turned to him.

'Their home's in Brunswick. That's not too far, eh, Franz?'

'No, sir.' Even then he'd had a feeling about the Countess von Bülow.

He could still see that scuffed and balding grass patch where the boys left behind on weekends played football.

Sweating boys, ribcages heaving, feet flailing the dust, while he booted the ball soaring in an arc to drop like a stone between the goal posts.

Sister Gabriel striding into the melee, the piercing blast of her whistle halting the game. 'You, Franz . . . You've a visitor in the parlour. Off with you now and get washed up.'

A hurried toilet. Then marching the length of corridor beside her, their two sets of footsteps echoing a tattoo as the sounds they made bounced off the walls. Her scanning eyes critically honing in on his hair. Hurriedly moistening his hands with saliva to smooth it down.

The parlour door swinging open, and there she was. The Empress Elizabeth, surely? Tall, willowy, sable fur draped about those elegantly boned shoulders, the fine Brussels lace pierced with a cameo at the throat . . . And the eyes – oh, those eyes! Green as his own with . . .

She traced his gunpowder scar with a hesitant touch.

Sister Gabriel hastily: 'An accident before he came to us, Countess.'

The Countess's eyes wide with – was it fear? 'I know. We must take special care of him.' She trailed those long fingers across the nape of his neck, leaving the stigmata he could feel to this day.

At last. 'Will you take me home with you now?'

'Mercy me,' Sister Gabriel chided. 'The Countess is our patroness. You're here thanks to her charity, child.'

He looked at Therése von Bülow steadily. 'YOU say it.'

Quickly, she lowered her lashes – were her eyes really moist? – and unpinned the violets from her muff. 'Keep these, Franz . . . Till Sunday?' A whisper.

Why hadn't she taken him home? *Was* he too untidy? Unacceptable? An embarrassment? A misfit? A mistake? Acceptance could be conditional. Rejection is an axe.

'Till Sunday?' she'd said. By then he'd run away to sea.

'Get those ruddy shoulders back! You're a midshipman in the Merchant Marine, not an orang-utan in a zoo! Back, I said!

In the mornings he'd wake rigid from having slept at attention.

He remembered being booed in a boxing match for hitting after the referee's whistle. And he remembered being cheered at the others he'd won. The envy of his victories. The scorn at his defeats.

He'd also filched things. The photograph of another midshipman's family because the mother wore her hair like the Countess von Bülow.

And he'd remembered all the other women in his life thereafter. The promises he'd carelessly uttered. And carelessly broken.

'Too far?' Charlie had asked. Was around and around the world far enough? The misdemeanours compounding until Herr Kaufmann traced him and entered him at the Kiel Naval Academy as plain Kurt.

Kurt, first up the mainmast. Kurt, captain of the rowing team with a trophy to show for it. But show to whom?

'Kurt!' Marine-Offizier Willi von Veltheim, jubilant, waving his letter from home. 'Kurt, Papa writes that he knows your guardian. Asks if you're free for Christmas. You are, aren't you?'

That first Christmas at Bielorat – jewel of the district on the Vienna-Prague road.

The snow so wedding-cake white it hurt your eyes. The wild boar hunts by day. Evenings around a log fire with pine cones that spat gum and spewed sparks that baked your cheeks red and your heart warm as oven-fresh bread.

Evenings perfumed with cinnamon and mulled wine.

Evenings filled with chess matches against the Freiherr Rainer von Veltheim. Evenings filled with talk.

Healing. Belonging.

And finally the gifts.

Christmas Eve. In the corner of the gun room the fir hewn from the woods and studded with the parchment-coloured wax candles they'd melted on the great porcelain stove, and poured into the moulds to cool.

He'd been the first in with a proud gift for Rainer – the set of antique Indian carved ivory chessmen – a panoply of elephants and foot soldiers.

Then it was Rainer's turn. He had made him cup his hands and dropped into them the gold fob watch and the ring engraved with the von Veltheim crest he now wore on the little finger of his left hand.

Bewilderment. No, that's not really true.

Rainer explaining, 'You remind me of the son I once lost.'

'And I lost a father.' His eyes reproached the older man. 'I think you know Therése von Bülow?'

'Her picture's in every tabloid.' Cagily.

A penetrating look. You, too, found me an inconvenience? Tell me.

'Willi's mother was still alive,' Rainer pleaded.

Tell me? Von Veltheim stared him down, the eyes hungry for words that did not come. Tell me!

The older man seemed to age before his eyes. His hand movements were stiff and clumsy when he poured the mulled wine, and his voice dull. 'What will you do?'

'I'll certainly not threaten Willi.' An eggshell smooth facade to plaster over the cracks of his crumbling insides. 'I've these fine expectations . . .'

That was when they noticed Willi.

Willi?

Back at the ship – Willi dropping his own watch and ring overboard. Reporting them missing. And von Veltheim on the run without needing to ask why. He only knew with Willi the only von Veltheim aboard – officially – he didn't want to be around for any explaining.

And what expectations! What if you did start out the wrong side of treason, so long as you were the next administration's hero? It had all seemed so easy before the bridge.

Von Veltheim looked out of the hotel window and realised that the light was beginning to fade. Propping Charlie's letter in front of him, he took up his pen and wrote:

Hotel Metropole
London
23 April 1896

My Dear Charlie,

Devastated I can't join you and all those Rhine maidens.
But that last high-risk, high-yield venture I promised?
Best leave an itinerary with Molly so I can cable you poste restante at short notice.

Your friend,
Franz

PS: Have you dispensed with those terrible whiskers and window-pane spectacles you wore steaming out of New Orleans, leaving 'wanted' posters on every corner in Bourbon Street?

I hear they kept the police on the hop for quite a while.

He sealed the letter, and strode briskly out into the darkening street to mail it.

Scarcely two hours after his Johannesburg protest meeting Barney Barnato walked down Pretoria's Church Street and turned into the path to the President's house.

But for the two uniformed sentries at the gate, it could have been a farmhouse. The corrugated iron roofed single storey was a tight enough squeeze for the eight Kruger children, let alone the daily stream of visitors he received on the cement stoep.

This day was different. Paul Kruger chose to see him in his study and waved him to the chair across his desk. The massive build had grown ponderous with age, and his scraggy white beard, now streaked with yellow from years of smoking Magaliesberg shag, was the colour of the highveld grass in winter. But the eyelashes that grew perversely inward made his eyeballs tear, and gave him an expression of perpetual grief. Brooding in mood, he seemed like an old bear poignantly at bay.

Barnato ran a finger under his collar. 'A deal was struck, Mr President; and then Gregorowski sticks their necks in a noose! It's not right.'

'And stealing my country *is*?'

'In gold law . . .'

'*Gold* law?' Kruger shifted his weight irritably. 'What counts is what's on the ground – farms, cattle, stone kraals. But it's going to cost those farmers their lifeblood defending them. And you talk to me about *gold*?'

Barnato's affable manner suddenly changed. 'Then how about numbers, Mr President?' Tonelessly he counted off: 'I've twenty thousand whites and a hundred thousand blacks on my payroll. If I close down, I put more men out of work than you've burghers in your whole Republic. Then where'll they be with their farms and stone kraals? Stone broke!'

Across the way some washing strung on a clothesline between

the new Dopper Church and the old Dopper Church flapped in a sudden gust of wind. 'Now this Jameson fiasco. Compromise . . .'

Kruger's grizzled eyebrows rose. 'With a farmer with a gun in his hand? On *treason*?'

Barnato stood and leaned his fists on the desk, reducing the space between them until Kruger could smell on his breath his before lunch beers, the wine he'd had with it and the brandies afterwards. 'We could go up and down all day like a tart's knickers with this, so I'll tell it to you straight. Reprieve, and we all get a second chance. Refuse, and I'll bankrupt you, and buy Piet Joubert the presidency. Just like a sack of mealies.'

And he turned and left.

3

Von Veltheim started down to the stables, periodically breaking into a half-trot. At the bridle path he turned to look back at Bielorat.

For over two centuries its citadel walls had been scoured by snow and bleached by sun, and in the spring morning light they gleamed like a freshwater pearl. Beyond the lawns as far as the Vienna road rolled a patchwork of fields – some freshly ploughed chocolate loam, and others brocaded with the new season's rye.

He could see Rainer von Veltheim and two Cossack-capped stable hands schooling a yearling in the lunging paddock, and he quickened his step. The thicker-set man held the lunging rein, but the bespectacled youth leaned on the rail, head bent over a pencil and pad. Of course! Rainer sponsored that school for his labourers. Von Veltheim dropped a hand on his shoulder. 'Allow . . .'

But the head swivelled with a toss, and the cap slid sideways, unexpectedly releasing a glossy dark braid. More confusing, the spectacles had slipped down the nose and there were fascinating golden lights in the startled brown eyes that gazed into his. Intelligent probing eyes he found faintly disturbing. Slowly he took in the bee-sting breasts that thrust ever so slightly against the front of the homespun smock. 'Why, you're a girl,' he said stupidly.

'And you, sir, are impertinent,' their owner flared.

'Not only a girl, but a shrew-tongued one,' von Veltheim chuckled. It was an infectious chuckle with overtones of sensuality that women found irresistible – with the clear exception of the one whose shoulder he was still clasping.

With a twinge of regret he released it and retrieved her cap, returning it to her with a formal little bow.

'Thank you. You were saying?' Her voice was equally mocking as she held out her pad.

Von Veltheim studied it. It was a remarkably revealing sketch of Rainer von Veltheim. With startling economy of line she had caught the essential presence of the man. There was the fine upright riding seat, the greying hair and the mutton-chop side-burns worn longer below the chin. But there was also his vigour and the beak of a nose that emphasised his hawk-like loneliness.

'Be right with you, Franz,' he called from the paddock. He checked the colt until it changed feet and trippled in the opposite direction.

'So you're Uncle Rainer's Franz?' She extended her hand. It was slim and warm, and he didn't want to let it go. 'I'm Anne-Marie.'

'And I'm enchanted.' Von Veltheim handed back her sketch. 'And impressed. *Is* he your uncle?'

She shook her head. 'Didn't you also grow up without parents? You must know how a guardian's close friends get . . . promoted . . .?' The question trailed off as she covered the upper half of the likeness and looked at him thoughtfully. Again the coolly observant eyes. 'You have the same jaw, you know?'

'Where did you learn to sketch like this?' he asked hastily.

'Paris.'

'At the *Ecole des Beaux Arts*?'

'I did political studies at the Sorbonne. In fact . . .' She broke off with a wry glance at Rainer who had dismounted and was making for them at an exuberant trot.

'In the nick of time, my boy . . .' He flung an arm around his shoulder. 'That dratted Flora Shaw's just offered Anne-Marie a post on *The Times*. Tell her how awful London is over Easter.'

'Unspeakable,' von Veltheim obliged.

'You *men* . . .' Anne-Marie exploded.

But Rainer firmly tucked her arm through his. 'You're too ready for a fight, and we're all parched.' And looping the other around von Veltheim's shoulder, he steered them back to the Schloss.

A military-looking figure stood waiting on the terrace, and von Veltheim bounded up the steps. 'Willi!' He clasped the broad shoulders and then held him at arm's length, hoping the vigilance he felt didn't show in his smile. 'Let's look at you.'

Marine Offizier Willi von Veltheim wore riding breeches and a loose homespun smock like his father, but his military haircut and stiff-backed stance were more suited to his gold garlanded officers' blues. He also wore his moustache trimmed short, tips waxed sharply like the Kaiser's whose yacht he'd skippered to victory at the last Cowes regatta.

'So, Willi? . . .' Von Veltheim squeezed his shoulder. 'Master of the Kaiser's escort cruiser?'

Willi grinned happily. 'And that's only a start. Through Krupps', he's forging us into a great naval power. Ready to challenge England . . .'

'And thrust us all into a world war,' Rainer finished gloomily, pulling out Anne-Marie's chair at the coffee table. 'Not so, my dear?'

Her hands moved gracefully among the Meissen cups, pouring. 'Germany's already too full of tensions. *Judenhass.* Madmen promising to purify the country of Semitic polluters . . .'

Willi covered her hand with his. 'Forgive her. She has these eccentric ideas. The latest's wanting to leave precisely when Papa and I are due at Klimt's for the Kaiser's Easter gift. I dare say we could drive into Vienna together . . .' – he gave von Veltheim a sidelong glance – 'But we'll have to ask Franz to get you to your train.'

Von Veltheim inclined his head. 'I'm supposed to say "delighted", but that's an outright lie.'

'How's your steamship company?' Rainer asked him pointedly. 'The English and West Indian Pacific Steamship Company sent Franz to Santa Marta,' he explained to Anne-Marie. 'Wound up Honorary American Consul, in fact.'

'*Ex*-steamship company,' von Veltheim confessed. 'I've just been invited to take a look at the Witwatersrand gold reef . . .'

'By anyone we know?' Anne-Marie asked suddenly. 'Some of Rainer's financier friends have powerful South African interests.' She was looking at him with interest, and this time he felt a warning thrill.

Rainer suddenly stood and jerked the bell pull. A steward appeared bearing a silver salver with a bottle of Moët de Chandon 1891 and four tall-stemmed glasses. He opened the cork with a pop and a twist of vapour threaded the air. Rainer offered Anne-Marie the first glass. 'To your byline in *The Times*, my dear.'

'Big and bold,' she agreed.

He handed the second to Willi. 'Victory always.' He gave the third to von Veltheim. 'And Franz in South Africa . . .'

'Good fortune?' Willi prompted.

Anne-Marie looked at him thoughtfully. 'Settle for his just staying out of trouble,' she advised.

And Rainer filled the glasses so hurriedly the champagne bubbled over the top.

'Death by hanging.'

Kruger scanned the faces of the deputation of Lichtenberg burghers on his front stoep. Big-framed, bearded, sunburned men with burning eyes. And their words burned with the bitterness that had brought their fathers from the Cape in the Trek he'd made as a boy.

'Remember Slachtersnek.' Still smarting from Jameson's Raid, the young fiery Veldkornet Grobbelaar used the rallying cry over a previous injustice that had fuelled Boer anger for nearly three generations. 'Now do unto them as they did unto us.'

The President puffed stoically on his pipe. 'It was wrong eighty years ago, and it's wrong now.'

Yes, wrong. But Commandant Leendert Roux was thinking of the sun glancing off the golden head of a fallen British trooper in the Queen's Mine vlei on New Year's Day.

The President's wife brought coffee for everyone. In his old age Kruger seemed to crave sweetness, and he took his coffee with several spoons of sugar. He stirred reflectively, and then drank with his spoon in the cup. 'If a poor man's dog comes into my garden, I shoot it,' he grunted. 'If a rich man's dog comes? Well then . . .' And he knocked out his pipe on his boot and gave Big Leendert a cunning smile.

'Oom Paul's right about fines.' And there was a measure of relief in his answering grin. 'Heavy ones. It's been a hard year for us farmers.'

After they'd left, Kruger sat alone on the stoep watching a fat green fly crawl lazily across the wicker table towards his coffee mug. He remembered it all. The entry in the Kruger family Bible had read simply: 1835 – *Ons het die Kaap verlaat.* We left the Cape.

When *uitlander* boys were still playing with lead soldiers he, with a rawhide whip in his hand, had led his father's ox-wagon north in the Great Trek. And when the wagons outspanned at night, the men would talk around the campfire of how the English flag was being hoisted over more and more of the land.

He remembered how it had been when the wagons had crossed

the Vaal. It was a harsh land where the Magaliesberg had reared up against the empty sky, and there were steep *krantze* where duiker and gemsbok grazed. But mostly there were the sun-baked *vlakte* stretching to the horizon, studded with umbrella-shaped *kameeldoring* or flat-topped *haak-en-steek*, prickly pear and *wag-'n-bietjie*. Always the thorn trees. And his people had loved this unlovely Canaan whither their God had led them. And how ironic that although it did not flow that abundantly with milk and honey, it should yield the one crop the English lusted for – the English who worshipped the golden calf and whose ungodly equation held precious lives so cheap.

Kruger's hands lay on the table before him – huge hands with their liver spots, scars and the left thumb maimed in a fight with a lion. Hands with memories.

With startling alacrity, the disfigured hand crashed down on the fly near his coffee mug and crushed it. 'Thou shalt not steal. Yea, and thou shalt not *kill*. I'd always intended to reprieve those *verdomde* sentences. And not because of Barney Barnato's threats.'

Von Veltheim stowed Anne-Marie's scuffed suitcase in the luggage-rack of her compartment on the Orient Express. A moment later he stepped onto Franz Josef Bahn's Platform 2 and, with both hands spanning her waist, lifted her down. It was a fetchingly narrow waist, and encircling it while shielding her from the crowds clogging the platform was an arrangement he enjoyed.

Vienna was the crossroads of Central Europe and a cosmopolitan tide of people bound for diverse destinations for Easter and Passover ebbed and flowed about them – Oriental-looking Bosnians and Czechs with wide cheekbones, Hassidic Jews with curled ear locks and Aryan-featured Austrians.

A group of young radicals surged down the platform distributing pamphlets, and von Veltheim moved closer to Anne-Marie, In her tailored travelling suit, starched white shirtwaist and straw boater she looked like a swot from an English boarding school.

She looked pointedly at his hands still casually looped about her waist.

'You look far too young to be travelling alone,' von Veltheim said cheerfully, without loosening his clasp. 'I'd buy you a cuddly toy for the journey, but Easter's . . .'

'Easter eggs! Lordy, I forgot!' Disengaging herself, she took off for the confectionery shop, turning only to fling over her shoulder: 'Couldn't you rather make that a newspaper? Please?'

He watched her thread her way through the crowd until all he could see was the slim brown hand straightening her boater. It was bouncing in the sea of people like a bottle being carried away by the tide, and he focused on it until it disappeared.

When he found her again at the confectionery shop, he had copies of the *Wiener Tagblatt* and the *Neue Frei Presse* under his arm. He eyed her large package overflowing with exquisitely fashioned Easter eggs. 'At least you shop like other women.'

'For Rainer, Willi, and one for you for keeping the peace.'

'If you're squaring me, I'd rather have your London address.'

'That's something of Willi's I don't think you need.'

'Trust Willi to want it too.'

Anne-Marie had been having too much fun to notice where their banter was taking them. But now she looked at him, stricken. 'I thought you knew. We've been privately engaged since I was seventeen.'

Von Veltheim wondered whether the sun had really suddenly gone from the bright spring day. 'Then I must get you back safe and sound,' he said lightly. He took her elbow, and stopped short.

Directly in their path the pamphleteers had gathered in a knot around two Hassidic Jews. People gave passage and an uneasy quiet grew along the platform. The ringleader plucked the Jews' hats from their heads and tossed them to his comrades. They fielded them and trampled them underfoot, and the insidious chant began: 'Hep, Hep . . .'

Von Veltheim put a protective hand about Anne-Marie's waist, and she shrank back against him.

'Hep . . . Hep . . .' Repetitious and insistent. Feet scuffled, and arms flailed like crazed windmills, and there was the meaty sock of fist against flesh, and a despairing grunt.

'Come. You don't need to watch this.' Von Veltheim grabbed her elbow.

'No, I don't.' She tore herself loose and dumped her parcel. Holding her umbrella fast, she waded into the thick of the skirmish. 'Let him go, you great hulk . . .'

Grinning broadly and arms driving like pistons, von Veltheim roared into the melee and swung on the first with his left, splitting his lip. A straight right brought him to his knees, and a left uppercut flattened him. He spun to see if Anne-Marie was in trouble.

Wielding her umbrella like a cudgel, she swiped a fresh opponent across the knuckles. It made the sweet brittle thump of a truly hit cricket ball, and he moaned and doubled over, nursing his shattered hand.

Astonished, von Veltheim looked again. The thwack? The crippled hand? Only a weighted weapon could have done that!

Anne-Marie caught his knowing grin, and flushed. Then, with a defiant toss of her head, went after her next victim. 'A lady's got a right to . . .' Thwack! She clubbed him square on the chin. '. . . to defend herself,' she panted.

'When the other side drew Atilla the Hun?' It had been far too long since he'd had a good punch-up, and suddenly they were a team.

Swinging her umbrella handle like a gladiator's mace, Anne-Marie set upon another thug, belabouring him furiously. He spun sideways and dropped, leaking blood from his crushed nose.

His comrade lurched straight for her, and when she split his cheek like an overripe fig he wrenched the umbrella away and pushed her roughly against a lamp standard.

Winded, she leaned against it gasping, and twisted to look for von Veltheim. Her eyes widened and she filled her lungs and yelled, 'Watch out!'

Four men were closing in on him in a pack. Von Veltheim grabbed the first two by the scruff of the neck and crashed their heads together like cymbals with the satisfying crack of a well-shied coconut. Their knees buckled, and their eyes rolled back. 'Two down, two to go!' he crowed.

He swung on the third with a vicious jab to the kidneys. It felt good, and he repeated it again and again like a conscientious dancer practising a routine, then socked him on the jaw and he crashed. That left one.

Anne-Marie saw that the fourth man had circled him, ready to club him from behind. Eyes narrowing, she thrust herself away from the lamp standard. Like a shot-put athlete, she backed off three paces in a semicircle and, unwinding with the recoil of a slingshot, launched herself in an almighty kick to the groin.

Face contorted with pain, he let out a strangled sound halfway between a yell and a cough, and doubled up and dropped.

The leader of the pack grabbed her shoulder in one hand, spun her to face him and arced the other fist high like an executioner's axe.

Her brown eyes widened, becoming almost too large for her face.

His clenched fist poised menacingly in line with her jaw, and then lost momentum. With a curse of exasperation, he swung her up in his arms and in three strides, without ceremony, dumped her on the platform floor, well out of range.

Frantic, she watched him lurch after von Veltheim.

A huge bruiser of a man weighing in at over two hundred pounds, he drew back a few paces like a rugby player before a try. Using his great bullet head, he came storming back to butt him in the gut with the force of a battering ram.

It drove the air from von Veltheim's lungs and he staggered back gasping, the whole platform swinging about his ears like a merry-go-round. Weaving like a drunken matelot, he dodged, intent only on staying out of range.

Then suddenly focused, in one movement he leapt and drove his left into his opponent's throat, expelling the breath from his windpipe in a sound somewhere between a grunt and a roar. His right swung back and walloped his chin with the force of a hammer.

It made a sharp sound like twigs snapping, and he dropped like a felled oak and lay drooling blood and spitting teeth.

Nobody moved. A sullen silence spread through the gang skulking uncertainly on the perimeter of the crowd. Then, painfully, the injured man dragged himself farther out of range until, in sudden decision, two of his comrades swooped down and hauled him to safety.

Von Veltheim saw Anne-Marie unsuccessfully trying to scramble to her feet and he retrieved her boater and staggered back to her. 'Did they teach you that at the Sorbonne?' he panted.

Her breath was also ragged. 'In the streets of Salonika . . . before . . . before . . . I was packed off to a convent.' She took the boater and rammed it on with dignity. 'Thank you.'

He hauled her up and set her on her feet. She tried a step, and winced. 'Ow! It hurts.'

'I'm not surprised.' Von Veltheim's grin was wider than that on a Halloween pumpkin. He inspected the injury, and announced, 'A sprain. But I've seen worse.'

'Sprains?'

'Ankles, woman.'

'Too bad I can't say the same for you.'

He examined his jacket and saw that the lapel was torn and one sleeve hung by a few threads. 'Damn!'

She giggled more easily than she breathed. 'Your face, idiot.'

He felt his cheek where someone's knuckles had abraded the skin. Ruefully, he inspected his own bleeding knuckles. 'Unwise, perhaps. But it sure as hell was fun.'

'The best.'

Von Veltheim gathered up their belongings, and thrust her umbrella and the bulky parcel back in her arms. He managed to swing her up and hold her against his chest. The rubbery feeling left his legs and he carried her to the carriage as though she were a child. Anne-Marie dimly remembered that her father had carried her to bed like that long ago. It had felt so safe and warm and comforting. She closed her eyes for an instant to lean her head against his shoulder, but her boater tipped askew.

He set her down on her coach balcony and jerked his head at her umbrella. 'Does that thing work as a walking stick?'

'At a pinch.' But the attempt at gaiety was betrayed by the tremulous shadow in her eyes. 'Look . . .' she began haltingly, 'even if we can't be . . . be . . . Well, lovers . . .'

'Don't anyone lay odds on that,' he advised.

'Can't we be best friends?' she pressed on doggedly.

'I sincerely doubt that,' he said solemnly. But she looked so desolate, he promptly amended, 'But you can always count on a place in my football team.' He gave her a magnanimous grin.

'*Best* friends?' she insisted. '*Swear*? . . . In sickness and health? . . .'

The grin softened. 'Wouldn't Willi find that highly inappropriate?'

Absolutely. She needed to think. She reached up in an involuntary gesture and touched the parenthesis lines at his mouth, her fingertips as sensitive as a braille reader's, her eyes photographing him for her memory to take with her.

The guard was waving the green flag at the rear of the train, and the whistle shrilled. Anne-Marie flinched, as if she had taken a blow to the gut. The train gave a mighty lurch, and he leapt down onto the platform as it began to slide forward.

They both spoke the same words at the same moment. 'Take care.'

She could not wave. She stood, boater askew, one hand steadying herself against the balcony rail, and the forgotten Easter eggs clutched to her with the other as though to hold her insides together. Gradually the train picked up speed and, as it streamed out of the station carrying her away, her white face melted into the sea of faces. Von Veltheim suddenly remembered that he still had her newspapers.

'Damn!' He struck them on the palm of his free hand so sharply it stung. 'Damn it to hell!'

He slowly removed his damaged jacket and folded it over his arm. The gang of ruffians had vanished, and he wondered what had become of the two Hassidic Jews. It was early in the day, but he needed a beer.

Sitting at a pavement café on the Danube Canal five minutes later, he opened the *Wiener Tagblatt.* A headline caught his eye and he read it twice. *All Barnato's interests in South Africa to be auctioned.*

4

'And I'd have gone the whole hog, if he hadn't backed down.' At 26 Park Lane Barnato surveyed the lie of the balls across the full-sized billiard table with one eye slightly narrowed.

Beit passed him the chalk. 'Don't I know?' he agreed feelingly. Their negotiations leading up to the De Beers' diamond amalgamation had been an example of the immovable object against the irresistible force. But he also knew how orchestrating the ivory balls across the green baize, and the discreet thwack of the ball as it was pocketed, could be as final as the signature on a contract. And just as binding.

Barnato's misspent youth had included a tough apprenticeship in Whitechapel's poolrooms and he privately approached this game as the East Enders taking on the toffs. He chalked his cue and took a practice shot in slow motion in the air. He was trailing five points behind, and the black – seven points worth – nestled annoyingly among the whites. He made a tripod of his left hand and carefully slid his cue through the valley of thumb and forefinger. It struck the white sweetly in plumb with the black, propelling it lethargically to the lip of the pocket. There it hesitated for a long excruciating moment, as though reconsidering, and then rolled gracefully over the edge to drop with a satisfying click.

'It's called flair,' he said smugly.

'Don't I know?' Beit repeated. Winning would put Barnato in a more receptive mood for the other fish he had to fry. So, he poured two Napoleons and settled into his chair with Jackie at his feet. 'And with your flair and our vision . . .'

It was three quarters of the way through his proposition that Barnato began to fidget uncomfortably.

'Look, I don't like the idea any more than you do,' Beit said reasonably. 'But it's a damned sight better than war.'

'What happens to Oom Paul?' Barnato demanded suspiciously. And in that question was not only the swaggering aggressiveness of the one-time bantamweight boxer, but the Whitechapel barrow boy's outrage against bullies.

Beit gave a sheepish little shrug.

Barnato had raised his snifter, but the gesture froze in the air and his eyes gleamed hard with the freight of other questions.

'Unharmed,' Beit added hastily. 'Should've happened months ago with the Boers so evenly split. Jameson's Union Jack turned a practical bid for the mines into an impractical one for the territory. Now we've no choice.' He scratched Jackie's stomach with a black-patent slippered foot. '*Any* of us.'

'*Us*?' Barnato's derisive hoot was inspired by an image of himself fifteen years back selling cigars while Rhodes and Beit, dressed in riding togs, swopped yarns and black velvets at the Kimberley Club. And it still hurt. 'Did *you* ever have to put on the gloves for the purse? And then sleep on the floor behind a counter instead of a bed?' There were the audience and the boxers – the haves and the have nots – and there were still recesses in Barnato's geography where never the twain would meet.

'And don't forget, I walked to Kimberley behind a Boer wagon, my man,' he reminded Beit. 'They're nice simple folk. A bit potty maybe about their soil and thorn trees and stuff. But *nice*.' He fished out his gold cigar case and distractedly removed a Roméo y Juliéta for each of them. 'Country's been good to me, Alfred, and it ain't been harf bad to you lot at Number One London Wall Building, either. I reckon we owe it. There's got to be another way.'

'Like Kruger's turning all that gold into arms and forcing us out?' Beit asked gently. 'Britain won't stand for that, Barney. Then it's an all-out fight with the whole might of the British Empire set to crush your Boers. Nice won't even come into it. England learned a thing or two last time around. And this time the wholesale carnage'll make the Transvaal War of Independence look like a Wanderers Club boxing match. That's why Erich and I are ready to put up half a million . . .'

'Cheap at double the price, but beside the point.' Barnato stubbornly jammed a Romeo y Juliéta into his mouth and spoke around it. 'I don't mess in politics.'

'You cast your vote when you put your mines up for auction,' Beit reminded him mildly. 'We just need a payment scheme operable only after Joubert's installed.' Barnato was distractedly searching his pockets for a light and he placed the matches on the whisky table next to him. 'You know your way around the Rand like the back of your hand.'

Barnato felt as though he'd gone just too many rounds with a younger, stronger opponent. He abandoned the cigar and abruptly knocked back his drink. 'Any more of that French grog?'

Beit poured him a heftier tot. 'Then you won't join us?'

'I didn't say that . . .' Barnato slumped in his chair, one hand shielding his eyes like a tired child. He had crept to the edge of the chasm Beit bestrode and found that it yawned like a gaping hole. 'And you know, my little nipper Jack's just begun to talk and understand things,' he said brokenly. He removed his pince-nez and wearily massaged the indentations on either side of his nose where they'd nipped the skin.

'Just a scheme for payment, you say?' he murmured vaguely.

'To start with, £1,000 a month plus expenses . . .' von Veltheim suggested.

Barnato concentrated on whirling his Indian clubs in his personal gym faster and faster until they traced patterns like twin propellers in the air. Beit perched on the box ottoman and, there being no seating arrangement for von Veltheim, he stood. But what the venue lacked in comfort, it made up in privacy. Barnato'd actually dispensed with his Hottentot valet for the occasion, and he didn't look happy about it.

'. . . And quarter of a million when the contract has been carried out,' von Veltheim finished.

'In gold?' Barnato enquired.

Gold. Von Veltheim felt gripped by a sense of purpose that exceeded anything he'd known. For days and nights he'd been preparing himself consciously and subconsciously for this moment. Relishing it. Planning it. Fearing it. If they propose this, I must be ready to counter with that. If they are uncertain, I must know how to reassure.

'And with a diplomatic posting with the new administration.' He bargained on principle. But he also suspected that Barnato, like himself, didn't trust those who didn't.

'Blimey, *you're* not bad.' But there lurked in Barnato's eyes the grudging recognition of a fellow graduate of the marketplace of life. He wound down his routine to eye him narrowly. 'Point is, can you deliver?'

'If you'd any doubts . . .' von Veltheim began.

'Mr von Veltheim was in Santa Marta last December,' Beit hastily pointed out, 'and the Colombians are eternally grateful.'

'So?' Barnato shot von Veltheim a suspicious look. 'Convince me.' He was toying irritably with his jar of boxing liniment. He had this twinge in his deltoid that he just couldn't reach.

'May I?' Von Veltheim reached for the boxing liniment, unscrewed the top and the smell of wintergreen perfumed the air. It was nervous time. Like crossing unchartered desert with a compass acting up. Like crawling across snowy wastes when the enemy artillery has you in its sights. Like laying charges on a bridge across a gorge knowing your judgement's already shot. Please God . . . only this once more?

'The Transvaal's a natural Boer fortress,' he began hesitantly. 'To seize the President and get him out fast, we use their own tactics: speed and mobility . . .' He spread neat dollops over the freckled skin and, working on the tension knots with deep firm strokes, he began to elucidate.

It was a good half-hour later that he used the blade edge of both hands to conclude with a brisk tattoo from the nape of the neck to the small of the back. 'It's neat and clean and in everyone's interests, including the Boers. You don't need a knockout punch when you can win on points.'

Barnato had closed his eyes and was giving himself up to the delicious sensation. 'Throw in the massage for a round £12,000, we see about that posting' – he shrugged experimentally several times, and then beamed expansively – 'and my lawyers take care of the bread and honey,' he purred.

Von Veltheim's brow furrowed in uncertainty.

'Money,' Beit interpreted.

'Then where do I contact you?' von Veltheim enquired.

'It is *we* who contact *you*. We just need to know where.' At last Beit felt comfortable enough to raise his legs into a lounging position on the box ottoman.

Von Veltheim wasn't quite so comfortable. 'In an emergency?'

'Like you said, if we'd any doubts . . .' And Barnato's face twisted in a *moue* of mock reproach at this heresy. 'Course, it may take a bit o' this and that to set up. Till we meet then at the Cape . . .' He stuck out his hand. '*Mazel and broche*!'

Von Veltheim recognised the diamond dealers' Yiddish jargon used to seal a pact. '*Mazel and broche*!' He gripped his hand and then Beit's.

'All that's left is to decide exactly how payment is to be made,' Barnato agreed.

That was when it struck von Veltheim that it was Barnato who had failed to bargain.

Purring down the Essen road in the rear seat of the custom-made Viktoria Benz, Erich Wernher sat back and studied its owner.

The car, the chinchilla-collared coat and the manicured beringed hands suggested a dilettante. But he also noted the cat-like stillness in the portly frame; and he'd seen the eyes. The banker to the bankers, had heavy-lidded dark eyes that could be acutely observant. And his way of listening only seemed absent-minded. He listened intently – and not only to the topic – but to all the nuances that gave away far more than the speaker guessed.

Wernher stroked the automobile's upholstery. It had the pleasant smell of new leather. 'They're here to stay, and you can't beat German engineering. I must stop shillyshallying.'

'Rather wait. There's a new model on the drawing board with pneumatic tyres.'

'The Benz Comfortable?'

'Exactly. Now that Karl Benz's partners oversee the administration and sales, he concentrates on design and production. All Europe'll soon be speeding about on his wheels.'

Wernher leaned forward for a better look at the instrument panel. 'They tell me vehicles leave his factory in their hundreds. And not only motorcars. What his bus is doing for public transport, his van will do for trade. *Zut*! Imagine how this'll affect commerce and industry?'

'And not a moment too soon if it's to be harnessed to armaments.'

'I've never thought much about armaments. Too busy with diamonds and gold.'

'Then think about it, Erich. Think. Mechanised warfare's just around the corner. Krupps manufactured the first gun and introduced the Bessemer steel process only in the early sixties. And then Bismarck's wars gave us ample opportunity to test them . . .' – the banker darted a quick look at Wernher – '. . . selling to both sides.'

Wernher felt like a man trapped in the thrall of a python's gaze. 'I'm a Franco-Prussian war veteran. Forgive me if I'm squeamish.'

'Forget all that sentimental claptrap, Erich. What if the Kaiser were encouraged to compete with England for naval supremacy? And then piff-paff.' The banker sliced the air twice with the flat of his hand. 'One incident is all we need to set Germany at England's throat.'

Wernher looked out of the car window at the countryside reeling past like landscape viewed from a train. It was all going too quickly for him to grasp.

The banker to the bankers laid a pink hand on Wernher's cashmere sleeve. 'But first we need just a little war to test everything. That shouldn't be too difficult, Erich. England must still want the Boer gold?'

From the Ruhr catchment lake Wernher could see Essen in silhouette. It was a town he knew well, and yet he dreaded getting there. 'The Boers are too pastoral to test your new arms,' he blurted out.

'Nonsense. They might still fight on horseback, but I assure you they're happy to do it with the most modern weapons we can sell them. And they're buying.' The banker leaned forward and tapped his chauffeur's shoulder. 'This will do nicely, thank you, Guenther. We'll walk from here.'

The two men climbed out. Up ahead reared the pile of the Krupp's Institute for Chemical and Physical Research.

'We already have armour plating. Now . . .' – the banker jerked his head at the building – '*Right now* they're busy with the most exciting chrome-nickel steel research. It'll revolutionise warfare, Erich. But we need experience. Plans. Options.'

'Let's suppose your first option was the Raid.' Unconsciously, Wernher was trying to match his pace to the banker's. 'And once that failed, your second was a war between the British and the Boers. What would you say if I told you there won't be one? *Je t'assure*, Alfred's already got a professional to abduct Kruger, and Barney Barnato's leaving for the Rand to arrange his payment.'

The banker to the bankers smiled indulgently and shook his

head. 'For every plan they make, we've a contingency one. There'll be war, my friend, because we need it. And then a breathing space to correct faults. Refine strengths. Mass produce . . . before moving on.'

'On? To *what*?' Wernher stared at him with growing unease.

'To world war. But a dozen or so years into the twentieth century,' he said gently. And taking Wernher's elbow, they began to climb the steps to the Krupp's Institute. 'Come, Erich. Let's show you the shape it's going to take.'

5

Von Veltheim stood watching Anne-Marie sketch the spires of Westminster in the fading light. In her grey worsted suit with the mannish tie, the reading spectacles and the worse-for-wear boater she just missed being dowdy. I know a dozen women who'd leave her standing, he decided.

Rot! his traitor's heart contradicted. She's the most appealing woman you've ever met. 'Sorry to hear about your engagement,' he said.

She spun around in surprise, almost dislodging her boater. 'Really?' Her spine had straightened to boarding-school approved deportment and he could tell she was aiming for cucumber cool.

'Really, more sorry for Willi.'

Suddenly her smile was a mile wide, and when she removed her spectacles it squeezed those curious gold-flecked eyes into crescents that were more disturbing than he'd remembered.

And now they scanned him.

In his Jermyn Street suit, Turnbull & Asser shirt and hand-lasted boots boned to a high military gloss, he looked every inch the dandy Willi had described to her. But Willi had neglected to mention the indolent fencer's grace with which he moved. He'd harped instead on his reputation with loose women with whom she now unexpectedly found herself in fervent accord.

Von Veltheim moved in closer to examine her sketch. 'Mmmn . . . The Terror of Fleet Street reports on the Jameson Enquiry! Exciting?'

'Confusing is closer.'

Closer, he had the look of a weary seafarer. Rainer had spoken of the rolling stone the Royal Geographic Society had commended for exploration in the Far East and Australia, and had been much less forthcoming about shadier exploits among the revolutionists in Central America.

'Confusing and worrying.' She hesitated. 'My editor . . . Flora

Shaw . . . You see, she . . . I mean, I . . . Oh, darn!' The stumbling words stuttered to a halt just as Big Ben chimed the quarter hour. 'Oh, *darn!*' In a flurry, she began packing away her drawing materials. 'As part of our orientation they're allowing some journalists through Westminster,' she explained in a rush, 'and I've got to *go!*'

'One travel article hardly qualifies me as the *The Daily Telegraph* correspondent.' He gave her a conspiratorial grin as he offered her his arm. 'But nobody but you knows that.'

She righted her boater, slipped an arm through his and they began to walk.

'Your Miss Shaw?' he prompted.

'Did you know that inserting a full stop can change a sentence?'

'Evidence tampering?'

The outrage came pouring out as though from a faucet. 'Like Jameson's dating the Reformers' letter to cover himself. Like Miss Shaw's covering Messrs Rhodes and Chamberlain, and liaising between them. And when Westminster subpoenas her, how much'll come out?' She answered her own question by holding up her finger and thumb linked in an 'O'.

'That subpoena's giving you your chance on the Colonial desk,' he reminded her.

'Lordy! Fag the Colonial desk! I'm focused on the mining men.'

'Not as focused as they'd be on silencing you.'

'With my ammunition to stop them in their tracks?'

Von Veltheim managed to hold his grin, but he felt as if a fist had closed around his heart.

Their footsteps made a hollow echoing sound as they entered the Great Hall of Rufus and gazed up at the curving ribs of the vaulted ceiling soaring above.

'This is where the first English Parliaments and coronations were held,' she breathed.

'You know, I missed you?'

Willi was right. Making a woman feel wanted was probably standard procedure. 'The King's champion would ride round here in full armour to fling down his gauntlet . . .'

'Badly.'

'To challenge to mortal combat anyone disputing his Sovereign's title,' she finished desperately. 'It's also where Charles I was condemned to death. But you probably know that?'

'I had to come after you.'

'It led to civil war.' Her somersaulting heart seemed to have taken on a life of its own. 'Remember that painting of the Roundheads interrogating the Cavalier boy?' she babbled on. '*When did you see your . . . your father*? I . . . Oh! . . .'

The torrent of words was abruptly cut off. Suddenly she found herself wrapped in his arms being thoroughly kissed. What's more, she'd never been kissed like that before. She felt as if she was floating. No, drowning and going to heaven. 'Oh, my!' she sighed when he released her.

'So if you'd rather not talk here?' He cocked his head in the direction of the hansom cab stand at Westminster Bridge and again offered her his arm.

A roué through and through, she told herself as the cab driver flicked his whip at a dappled rump, and their cab jolted away from the kerb.

But who cares? Her reckless heart thudded as they swayed together and she succumbed to the delicious thrill.

The clip-clopping of the horses' hooves slowed and then stopped outside 55 Gower Street and he sprang out and lifted her down. She made no attempt to break the physical contact, and stood quite still in the circle of his arms. The lamplighter lighting the gas lamps came and went. Von Veltheim tried to read her eyes. Then for the third time that afternoon she slipped her arm through his. But this time they went inside.

Breathless, she closed the bedroom door behind them.

He fumbled for matches to light the gas lamp, but she came into his arms so swiftly their noses collided in the dark. 'Blast! I've dropped the matches. Everywhere.'

'Never mind. I . . .'

'Let's not talk,' he whispered.

'No . . . I . . .'

Then he found her mouth.

'There now.'

Much later the match flared and he touched it to the candle on the bedside commode laden with books and an outsize atlas. The bedclothes were tumbled, and their clothes lay in heaps on the floor.

'I liked it like that in the dark,' she sighed.

He rolled his head to look at her. 'Me too. Did you also learn to kiss like that in Salonika?'

'No, silly.'

'In the convent then?'

'Really, Franz . . .'

'Well?'

'Well, my guardian chose this Swiss finishing school, and I wanted to study . . .' She rolled onto her belly and propped her chin on her hands to study him better. 'What are you really like, Franz von Veltheim? I don't even know the things that please you.'

'That's easy. My Château Neuf du Pâpe at room temperature and my Chablis chilled. Sunrises in the desert, but in the southern latitudes I enjoy watching it set into the sea. Chess in front of a roaring log fire, particularly if I can take my opponent's queen in five moves with two knights. Beethoven's glorious sixth . . .'

'The slow movement,' she agreed. 'It's so sad.'

'*Swan Lake* at Covent Garden when I'm escorting a lovely woman in a Poiret evening gown . . .' He caught Anne-Marie's raised eyebrow. 'On second thoughts, fag the gown.'

'All sensual things,' she observed. 'Does nothing touch your heart?'

'I believe not. I'm told I have impulses, not feelings, by a lady who also says that in London and Paris a lady changes her gold jewellery for diamonds after dark. And she proves it by doing so. Shows she's not only knowledgeable, but sincere.'

'And in my opinion, misguided. What are impulses if not the first stirrings of feelings? But *what* stirs you?'

His eyes grew sober. 'Afraid more things I dislike. Injustice. Lapses of integrity and courage . . .' His gunpowder monocle tightened. 'In particular, my own.'

'With the *The Daily Telegraph* requesting your account of overland from Japan to Sumatra?' she teased. 'Or the Royal Geographic Society's award for that record-breaking expedition through the Never-Never country? Am I going the right way for an interview?'

'I'm not that partial to reporters. But play your cards right, and we'll see.'

'Then you traded exploring for more dangerous fare. Coups d' états in Colombia provoking changes of government?'

'Ahah! The intrepid newshound trails a scoop!' He tried changing the subject and leaned over and touched the atlas. 'Is that what this monster's doing here?'

'What made you do it?'

'Don't know. You get an attractive offer one day and you just do it.'

'No, you don't. You're not a jungle predator acting on instinct. You *choose* what you do.'

'Unless something chooses you. Something that drives you.'

'*What* drives you, then? What makes it stop driving you? Could it drive you again?'

Von Veltheim took a breath to speak, but for a moment no utterance came out. 'If a country takes what it wants by force,' he began, 'and the casualties are out of all proportion to the prize . . .'

'Having been such a casualty yourself?'

'I won't have you turn me into a bloody hero. I'm telling you I did it for the money at first.'

'And now?'

'Forget that interview. I don't like the questions you ask.' He was breathing hard because he was rattled and he didn't know why. He realised that all her probing had given her the capacity to penetrate his guard and wound him. At the same time she was the only antidote to his loneliness he'd ever known. Was she salvation or nemesis? With a feeling of desperation, he gathered her close.

She relaxed against him and breathed in his man odour. 'Oh my, I didn't know it would be like that just now.'

'Nor did I. I think you just deflowered *me*.'

'Is that bad?'

Was it? Salvation or nemesis? He shut out the thought and inhaled the scent at the nape of her neck. 'You know, you've a whole bouquet here. I smell lemon.' He moved on to her armpit 'And here you're musky.'

She rolled on top of him, nuzzling his chest hair. It was curly and crisp to the touch. 'Yours is good and gamey.' Her tongue peeped out, pink and inquisitive as a kitten's. 'And you taste of salt.'

He rolled her on her back, and felt her fingers, light as butterfly wings, in the small of his back.

He touched her ribcage. Her skin was drum tight and silky, and his finger pads slid lingeringly over each rib, reading them like braille. His head moved over her taut belly muscles and down. And down. 'And here you have the most delightful anchovy smell . . .' She ducked her head sideways, watching him in disbelief. '. . . And taste . . .'

'Franz, you can't mean to . . .'

'Can't I?'

'No, really . . .'

'*No?*'

'No . . .' She felt the breath snatched from her body, as she gasped, 'Oh . . . Oh my!'

The banker to the bankers liked to work at the window with its fine view of the Elbe. He enjoyed its moods, its movement, its industry. And the ferry.

'Thank you, Friedrich.' He took the cardboard dossier his secretary had compiled for him, and began to read.

Braun, Karl: Born in Bremen, son of a tobacco merchant. Now aged 36. Emigrated as a child with his family to the USA. As a young man he drifted into journalism, covering frontier stories and Mexican disputes for the Missouri Democrat. *While thus occupied, he met Adolf Luderitz (also a German expatriate travelling in the USA) and joined his exploratory expedition to the no-man's-land of South West Africa in 1882 where they hoisted the German flag in 1884, and renamed the Nama territory German West Africa.*

In 1886 Luderitz sold out the concessions he'd acquired to the 'Deutsche Kolonialgesellschaft für Südwestafrika' and they turned to prospecting along the Orange River. Luderitz tired of waiting for supplies by ox-wagon, and set off by canvas boat along the Orange River, never to be heard of again.

Braun made his way overland to Kimberley and then to the Witwatersrand gold fields.

In 1892 he returned to the USA where he found interim work while trying to raise capital for mining ventures in South Africa. These negotiations were cut short when he left the USA suddenly.

The one-eyed tortoiseshell cat the banker had rescued from a neighbour's trio of snapping Weimaraners lay grooming itself on a flocked velvet pouffe at his side. He picked her up and caressed the ruff at the back of her neck. 'Resourceful, a renegade, with a healthy respect for money. I think he's worth meeting, Kitty-cat,' he said softly. 'Don't you?'

Newmarket!

Barney Barnato stood with Woolf Joel watching the horses circle the Rowley Mile parade ring at the autumn sun gleaming on their polished coats. His golden chestnut filly, sleek muscles rippling, prominent veins like silken cords, pranced in the circle and kicked out with her back legs.

'Looks a tre-eat,' Woolf drawled in the plummy proletarian-to-Park Lane accents of the rather-recently-rich.

'Not 'arf the treat she'll look in there.' Merrily dropping his 'h's', Barnato jerked his thumb at the winning enclosure and turned back to favour his favourite nephew with an affectionate beam.

But it was not for his Byronesque good looks nor his ever-so-English stance – one knee slightly crooked, one manicured hand resting elegantly on his sleek Savile Row-clad haunch. It owed more to the camaraderie they had cultivated in their rags-to-riches safari from Whitechapel to the West End. Back when Barnato had first struck it rich on the Kimberley diamond fields he'd sent for his three nephews, one by one. But it was finally Woolf's blend of acumen and courage that welded them both into a formidable team.

Woolf was doing a quick comparison between Barnato's Primrose Gold and the favourite top weight. 'Competition's Rothschild's grey,' he pronounced.

Pewter-coloured, dappled silver to anthracite, with the muscled shoulders and quarters that belonged on a Greek frieze, Excalibur threw out his forelegs and rolled his eyes.

'Huh!' Barnato sniffed, 'My old sweetheart'll give those toffs a run for their money any day.' And this time when he jerked his thumb it was at Leopold Rothschild and his entourage.

He looked about nervously. Then, in sudden decision, he led Woolf out of earshot of the racing crowd milling about. 'Fancy the biggest punt of our lives, Woolfie?' he breathed.

'I'm listening.'

So he spoke to him rapidly in low urgent tones.

Woolf stared at him, flabbergasted. 'But we've always supported Oom Paul.'

'Alfred says it's become a matter of who gives us the squarer deal,' Barnato said with defiance.

But when he lit a fresh cigar Woolf noted that he needed both hands to steady the match. And now he also noted the tracery of new anxiety lines superimposed over a skin grown suddenly slack. Does a man age so suddenly at forty-five? he wondered. He felt the cold clutch of fear. This time Barney's bitten off more than he can chew, and I'm blowed if I know how to head him off. 'Ever heard how the Prince of Wales took the Derby?' he asked casually.

'Ah, but that time it suited Rothschild to do the pulling up. One hand washes the other, Woolfie. That's smart.'

'But not smart for us? Noticed the balance sheet since I've joined his grouse shoots?'

Barnato's grin hardened into an obstinate scowl. 'You can tell him with knobs on: not with my filly you don't.'

Woolf gave him a 'You're the boss,' shrug and obediently sauntered over to the Rothschild clique.

Their trainer bustled into the ring with a slight youth in Barnato's black and gold silks, and the lad touched his cap respectfully. 'She looks on fine form today, sir.'

Barnato had been expecting the champion jockey, and he raised an enquiring eyebrow at his trainer.

'Taffy Jones pulled a back muscle,' he explained hurriedly. 'But young Patrick here's our most talented apprentice. Rides Primrose Gold in work.'

Barnato took in the pint-sized muscled frame and the hands that belonged on a much bigger man. He'd always had a soft spot for a boy who was keen-eyed and strong. 'Then win for me, young Patrick, and you've five hundred guineas,' he said suddenly.

The 'get-mounted' bell clanged, and all at once trainers were giving the jockeys a leg up, and muttering last minute instructions:

'Take her out nice and easy . . .'

'Break clean and don't get boxed in on the bend . . .'

'Don't wait for someone else to make the running for you . . .'

Barnato saw that Woolf had strolled over to Primrose Gold and was stroking her glossy flank and talking earnestly with the jockey.

A broker raised his topper. 'Say, Barney! How's a pony on Primrose Gold?'

'Safe as money in the bank,' he grinned happily.

Jockeys up. Horses, ears pricked, nostrils quivering, trippling like circus ponies in their final circuit.

Woolf suddenly back, grabbing Barnato's arm. Threading their way through the crowd and up the steps of the members' stand to see the horses canter past.

First on the track the top-weight jockey in Rothschild's blue-and-yellow colours trotting Excalibur down to the start on a tight rein that arched his neck like a knight errant.

Apprentice jockey in Barnato's black and gold trailing him, and Primrose Gold's beautiful daisy-cutter action scarcely skimming the ground.

The rest of the field spreading out in Indian file. The gaily coloured silks receding up the track like confetti in the breeze.

'Never thought I'd be so set on my colours,' Barnato murmured. 'When you get on a bit the gee-gees or the gloves makes no odds, Woolfie. Life kind of gets the bit between its teeth, and next thing you know, you're just trying to hang on.'

'*You*? The terror of the ring and the turf?' Woolf scoffed. But he was worried. Cocksure Barney, afraid he's losing his grip? Confidence eroded and direction confused? His heart went out to him. He wanted to marshal all his ebbing courage and energy for him, and bring it back. But he didn't know how.

Bookmaker's voice carrying over the hum, 'Excalibur two-to-one on. Primrose Gold even money. Ten-to-one the field.'

Barnato training his binoculars on the starting-post. 'Red flag's up!'

Commentator's patter over the megaphone: '... horses are under starters' orders for the Caesarevitch ...' Bell shrilling momentarily cutting him off. Commentator shouting, 'They're away and racing!'

Barnato focusing his lenses on the frieze of flying horses, a rippling string of beads between rail and sky.

Voice on the loud-hailer calling, 'The four-furlong post coming up, and it's Primrose Gold and Excalibur out in front with hardly a whisker between them ...'

Barnato pleading, 'Let's see you foot it, my little love.'

The field spreading out as they take the bend.

Commentator roaring, '... and it's still a two-horse race ...'

Horses thundering like a cavalry charge for the two hundred-metre mark.

Barnato hysterically punching Woolf's shoulder. 'Go, Primrose Gold!'

Jockeys, hands and heels working like pistons, crouched so low that horse and rider blend into one.

Crowd whooping, 'Ride him, Patty!'

Barnato howling, '*Go!*'

Into the straight. Primrose Gold, a length of copper silk streaming in the wind, opening up a lead.

Excalibur, ears flattened, flying hooves churning up sods of dirt.

Barnato bellowing, 'Use the whip, damn it!'

Crowd screaming, 'The stick!'

One and a half lengths to go, and now the crops are flailing, horses' coats afroth.

Chestnut abruptly checking her stride. Changing feet.

Excalibur exploding in a burst of speed and streaking up the inside, first past the post.

Crowd roaring. Rothschild mobbed. The press of bodies ecstatically opening up a path to the winning enclosure for him to lead in his winner.

Barnato stood with his binoculars clutched to his chest wistfully watching the jockey trot Primrose Gold back to her groom. 'He bloody gave up the ghost,' he mumbled.

'No harm done,' Woolf said cheerfully. 'Run'll bring her on.'

But Barnato was glowering at him. 'How much to the lad to see she didn't finish?'

A sheepish smile. 'Thousand guineas. Said we'd put our shirts on the grey.' He looped an arm around Barnato's shoulder and steered him towards the Members' Bar. 'She'll win next time out, Barney. And you'd be chuffed no end to lead her in. How about watching things here while I take a gander at the Rand?' he pleaded. 'Deal?'

But Barnato's mouth had set stubbornly. 'I've just told you why I can't.' Aching, he looked at Woolf. 'We see things so differently now, Woolfie,' he said dully. 'And you say, "*deal*"?'

Woolf ached too, but with a nameless dread.

6

The murky fog that rolled down from the Thames over the City of Westminster that February morning was enough to make Anne-Marie turn up her coat collar against the chill.

Outside the Houses of Parliament carriages were banked up in the thick peasouper two and three deep, with half a dozen rain-caped Bobbies trying to unsnarl the jam. An enterprising coster-monger in mittens and a too-large overcoat worked the perimeter doing a brisk trade in miniature Union Jacks.

There was a flurry of sheet music, and a brass band smartly erupted in *God Save the Queen* just as the closed carriage with the Royal coat of arms rattled to a halt.

On the adjacent pavement a uniformed nursemaid lifted a small boy in a sailor suit on high and squealed, 'Oo-ooh, look! It's the Prince of Wales!'

The sergeant manning the door to the committee room waved a list and kept apologising: 'Only select members and the press this way.'

Breathless, Anne-Marie ground to a halt at his elbow.

'Do move along there, Miss,' he pleaded.

With an indignant flush, she firmly poked her press pass under his nose.

He scanned his list doubtfully. No one had said anything about a woman.

'You've surely read Miss Mavrogordato in *The Times*, my good man?'

Anne-Marie recognised the bewhiskered man with the merry eyes as Melton Prior, correspondent for the *Illustrated London News*. His reputation in trouble spots had given him celebrity status, and she flashed him a grateful smile as he swept her through the door.

Inside, she hauled out her sketch pad to draw a quick diagram. The witness's rectangular table enclosed the open end of the committee's horseshoe-shaped table, behind which sat select members of the house and the press.

Big Ben struck one, its chimes muffled by the fog. Inside, the creaks and silences seemed amplified as the committee filed in and took their seats. Under her boater Anne-Marie could feel the hair on the back of her neck come erect. Rhodes . . . Beit . . . Chamberlain . . . The Prince of Wales . . . 'Lordy!' She clutched Prior's sleeve. 'Ever see so much power in one room?'

Prior was busy impaling Chamberlain with cruel telling pencil strokes – orchid in his buttonhole, eye behind his monocle as keen as Birmingham steel. 'Pushful Joe,' he sniffed. 'And my old father once voted for his social reform.' Leaning closer, he indicated a burly man with a troubled face, and muttered, 'That's Graham Bower. Secretary to the Cape High Commissioner during the Raid.'

Anne-Marie eyed him with frank interest. 'They say he's got enough dirt to turn this whitewashing party a nasty grey,' she whispered.

Deftly she sketched the Prince of Wales lounging before the wall-to-wall backdrop of the South African map, as casually at ease as though he were in his box at Ascot. Russet-bearded chin in one manicured hand, his merry blue eyes were fixed with interest on her. 'One minute his head's blocking "Cape", she grumbled under her breath, 'and the next, "Town".'

'Rhodesia's too high,' Prior hissed. 'We're here to praise Caesar, my dear, not to bury him.' He sneaked a look at the far end of their bench. 'Careful, your editor with your boss.'

Flora Shaw ensconced at Moberley Bell's side was also studying her curiously. Anne-Marie smiled at them sweetly just as the Sergeant at Arms ushered Rhodes to the witness table, and she flipped over a fresh leaf for him.

An urbane giant, his expensive grey suit rumpled on his loose-limbed frame, he looked a man of the veld, astonishingly rejuvenated from his year's African Sabbatical and unnervingly impassive. And the eyes ... Her pencil poised above the page. They were quite messianic. 'No wonder everyone's ready to follow him to hell and gone,' she breathed.

Copies of his prepared statement were being circulated, and she just had time to scan hers before he stood and cleared his throat to speak.

'My Lords, gentlemen,' Rhodes began in that light voice, deliberately pitched a couple of decibels below those of most public speakers to make people strain to catch every syllable. 'Discontent in the Transvaal began with the discovery of gold there . . .' For the next half-hour he compellingly chronicled his highly personalised vision of the Witwatersrand.

'The English-speaking majority owns more than half the land, nine-tenths of the wealth and pays nineteen-twentieths of its taxes.' His eyes swept the committee table, reasonable, intimate, and hypnotically persuasive. 'Redress through constitutional means having failed, I placed Dr Jameson's column on our border . . .'

Sir William Harcourt stood. 'What right had *you* to send Rhodesian troops to South Africa?'

Rhodes tossed his leonine head in a gesture of dismissal. 'The same right England's got sending aid to Crete right now,' he snapped. 'I dare say that's wrong too, but it's still going.' With neither horse nor helmet, he'd flung down the gauntlet in his sovereign's name in a challenge none dared dispute, and as he stood down, several members exchanged nods of approval.

'Game, set and match to Mr Rhodes,' Anne-Marie whispered. Then something made her glance up at the committee table. Chamberlain exuded a mix of ruthlessness and charm; but the eye behind his monocle was fixed piercingly on her. She looked back defiantly and then turned back to her pad to add a note.

'I'll pay double for your crib notes,' Prior hissed.

Anne-Marie shook her head firmly.

He smiled winningly and held up three fingers.

She tossed him a grin and read under her breath, 'Only witnesses meant to cover the Colonial Office's complicity . . .'

Prior had heard enough and he swiftly put a cautionary finger to her lips. Just then a hush fell with the suddenness of guillotine blade, and they turned to see Beit take the stand.

White, with a sickly sheen of perspiration accentuating his pallor, he faced Sir William Harcourt. 'If you please, sir, I'd also like permission to read a prepared statement.'

A jerky nod.

'I'm German by birth,' he began shakily. 'But I truly believe that in trying to reform the Transvaal Administration I was promoting the interests of both England and my own country.' A nervous Hamburg sibilant had begun to plague his 'th' sounds.

'You're not a naturalised Englishman?' Harcourt looked as if he'd just made an unsavoury discovery.

'Not yet.'

'And you fancy both powers have mutual interests?'

'It's in everyone's interest to replace an incapable government with a capable one.' The fish eyes blinked nervously. 'A rising in Johannesburg was inevitable. We sent that force to avoid full-scale rebellion.'

'And to avoid it, you *promoted* it?'

Beit darted a pleading look from Rhodes to Chamberlain.

Chamberlain looked back. Inscrutable.

'You also sold certain shares short?'

Beit opened his mouth to reply, but no words came out.

'A bear transaction?'

'I tried to save the industry,' he said softly.

The expression in Harcourt's eyes reminded Anne-Marie of the feverish look on the faces of the crowd of ruffians she'd recently seen plaguing two men on Vienna's station.

Her shorthand leap-frogged from verbatim reporting to her own comments. '*Which is the more heinous crime – being a natural businessman or not a naturalised Englishman?*' She would never remember at which point she began reading her notes under her breath to Prior.

'Mr Rhodes's Raid, fought with cloak and dagger tactics, live ammunition and diplomatic double-dealing is one thing: but Mr Beit's, with its book entries, Teutonic origins and less support from Chamberlain . . .'

Prior realised her voice was carrying, and he nudged her. It was useless. Anne-Marie had recognised something else in his expression. Admiration. And it was spreading like a veld fire among her peers. It gave her a heady sensation of her own worth, and she felt strong and vital in her crusade.

'Does the Radical Member *really* believe Mr Beit's action a Stock Exchange manoeuvre?' she demanded. 'And why does the Liberal Member avoid questions about the real perpetrator – the Colonial Office?'

The silence was broken only by Prior's despairing, 'Hush, now!'

Anne-Marie was beyond caring. She was on her feet, glaring at Chamberlain. 'And why are Messrs Rhodes and Beit covering *your* part in this scandal, sir? The Prince of the realm sits here, and he wants answers.' Eyes blazing, she swivelled to face the Prince of

Wales. 'Or does he?'

Edward liked spirited women, and had been trying to catch her eye. Now he was sorry.

Prior caught it all.

Chamberlain trying to look outraged, but too shifty to be convincing. Beit looking helplessly from Chamberlain to Rhodes.

Rhodes avoiding his eyes.

Beit betrayed.

Graham Bower silently approving.

The buzz of shock among the members.

Flora Shaw appalled.

Moberley Bell and the Sergeant at Arms ready to close in on her from both sides of their row.

With a covert signal from Prior, the press corps closed ranks. As in a superbly rehearsed troop manoeuvre, the reporter immediately behind her swiftly vacated his seat, and Prior swung her into the space, vaulting into the neighbouring one – now magically vacant. But a moment later the Sergeant at Arms had wrenched her from his protection. And now he had her by the elbow, and was bundling her along the row to where Moberley Bell stood waiting in the aisle.

He gave her a curt little nod and held out his hand for her notebook.

'So when he asked for my resignation, I told him to consider it rendered.' Anne-Marie loosened the pins and allowed her hair to tumble over the pillow.

Von Veltheim saw that it had a thread or two of grey and realised that it was the first time he'd seen it quite loose in the daylight. He thought of the coming months, and he felt a pang for all the other little things about her there'd been no time to know. The changes he wouldn't be there to see. 'And then?' he prompted, his casual voice giving the lie to the ache in his soul.

'He strongly advised me against accepting a position with a rival concern. So I told him not to worry, I had other plans. And anyway the trustees of my father's estate wanted me back on the Continent where my estranged fiancée was pressing for a reconciliation.'

'Sounds damned convincing.'

'Good?'

'Not the part about Willi?' He frowned in mock alarm. But his heart plummeted with the realisation that if there was anything worse than his taking her from Willi, it was Willi taking her from him. 'At least with you out of the way the Colonial Office can get some peace.'

'Not if I go after Chamberlain. Presiding where he belongs in dock? It's actually hilarious.'

'No, it's actually dangerous.' He examined a hank of her hair for further grey. 'You're out of your depth accusing Westminster.'

'And you're not out of *yours*? You think *you're* safe because you're apolitical?' She captured his hand and clasped it in both of hers. 'Listen to me, Franz. Everyone knows the mining men are ready to go to war for their gold fields. And my guess is you're their soft option. But England's not the only colonial power. Who knows what others are pitted against you? And then you can't discount the other money men. Those who profit from war. The arms manufacturers . . . Merchant banks. I've *met* some of Rainer's financier friends. Believe me, this isn't the first time they've kept hostilities on the boil with credit for arms to both sides.

'They're like the legs of a powerful nutcracker. And you?' she steepled her fingers and brought her palms sharply together. 'In the middle. That's *worse* than being aligned with either side.'

She reached out and touched his cheek. 'Then there's also me. I just *have* to expose what I can. And that includes the mining men and their secret agenda.' She helplessly dropped her hand. '*Please* get out before it's too late.'

'Or?'

'Or have the good sense to stop seeing me,' she whispered.

That would happen soon enough, he thought grimly. Taking her face in his hands, he kissed her on the lips. 'You talk too much, woman,' he said gruffly, gathering her close. 'And especially about Willi.'

'I'm unemployed now,' she reminded him from the depth of their embrace. 'Temporarily, anyhow. And with this useless inheritance for which I've got to be either twenty-five or married.'

'Well, I'm glad you're neither.' Achingly, he nuzzled the nape of her neck.

For an instant she succumbed to the delicious frissons this provoked before twisting and holding him away. 'I'm trying to tell you something, Franz! That darn will's why I first agreed to marry

Willi,' she finished in a rush.

'Any marrying you do, will be to me,' von Veltheim said flatly. He felt as if a huge spring-cleaning had taken place in his mind, and he was clear about what was important in his life and what was not. But the thought of Molly twisted like a warning in his gut. He stood and began to pace. 'Unless your guard . . .'

She shook her head soberly, cutting him short. 'My guardian's why I *need* the marriage certificate.'

A marriage certificate. Von Veltheim's thoughts took off like a roller coaster. 'A temporary one then?' he urged. 'Just till I get back?' He had both hands on her shoulders, and his words were like rapid-shooting on a river in spate. 'I know it's fraudulent, but you're *not* marrying Willi!' He gave her a little shake. 'Damn it, woman, we've no time to argue.'

'Who's arguing?' she sighed helplessly.

Instantly, they were locked in each other's arms, and he still couldn't shut out all the emptiness he'd ever felt. And he couldn't shut Molly out. And though he knew he should tell Anne-Marie, he couldn't even do that. Helplessly, he listened to their hearts beat . . . until she pulled the sheet away.

It was much later when he awakened from a relaxed doze that he found her putting the finishing touches to a line drawing of him. She'd captioned it *Soldier of fortune – caught off guard.*

He stood and swung her up in his arms. 'Come. We're going to get you married to the right von Veltheim,' he announced, 'and the hell with 'em all.' But he added a silent *please*?

She read his eyes, and anxiety and desire warred in her and made her voice husky. 'Well, so long as you're right here . . .' – she interlaced the fingers of his one hand with hers, locking them tight – 'what could happen now?'

'And so the fewer people who know about this, the better,' Barnato finished. 'That's why I'm glad *you're* driving us out to Rose Deep today.'

'It certainly means acting without the other partners,' Oscar Beit concurred.

Barnato noticed that he drove the spider through the East Rand like a man used to horses. In his pith helmet with its white silk puggaree, he was physically a younger and more athletic version of his brother, yet in some ways he reminded him more of Woolf. They were the same age; and that made the difference. The older men accumulated and the younger ones consolidated. Only without worrying it could all vanish as easily as it had come.

Oscar whistled to the mare and braked on a *bult* with a panoramic view of the Rose Deep complex melting into the horn of the East Rand. Out of the saffron haze of cyanide dust a score of golden mounds were strung like a necklace across the veld, and the tall wooden headgear of half-a-dozen mines reared up against the midsummer sky.

He turned to Barnato. 'A bit different from twelve years ago, eh?'

'Cor! This was all bare veld crisscrossed with wagon tracks, and a few pegged-out claims,' Barnato agreed. 'Our cuttings and tailings dotted the whole bleeding veld. And there was this muddle of wagons and Scotch carts and corrugated iron shelters where everyone lived, see?' A dreamy smile superimposed itself over his features, gradually eroding the anxiety from the eyes and mouth. 'But all along the reef you could hear the exploding dynamite. Crump-crump . . . Crump-crump. Like that. Hell, we were bang in the middle of this mucking great gold field.' He spread his arms wide. 'Now this's all mine dumps, and those tents . . .' – he jerked his thumb over his shoulder at Johannesburg – '. . . are all office buildings and banks and shops. And our drawing boards are full of parks and theatres . . .' He twisted to look back as if he could see his metropolis in the veld metamorphose from his dreams. 'That makes a man feel good, Oscar. Too good to . . . Well . . . you know?'

'To risk?'

Barnato nodded soberly. 'Cept there's Oom Paul and his folk and their talk of soil and thorn trees and stuff.'

'Against the might of the British Empire?' Oscar cocked a gently ridiculing eyebrow.

'I wish I knew,' Barnato said miserably. 'When I think of Oom Paul I keep remembering my trek to Kimberley behind that old Boer wagon. And how that old *oom* was kind.'

'Seeing both sides hardly makes Joubert Irish. And there's growing support for him among the Progressive Boers.'

Barnato searched Oscar's face for courage.

'They'll owe you,' Oscar assured him. 'If war doesn't overtake us first.'

Then he turned and indicated with his pith helmet. 'That's Rose

Deep's security area over by those bluegums. The cyanide shift boss – a man called Bracer – is authorised to transfer those gold ingots from there to your agent. And it'll stay confidential.'

Barnato gave him a sceptical look.

'See there?' Oscar pointed to a corrugated iron roofed brick building in the distance opposite Elandsfontein Junction. 'That's Michael's Railway Hotel. It's not the Rand Club, but they brew a decent draught beer. It's also got a nice shady stoep where some of the men play poker when they're off shift.' He winked. 'So happens, I've taken a good few pounds off Bracer there.'

'I'm a *klawerjas* man, myself.' Barnato grinned. 'But you did mention beer?'

Oscar let off the brake and flicked his whip above the mare's rump. 'Giddy-up, my old sweetheart,' he crooned. 'Let's get Mr Barnato out of this frazzling sun.'

Leaning perilously out of the hansom cab, Anne-Marie waved her new spring Luton straw hat to her landlady, Mrs Merriweather, who threw one last handful of confetti as it lurched around the corner of Gower Street.

'A bridal couple?' a young woman enquired.

'Oh, yes,' Mrs Merriweather sighed sentimentally. 'You know, I'd never have thought her his type? But there she goes now – the Baroness von Veltheim – and don't she half look the part.'

'Von Veltheim?'

The catch in the woman's voice made Mrs Merriweather turn in time to see the blood drain from her face. 'Oh, my dear. Do you know him?'

Her mouth shaped the word, 'Yes,' but her lips were trembling, and her bleak eyes searched the corner where the cab had disappeared.

'Lord knows when they'll be back. But whom shall I say called?'

'Tell him Madame von Veltheim from Weston-super-Mare,' she whispered.

Mrs Merriweather clucked sympathetically. 'There now, you're all upset you missed them. You being a relative and all.'

'Yes.' She gave a thin little smile. 'But I've never met the bride.'

'Why, she's Anne-Marie Mavrogordato of *The Times*, dearie – or at least she was until an hour ago.'

'Anne-Marie Mavrogordato,' Molly von Veltheim murmured. And the way she said every syllable told Mrs Merriweather that it was a name she didn't mean to forget.

7

It looked like an oversized piece of rock candy shaped like the map of Africa; but it catapulted Beit back to when Kimberley was still called Colesberg kopje. And he thought of how he'd seen the kopje disappear.

How a thousand picks and spades had gnawed and chewed their way through the earth's skin, devouring first the yellow rind and then the blue ground to tear its carboniferous core free.

That same kimberlite core had been fired millions of years ago, in a demon furnace deep in the bowels of the earth. It had been subjected to the same intense pressure that had forged the Alps and the Himalayas, the Rockies and the Andes. From India to Brazil it had lassoed the oceans with a ring of fiery volcanoes. From the Jordan to the Zambezi it had ripped open the Great Rift Valley like a housewife splitting poultry.

With the heat so savage and the pressure so intense, the molten lava had convulsed in a fiery holocaust. Forced upwards through a hundred-and-twenty miles of the earth's crust, it had exploded in a burning cone of molten magma. And locked in its hard blue heart was the hardest and most precious of substances that would sparkle with the light of a thousand stars.

What now lay before Beit on a bed of snowy tissue was a diamond with the capacity to refract its myriad colours in dazzling translucence. The very first time he had looked into a diamond's heart of blue-white flame he'd understood the passion they had inspired since the beginning of time. Here was beauty, and brilliance and power. They aroused an almost sexual love in those who handled them and cut them and traded in them. And he became a convert, a supplicant, a disciple to an absolute truth he would never forget.

'Do we cleave or saw?' Wernher's voice broke into his thoughts.

The giant *Reitz* diamond had been mined at Kimberley's Jagersfontein Mine. Originally named for the Orange Free State's

President F. W. Reitz, it was about to be recut for Queen Victoria's Diamond Jubilee.

That it lay on a bed of white tissue on the table between Wernher and Beit in the premises of one of London's finest master cutters was a tribute to both the cutters and the experts.

It was huge, and Beit used two pairs of tweezers to lift and examine it.

Awed, he glanced across the half-glazed partition at where the white-coated master cutter and the polishers were retesting the diamond-dust impregnated cutting edges of their saws, for only with diamond can you cut diamond.

He replaced the stone and shook his head dumbly. 'My mind's too distracted, Erich. Frankly, I'm scared.'

'You, scared?' Wernher chuckled. '*You*? You once recognised the same parcel of Kimberley diamonds being passed through your hands twice in a *schlenter* deal? The newspapers were full of it.'

'Well, now they're only full of caricatures captioned "Herr Beit". '*You* try being tried by the press.'

'*Zut*! You didn't expect Westminster to treat you like Rhodes? And if a sanctimonious little rag like *Punch* smears you, fight fire with fire.' He picked up the tweezers and turned the stone over to examine the underside. 'I've contacts with *Figaro* and *Der Spiegel* who'll be only too happy to do an article on your advising on this.'

'You think it'll help?'

'I think the Queen will like it if you rename the stone the *Jubilee.* A change of focus, and the whole Marlborough set will not only be buying De Beers', they'll be vying with each other to have you at their grouse shoots and balls again.'

Beit picked up his loupe. 'I have to admit it beats being a pariah.' He lifted the gem with the tweezers, studying it. It looked soapy, yes. But in his mind's eye he could see the whole African firmament on a dry Kimberley night. 'Irregular,' he murmured. 'A flattened octahedron, but without definite crystal faces. How much did you say it weighs?'

'Six hundred and fifty points, eighty carats of Kimberley's finest blue white.'

'Enough to sacrifice weight for lustre.' Beit spoke in the caressing tone other men reserved for a beloved woman. 'Enough to go for a brilliant-cut cushion shape . . .' In soft seductive words, Beit outlined his vision of the Jubilee. 'And with such perfect symmetry it'll balance on a culet two millimetres in diameter,' he finished, laying the stone back on its snowy tissue nest.

'It'll do us all proud,' Wernher congratulated him.

'Barney too,' Beit agreed.

'Oscar's put him in touch with Bracer?'

'Put him in *touch*? They've already half von Veltheim's gold bars at Rose Deep awaiting collection.'

'And you think he'll bring it off?'

'No question. But this time the Transvaal will be ours.'

'*Ours*, Alfred. Not England's.' Wernher emphasised. And he stood and opened the glass partition door.

The St Pauli ferry hooter blasted. The banker to the bankers finished his coffee and pastry at Wiezel's, shrugged on his chinchilla-collared coat and sauntered down the Stintfang along the old Hamburg wall to the Spielbudenplatz.

At precisely the same time a man with a duffel bag disembarked from the ferry and, leaving the grey waters of the Elbe behind him, also walked unhurriedly to the Spielbudenplatz. He saw the portly middle-aged man in the tall silk hat and chinchilla-collared coat watching the trained chimpanzees; and when he bought a packet of nuts from a vendor, the traveller did likewise.

The chimpanzees swooped around the miniature arena on midget bicycles to the zither's finale, and the banker raised his eyebrows for the trainer's permission to reward them. He nodded, and they jostled around him until they spotted an alternative source of supply and re-formed. The banker shrugged good-naturedly. 'Their luck's in today.'

'And hopefully ours, *mein Herr*.' The traveller gave a formal little bow and extended his hand. 'At your service, sir. Karl Braun.'

'Shall we?' The banker nodded at the benches under the lime trees.

He looked at Braun sideways as he fell in beside him. He was pretty much as he'd imagined from his dossier. The athletic build of a gymnast. The pleasant smile of a Sunday-school teacher. Unless you caught the flatness in the grey-flecked eyes. A stillness. Secret. Like water over stone. 'So, Braun? You left the States suddenly? Trouble with the police?'

'Broke the superintendent's arm,' he agreed cheerfully. 'Wouldn't fancy going back though.'

'And South Africa?'

'Ah! Like a warm woman and a cool bottle of wine.'

The banker subsided on a bench and patted the vacant space beside him. 'I'll be frank,' he confided. 'The mining men are being foolish. The dust hasn't even settled, and already they've designs on Kruger.'

Braun thought a moment. 'It *is* possible.'

The banker to the bankers smiled enigmatically. 'Not if there's no Paymaster Barnato.'

'Barney Barnato?' Deep in the flat grey eyes a spark ignited.

'One can't make omelettes without breaking eggs. A small accident, perhaps?'

'Suicides are my forte. Fewer questions asked.'

The banker nodded like a benign mandarin. He pressed a stout Manila envelope into Braun's free hand. 'Go on. Open it.'

Braun glanced about warily. The crowd was now engrossed in the tumblers, and he cautiously withdrew the contents. As he began to count, his expression changed. He looked at the banker uncomprehendingly. 'Why, this is most . . . generous.'

'In your business?' Smiling, the banker arched one eyebrow.

Braun slid the envelope inside the duffel bag. 'It's still twice what we agreed.'

'So is the job, actually.' And although he didn't elucidate further, the banker's chuckle was rich with amusement.

From the rail of the *Ionic* the land mass of Africa rose steeply from the south. Closer, the great solid grey pile of Table Mountain was riven halfway down by gullies and choked with dense cushions of Mediterranean pines, and over the huge flattened summit a froth of milk-white clouds broke like the surf.

'A bleeding tablecloth exactly!' And the man beside him punched von Veltheim's shoulder in glee.

Four weeks earlier when they sailed from Plymouth he had told Fred Foster all about the southern latitudes. Once he'd explained how the streets of Johannesburg were only metaphorically paved with gold, the conversation turned – as had so many others – to gambling. The *Ionic* was no luxury liner with sports committees and deck games; and von Veltheim knew that without his mother-of-pearl card case and ivory chips, it could be a long trip.

'Call me Fred,' Foster invited. 'But I didn't catch yours?'

'Why, Kurt.' And picking up his Gladstone, von Veltheim had started up the companionway with Foster at his side.

Now, a month later, they clattered back down the gangplank together to an unofficial welcome committee of quayside 'skollies' prancing and strutting, whistling and crowing:

Daar kom die Ali-ba-ama . . .
Die Ali-ba-ama kom oor die see-ea!

It was a Malay song dating back to the flying visit in their waters of an American ship during their Civil War; but it had such a catchy tune von Veltheim found himself whistling along.

Foster gripped his shoulder. 'One for the road?'

But von Veltheim shook his head in regret. He had an important message waiting at the Grand Hotel. 'Tomorrow,' he promised, tossing his Gladstone into a waiting cab. 'After a prior engagement at the Queen's.'

At 9.30 next morning Barnato's Hottentot driver-cum-valet called at the Grand Hotel to drive von Veltheim to a meeting with Barnato at the Queen's Hotel.

Along the Beach Road gulls spread their sparkling white wings full-span and skimmed the waves, while scurrying sandpipers left chevron patterns across a milky shoreline with mounds of kelp. Von Veltheim breathed the ozone and filled his lungs with salty shiver.

Jan Bakoven glanced behind them. Cycling was the newest craze and several cyclists were taking the air. 'Just checking,' he explained. 'Mr Barnato's kind of nervous.'

'About being followed?'

'So would you be, sir, if you'd got on the wrong side of President Kruger's *Geheime Dienst*.' Jan Bakoven's tar-coloured eyes narrowed. 'Wherever this carriage goes. I can usually spot him. A tall, well-built gentleman like yourself, sir. And always whistling the same awful tune.'

The Queen's Hotel sprawled like a cub beneath Lion's Head, a string quartet's rendering of *Beautiful Isle of Somewhere* rising reedily from its colonnaded verandah. The wine steward poured a freshly popped Veuve Clicquot into two long-stemmed crystal glasses and retreated.

Von Veltheim studied Barnato, and noted that the ginger hair was more heavily threaded with grey, the choirboy blue eyes with a deeper network of crow's-feet, the adolescent button nose with more booze-artist veins. He wondered what had eroded his cockiness and left him so undermined.

'What's next?' Barnato's question refocused his attention on the job in hand.

So von Veltheim told him about a new kind of warfare that was scarcely warfare at all. And he glossed over the guerilla tactics, the split-second synchronisation, Charlie's sensitive musician's fingertips and the unmusical devices they wrought with such skill. 'So, we rendezvous any day,' he finished. 'I suppose that brings us to Joubert?' He eyed Barnato, waiting.

Barnato glanced about uneasily, and then hunched deeper into his jacket as though trying to disappear. 'Ever been to the "gents" knowing one of those plain-clothed sods is using the next urinal just so he can report to Pretoria how you peed?' he demanded.

Von Veltheim had the general picture, and he didn't like it. He decided to shop around for a hostelry in the suburbs that would be less conspicuous than the beachfront or town. 'What about *Mrs* Joubert?'

'Seeing as how you fancy yeself a ladies' man?'

'No. Seeing as how she's a commando veteran.'

'Either way, she's the person to get him to see you,' Barnato agreed.

'I hope so, because we'll need a diversion in Pretoria. And it's going to take contacts and money. We've still a private army to recruit and equip.'

'The quarter've a million in ingots at Rose Deep'll cover that twice over. The cyanide shift boss – a man called Bracer – will hand 'em over.'

'And cash them?'

'After the takeover? Certainly.'

'My problem is without cash there can't be one.' Von Veltheim tried for the note of rapport they'd struck on the massage table. It didn't come off.

'And not reflecting it in the books is mine.' Barnato matched his smile. Also edgy.

The wind sharpened, and the sand blew up in a sudden curtain shrouding the merry-go-round. Barnato stared thoughtfully at the galloping horses frozen in midair, the southeaster whistling through the canvas. 'I'm to be home for the Queen's Jubilee . . .' – he seemed to be thinking his way through a fog in which he just could not see the next step – '. . . but I'll have answers for you by Madeira. Just bring it off. I mean, 'twould be a crying shame to howl it off for only £12,000.' He upended his domino box on the table and turned the contents face down, shuffling them as he spoke. 'With what's at Rose Deep.' But when he slapped down a roll of bank notes, the smile was a pale imitation of his old cheeky grin. 'Care to draw?'

A knot of interested spectators had gathered nearby. Foster noisily cleared his throat. He was laying a book. His usual cut? Von Veltheim removed his gloves from the table, and Foster immediately engaged his neighbour in a whispered conversation. Von Veltheim's hand hovered for a second, and then smoothly turned up the double six.

Several games later Barnato peeled off the last of his bank notes. 'So you're lucky in gambling too?' He suddenly flashed a frown at Foster. He was chatting innocuously in the doorway with a young man twirling his moustache. Von Veltheim shot him a glance, and studiously examined his glove.

Then Barnato leaned closer and spoke to him very firmly and rapidly of Foster's companion. 'Solly was daft enough to sign on with the Reformers, so even if he's a good lad,' he finished, 'he stays out of this. It's his older brother, Woolf's, my number two. He topped up their glasses. '*L' Chayim*?'

Von Veltheim clinked his glass. 'Your health.'

'You don't appreciate it till you haven't got it,' Barnato said wistfully. 'Not so long ago with a pair of boxing gloves I was every bit as fit as a geezer like you.' Then he looked him over almost cockily, as if sizing him up for a match. 'In the ring it's not how tall you are, it's how fast. And how hard you hit.'

But as he walked von Veltheim out to the carriageway where Jan Bakoven waited with the spider, he shivered.

The little Hottentot's tar-coloured eyes sharpened in his coffee-tinted face. 'Not coming down with the grippe, boss?'

'Just a shiver.'

'Must be someone walked over your grave,' Jan Bakoven said cheerily.

Barnato blanched. 'Knock on that.' He thumped the spider's wooden body work.

'Yess-sir!' And Jan Bakoven knocked.

Von Veltheim knocked, too. And this time it was he who shivered.

At that moment Barnato's white face was captured in the twin lenses of the binoculars trained on him from Lion's Head.

Braun watched Jan Bakoven taking von Veltheim back to Cape Town along the Beach Road. He'd assessed his tall muscular frame, and knew he was a man who could use himself. He also knew that he'd only recently arrived, and would be in no hurry to leave. There were easier ways of doing for Barnato.

He turned his bicycle around and took the higher level track at the base of the mountain to Cape Town's dockland to arrange it.

8

The Union Steamship *Scot* rode proudly at anchor in Cape Town's Empress Dock, pennants whipping in a stiff southeaster. From the quayside wafted the strains of a brass band belting out: '*We're the soldiers of the Queen, m'lads . . .*' Steps lilting to the beat, the first-class passengers streamed aboard, their entourages of valets and butlers bearing polo sticks and golf clubs bringing up the rear.

For Barney Barnato the real music was in the way men talked stocks and shares or racing. The way women laughed and chattered or flirted with men not already talking to other men. The *Scot* putting out to sea for Queen Victoria's Diamond Jubilee was one great party with all the excitement of the voyages of discovery and the pomp of a royal gala.

The all-ashore hooter sounded, and visitors streamed back down the gangplanks, the southeaster snapping the red, white and blue bunting behind them.

The band struck up *Land of Hope and Glory*, and ecstatic passengers hurled paper streamers that unfurled in a giant multicoloured spider web between ship and shore. As she weighed anchor and began to slide away, they stretched and broke.

Barnato, standing at the rail with his party, lifted his little daughter up in his arms and pressed her petal cheek against his weathered one. 'Wave goodbye to Table Mountain, my little love,' he whispered in her ear. 'It's a sight you never forget.'

Fanny Barnato squeezed her husband's arm. 'I never thought I'd feel this way about England. I'm actually glad to be going home.'

'Home!' Solly exulted.

'Home?' Jan Bakoven echoed. 'Home *se voet*!'

One flight down, the steerage class passengers were also hanging over the ship's rail. A Cockney miner with a phthisis cough, returning to London, thumped his neighbour's back. 'It's good to be going home for the Jubilee, eh, mate?'

The man was tall with shoulders broad as a crossbeam, and a flat, muscled belly. He shrugged good-naturedly. 'Looks like half South Africa thinks so too.' And they both craned their necks to look up at the first-class passengers.

'Cor, there's Barney Barnato. Don't you wish you was 'im?'

'No,' Braun answered truthfully. And he picked up his duffel bag and went below.

Every morning after breakfast Barnato walked briskly three times around the promenade deck before Solly joined him. To the rear of the deck cricket he spotted an athlete going through his paces with Indian clubs, and he ground to a halt. Round and round they whistled, drawing figure eights in the air.

'Used to be a bit of all right with those meself,' he said wistfully.

'Well then . . .' Braun had stopped and was holding out the clubs with an inviting grin.

Barnato started to peel off his jacket just as Solly hove into view. His eager smile vanished as though at the flick of a switch. 'Tomorrow?' He gave Braun a wink. 'And no chaperone.'

Solly fell in at his uncle's side. 'Soon's I turn my back, you're off with some rum-looking customer . . .' He jerked his thumb over his shoulder.

'A clean-cut athlete, Solly. Get a gander at those clubs.'

'They're always clean-cut – those geezers you pick up . . .' Solly remembered the tall man with the gunpowder scar at the Queen's, and he scowled at Braun. 'But I wouldn't trust 'em farther than I can throw 'em.'

Von Veltheim's smile faded, and he turned away from the Wynberg poste restante counter.

He trudged home to the Vineyard Hotel under oaks still leafy with the Cape's autumn finery and already swollen with the nodules of next spring's growth. It was mid-June and no word from Anne-Marie since her train swept out of Waterloo Station, carrying her away.

He'd thought he needed to be without encumbrances right now. But without her his life was empty. A void. A meaningless shell. His need wasn't the burgeoning explosion he'd known with other women, but a gentler, healing need. And fear had given it an edge sharper than a Toledo blade.

And now when he lay awake at night a new thought plagued him. In those last months of their lovemaking he'd lost track of her physical cycle. Suddenly there were questions he needed to ask, and there was only this image of another empty railway track and this silence. Why no word? His thoughts drummed in his head. *Why?*

'I say, Kurt!' Q.C. Salamons called to him across the Vineyard verandah. 'Do join us in some wine?' He beckoned him to the table where he sat with his niece.

Von Veltheim gratefully dropped into the vacant seat. He clinked his glass with theirs. 'Your good health, sir. Ma'am.' He noted with wry amusement how the nubile young woman flushed.

'Heloise,' she corrected him breathlessly. She indicated the turf clinging to the soles of his well-dubbined boots. 'I see you like hiking, Baron?'

He put a discreet finger to his lips. Women were intrigued by the 'baron' he'd let slip even though he'd signed the register plain F.L. Kurt. 'With such beauty, how can a man resist?' His innocent glance at the scenery failed to cancel the teasing note in his voice.

Heloise lowered her eyelashes seductively behind her fan.

Salamons glared at her for behaving like a hussy. He turned back to von Veltheim. 'Do yourself a favour, Kurt. Take the path up the back of Kirstenbosch to Devil's Peak. Excellent view of Rhodes's estate.'

Heloise smiled demurely. 'And don't you ride, B . . .' She broke off in time. '. . . Sir?'

'Only when I'm hunting.'

'Mercy me! And I took you for a cavalry officer!'

'Afraid I missed out there. What with a stint in the navy and another with the infantry in the Bulgarian campaign.'

'There's always the Bechuanaland Border Police for a spot of cavalry,' Salamons advised.

'That's miles away,' Heloise wailed.

Von Veltheim smothered a smile. 'My dear Madame, *you* pointed out the omission in my career.'

Salamons cleared his throat noisily. 'The BBP'll soon remedy that, Kurt . . . Got a camel patrol . . .'

Heloise fanned herself, frantically. 'Oh no, Baron, you've only just arrived!'

'*Baron*?' Salamons looked from one to the other sharply. '*Is* it Baron, or is it Kurt?'

Von Veltheim gave him a conspiratorial smile that failed to enlighten him.

'Well, whatever,' he gruffed. 'The BBP'll kill two birds with one stone.'

Barnato stared at the *Scot*'s smoking-room calendar and read: 14 June. He looked quickly at the officer on duty. 'When do we get to Madeira?'

'Tonight some time, sir. Twelve knots in a sea like this is actually good.' Fourth Officer Clifford darted a look at Solly to see if he'd noticed that Barnato was trembling.

'Let's get you some fresh air.' Solly took his elbow and steered him up onto the promenade deck, and they began to walk. Past the deck games. Past two small boys with a hoop. Past the nursemaids with their charges. Near the rail Barnato hung back to watch the man swing his clubs.

On past the swish and tap of the deck billiards. On past the whoosh and plunk of the deck quoits. Solly wrapped in uneasy thoughts of Barney's nerves. His phobias about being followed. And again past that rum-looking customer with the swinging clubs.

Officer Clifford came off duty. He subsided into a steamer chair on the quarterdeck and pulled up a plaid travelling rug to doze.

Barnato caught Solly's envious look, and felt a twinge of guilt. He'd had him on the trot since breakfast. 'What's the time, Solly?'

Wearily Solly consulted his pocket watch. 'Three-thirteen.' He collapsed into a steamer chair like a puppet released from its strings and patted the empty one beside him. 'Sit a bit, Barney. I'm done in.'

Barnato sat and moodily watched the deck cricket, fingertips drumming restlessly on the armrests. He glanced back at Solly and saw his eyes droop closed. Near the ship's rail that lad with the ready smile was still flying clubs. And now Solly was fast asleep. He stood up.

Braun saw him and accelerated. Barnato started towards him, pace quickening, grin broadening. Braun grinned back.

Only close up it wasn't a grin anymore. Barnato saw that his face had contorted in the vicious rictus of a man summoning his last ounce of strength, and he wielded one club like a mace until it whistled in his ear.

THWACK! The blow was a bombshell exploding in his head. As it knocked him off his feet, a pair of powerful arms scooped him up like a doll and hefted him over the side. Barnato just had time to fill his lungs and yell, '*Murder*!'

It was the last sound he would utter. He was already rocketing into the rampaging sea.

'For God's sake, save him!' The words sliced through Clifford's sleep; and he was on his feet, legs pumping, his chair skittering across the deck to collide with the bulkhead. 'Save whom?' There was the line of deserted deck chairs, the heave and roll of the deck, and the empty horizon.

Then he saw Solly Joel hunched over the rail, rigid with fear. He reached him in three strides. Close up, his eyes were screwed up like a child's in a temper tantrum, tears coursing down his cheeks. He was mouthing the words, 'For God's sake, save him,' scarcely a decibel louder than a whisper, and far below them in the churning wake a head bobbed like a top.

Clifford ripped off his jacket, spun to the lookout and, hands cupped around his mouth, bellowed, 'Man overboard!' But a squall was coming up, and his voice was hoarse and blurred with the roaring sea.

The alarm siren sent the rescue detail pounding across the deck to the lifeboat, dragging on their life belts as they ran. Dr Mascus Wilson checked his surgical bag and snapped it shut. Hands thrust him into his life jacket, dexterous fingers tying the tapes as precisely as a fly fisherman's knots.

The lifeboat teetered above their heads. As it drew level they clambered in. The hawser grunted and squealed, unreeling like a spool of cotton as it slithered down to hit the pitching sea like a bomb.

The squall enveloped them in a curtain of rain, but from the peak of the first swell the coxswain was already straining to scan the ocean. Clifford? Mr Barnato? Where were they? Search the first quadrant. Extreme left to dead ahead. Nothing. They slid into a trough. A second swell lifted the boat, and the horizon stretched farther away. Second quadrant. Dead ahead to extreme right. Nothing. Trough. Swell again. There was somebody at 150 degrees. Clifford?

'Ship's Officer ahoy!' he roared into his megaphone. 'Heave, lads. *Heave*!'

Shoulder muscles bunching, knees bending and flexing, they stretched and pulled. Stretched and pulled.

Third Officer Stuart braced himself and, with an expert oval motion as though throwing a deck quoit, he sent the life buoy skimming into the sea near enough to strike Clifford a glancing blow.

'Grab it, man. *Grab* it!' he commanded.

'Stretch out, laddie,' the coxswain urged. 'We'll do the rest.'

Clifford grasped the ring in both hands. He ducked his head under it and, forcing both arms through, hung there exhausted. Arms gripped the rope and, hand over hand, dragged him into the lifeboat.

'Mr Barnato . . .' Chest heaving, he pointed, and gasped, 'Over there.'

The coxswain screwed up his eyes and scanned the sea doubtfully. 'Looks like flotsam to me.'

'It's a man. And he's not taking a dip for a lark.'

The sergeant cut the patrol boat's motor. He peered through the early morning mist rising in ghostly plumes from the Thames. The constable was pointing at a floating mass just ahead.

Using grappling hooks they inched closer and stopped.

The Wapping river patrol was used to corpses in the Thames. Old soaks called from a last alcoholic haze to meet their Maker. Young women without wedding rings declared five months pregnant on the postmortem slab. This one was different, and both men shrank back.

A naked giant of a man had been trussed with a ship's heaving line as efficiently as a Christmas turkey. And the same steel rope embedded in the swollen waterlogged throat pinioned the once muscular arms behind a once powerful back.

Fighting down the urge to gag, they forced themselves to manoeuvre him aboard. Their grappling hooks prodded and guided. Heaved and tugged. Once they lost him, and their gruesome prize bobbed away playfully. At last they managed to lodge one hook in the knot of the steel hawser and with the second nudging it closer, they grabbed it and hauled it aboard.

The waterlogged cadaver thudded on the planks like a sack of ballast, and lay streaming puddles of murky water at their feet. Staring, they felt the bile ooze up from their bellies. The violence of the strangling line had conspired with the impersonal waters of the Thames, swelling the limbs and sloughing off the skin like a sweet wrapper.

The constable stared dumbly. 'Whoever wanted him dead, sir, must've wanted it real bad.'

The sergeant crossed himself. Between the fish and the water rats he'd take some identifying. He shuddered, and quickly pulled the canvas sail over the decomposing corpse.

Oars dipping and lifting mournfully, they moved sombrely through the funereal waters to Carron Wharf.

9

The climb down Devil's Peak took von Veltheim past the back of Rhodes's estate, Groote Schuur. And past the silver-leafed trees and the great rose-coloured pincushion proteas that clothed the base of Kirstenbosch. But once he crossed the Liesbeek River he was in the valley at the bottom of the Vineyard garden. He crushed a leaf of wild almond and inhaled. Cape mountain smells. The southern hemisphere sun was an elixir to him, as if he inhaled sunshine as well as air.

The clatter of carriage wheels in the Vineyard driveway made him look up from the boots he was scraping on the cast-iron foot scraper. Salamons leaned out of his carriage, waving his newspaper. 'Bloody awful news . . .'

Von Veltheim went to greet him.

'. . . About Barney!' He handed over his copy of the *Cape Times*. 'Suicide at sea. Tsk, tsk, tsk.'

The shock was an earthquake that shattered his centre. Left direction disorientated. Navigational function wrecked. Despair engulfed him and warred with his refusal to believe what he was reading. 'It's an error,' he muttered. And his knuckles were white where he gripped the paper. 'It's got to be an error.'

Salamons looked at him curiously. 'But you never knew him, Kurt?' He frowned. '*Did* you?'

Charlie waited at the poste restante counter of Funchal's post office while the postmaster slid a telegram under the grille.

'Good news, Señor?' The postmaster was a fat, sweating, Portuguese with one gleaming gold tooth.

Charlie grunted something noncommittal and tore open the telegram.

The postmaster proudly recited: '*Rendezvous Grand Parade, Cape Town. Tight security. Top pay. Kurt.*'

Charlie looked at him accusingly. 'That was confidential.'

He nodded vigorously. 'I learn that from the "tight security" part.' He noted Charlie's irritation. 'Funchal is so big,' he explained hastily, indicating half an inch with finger and thumb. 'And the rest of Madeira is not much bigger. Here, I receive the cables . . .' Proudly he counted off on his fingers. 'I write them out. And I also try to improve my English. Is that not good for a man who looked after his father's goats until he was twelve?'

Charlie thought this over, and smiled. 'Such a man must know which tavern sells the best Madeira?'

The postmaster glanced about the empty post office, and then at the clock that said 3.55. 'I've worked hard today,' he sighed. 'That can give a man a terrible thirst.'

Five minutes later the tavern keeper put two fresh glasses in front of them and opened a bottle of house wine. It was almost empty and their speech was beginning to slur when the postmaster raised his glass to toast the *Scot* steaming out of port. 'The albatross of the north, they call her. She has very much power because she's got twin . . .' His brow furrowed like a troubled spaniel's. 'Twin crews?'

'Twin screws. And they can keep all that albatross nonsense. It's unlucky.' Charlie gave the *Scot* a baleful look. It made him morbid and he poured himself another drink. 'I'm going to South Africa on a job that'll make me very, very rich.'

'See there . . .' The postmaster gestured in the direction of the horizon where the *Scot* was now steaming. 'Señor Barnato was very, very rich when he left South Africa. But he's now very, very dead.' He crossed himself, and muttered a hasty '*Ave Maria*'. Then he beckoned Charlie closer to speak in confidence. 'My brother-in-law, he is the undertaker here. *He* says someone killed him.'

Charlie hiccoughed. 'Now why would anyone want to do that?'

An unseasonable squall whipped the grey waters of Southampton. The *Scot* was scheduled to dock at noon, but the first mourners had begun arriving at the South Western Railway Hotel since breakfast.

Across the way the Southampton Synagogue choir voices rose sweetly in unison: '*Schema Yisroël, Adoshem elu`kim, Adoshem Echad.*' In the hotel lounge the voices at the press conference were low.

Woolf Joel looked around at the score of faces in the outer office, and spotted a familiar one. 'May we start with you, Mr Prior?'

'Sir, your comments on the rumours that Mr Barnato's death was no accident?'

Someone was bound to ask that, but hearing it was like a gut kick. 'You called it a rumour. At present, I second that.'

'And that he wasn't of sound mind?'

A greyish pallor faded Woolf's Monte Carlo tan. 'Only know he'd overworked and was mentally exhausted.' He turned to a reporter in the front. 'The *St James Gazette*, I believe? Can I help you, sir?'

'You don't suspect foul play, Mr Joel?'

Woolf shook his head pityingly. 'Thank God, there's an inquest. Need to scotch all this gossip for good.'

Prior surveyed Barnato's next of kin. The women wore their furs clutched around their shoulders like ragged shawls. Their eyes swam and their noses leaked as unbecomingly red as anyone else's as they huddled mournfully over cups of tea. The men, restrained in manner, spoke in brief sentences and hushed tones. It was Old Testament grief where men smeared their brows with ash and rent their garments as they had for 5 000 years.

Prior sketched them. Power? Death is the final leveller. In time of bereavement there are no advantages.

Woolf conferred with the company secretary, Thomas Honey, and within minutes the entire family had disappeared.

Prior raised an enquiring eyebrow at Honey.

'All repaired to the *Dunstall*,' Honey indicated. 'One with her flag at half-mast. More private, you see.'

Southampton's waters stretched before them luminous with fog. There, shimmering in an aura of its own, spectacularly stage lit by a watery ray of sunshine, lay the yacht that would take more than a half-masted flag to detract from her fairy-tale splendour.

Power? Prior decided. Yes, even in bereavement, it had its advantages. He glanced at his line drawing of the family – their trappings of wealth and their naked grief – and found it obscene. He looked up and sketched the *Dunstall* instead.

Through the porthole Dr Mascus Wilson could see the *Scot* anchored in Southampton's Empress Dock. Woolf handed him a snifter of vintage Napoleon and another to his brother. 'Lot of tommyrot, Solly,' he drawled languidly. 'Neither you nor Officer Clifford saw anyone else?'

Solly shook his head uncertainly, and began to weep in great racking sobs.

Woolf turned to the ship's doctor. 'Coroner Coxwell's insisting on this senseless inquest. If you'd care to give my brother some kind of sedative, my cabin's through that door.'

Wilson took his medical bag and helped Solly to Woolf's cabin. He returned a few minutes later. 'That should do the trick.'

Woolf looked in on Solly, and then closed the connecting door. 'So, you were in the lifeboat?'

Wilson nodded. 'I applied artificial respiration both there and afterwards on the *Scot*. Uselessly. Shocking business.'

'Rather thought so, too – when the Coroner had the coffin prised open in that luggage shed.' Woolf shook his head, trying to obliterate the image of Barney with the livid discoloration on his cheek. 'Bruise on the left side of his face? Caused by the force with which he hit the water?'

'Or the force with which something hit him?'

Woolf looked at him levelly. 'My uncle was known for his philanthropies. Had no enemies.'

'Well, *some* lunatic must have administered that blow.'

'He *had* no enemies.' Woolf's jaw muscles had bunched, but he spoke very distinctly. 'Family doctor'll confirm this. Has this thriving practice in Wimpole Street. So much so, thinks he needs a new partner. Might appeal to you, Wilson?' Woolf swallowed some brandy. 'More than those weeks on end away from your family. Lead to tensions, you know.'

Wilson drained his snifter and put it down. 'Mr Joel, if I didn't know better, this could sound like a . . . proposition?'

Woolf gave him one of his poker player's smiles and shook his head. 'Now, if I'd mentioned that little operation you performed on that young lady last trip? The one due to a dalliance? *That* could.' Woolf's expression hadn't changed, but he noticed Wilson had blanched, and he poured them each another tot. 'Facts are just too inconclusive for a verdict, wouldn't you say?'

Wilson took a deep swallow, and his hand holding the glass shook.

'Thought you'd rather slip away on the boat train. Time they call you, you could be steaming into Waterloo.'

'Poor Barney.' Beit took Jackie off his lead and watched him scamper along the bank of the Rhine.

He loved Andernacht, that exquisite jewel of an ancient walled town. Its maze of winding streets. Its orthodox Jewish bathhouse. The tendrils of its newer shops and businesses reaching out along the routes to the big cities – Cologne, Bonn, Frankfurt, Hamburg. A weekend at the banker's Schloss was relief from London's recent tabloids, with all those caricatures of 'Herr Beit'.

'If the inquest said, "*Death by drowning while temporarily insane*", why do I feel I pushed him?' He looked from the banker to Wernher and shook his head dumbly. 'I keep thinking: but for me, he'd still be here.'

'You can't make omelettes without breaking eggs,' the banker said soothingly. 'Perhaps it's simpler for England to settle with the Boers? A few months won't harm your gold production much, and you can hedge . . .'

'Who gets hurt?' Beit cut him short.

'No one who wouldn't get hurt in any case,' the banker replied reasonably.

'Erich's told me all about your little tour,' Beit grumped. 'And if you're investing in that kind of market, presumably it's for countries to go to war?'

'We're in business, not politics, Alfred. We're interested in balance sheets,' the banker said patiently. 'In Kynochs' dynamite and Birmingham Small Arms.'

'*We*? I haven't committed myself to anything yet,' Beit reminded them. 'Besides, von Veltheim's plans are too advanced.'

Wernher raised one eyebrow quizzically. 'Without Barnato?'

Beit frowned. 'He's a professional.'

'But is he still useful?' the banker to the bankers asked softly.

Useful? Can a man be disposable like garbage? 'He'll *do* it,' Beit said doggedly. He whistled and Jackie came bounding up. 'And without incriminating us.' He fastened his lead, and looked sharply at the banker. 'He's honourable. He gave us his word as a *Freiherr*!'

The banker squatted and tweaked Jackie's ears playfully. 'So where's this *Freiherr* now?' he asked.

'At the bottom of the *Thames*?'

The *Lloyds's* printing press hummed and clattered, its giant rollers spooling out the news of the day.

The editor looked at the fetching young widow seated next to his senior journalist on the opposite side of his desk. Owen found himself wondering inappropriately how she'd look if her widow's weeds were a black décolleté ball gown instead.

'Madame von Veltheim believes her husband to be the Thames victim.'

'Do tell us, my dear.' Owen lit his pipe and settled back to admire Molly's trim ankles while she spoke. But against the background clap and bray of printing machinery, both newspapermen had to strain to catch her words. 'So, how would I go about identifying the body?' she finished.

'We could apply to the Home Office to have it exhumed. Grisly business, I'm afraid.' Owen leaned across the desk and laid a gentle hand on Molly's black bombazine sleeve. 'Think you're up to it, my dear?'

Molly managed a brave nod.

'I'd be happy to accompany you to Little Ilford mortuary,' he said softly.

Whitfield frowned. He'd meant to do that himself. 'Before the Home Office acts they require a motive,' he said testily.

'Indeed.'

Both men turned to her, eyes gleaming. Suddenly they were newsmen again.

Molly pressed her white lace handkerchief to her quivering lips. '*I* believe he was the victim of a Greek vendetta.'

'How so?' This sounded like a scoop.

'My husband was attractive to women. It was inevitable he'd make the wrong one pregnant some day. Then foolishly . . .' A sob threatened to derail Molly's monologue, and Owen poured her a glass of water from his flask.

Molly sipped, and began again. 'Foolishly, he married her under a false name. Her guardian was incensed.'

'You know the lady's name?'

She told them.

The men exchanged a look of surprise.

'Not the *The Times* correspondent?' Owen queried.

Molly nodded.

'I know she left hurriedly,' Whitfield murmured to his editor under his breath.

'I've no doubt she did,' Molly said so crisply that their eyes swivelled back to her, and Owen nodded to her to continue.

'She filed a decree of nullity in May. But of course my husband failed to defend it and the case was remanded.'

'*Of course*?' Owen raised his eyebrows.

Molly's eyes brimmed, and this time she swayed slightly.

Owen automatically reached into his desk drawer and felt among his arsenal of panaceas for his smelling salts. 'Why, of course?'

Two fat tears trembled like dewdrops on Molly's eyelashes, and both men leaned forward to catch her whisper.

'I've told you. By then he was already at the bottom of the Thames.'

'The Transvaal's a natural Boer fortress,' von Veltheim warned. 'We'll have to *move*.'

'Did you know that the early settlers fired that cannon to summon farmers to bring provisions for the ships?' The non sequitur came dreamily. Charlie lay on a grassy patch halfway up Lion's Head, coaxing a rock rabbit with a trail of nuts; and this bucolic prospect was causing von Veltheim to look at him with a touch of impatience.

'*Concentrate*, Charlie!' he commanded. He had gathered some loose pebbles and was busy separating the dark granite from the lighter shale. 'From Pretoria we go west in relays to the Rhodesian rail link. We're going to need fully equipped relay stations between Pretoria and Mafeking.'

'Simple. A few picks and shovels lying around, and *voila*! They're harmless prospectors' camps.'

'Once across the Bechuanaland border, we make for Beira. Now what about a small boat to get him from there to Europe?'

'A question of reviving some old friendships.' The dassie warily nibbled the outer nuts, keeping its escape route clear, and Charlie rewarded him.

'He'll embark, the new president'll be sworn in . . .'

'And the Boers think it's a palace revolution,' Charlie finished for him. 'And recruits?'

'Two kinds. Regulars . . .' Von Veltheim set up a line of shale. 'And a super posse.' A smaller line of granite.

Charlie nodded.

'You infiltrate the Rand mining camps for our camp personnel. I recruit the super posse.' Von Veltheim nudged the granite pebbles farther away from the others. 'Soldiers with enough combat experience to handle a gun, and enough style not to need to.'

'Trained mercenaries, Count? You're a hoot.'

Von Veltheim scrambled to his feet. 'Then laugh, you bastard. From tomorrow you write me c/o Trooper Kurt, Genesa Barracks.' He aimed a playful kick at Charlie's rear. 'Then the fun will start.'

10

When the wind blew at Genesa it shrouded ragged spirals of long-dead vegetation in particles of grit, and drove them across the veld like demented spirits. 'Dust devils', they called them. Von Veltheim reined in his Basutoland pony on the empty winter-dry veld, and watched them with slitted eyes from the protection of his slouch hat.

He focused his field glasses on the barracks. Whitewashed, thatched and godforsaken looking, its Union Jack fluttered dismally in the wind. 'Let's hope it's worth the ride, Laddy-buck,' he muttered, and kicked his horse into a canter.

Twenty minutes later Colonel Raleigh Grey looked up from the enlistment form he was filling in. 'Spot of naval experience, I see?'

'Good way to see the world, sir.'

Von Veltheim studied the greying Bechuanaland Border Police OC behind his desktop-fitted military chest with all the sundowner and ink stains acquired on his Indian and African campaigns. The quintessential British career officer, impeccably groomed even in this last outpost of civilisation, he had the unmistakable deportment of an ex-guardsman. Had he been at the Kiel Naval Academy, he'd have made sword of honour cadet.

Grey consulted von Veltheim's résumé. 'Been around a bit, what? Europe, Java, Australia, the Americas?'

'Bit of an explorer, sir. Just missed Stanley's African expedition.'

'Curious mixture, exploring and the service. Served in Bulgaria?'

'On Prince Alexander's staff until I was wounded.'

'Next of kin resides in Bohemia, I see?'

'Neighbouring one of the Battenberg country estates. That's how I came to be there.'

Grey's eyes filled with sympathy. 'Ah well, foreigners lack opportunities the Empire offers,' he consoled him. 'We're all ex-guardsmen here or veterans of the Chinese and Indian campaigns. Disciplined. No nonsense like calling officers by their first names.

A privilege to serve with them, if I say so meself.'

'I'll look forward to that, sir,' von Veltheim said feelingly.

'And if it's action you're after, there'll be . . .' The staccato dot-dot-dash of Morse Code from the adjoining room interrupted Grey, and he cocked an ear. 'Hmmph! Reports of rinderpest,' he interpreted. 'With orders to slaughter and repel . . .'

The Batlapin people would always remember 1897. A year after Doctor Leander Starr Jameson crossed the Rhodesian border, it brought a far more deadly scourge from the north.

The rinderpest plague decimated their herds. Attacking their mucous membranes and gastric organs, it caused them to die cruelly with their empty bowels voiding, their lungs drowning in slime.

Carried by the carrion birds that gorged on their diseased flesh, it swept south across the game lands like a pitiless scythe. The mighty kudu buck and the little duiker, the black wildebeest and the brindled gnu had once been prey only to the great cats. Now the natural predatory culling ceased. The scourge ravaged the land all the way from northeastern Rhodesia through the Bechuanaland Protectorate. It would have swept even farther south had the British Government not decreed wholesale slaughter, compelling helpless farmers to destroy the herds they prized.

Then some of Chief Galishwe's animals strayed over the limits of Border Siding.

A patrol of sharpshooters stood silently around the district veterinary officer in the Batlapin *stat*, their BBP guinea-fowl patterned puggarees protecting the backs of their necks from the noonday sun.

The veterinary officer straightened from his crouch over a doomed bull, and looked broodingly at the *kameeldoring*.

Grey also looked at the tree on which half a dozen huge vultures squatted obscenely, naked heads sunk in their hunched feathers. 'Now is it sight or smell that attracts them?'

The vet had seen too many that week to have time to philosophise. He massaged the ache in the small of his back, and looked at the cattle again. 'I suppose it's more humane to start with the dying ones.'

'I don't fancy telling them.' Grey glanced at the knots of Batlapin anxiously watching him, their faces still flickering with hope of reprieve.

'Poor beggars just can't grasp it.' Von Veltheim knew the man who made the remark as Captain Spencer; and now he saw how his eye sockets were underscored with weary shadows. 'Cattle's their wealth and ruin all in one,' he murmured to no one in particular.

Von Veltheim noticed Grey now conferring with Sergeant Sullivan. He was roughly ten years older than himself, every bit as tall, and a whole lot bulkier. A veteran of the Indian campaigns, his beard was rolled Sikh-style under his chin, and the shock of wild red hair beneath his brown felt smasher was shot through with grey.

'Dirk Fish, you lazy savage!' he called to his half-caste Hottentot-Batlapin scout. 'Let's see you earn your keep.' But everyone including Dirk Fish recognised that it was his way of saying, 'Let's show 'em what you can do.'

Dirk Fish was a slight coffee-coloured man with a cap of peppercorn hair, a singsong voice and a wicked flair for mimicry. In another place at another time he would have been an actor or a poet. He took his place between Sullivan and Grey, and dutifully began in Batlapin, 'My brothers, these cattle are infected with a terrible plague.'

'And the British Government decrees slaughter to prevent it spreading,' Grey prompted.

'The Great White Elephant Queen across the sea sorrows that her people are so afflicted,' he rendered diplomatically.

Grey gave Dirk Fish an approving nod, which he took to be a carte blanche poetic licence, and he applied himself with feeling. 'The English Queen promises shining stones and other riches until the scourge is wiped out.'

'Whoah!' Sullivan growled out of the corner of his mouth.

Dirk Fish shrugged philosophically. 'For your wisdom in helping her soldiers stamp it out, she promises healthy young cattle to replace these we have to destroy . . .'

The Batlapin headman strode forward, eyes blazing, and made a chopping gesture with his hand. 'No touch. No tricks.'

The vet turned to Dirk Fish. 'Explain we've no option.'

Dirk Fish nodded at him deferentially. 'For such wisdom, you'll be repaid in fine healthy bulls, fertile heifers and many, many calves.'

Perhaps Dirk Fish knew best. Get it over fast. Worry later.

More and more vultures were circling on high, and planing down to augment the profile of the *kameeldoring*. The patrol's gaze swung from the gathering carrion back to Dirk Fish, and so no one saw the induna in whispered conference with a youth on the blind side of the tree. Nor noticed how the messenger crept away under cover until it was safe to lope off to where the land melted into the sky.

Grey's bark split the noon stillness. 'Loaded and cocked?'

Musketry rattled.

'Right. Start firing, and keep going until every last animal's dead.'

Sullivan held his pistol to a stricken cow's temple, and shot. The animal, suddenly released from the convulsion that twisted back its neck, stiffened and contorted, then rolled over, dead.

Von Veltheim cocked his Colt 45, and his shot joined the cacophony that spat and blasted, weaving back and forth like a shuttle sowing death.

A wizened crone began to ululate. It was the ancient sound of Africa, known to strike at the heart of every white man who heard it. And it rose from a score of throats – some smooth, others wizened. It tripped from their tongues like the peal of a bell, trilling and rippling, rising higher and higher. It was a torrent unleashing: a dam bursting. And it swelled and swelled, carrying in its wake a chorus of ancients' wails and children's sobs.

In silent anger, the men watched:

Their families weep . . .

Their domestic animals slaughtered . . .

Their herds wiped out.

Finally there were only those animals not yet in extreme stages of suffering, but surely infected. Sullivan started on the first cow with great trusting eyes. Next to him, Spencer's glance flicked nervously from the cattle to the Batlapin and back. He took aim . . . But the headman fixed him with burning eyes that exerted a hypnotic pull. He tried to aim again, but his face crumpled and his hands shook so uncontrollably that he had to lower his gun.

Sullivan fired on and on.

The headman strode up to him and seized the smoking barrel. With a shrug of his powerful shoulder, Sullivan shook him off like a summer fly and kept firing.

Dirk Fish put a hand on the Batlapin's shoulder. 'Do not grieve, my father. By tomorrow they would all be dead. And more horribly than this.'

'*Father*?' The headman spat. And his eyes were blood-mad with rage. '*Yours*? The white man's dog?' With one sinewy arm he indicated the carcasses that littered the veld. 'These were Galishwe's herds.' Raising a clenched fist on high like a mallet, he croaked, 'Before the moon wanes, you who mercilessly sow death will be as mercilessly slain.'

The sob Spencer choked down sounded like a hiccough. But the other men stared the headman down, unflinching.

Von Veltheim looked from one to the other. He was thinking: I've found my elite posse, but it's going to take a damned sight more than a fat bonus to recruit them.

There were more than a score of vultures now sailing above in slowly decreasing circles. One flew lower and planed down to waddle towards the others crouched on the *kameeldoring*.

The vet looked at them wearily. 'Time to burn.'

This time when Dirk Fish spoke to the Batlapin his voice was ragged. 'We must ask you also to leave your homes . . .' The words trailed off.

Speaking in the Batlapin tongue, Sullivan finished for him, 'Gather your cooking utensils and bedding. Your grain and *tswala*. Anything you can carry you may take to the caves in the kopjes over yonder. But take no livestock. Her Majesty's Government will compensate you.'

'*Compensate*?' The headman gave a harsh laugh. 'How does she compensate a peaceful people for lives she has sundered?'

Sullivan had been wondering the same thing, but he only said, 'I'm sorry, but we're going to have to help you evacuate this *stat*.'

Young women with gazelle-like necks gracefully balanced heavy jars on their heads and then slung babies onto their backs with ease. But there were also the ancients who struggled with the help of a child or a cudgel.

The Batlapin men formed a human shield around the evacuees, shepherding them out of the flare path where Dirk Fish was dexterously fashioning piles of kindling into torches.

Sullivan ignited the first two and tossed one to von Veltheim. 'Prince Alexander likely had no call for these,' he grunted, 'so try not to scorch your shirt-tails.' He sent his torch arcing through the air to land on the roof of a hut. It fed hungrily on the tinder-dry grass, until it crackled and snapped, billowing into a roaring flame.

Von Veltheim estimated the spread and then calculated his aim to land precisely where it would link with Sullivan's. The next one followed, and then the next, until there was a daisy chain of fire all along the perimeter of the village.

The branches of a tree caught alight with the roar of a lyddite explosion, the flames red as a furnace and high as a sailing ship's mainmast. It took one gust of wind to leap the firebreak, and then its neighbour flared, in a huge hellish tongue. It licked and slobbered, and spat and hawked until the branches cracked, split asunder, and hurtled across the veld in a demon dance. All at once the veld was an inferno; and in its path sobbing families clung together paralysed with fright.

Von Veltheim caught the despairing look of a small boy trying to support an aged crone. He swept the old woman up in a fireman's lift and, tucking the boy under his other arm like a parcel, yelled to Dirk Fish to grab a toddler and follow him downwind. Coughing and choking, his lungs felt ready to burst and his muscles were like dough. Staggering and stumbling, at last they reached the sanctuary of an outcrop of *ouklip*, delivered their charges and collapsed like tents released from their guy ropes.

Gulping in the sweet air, they watched the insatiable flames consume the carcasses. They blackened, then twisted and changed shape in a macabre ballet as the gases released from their swelling bellies escaped with a hiss, the fire crackled on, blanketing everything in smoke.

Von Veltheim looked at the frightened faces of the very young who were seeing the spectacle for the first time, and then at the haggard ones of the very old who had seen destruction all their lives. He thought of Bielorat. Of Rainer's sleek herds and fertile lands. Compassion welled up inside him, and with it the sinister doubt that questioned the humanity of this mission. And if he did not know whether he was saviour or vandal, could he really believe in his mission to avert war?

He felt Dirk Fish nudge him to his feet and, with surprise, he saw that the sun hung low in the west. Weary unto death, they trudged back to the posse together.

Then through the heavy smoke pall, he saw the Batlapin men. Their anger. The menace in their eyes.

'Spencer's gone soft.' Sergeant Webster was tough-skinned but tenderhearted, and though he jerked his thumb over his shoulder to where Spencer was riding, his face had clouded with concern.

'*Soft?*' Sullivan glanced back at the white-faced Spencer. 'Battle weary, son. Leave's overdue.'

Charcoal smeared and uniforms scorched, the BBP were headed back to Genesa, wearied by their exertions and weary of heart. Each man in his own way felt a helpless anger at the pitiful order they were trying to impose on an implacable nature, and a black cloud of post-action depression engulfed them like a malignant blight.

'May I join you gentlemen?' Webster and Sullivan rode just ahead of von Veltheim, and he wheeled his mount forward. 'Fine teamwork, that was, Sergeant. Really professional.'

'Professional's right,' Sullivan agreed sourly. 'Beats me why the Colonel wants a bleeding remittance man along.'

Webster hastened to his defence. 'I thought you did fine.'

'I've the greatest respect for the Colonel's judgement,' Sullivan continued. 'Usually.'

Von Veltheim ignored the slight and threw a curious look at the rear of the column towards the elegantly tailored Forsythe with the graceful riding seat. 'And him?' He raised an enquiring eyebrow.

'Skeletons in every locker here,' Webster said cheerfully. 'Only wish I had his troubles.' He glanced back and took in Forsythe's gentlemanly style and the devil-may-care smile. 'Course Forsythe's not his real name. He'd have still been Master of the Hunt on his – I'm not saying which – country estate back home if he weren't such a lad. But his brother's standing for re-election. House of Lords. Cost the family a pretty penny in severance pay.'

Von Veltheim threw Webster a grin. 'And you?'

'I grew up dirt poor,' Webster admitted. 'I'd still be a rag-and-bone man, but for the BBP.'

Sullivan punched his shoulder in jest. 'Fifteen years' service, son? Me aside – beat that.' He looked von Veltheim over. 'You're as nosey as a woman. Apart from Prince Alexander's Bulgarian campaign, where'd you be from?'

'Nowhere in particular,' von Veltheim said cagily. 'Bit of a jack of all trades, I'm afraid.'

'No need to be afraid, Boyo. There's plenty of us didn't arrive here via Sandhurst. But since ye're clearly not something the fairies dreamed up, you must be from *somewhere*?'

'Abroad.'

'What part of abroad, then? There's also a good few of us here hail from abroad. It's a pretty wide margin ye've given yourself. If you ask me, you're as slippery as soap in a bath.' He leaned forward in his saddle and a glint of suspicion ignited deep in his eyes. 'It wouldn't be that ye've something to hide?'

'Not unless you've something against travel?' Von Veltheim had called men out for less. Pistols or sabres at dawn.

But he had reason to grin equably. In his head he was marshalling his super posse. Forsythe's speed and cool would qualify him to ride with him in the initial snatch while Sullivan, the insolent seasoned campaigner and his bush-blooded scout, would take over at the border crossing and on to Beira, where Webster and Charlie would escort Kruger to a safe house. There they could all go to ground until it was time to rendezvous with the boat.

But he smothered that equable grin and simply said, 'Nothing to hide but a bit of exploring. And in the German Marine . . .'

'See?' Sullivan turned to the others in triumph. 'A bleeding remittance man!'

'Guilty as charged.' Von Veltheim spread his hands in mock despair.

He glanced over his shoulder at the Batlapin *stat*. 'Think there'll be reprisals?'

Sullivan twisted in his saddle, and stared. In the distance the smoke rose to the heavens like an accusing finger. 'Do horses eat hay?'

11

Galishwe's kraal clung to the slope of a hill near a tiny trickle of a stream. His thatched beehive hut and those of his wives were arranged in open-ended concentric circles that looked like a triple-stranded gold necklace in the afternoon sun.

In the open area his wives prepared his meal, ground his maize and brewed his *tswala*. Over a pot of it outside his hut his councillors sniffed snuff, smoked dagga and discussed changing times. Especially the changes the missionaries had brought. It was in this fashion that he watched a plume of dust no bigger than a dust devil cross the wide empty landscape approaching ever closer until the youthful runner finally dropped into a crouch in their midst.

'I salute you, my chief.'

'I salute you, my son.' Galishwe took in the dried runnels of sweat on the messenger's dusty skin and his rasping breath, and he listened gravely to the tidings he gasped out.

'The white Queen's medicine man tells of a plague spreading south from Lo Bengula's herds.'

'I have heard of it.' Galishwe received the gourd of *tswala* from the man on his right. 'We are under the white Queen's protection. But I sometimes wonder for whose good.' In his mind's eye Galishwe could still see the herds he'd tended as a boy in his father's kraal. They were fatter and more numerous than his own today because the grazing had been so much richer. 'Aai!' He sighed, and drank deeply from the gourd.

'His orders are to halt the scourge. The Queen promises compensation for slaughtering our cattle.'

Galishwe paused with the gourd in midair and fixed him with such burning eyes he had no need of the utterance: 'How?'

The messenger kept his eyes lowered. He feared the chief's wrath. 'The animals are already slaughtered, my lord. A great fire now consumes the remains of herds we once prized.'

A rumble of indignation stirred among the councillors, and their eyes flashed anger.

'Where?'

'The *stat* near Border Siding.'

'The white Queen's *protection*?' An induna spat in the dust.

Galishwe nodded impassively.

A second elder took a leisurely pinch of snuff, and sneezed. 'Pokwane trading store lies close to Border Siding,' he said delicately.

Galishwe stood. 'The missionaries were right. It is time.'

His kraal had grown quiet as the younger warriors drew closer. They had spent some weeks in the veld learning, along with their other lessons, to master the front loaders the missionaries had brought. The moment was nigh? They looked at their chief for confirmation.

He nodded once.

He watched them gather their mounts and rifles, their pride fierce. One youth brought his horse, another his bandolier and gun. Face alight with the unearthly glow of a demon hunter, and ululating until his blood flamed like a furnace, he swung into the saddle, and kicked his horse into a gallop.

His men followed, their horses' hooves thundering. Their roar mixed with the men's blood-curdling cries, that built and built until the whole valley reverberated and they disappeared in a shroud of dust.

The strident bleep of Morse code brought Grey at a trot. He glanced at the message von Veltheim was still scribbling. 'Reprisals?'

Von Veltheim nodded. 'At Pokwane Store.'

Grey looked out at the salmon sky trailing twists of ivory cloud and luminous apricot where the sun dipped into the horizon. 'Quite sacred looking, really,' he murmured half to himself. 'Have the bugler sound assembly, Kurt. Column leaves at first light.'

The bruised July night sky had scarcely faded when the double column rode out from Genesa across the frosted veld. Before them lay miles of southern Africa's semiflat landscape. Its plains and plateaus were pimpled with the occasional kopje, and a single sweep of *kameeldorings* stretched from the western border near

Genesa almost as far north as Mafeking.

Riding knee to knee, Grey and Sergeant Webster trotted at the head, and von Veltheim a length behind them with Sergeant Sullivan. Dirk Fish always started on horseback, but closer to target he'd dismount, toss his reins to a trooper, and fall into a lope. He scouted better closer to the ground.

Von Veltheim lowered his felt smasher against the early morning glare. 'Wonder what we'll find at Pokwane?'

Sullivan frowned. 'Hard to say. The Batlapin might be quarrelsome, but hardly warlike.'

'Unless provoked,' Dirk Fish corrected him. He flashed a smile that lacked two front teeth at von Veltheim. 'But the new trooper knows nothing of this.'

Sullivan knew he was waiting to be invited to enlighten von Veltheim, and he shrugged. 'Go ahead. You'll talk the hind leg off a donkey anyway.'

'You know Shaka was paramount chief of the Zulus?' Dirk Fish enquired of von Veltheim.

'Oh, yes.'

'And that he drove out the pretenders and their worthless followers? One cousin he drove right into our territory.' His narrative fell into a rhythm that sang with his lope. 'Now the Zulus were warriors and my grandfather's people, not fools.'

'That the Good Lord saw fit to bestow you on me, makes me wonder,' Sullivan said gloomily.

'Hau!' Dirk Fish threw him an indignant look. 'Few people live to win an argument with a Zulu.'

'True. So, get on and be done with it.'

Dirk Fish muttered indignantly to himself in his own tongue, and then lapsed into a sullen silence.

Von Veltheim prompted, 'Your people travelled far?'

Dirk Fish nodded disdainfully and jogged on.

'Far as the Witwatersrand?'

'Not that far. In Egoli lie other evils.' The thought seemed to placate him. 'But our gods respect good sense, and they showed it by sending our people a great harvest of fish.'

'But isn't "batlapi" the Tswana for "fish"?'

Dirk Fish clapped one hand to his cheek in pantomime of his admiration. 'This man with the tattooed eye has been here five minutes, and already he knows more than me.' He turned back to von Veltheim. 'That's why, in reverence to the gods, we call ourselves people of the fish.'

'But if these are also Galishwe's people, then we're pursuing runners, not fighters. Right?'

'Perhaps so,' Dirk Fish shrugged eloquently. 'But the Zulus are long gone. We, like that tortoise who had that race with the hare, are still here at the end.'

'And what they've been up to, we'll know soon enough.' Sullivan thrust his red-bearded chin at the thatched-roofed hut up ahead. 'That's Pokwane store over yonder.'

Pokwane trading store was one of hundreds of such shacks all over Africa nestling at the junction of a road and river, and shaded by a peppercorn tree. Mostly built of corrugated iron sheets pasted over with hoardings, they advise the very few who can read: 'Mazawattee Tea' or 'Carters' Little Liver Pills sold here'. It looked quiet and peaceful as the column reined in.

'Patrol dismount!' Grey barked.

The men tethered their animals in uneasy quiet and cocked their Colts. Sullivan and von Veltheim leading, Webster, Forsythe and Dirk Fish bringing up the rear, they moved cautiously through the open door into the store.

Nobody inside. There was a packet of candles on the counter and some silver coins beside the open till. The upended tea chest trailing a meteor tail of spilled tea leaves might have been an accident that someone was fetching a broom to sweep up.

Von Veltheim held his breath and listened. Too quiet. In the years he'd hunted and campaigned, he'd learned to sharpen his senses. To trust his hunter's instincts to take over from reason.

With the unconscious grace of a leopard, he moved to the rear of the store. There was a crunching sound like sugar underfoot and a spill of crushed glass glinted like tiny diamonds in the shaft of sunlight at his boots. Then he saw that the rear windowpane was shattered with ugly jagged shards. And across the newly limewashed wall a bloodstain bloomed like a giant poppy.

The back yard was deserted except for a well, but the smell of putrefaction rose from it like a miasma.

Sullivan turned to Grey, and jerked his thumb towards it.

Von Veltheim, red bandana neckerchief already secured over his nose, peered down. Stuffed into the bottom were what he took to be bundles of washing until the reality penetrated. The coppery taste of bile rose at the back of his throat, and he swallowed hard.

'It's the victims, sir. Mutilated something horrible,' Sullivan reported. He glanced back at the store, already making a mental inventory of equipment they'd need. 'And begging your pardon, we'd better not waste time.'

Grey nodded brusquely. 'Detail some men to requisition rope, wire, hessian - any damned thing to get the poor souls out.'

Twenty minutes later von Veltheim stared at what was left of the store owner and his half-caste assistant laid out on a wagon sail. The faces of Blum Bolton and Piet Plaatjies were a meaty pulp with noses and ears amputated. Their ripped trouser fronts were sodden with blood where their genitals had been hacked away, and their stomachs had been slit open so that their entrails spilled out.

The violence of the desecration tugged at von Veltheim's own viscera as though they'd been wrenched from a common pool. He kept thinking: yesterday they were as alive as me. And although the sun beat down, he shivered.

'I'm afraid it's a grisly sight, my dear.'

Supporting Molly, Owen felt her legs buckle and he took the precaution of slipping an arm about her waist.

The corpse laid out on the Little Ilford Cemetery mortuary slab was draped with a clean linen sheet, but everyone stared with morbid fascination at the protruding feet with the label attached to one big toe.

The district surgeon, Dr Metcalfe, took his own precautions at these exhumation identifications, which consisted of a bottle of Glenlivet decanted into a medicine flask. This particular case had been so gruesome he'd already been obliged to resort to it twice.

The manner of death had been violent enough. But the natural putrefaction had been compounded by weeks of submersion in the Thames. Extraordinary that a man who belonged to such a lovely woman would ever have strayed from her side.

He took Molly's arm. 'We're going to peel back the sheet from the head, my dear,' he announced. 'Take a deep breath and say when.'

'Ready?' Owen chimed in from the other side.

Molly pressed her handkerchief to her mouth, and nodded. The quick intake of breath was a soft little gulp. 'Franz!' The cry was wrung from her heart, and both men moved to catch her as she crumpled.

'Dear God, what have they done to you?' she sobbed.

'Get them buried like decent Christians, then follow,' Grey snapped at Webster. 'The rest of us are going after those bastards now.'

Leaning forward in the saddle, poised like a sniffer dog, Dirk Fish pointed to twin parallel kopjes in the distance.

Grey focused his field glasses on the base where a line of mounted Batlapin were disappearing as though into a tunnel. 'Follow me!' He kicked his horse into a gallop, and the column spun and pounded after him in a swirl of dust.

'Just too bloody convenient,' von Veltheim muttered. Abreast of the kopje he followed Dirk Fish's gaze from one crest to the other. They both saw the tiny sawtoothed edges grow on the promontory at the same moment.

Grey saw it too and bellowed, 'Ambush!'

In one movement von Veltheim flung himself off his horse, dragging Sullivan down into a donga between him and Dirk Fish. The high ground was alive with Galishwe's men firing into the column trapped in the valley like flies in a flask.

He had been pinned down before, the enemy pounding away at a snowscaped field on the outskirts of Pirot, his thigh slit open from kneecap to femur while he fought down the terror. On a bridge across the Sierra Santa Marta gorge just plain paralysed with fear. It was a black bat beating its wings in his head, battering at his ribcage where his heart should have been, flailing his soft vital tissues where his viscera pooled. He could lie there and be annihilated, or . . .

Breathing hard, he forced himself to his feet, expecting a sniper's bullet to mow him down any second. As though in a rugby tackle, he launched himself at a thorn tree in a cleft rock. From its cover, he steadied his Lee-Metford on a natural rock tripod, aimed it at a spiked buttress and fired. The blast rent the quiet, and he was surprised to see a diminutive black figure tumble from behind his cover, gun clattering down the ironstone rock face like a tin can in a gully.

Then Sullivan was suddenly beside him shooting through a saddle in the rock, and another of Galishwe's men fell forward, flattening the winter-bleached grass. His eyes combed the outcrop. 'All over the high ground,' he grunted, 'like ants over honey.'

For von Veltheim the adrenaline was suddenly a furnace in his blood and it burned away his fear. He clamped a thin black cheroot between his teeth and lit it, and felt his hands steady. Methodically, he set the rear sight of his Lee-Metford at a thousand yards and shot blindly, his fire raking the grass of the summit and silencing two guns. He saw a third man fling up his rifle with a scream, stagger a few paces down the kopje, crumple, and lie still.

After that they stopped counting. Emptying magazine after magazine, von Veltheim felt the recoil bite into his shoulder and the barrel smoked hot enough to blister his hand.

'Like pigeons on a fence,' Sullivan purred and heaved his great bulk a bit higher.

In a flying tackle, von Veltheim flattened the huge man just as he felt a bullet graze the back of his uniform jacket. The next instant he was on his belly beside Sullivan. 'You shouldn't have done that. I'm particular about what I wear.'

Sullivan didn't quite know whether he was talking to him or the man who'd just fired.

Without taking his eyes off the promontory, von Veltheim squeezed the trigger again. The figure half hidden behind the outcrop staggered into full view, this time an easy target, and von Veltheim shot for his gut. The Batlapin stood, stupefied, looking at his spilling entrails, hands clasped about them to hold them in. Then he tottered and fell from the rock ledge, his body cartwheeling and bouncing off the cliff face like a loosened wheel.

The firing tapered off and the kopje was silent.

So gradually that at first they thought it was a bird call, a voice began to ululate. A second joined in, and then a third. Soon the whole kopje reverberated with the sound of voices keening in grief, and then slowly diminishing as the Batlapin retreated.

In the short South African dusk that falls as suddenly as a roller blind, von Veltheim and Sullivan followed Dirk Fish to where the last Batlapin lay dead.

'Galishwe, is it, Dirk Fish?' Sullivan asked hopefully.

'No, it's his brother, Piet Gasibone.' Dirk Fish straightened and looked south where the Batlapin were retreating. 'He flees now to the Langeberg range.' He turned and gazed north where the Kalahari encroached. 'But to capture him, he'll lead us deep into the wilderness yonder.'

'Good work.' But there was weariness in Grey's voice at Dirk Fish's prophecy. 'We camp tonight at Schapfontein and head back to Genesa in the morning.'

The campfire embers had burned low when they bedded down for the night. Sullivan stuck his grizzled ginger head out of his blanket roll. 'Sorry about your jacket, Kurt,' he said gruffly.

'I'll take an IOU,' von Veltheim replied sleepily. He had already rolled himself in his blanket like a Bedouin, and was tucking it about his ears.

But something in his voice told Sullivan that he would call it up one day.

'Darjeeling, milk, no sugar?' Mrs Merriweather passed the blue and white willow-patterned Spode cup and saucer to the Captain.

'By Jove! Scones are spiffing.' Spencer folded back the morning paper at the large breakfast table. '*Baron*? Bless my cotton socks! That's Kurt.'

'The Thames Murder Mystery victim?' Mr Merriweather took Spencer's copy of *Lloyds'* newspaper and, frowning, he scanned it for half a minute before passing it on to his wife. 'Isn't this Miss Mavrogordato's young man?'

She studied the three-column spread with particular attention to the portrait. But although she opened her mouth and nodded, no sound came out.

It was Mr Merriweather who read aloud:

'*Madame von Veltheim explains that she was aware of her husband's bigamous marriage to Miss Mavrogordato. And that when he went missing and the Thames Murder Mystery occurred, she was convinced he'd been the victim of a vendetta on the part of Miss Mavrogordato's family.*'

Mrs Merriweather found her voice. 'Those turtledoves? Vendetta, indeed! I've a *pile* of his letters to be forwarded, but no address. And as for this portrait . . .' She gave the likeness a disparaging poke. 'If *Lloyds'* can't afford a better artist, their reporters can't be up to much.'

Spencer retrieved his newspaper and continued to read aloud:

'Madame von Veltheim says her husband was born in North Germany, had been orphaned as a child, and was raised by a wealthy uncle. Well educated and a proficient linguist, he served in the German Marine and with Prince Alexander Battenberg in Bulgaria. An explorer of note, he was the first man to walk across Australia to Port Darwin. From her home in Weston-super-Mare Madame von Veltheim . . .

'Madame von Veltheim from Weston-super-Mare!' Mrs Merriweather whispered. She was thinking of the pale tight-lipped woman staring after the carriage as it swept the honeymoon couple away.

Spencer looked up from the paper. 'A celebrity at Genesa? By Jove! Course . . . Wouldn't be the first black sheep sent abroad to save family embarrassment,' he beamed.

Mrs Merriweather considered the last paragraph Captain Spencer had read, but she didn't beam. She only said, 'I'd best advise *Lloyds'*. Before this other Madame von Veltheim embarrasses them further.'

12

It was the dust that got to you. That fine red powder that coated the walls and furniture sifted in drifts from the pages of books. It seeped into cupboards to film your underlinen and make it itch. It settled on the eyebrows, invaded the nostrils and scoured the membranes of the throat. It scored the skin on your hands with tiny cuts that split open and refused to heal.

Von Veltheim flexed his stiff fingers. Three months since he'd joined the BBP, and he still wasn't used to writing on dust-filmed stationery with ink that clogged in the pen and made it blot.

Genesa Barracks
September 1897

Anne-Marie Dearest,

Although I left a forwarding address at the Vineyard when I left Cape Town and have written regularly since then, only Mrs Merriweather has replied, saying she had no forwarding address. This means no contact since April. Five whole months.

Having caused such pain, we both agreed not to correspond through Rainer. That I do so now is a measure of my anxiety for you.

Am in the midst of a mission I just cannot leave. But I long to hurry back and give our marriage its true status. Despite the light-hearted way we approached it, I cherish it more than words can say.

Yours, always,
Franz

'Insulting poppycock!' Grey slammed down the Colonial Secretary's telegram on his military chest. 'Galishwe's inciting.

We've a full-scale war on our hands. And the Colonial Office has the gall to query the bill.'

Von Veltheim looked at Dirk Fish, straight-faced. 'While the cunning bastard's gone to ground in the Kalahari?'

Grey unearthed a briar pipe from his uniform jacket and waved it irritably. 'Dash it all, Kurt, it takes manpower to fight on two fronts!'

'Or cunning.' Dirk Fish intoned the Tswana proverb: '*Tau eiphutha methala elenosi enalemalwana mafaratlhatlha.*'

'Because the lion can look after itself, it doesn't mean the cubs can,' Sullivan interpreted smugly.

'Without Galishwe, the others won't last,' von Veltheim pointed out. 'And Dirk Fish could lead a decent posse to him like a homing pigeon.'

'While the column mops up Langeberg,' Sullivan agreed.

Filling his pipe with navy cut, Grey went through the exercise in his mind. 'There's a citation in it for you, Sullivan. If it works.'

'It'll work. Dirk Fish . . . Kurt, and . . .'

'*Kurt*?' Grey stuffed his tobacco pouch away and stared blankly at Sullivan. He'd not been that keen on him before Pokwane.

'Kurt,' Sullivan agreed. 'Webster and Forsythe. It's not going to be a weekend at the Connaught.' Which everyone understood to mean scarce water and night marches.

Grey scribbled out a requisition form. 'Would a dozen Basuto ponies and a week's supplies do?'

'I say, a mount per man,' von Veltheim cut in. 'And we survive off the land.'

'We're talking about the Kalahari, Kurt. Are you feeling all right?'

'*Especially* in the Kalahari.' And his smile gleamed white in his piratical face.

Von Veltheim squatted on his haunches and examined the ash with interest. 'Last night's campfire?'

Dirk Fish straightened. 'Galishwe and a small party like ourselves move east along the river bed. In a few hours we reach the Malopo. Two days' march and we have them.' He glanced up at the westering sun, and then at the Kalahari. 'It takes one jackal to catch another. Better we rest now and travel by night.'

They had been moving towards the setting sun for less than half an hour when Dirk Fish stood up from his last routine inspection. 'They either grow weary or careless. They no longer trouble to cover their tracks.' He flashed von Veltheim a grin as he tossed his reins to Sullivan.

Von Veltheim looked enviously at his bare feet. Impulsively, he stripped off his boots and socks and tied them to the pommel. Then his jacket and shirt. 'Here, catch.' And Webster found himself holding his clothes and then his reins as he fell into a trot beside Dirk Fish.

At first it was harder going than he made it look, and inwardly he cursed the fleet-footed half-caste setting the pace. He concentrated. Matching his stride and then his breathing, he fell into a relaxed momentum that made the second hour surprisingly easier.

And so the rhythm of their days and nights turned upside down. The waxing moon had lit the landscape with an unearthly light and still the Stellaland night sky was so sown with stars that von Veltheim could recognise those southern constellations by which he'd charted a course so many voyages ago. With the rhythmic swish and slap of their feet rose the sheer exhilaration of running and the heady sensation of oneness with the universe whilst paradoxically pitting himself against it.

'You sleep while you run. See.' Dirk Fish pointed to the east. The darkness had slid back to show the thin pencil line of the horizon. 'Useful. Another two hours of cool before we can rest. Use it.' They ran on watching a sliver of the sun's orange rind swell and flush the sky before the heat squeezed the thirstland dry.

As they stopped to fill their bottles, a flight of Namaqua partridges rose and flew in long formation along the Malopo. Forsythe raised his rifle, but Dirk Fish caught the barrel and shook his head. 'The bird you'd shoot today could lead us to water tomorrow. And I could pee more than this trickle that divides us from the Kalahari. Today we'll eat *rosyntjie* berries and roast *voetgangers*.'

'*Voetgangers*?' von Veltheim echoed.

'Locusts,' Forsythe translated gloomily.

'They fly west to east like the white butterfly,' Dirk Fish explained airily. 'And the taste?' Words failed him and he clasped his fingertips and floated away a kiss in tribute. But von Veltheim noticed that none of the men shared his enthusiasm.

An hour later he squatted again to examine the spoor. Under his creased forehead his eyes were troubled. 'Galishwe's bypassing Gaberones and making straight for the wilderness.'

'The dirty dog!' Sullivan exploded. He sounded disappointed in Galishwe for using unfair means.

Von Veltheim looked at the Namaqua partridges sailing above in a cloudless sky. 'No water?'

'Ai! And too much sand like the sea!' And again the posse failed to share his enthusiasm.

'There goes my mucking gong,' Sullivan groaned.

Von Veltheim looked off into the Kalahari. 'What if Dirk Fish and I were to outrun them and encircle them? Drive them back into an ambush? He says he knows a natural horseshoe in hilly terrain where they might rest.'

Sullivan looked dubious.

'You could make it by midnight if you don't dawdle, Sergeant,' von Veltheim prodded.

'This one might run like a sick hippopotamus, but he has the cunning of a jackal. An old one, perhaps,' Dirk Fish conceded. 'Together we'll drive Galishwe straight into your kraal.'

'It's tonight or never,' von Veltheim reminded him.

Sullivan looked broodingly at the desert. 'All right, Dirk Fish, just show us how we find this kraal.'

And Dirk Fish squatted in the centre of the posse to draw in the dirt.

Von Veltheim slung his canvas water bottle and holstered Colt 45 like crossed bandoliers over his bare chest and told Dirk Fish: 'I don't aim to become a spectacle like those at Pokwane. Come.'

Dirk Fish gave the Colt a disparaging tap. 'Let's hope that blue toy of yours works.'

At an easy trot they moved out across the Kalahari – that moon-washed sea of sand with tufted grass swells. This night there would be no rest.

Shortly before midnight Dirk Fish stopped to study the spoor. He smiled. 'Galishwe grows weary and has to be helped.' He pointed to the trail of three pairs of footprints almost abreast leading the rest. 'If we encircle them now to the north it will mean one hour – perhaps more before we can stop.'

Von Veltheim's throat was swollen, his breath coming in great laboured gasps. He nodded.

'Courage, my hippopotamus. We are not far from where these empty sands rise in a spine where those energetic ones might choose to rest. If we can find them there . . .' Dirk Fish tapped the Colt with an impish grin.

Von Veltheim nodded again.

'So then, empty your mind and breathe with me,' he commanded. And together they fell into a rhythmic jog.

It was a punishing marathon and von Veltheim felt his lungs beginning to rebel. He willed himself to separate mind from body and keep his legs moving at the same steady trot. Not to feel.

Over an hour later they breasted a rise and looked down on five little matchstick figures asleep around a dying fire. A guard sat facing them, his head drooping onto his chest as he nodded off.

'So?' Dirk Fish pointed to the Colt. 'Does this apology for a gun shoot any better than you run?'

Flat on his belly, von Veltheim slowly inched forward to bring the Colt within range. He held it in a two-handed grip, aimed at the guard's heart, and squeezed. The shot resounded like a thunderclap in the still desert night. The guard jerked to his knees as though intending to rise. He hung there for a long moment and then pitched forward, dead.

One man broke away from the group, examined him and peered into the night. He dropped to one knee and fired his shotgun in von Veltheim's direction. Someone shouted something in Tswana. The next instant they had smothered their campfire.

As von Veltheim and Dirk Fish grew accustomed to the dark where the fire had been, they counted five men receding into the distance. They were going south in a peculiar formation where two men flanked a third, while the last pair brought up the rear.

'It's nice to know Galishwe's also weary,' Dirk Fish sighed happily. 'Now we know this blue thing really works, you might try one more shot just to hurry them along.'

'*You'll* have to steady this blue thing then,' von Veltheim grunted sulkily. 'That sod got my hand.'

'Then you did all right for a man who runs like a lame tortoise and lacks the simplest skills of self-defence,' Dirk Fish retorted, examining the shattered hand. But he ripped his own shirt and began tearing it into bandages. And his hands were gentle as he lowered the hand into the sling he fashioned. 'I'll teach you some time. And to use a *sjambok* like a man.' He patted his handiwork approvingly. 'In less than an hour it should all be over, so stop dawdling or you'll make me miss the end.'

It was half an hour later that they observed it all from a rise. Galishwe's escort, taking it in turns in pairs to half carry their chief, entered a valley commanded by the five hills in the rough horseshoe shape. Sullivan fired a warning shot. 'We've got you buggers surrounded,' he called gallantly, 'Dead or alive, we're taking you in.'

No response.

'So, pick!' He fired another shot into the air.

Their rifles thudded onto the ground and Galishwe and his escort limped into a ring that closed about them like a noose.

It was already getting light when Galishwe was safely locked in the security section of Genesa Barracks and Sullivan escorted von Veltheim to Vryburg hospital. Soberly he watched the medical orderly disinfect the wounded hand. 'The doctor'll be here soon,' he consoled him. 'Lucky it's only your left.'

'I was still planning on using it,' von Veltheim grumbled.

Sullivan studied him curiously. 'You've been around a bit, laddie?'

'A bit.'

'I mean, you're not just wasting a spot of time here?'

'I sure as hell hope not,' von Veltheim said feelingly.

'Because my bet is, you were using that desert exercise as some kind of test?'

Von Veltheim shrugged.

'Has the cat got your tongue?' Sullivan demanded, exasperated. 'Just stop playing the giddy goat with me and tell me exactly what it is you're testing.'

The orderly was sterilising his instruments in the anteroom, so von Veltheim lowered his voice a couple of decibels. And, outlining the plan he'd been refining since the slaughter at Border Siding, he made Sullivan an offer he couldn't refuse.

13

Von Veltheim carried his shaving tackle and a bowl of hot soapy water outside away from the ether and formaldehyde smells. A peppercorn tree the Boer children used for their peashooters grew near the fence, and he slung his shaving mirror from a limb. He thrust out his chin and, spreading a section between middle finger and thumb of his left hand, he tried to manoeuvre the razor with his right. But the wounded one was possessed of a life of its own and he nicked himself twice. He cursed under his breath.

'Sure now, ye didn't think ye'd miss a weeny slice of finger that much?' Sullivan came striding across from the hospital building.

'Let's hope I shoot better one-handed than I shave.' Von Veltheim agreed gloomily. He glanced at the sheaf of mail he was holding. 'What's that you're clutching in your great hairy paw?'

Sullivan withdrew a letter. 'This came for you.' He awkwardly handed him an envelope with the von Veltheim crest. 'Thought you'd want to read it in private.'

'Why, thanks.' Von Veltheim stuffed it in his pocket and looked curiously at the newspaper Sullivan was twisting round and round. 'And that?'

'A newspaper.'

'Evidently. But what's in it that's got you behaving like a wall-flower at a debutantes' ball?'

Sullivan shifted his weight uncomfortably. 'Kurt, do ye know this von Veltheim fellow?'

His smile faded. Sullivan was holding out a copy of the *Cape Times* open and folded back at his own portrait. And it was prominently sandwiched between sensational headlines and a four-column spread. 'It *says*, "*Thames-Wynberg-Vryburg Conundrum. Puzzle in identities. Von Veltheim mystery*". That's *your* picture, Kurt. No arguments. This story's made headlines on two continents, and *it* says you're von Veltheim.' He looked at him like a troubled bloodhound. 'Now who *are* you?'

The shadow of peppercorn fronds dappled patterns on his likeness in the copy of the *Cape Times* in Sullivan's hand. He took it from him and read rapidly:

Trooper Kurt has been identified by Captain Spencer of the British Bechuanaland Police and by fellow guests at the Vineyard Hotel, Wynberg, where von Veltheim stayed (as Kurt) before entering the service. The Cape Times *has assured Madame von Veltheim of Weston-super-Mare that her missing husband is alive and well, and has despatched a correspondent to interview Trooper Kurt in Vryburg.*

Von Veltheim held the paper out to Sullivan, but he waved it away.

'Keep it, old son. Anything you say is good enough for me. Ye'd not be the first to serve here under an alias. Point is, what with the *Cape Times* and the OC both wanting answers, it's simpler just to tell one story and stick to it.'

Von Veltheim nodded, and watched him walk back through the hospital gate. Then he withdrew the letter from his shirt pocket and turned it over to read Rainer's precise Gothic script. 'You didn't waste much time,' he smiled crookedly. 'Or paper.'

Leaving his shaving tackle and bowl beside the peppercorn tree, he fixed his eye on a distant kopje, and walked through the gate and out into the veld.

It was summer and the weaverbirds were nesting. A black-beaked yellow-breasted male laboured, fetching and weaving threads of leaves and grass, and cementing them with his saliva into an igloo suspended from a *soetdoring* branch. His mate would probably reject it and shred it in a fit of pique as she had his previous efforts. Von Veltheim surveyed the pool of scattered greenery. 'Women!' he said feelingly.

He slit open Rainer's envelope with his pocketknife. 'The women in my life are giving me a hard enough time, so I can't say I relish a tongue-lashing from you.'

It was hours later that Dirk Fish found him on the kopje under the thorn tree looking across the valley at the crescented mud huts. He dropped two *sjamboks* on the ground beside him and sat. 'Women? Ai!' He loosened a leather drawstring pouch and spilled a few grains of snuff into his pink palm. 'Your wives, they are angry with you?'

'I have no wives.'

'And your father with the name other than the one by which you're called? The one in the newspaper?'

'Look here, Dirk Fish, he's more a kind of an uncle, see? And, yes, they're all angry, but not as angry as me.'

'And your new son?' Dirk Fish asked delicately.

Von Veltheim's sardonic expression softened. 'I can't believe it yet, but it seems I'm a father.'

'Truly wondrous. To have fathered a son with no woman?'

'All right. So the child has a mother. And they live on the farm with my father . . . I mean, my uncle. And my brother wishes to marry my woman and be as a father to my son. Makes sense?'

Dirk Fish pinched one nostril flat using thumb and forefinger and sniffed the snuff cradled in the palm of his other hand. He gave an almighty sneeze. 'Hau!' He looked at von Veltheim with open admiration. 'A half-caste Batlapin-Hottentot couldn't have managed it better. You have slaked the thirst of your loins, and you're still free to run with me as we did in the Kalahari. That's good news, for we've still important work in Egoli.'

Von Veltheim seized the front of his shirt and drew him close enough for his piercing green eyes to be level with those of Dirk Fish. 'Now, you're going to tell me where you heard that. The parts about my son and the Witwatersrand.' He shook him. 'Talk, man. *Talk*!'

Dirk Fish pointedly regarded von Veltheim's hand crumpling his shirt front, and then the remaining snuff cradled in his palm. Von Veltheim loosened his grip.

In a leisurely fashion Dirk Fish pinched his other nostril, sniffed and sneezed with satisfaction. 'The witch doctor over yonder . . .' He gracefully indicated the mud huts. '. . . threw the bones for me when I went to consult him about the story in the English newspaper.' He glanced at von Veltheim warily. 'It's good we're both angry with your women. It's always the best time to teach a man to fight.'

'*You're* going to teach *me*?'

Dirk Fish held out the *sjambok* he'd fashioned for him.

Von Veltheim examined the rawhide whip. Its pliability and craftsmanship.

'I made it for you to protect yourself from the *mabuni* in Egoli. When I was a boy, I led their ox-wagons with one like this.' He scrambled to his feet. By a feat of mime, before von Veltheim's eyes the years fell away, and he moved with the boyish agility of the *touleier* he'd been long ago.

'Lightly as a caress . . .' He flicked his *sjambok* at an imaginary ox. *'Kom,* Rooipens, my darling. You are the lead ox. If you don't tread carefully, those fools behind'll have the whole wagon in the *krantz.*'

He clapped his free hand to his cheek, eyes momentarily clouded at the prospect. 'There now. In the donga!' He shook his head disapprovingly. 'Tsk, tsk, tsk. Come, all of you, now! Show me how you can pull!'

He flicked it to snake farther. *'Kom,* Witbooi, *my skattie,* Rooipens and all of us need your sureness now. Donder, *my kind,* you have the strength of ten,' he purred.

'Kwaai-kwaai, no nonsense, eh?' he warned the rear offside. 'Pula?' With an air of finality embracing the whole span, 'Everyone, he-eave!' he commanded, *'Daar's sy.* He-eave!'

Like a magician with a repertoire of tricks, Dirk Fish changed technique. 'See?' He sliced the stalk of a wild flower and dropped it into von Veltheim's palm. 'Gently as a butterfly, it gathers *aandblommetjies* for your beloved. Or it can smite like this.' His eyes glittered with mock menace as he made the *sjambok* uncoil through the air, decapitating a snake.

Like a little goblin, he pranced and mimicked. 'It can disarm your enemy even as he aims his rifle. Or rip a revolver from an assassin's hand. And if one should come at you with a knife . . .' Grinning evilly, he leapt back, cracking the *sjambok* in one lethal movement. '. . . he would either be dead, or wish he were,' he chuckled. 'For he'd never sleep with his woman again.'

He cocked his head at von Veltheim. 'Come. Try.'

Like a sports coach, Dirk Fish demonstrated the elementary grip and the flexibility of the wrist. Von Veltheim's first try was wide off the mark. 'It's plain you never spent your youth guiding the *mabuni's* oxen,' he sighed. 'Never mind. Nothing teaches you faster than a woman making a fool of you. Again . . .' Again he adjusted von Veltheim's grip and flexed his wrist. He demonstrated by pruning the tip off a bush.

Suddenly von Veltheim reared back. The long rawhide whip, flying full length high above him, whined through the air and exploded with a crack above his shoulders.

'Hah! You want to play games?' Dirk Fish sprang back, flipping the pliant grip.

Although von Veltheim ducked under its flailing lash, it ripped open his shirtsleeve. But the sting inflamed his outraged pride more. He flung the recoil to full length behind him. Then with the easy grace of a fly-fisherman casting, he whipped the handle forward, the lash whistling as it flew, opening Dirk Fish's shirt from shoulder to belly.

'Whoah!' he cried, 'Save the rest for Egoli!'

They collapsed on the ground panting and sat, backs propped against the tree trunk, physically tired, but with all the tension gone from von Veltheim's face.

'From this job in Egoli, we'll no doubt earn much gold?' Dirk Fish asked tentatively.

'That's the general idea. But that was meant to be private.'

'But it *is*,' Dirk Fish's face was as serene as the full moon over the Kalahari. 'The witch doctor has no business there. And if you make enough gold, your uncle might be pleased to sell you back your wife and son.'

'That's not really our custom.'

'Then make haste and write to your family and tell them to wait. For this brother who covets your woman will never have such gold as yours.'

'The witch doctor said that?'

'He saw you with more gold than a man can carry. But he also saw many problems.' Dirk Fish tried to imagine that. 'Perhaps we, here, could help when the time is nigh?'

'That, too, was the general idea.'

As the shadows lengthened the tattoo of an African drum was borne on the wind. Dirk Fish inclined his head to listen. 'The people in the next village are having a beer drink and they summon those who wish to attend.'

'I've never tasted your *tswala*.'

'But in your country is it not the custom for the father of a newborn son to drink his health?'

'You're damned right, it is.'

'Come then. The place where the drums call us is a good half-hour from here.'

And the two men scrambled to their feet and, jogging to the beat of the African drum, set off together in the direction of the setting sun.

It was sunless. The damp penetrated the tartan cashmere travelling rug and chilled the two men in the carriage bowling along the Bedfordshire countryside.

Wernher cheerfully peered out at the near naked elms and oaks. 'Did you know that this is the centre of England's ancient straw-plaiting industry?'

'It's too chilly for sight-seeing,' Beit grumbled. 'Had I not something to show you, I'd never have come.'

'Nonsense. Everyone should get out into the country regularly.' Wernher craned his neck for a better view of the farmsteads they were passing. 'They say Anne Boleyn grew up in these parts. The whole of Luton just reeks of history,' he marvelled. 'And I, too, have something to show you. Yours, I suppose, is that sordid article about von Veltheim?'

Sheepishly, Beit began searching his pockets. 'The newspaper portrait's his, all right. But he says he has an idea of how it came to be in the so-called Madame von Veltheim's possession.' He hauled out a news cutting from the *Cape Times* outlined in red ink, and glanced at Wernher to see if he had his attention. 'It appears it was a fraudulent attempt on the part of his widow – quote, unquote – to attempt to collect insurance, and the lady has now had to resort to selling her story to the press. Notwithstanding, von Veltheim categorically disassociates himself from this unsavoury publicity, and refuses to answer questions about his family connections.'

'Closing the vault door now – to mix a metaphor – will hardly deter the Viennese gossip columnists from rattling the von Bülow skeleton in old Rainer's closet.' Wernher cheerfully held out his hand for the mauled cutting.

But Beit was already stuffing it back into his pocket. He gave him two manila envelopes. 'I took the liberty of collecting two copies – one for you and another to pass on to your friend.'

'If you think it's necessary,' Wernher agreed doubtfully.

'I told you he was resourceful,' Beit said smugly. 'He must have employed a nice little private army by now, and I've sent him the money to fund it.'

'For a competent businessman, *mon vieux*, you do jump the gun.'

'With no more Barney now, we need a new paymaster,' Beit reminded him. 'That means bridging finance until I finalise with Woolf Joel.'

'And you think you can?'

'For a start, we've a great deal of his bullion sitting in the vault at Rose Deep. And Barney's solicitor was to keep a record of von Veltheim's payments. Don't *you*?'

'Why, Alfred! I never thought you'd stoop to greymail.'

'Don't be coarse, Erich. Persuasion sounds better.'

The carriage ground to a halt at the top of a rise where the Bedfordshire countryside rolled away. Wernher leapt out and helped Beit down. There were hedgerows, an ancient stone bridge spanned a stream, and directly across from them stood a once stately home, now abandoned and in an advanced state of disrepair. 'Pure eighteenth century classic proportions,' Wernher rhapsodised. Robert Adam built it for the Earl of Bute. So? You think it's a gem?'

'I think it's too miserable a day for cavorting about the countryside,' Beit said shortly. He began to clamber into the carriage, but Wernher hauled him back.

'*Look* at it, you Philistine! It's an absolute treasure.'

'It's an absolute ruin.' But the glow in Wernher's eyes prompted Beit to study it more respectfully. 'Can't we rather come back in summer?'

'Oh, we shall.' Wernher helped him back into the carriage. 'By then – if they accept my offer – I'll have begun the restoration. And do you see where the lawns roll away from the west wing? That's where I'll grow the finest rhododendrons in England. If things go according to plan, our friend says we'll both need country houses for private meetings with European colleagues.'

The carriage started back along the London road. 'If I were to buy one,' Beit said thoughtfully, 'it would have to be less of an undertaking and more accessible.'

'With motorised transport, everywhere'll be accessible,' Wernher predicted.

'Poppycock!'

Colonel Grey poured the Lap Sang tea. They were on his verandah. 'We're only asking for your given name and an affidavit that you haven't broken Her Majesty's law as a bigamist. Try one.' He offered von Veltheim the plate of Karroo lamb sandwiches with a bottle of Gentleman's Relish. 'I'm dashed if I'll allow you to force me into asking for your resignation.'

Von Veltheim watched the flamboyant apricot sun sink into the cirrus-streaked west. 'I was thinking of leaving anyway.'

'Confounded waste of potential.' Grey scraped the Gentleman's Relish from the sides of the bottle and spread it carefully. 'What in the name of Hades were you planning to do?'

'There are also native disputes in the Transvaal, and I've never seen the Witwatersrand.'

'Of course. That dratted newspaper did rather bang on about your being an explorer.' Grey munched his sandwich thoughtfully. 'As for the Transvaal, General Joubert's a good man . . .'

'You've met him?'

'Knew him quite well when Vryburg was capital of the old Stellaland Republic. Fact . . . 'Twas dashed embarrassing for me . . . old Jameson's Raid . . .'

'Well enough to give me a personal letter of introduction?'

'Look, I don't like the idea of his raiding my officer material, but if that's what you want, you've got it.' Grey irritably upended the last of the Gentleman's Relish on the side of his plate and spread it recklessly on his sandwich. 'When were you thinking of leaving?'

'I'd like Christmas with the men and I'll head for the Rand for New Year.'

'Then you might go by way of the Wakkerstroom district. It's way off the direct route, but the Jouberts are spending the festive season on their farm before he starts electioneering again against Kruger.'

14

'No, dash it, Tom-Tom! We'll scratch the last paragraph and say sorry their bid came too late, but in the not too distant future . . . Blah, blah, blah . . . Then wire Paris express that we'll deal. Right away. And send in old Miles to finish this lot.'

Tom-Tom, formally christened Thomas Honey, was Barnato Brothers' company secretary. He was also an old Etonian and an Oxford cricket blue with a promising career lined up in the diplomatic corps. But his idea of high adventure had recently become his post as Woolf's number two in the Drapers' Garden offices. He believed that all their hectic days and often nights of bulling and bearing, buying long and selling short, forward, backward and sideways had put them at the *real* anvil of big business.

Honey knew that the other co-directors of De Beers' – Messrs Rhodes, Wernher and Beit – also headed up their respective Rand gold-mining houses. But he also knew that ten years back the Barnato-Joel duo had challenged them in the all-night marathon talks that preceded the Kimberley diamond amalgamation. Barnato's peers had wanted them out, but Woolf's far-sighted negotiating skills and poker-player's nerve had not only helped Barnato outmanoeuvre them in Kimberley, but pip them to the post in the development of the Rand.

Woolf was imaginative. He was energetic. He was the future. He was fun. A glance around his office told you that. A fresh bowl of roses, fennel and country flowers harvested daily from the Joel garden sat on his desk. Beside it glowed a silver-framed sepia study of the equally flowerlike Olive Joel – formerly toast of the West End – with their baby son, Geoffrey. A facsimile of Geoffrey's first pair of baby shoes cast in Primrose gold stood firmly astride the two piles of incoming and outgoing mail.

The Veuve Cliquot was always chilling at Woolf's elbow in a handsome silver trophy his colt had won at Deauville last season. His humidor filled with his choice Havanas shared space on the whisky table with a galaxy of framed photographs of the Joels with their family and friends at work and at play. With the Grimaldis at a charity evening at the Casino de Monte Carlo, the Rothschilds at Ascot, and the Barnatos at a Lily Langtry opening at the Prince of Wales. But most significant of all, a life-sized oil portrait of Mr Barney in his heyday, strategically placed on the wall behind Woolf's desk, warned anyone misguided enough to challenge his acumen that he was taking on Barney too.

'Back better?' Woolf enquired of the clerk who had taken Honey's place. 'Good show. Now, Miles, there's this auction coming up at Sotheby's of that pair of bronze horses Mrs J's taken a fancy to. Get a valuation from Bosie. We'll go twenty-five per cent higher and try to give her an anniversary surprise. And while we're about it, let's write to the Harbour Master at Ostend and tell him what a dim view we take of the condition of the jetty.

'Oh . . . The three o'clock already waiting? Business acquaintance of Mr Barney's?' His forehead wrinkled uncertainly as he examined the business card. *Houldsworth & Page, Attorneys at law. Serjeant's Inn.* Barney'd always retained Houldsworth to settle confidential odds and ends like personal philanthropies and bookmakers' accounts. 'Well, yes . . . By all means . . .' And Woolf indicated for him to be shown in.

Houldsworth, a contemporary of Barney's, had also been a keen boxer and, upon discovering their mutual passion, they'd begun sparring together and had continued to do so until long after they were both a bit past it. Woolf exchanged greetings with him, then pleasantries, and finally got down to brass tacks. 'Some charity Barney overlooked, is it?' he prompted. 'And squealing no end, I'll bet?'

Houldsworth shook his head gravely. 'Nothing overlooked. And regrettably not a charity commitment.' Houldsworth meaningfully lifted his attaché case onto his knees. 'A stop order paid regularly to a certain foreign gentleman on the Rand for services rendered. Highly confidential ones like funding the next election. And for which the £12,000 mandate has just about run out.' He stroked the polished calf surface of the attaché case. 'Question is, do we extend it?'

Highly confidential services rendered? On the Rand? The words were like meteors shooting around Woolf's brain. He automatically reached for the tantalus. 'Cognac? No? Sherry then?' He poured one for Houldsworth and then took a swallow of cognac himself. 'Can't possibly extend a mandate when I don't even know the scope of these services,' he muttered distractedly. 'Probably a day's work of odds and sods there need tidying.'

Houldsworth snapped open the attaché case and produced a file. 'Current? Or archives?' he was asking. 'It's your choice now.'

Woolf regarded the file with unease. It reached out to him, malignant as a leper's touch and he thrust it away. 'Archives, old chap,' he said promptly. 'Positively your archives.'

'Think that's wise, Mr Joel? You may need to refer to facts not necessarily on record? . . .'

But Woolf had already stood up to see him to the door. 'Doubt that,' he smiled winningly. 'You see, for it *not* to be would be against the law.'

The smile faded as soon as he closed the door behind Houldsworth and he stood at the window for a while looking out. The crescents, colonnades and archways of Drapers' Garden were a maze. Some said a man could cross it without an umbrella in bad weather without getting wet. He watched the rain douse it. 'Regular payments to a foreign gentleman on the Rand?' To fund . . . What?

His mind reeled back to the Caesarevitch. What was it Barney'd said? 'According to Alfred, it's now a matter of who gives us the squarer deal.' He stared out at the street sweeping around in a broad arc where London Wall Building rose like a citadel. It came to him in a blinding flash. Alfred? It was a terrible thought. A monstrous thought. And it would not let him be.

He scribbled a brief note and rang for his clerk. 'I say, Miles, be a good fellow and have a messenger deliver this to Mr Beit.' He looked out at the drizzle. 'And have him take a brolly. It's actually coming down harder than you think.'

He looked up at the imposing oil portrait on the wall. Barney was half-seated on a table in a pseudo casual pose, one leg dangling not quite casually enough, chin set at the prescribed resolute angle. But the eyes suddenly struck him as desperately irresolute.

'Barney, the bastard who sold you that one answers to me,' he promised. Then covering his head with his hand, and rocking back and forth in accordance with ancient Jewish ritual, in a ravaged voice he began to intone the Kaddish prayer: '*Yit-ga-dal Ve-yit ka-*

dash she-mei ra-ba . . .'

Beit looked around Woolf's study at the silver racing trophies, the framed watercolour of the *Dunstall* at dawn, and the family photographs. It smelled of dubbin, Havanas and Olive Joel's potpourris of last summer's roses. Loose on the desk a sheaf of snapshots of Olive holding young Geoffrey on a Shetland pony, in a Coleport bowl a handful of small change in half a dozen currencies, a tipster's list for the coming meeting at Newmarket, the current wine list from Hatch Mansfield & Co.

The sterling silver tea service and flowered bone china tea set was accompanied by a plate of his favourite bagels and chopped herring, and Beit accepted one from Woolf. 'It was just a matter of time, Woolfie, before Houldsworth contacted you.'

'Now that he has, I had him close the file.' Woolf always sat in one of a pair of identical hide chesterfields at right angles to the fireplace, and still thought of the other as Barney's. 'Consigned it to the archives,' he smiled apologetically. 'So, that's that.'

'Not that simple, Woolfie. Houldsworth's payments were for services rendered. Services that couldn't just terminate with poor Barney's death.' A searching look trying to estimate exactly how much Woolf really knew. 'He didn't confide in you?'

'Important matters, Mr Beit. But I'd never met Houldsworth face to face before today.'

'But Barney *must* have mentioned our plans for the Rand? At least in broad outline?'

'Funding the Progressives' election expenses's like insurance.' Woolf sliced a bagel in half and picked at it. 'Barney probably did the same for Oom Paul.'

'Not quite, Woolfie. Houldsworth's payments were to unseat Oom Paul. To see that no real election takes place.'

There it was. Woolf stared across the chasm Barney had bestrode, and he was breathing hard. He felt as though he'd taken a blow from a battering ram full in the chest. ' 'Fraid not our style.' Miraculously, he managed to sound casual. Almost bored.

'It's your style, all right, Woolfie. A quarter million's worth of your gold bullion's already at Rose Deep because Barney transferred it.' Beit helped himself to the second half of Woolf's bagel. 'It'll be in your Johannesburg records. Hidden, of course. Still, they're public property. Finding it would be easy.'

'If that's so, he neglected to tell me.'

'He *meant* to. The tragedy is, his nerves gave way.'

'With a quarter million committed to what you're suggesting, I'm not surprised. And the tragedy, Mr Beit, is that he was only forty-five.'

'The night of the De Beers' merger you called me Alfred.'

Woolf seemed to be remembering. 'You're right,' he said slowly. 'I'll need to go out meself and wrap up the loose ends.'

'Barney would have wanted it that way,' Beit smiled happily. 'I'll never forget Kimberley – you two against Rhodes and me. You were a team, Woolfie. You were *close*.'

Woolf beckoned Beit to the long-skirted whisky table covered with silver-framed photographs. He picked one up. 'Barney and me beside Kimberley's big hole in the early days.' Another. 'Barney and me at the roof-wetting of the JSE.' Woolf held out another so Beit could get a closer look. 'Barney and me fooling around with the old boxing gloves on the *Dunstall*.'

'Even as a youngster, he loved to box,' Beit sighed sentimentally.

'He loved to box. And he loved to live. But he's not coming back.' Woolf's eyes hardened with all the grief and frustration of that unalterable fact. 'You're right. We were very close. And you're asking *me* to support *you*?'

Piet Joubert thought that the Wakkerstroom district was the finest cattle country in the Eastern Transvaal. As a shrewd land agent, hard-working rancher and prosperous owner of several farms, he was in a position to know. The grass in the cattle camps was lush and dappled with his sleek Afrikaner herds. Clumps of wattle and camel thorn provided them with shade, and windmills whirred and clanked, pumping the sparkling stream water, from which the district got its name, into the troughs he'd made.

The large whitewashed homestead with open beams, thatched with last season's grass, was built to house three generations of Jouberts over Christmas. And in his workshop just off the kitchen Joubert patiently sawed and planed, glued and polished most of the furniture they used in the house.

Hendrina Joubert came forward to help von Veltheim tether his horse. She was an elegantly boned woman with light intelligent eyes that gleamed behind her steel-rimmed spectacles, and there was a determined look to her mouth and chiselled jaw. She and von Veltheim exchanged frankly appraising looks, and liked what they saw.

'Mr von Veltheim? Colonel Grey wrote us you were coming.' She led the way to Joubert's workshop just off the kitchen. 'My husband's making furniture.'

'His hobby?'

'In as much as a man who has to snatch time from soldiering and politics to farm can have one.'

Joubert was weaving the *riempie* seat of a chair with strips of creamy raw oxhide when his wife showed von Veltheim in. Stockily built, and excessively neat, even in his corduroy working trousers and faded cotton shirt, his white spade-like beard contrasted with his dark hair just faintly threaded with grey.

'Ah, Meneer von Veltheim it must be.' The deep-set grey eyes that looked up from his task crinkled at the corners when he smiled. 'Colonel Grey's friend!'

'I've warmest regards from him.' Von Veltheim extended his hand.

Joubert grasped it in a bruising handshake, and then scanned the credentials he'd offered and returned them. 'So? Honorary American Consul to Santa Marta, were you? But now, is it as a diplomat that you seek us out at Rustfontein? Surely not as a farmer?'

'I should hope as a welcome guest,' Hendrina said tartly, and put down the coffee tray with a fresh batch of vetkoek with a thump. 'Meneer von Veltheim's a foreigner, a friend of Grey's, and after six months of Stellaland border patrol, the least we can offer him is some decent Boer hospitality.'

'Oh, *ja*. You must stay the night,' Joubert agreed hastily. 'So, how goes it in Stellaland?'

'The border unrest continues, but now it's England's problem.'

'Stellaland should have been a Boer Republic.' Hendrina's eyes snapped with impatience. 'That it's not, still sticks like a thorn in a person's side.'

'Come now, *duifie*. Meneer von Veltheim didn't come here to listen to political nit-picking.'

'Don't *duifie* me. Whoever sits drinking my coffee must have the manners to listen when I talk. You, too, Piet Joubert.' Her scowl softened as she looked at her husband. 'You know Piet was to have been Special Commissioner of the whole Western Border? Till Kruger replaced him.'

'*Ja* well, in any case it was time to come home.' Joubert looked up from his riempie work, and von Veltheim detected in his eyes the look of a man who has known more than one kind of defeat. 'The land restores a man's perspective. Not so, Meneer?'

'I've never worked with the land.' Von Veltheim looked out at the sea of grass rolling away to the horizon and wondered if he hadn't missed something quite fundamental. 'Perhaps some day.'

'A man can follow the *trekgees* only so long,' Joubert said gently. 'Get yourself some farmland and put down roots.'

'A wife and children, too,' Hendrina advised.

'I've a baby son in Europe,' von Veltheim heard himself say.

Hendrina looked at him sharply. 'It seems to me that a man who went after Galishwe wouldn't be so mealy-mouthed as to leave his woman and son without a good fight. Fetch them here, I say. This is the country for a man to rear his young.'

'You know, when I've finished my business I might just do that.' He nodded deferentially at Joubert. 'It's not everyone gets advice from the hero of the hill of doves.'

'I'll let you into a little secret. Truthfully, the hero of Amajuba – as the Zulus call it – is Hendrina here.' Joubert gave her an affectionate little smile. 'We were camped down by Laing's Nek when she rose at daybreak. She looked up at Majuba, and called to me that there were figures moving around. So, I called back that they must be our reinforcements. Then she really snapped at me. "*Look*, old man with your *verkykers*! Since when do our men wear red coats?'

'We Boerevolk are too smart to go in for this uniform nonsense,' Hendrina told him smugly. 'Our men always wear homespun. So, using boulders for cover, they managed to scale the summit by noon. Then it was the *rooineks*' turn to be surprised,' she chuckled. 'And if I'm not mistaken, that was the last time the British wore red.'

'Of course, you're a commando veteran, Mevrou!' von Veltheim reminded himself. 'And the Commandant-General is most proper to accord you the credit.'

'There isn't a kinder man, but *proper*? Once he'd taken my

apron and petticoat for bandages for the English wounded, he wouldn't have stopped at my dress.'

Her relish at the story made her eyes sparkle. But von Veltheim's close attention embarrassed her. 'We Transvalers are supposed to be rough-grained like our landscape,' she explained self-consciously. 'I might be Piet Joubert's wife and Paul Kruger his opponent, but in the end, we're all children of the Trek.'

She removed her spectacles and looked off into the distance as though she could see the past. 'You see, when the first wagons left the Cape . . .'

She was a raconteur of the veld whose tales teemed with diamond diggers and cattle smugglers, missionaries and witch doctors, deeds of great cruelty and of even greater heroism. She spoke of a life which, if it was rough, nevertheless offered a physical freedom of which the city-dweller could know nothing – and bestowed on the spirit a quality not of breadth but of intensity. When she'd finished the shadows were lengthening.

Joubert laid down his work as he would a burden. 'We've seen too much blood flow. Too many tears.'

Hendrina adjusted her spectacles. 'That's why Piet's Commandant-General under protest. He's a pacifist who only fights when necessary. Like with Kruger.'

'Nine times out of ten it's because he's wrong,' Joubert grunted.

Von Veltheim sat forward and deep in his eyes a raw flame burned. 'You've actually fought with him?'

'And resigned,' Hendrina said crisply.

Joubert began to pack up his tools. 'Before we left Pretoria, I returned a pair of binoculars, a sabre and revolver to the State. He presented me with the sabre and binoculars, but he gave Hendrina the revolver . . .' He smiled slyly. 'Now why would a man's political opponent present his wife with a gun when it's common knowledge she's quick-tempered?'

'And not at all a bad shot,' Hendrina put in. 'But come, it must be some time since you've tasted decent beef?' And she led the way into the dining room where the long polished yellowwood table gleamed with fine Dutch East India Company china and old Cape silver.

They clasped hands in their fashion and Joubert said grace. Then he opened a bottle of Cape estate wine while Hendrina piled their plates with succulent sirloin, with that old Boer economical stand-by, crisply fried potato peelings and Joubert's favourite spiced beans which they called *sousboontjies*. And then it was von Veltheim's turn to fascinate them with an edited account of his own experiences in far-off places.

'But as Honorary American Consul in a turbulent country, an explorer of unchartered territory, and more recently a guerilla fighter in Bechuanaland, you're surely overqualified for work on the mines?' Joubert quizzed delicately.

'My mission on the Rand is more a political feasibility study.'

'Mission?' Hendrina shot von Veltheim a penetrating look. 'Sounds very focused?'

'*Magtig*! But it's late,' Joubert interrupted hastily. 'We leave for Pretoria tomorrow for the elections,' he explained to von Veltheim. 'We're also sending cattle to the Johannesburg market. If you're headed for the East Rand and you don't mind travelling by ox-wagon, our manager, Van Aswegen, will be glad to set you down at Elandsfontein Junction.'

'But this is sad,' Hendrina protested. 'I hope you'll take time from your business to visit us in Pretoria?'

'Honoured, Mevrou. Depend on it.' But in von Veltheim's gleaming green eyes was the promise of talks yet to come. Highly enlightening ones. And Hendrina smiled back, cementing a wordless pact. 'Meanwhile we drink to a victorious election?'

Joubert studied the ruby wine soberly. 'It would have to be a miraculous one this time. Since the Raid the country stands behind Kruger.'

Hendrina raised her glass to the men's. 'Then to a narrow margin and an honourable defeat,' she said briskly.

Von Veltheim clinked his glass against Hendrina's and then Joubert's. 'If the presidency's always eluded you, why not drink to the one per cent chance?' And his eyes glowed hot as a branding iron as they locked on Joubert's.

15

Seen from afar, it didn't look that different from a dozen other lo *bults* that veined the veld. Lodewyk van Aswegen stopped the ox-wagon on the crest of a hill and there it was.

'The Ridge of White Waters,' von Veltheim said softly. For almost a decade since he first heard the name whispered with a kind of religious awe, it had beckoned him with its siren's call.

Twin ridges curved in a great horn from east to west as far as the eye could see. The gently undulating veld between was generously pimpled with yellow mine dumps and slimes dams, and beside them tall cat's cradles with wooden wheels and spools of steel rope stood like fretwork against the sky.

'Winding gear.' Van Aswegen spat a stream of tobacco juice onto the veld at the side of the wagon track. 'The *verdomde* things reach right down into the belly of the earth to fetch out the gold. Listen.' He cocked his head and they could just hear the faint crump-crump of an explosion. 'That's dynamite blasting it out.' He knocked out his pipe and looked at von Veltheim curiously. 'I suppose there's no point in asking if you'd rather move on?'

'We've been talking exploring all morning. Now would I come halfway around the world to pass this by?'

The information had been gleaned in seductive snatches around campfires or in officers' messes. In drawing rooms or dockside pubs. About how when it twinkled its bright sunshiny smile some men responded with the love they would have reserved for a special woman, while others worshipped it with the reverence of the religious devotee.

Billions of years ago the hundred-and-fifty mile arc of outcrop was thought to have been the northern rim of a vast lake of molten conglomerate. It had petrified under the enormous pressures of the earth's cooling, and had tilted up until its perimeter had broken through its crust in the ridge of the Witwatersrand.

The reefs of banket – so called for the sweetmeat of toffee and nuts and cloves it resembled – were layered like a sandwich cake. Made up of the thick sedimentary beds of ancient buried lakes, they were part of a mother lode said to be rich enough to be mined for a century without exhausting its reserves.

'It's so rich, they say it's one of the wonders of the modern world,' von Veltheim explained.

'You make a living from this exploring?'

Von Veltheim shrugged philosophically. 'That's why I'm also looking for opportunities in the horse relay-station business.'

'First finish your exploring. Then you can talk business with my kin.'

Van Aswegen let von Veltheim off and handed down his Gladstone. 'Many's the heathen I've left here with a look of unearthly joy in his eyes, but you're the first dressed like a gentleman.'

The rawhide whip snaked through the air and the wagon moved off, the *middelmannetjie* of grass flattening and springing back again after it had passed.

The first farmer who watched the short-horned black-tufted eland drink at the water hole felt the *trekgees* leave him. He outspanned his wagon and called his farm Elandsfontein.

But since the discovery of gold a rash of mine dumps sprawled across his grazing lands. Instead of the cricket chorus by night and bird song by day, man-made noises tolled the monotonous seasons. The men who later toiled under the ground the farmer had tilled knew only the roar of the dynamite explosions and the rasp of shovels scraping the tunnels clear.

Now 'Michael's Railway Hotel' was painted across the corrugated iron roof of the brick double-storey that stood roughly where the farmstead had been; and a fine draught beer, brewed from the same water that once flowed for the eland, quenched the thirst of the mining folk in the bar.

There were the old hands who had panned gold everywhere from California to Barberton, and bright young hopefuls from Europe in search of a claim that hadn't already been snapped up. There were fast-talking option hunters and slow-off-the-mark land agents. New men, like Fred Foster, learning the trade, and one of the most experienced cyanide shift bosses in the game. Thomas

Bracer was also famous for once having lost a charity boxing match on points to Barney Barnato, and had thereafter been reciprocally more fortunate at *klawerjas* and dominoes.

From a shadowy corner von Veltheim watched the smoke of his pipe and Foster's cheroot curl upwards from the corner table as he trounced his friend at dominoes a second time.

'You beauty!' He swooped in for his kill, and began flipping the pieces face down again. 'Double or quits?'

In reply, Foster wryly turned out his empty pockets.

Von Veltheim's hand seemed to come from nowhere. It hovered a moment and turned up the double six.

'You motherless reprobate!' Foster was on his feet punching his shoulder. 'Meet the man who cleaned up Barnato,' he crowed.

'Draughts all round, Mike?' The winner slid his empty tankard across the bar, and extended his right hand. 'Von Veltheim, I presume? I'm Bracer. A tall *ou* called Charlie's been asking for you.'

He followed Bracer through the cavernous labyrinth, the click and crash of the double security doors unlocking and relocking marking their passage as they went. Bracer disappeared without warning, plunging him into inky darkness to reappear a moment later with a lamp.

Von Veltheim caught his breath. The sight was awesome. Pyramid upon pyramid of gold bars gleamed within the perimeter of lamplight, melting into the dark beyond. He felt his spine prickle with the fever of a hundred nights of thinking and planning. He stooped to lift one. It seemed cemented to the floor. 'God, it's heavy.'

'Sixty-two-and-a-half pounds each,' Bracer smiled proudly. 'Thanks to cyanide extraction, God bless it.' He ran a loving hand over an ingot and looked at von Veltheim. 'Instructions say four dozen, so I'll get some labour.'

'And then?' It came out less casually than he had hoped.

'By law, it's got to be redeemed through proper channels.' Were there any? With Barnato dead, was this unfinished business that was bringing Woolf Joel to the Rand? 'If you're short meanwhile, it'll have to be a pawnbroker,' he decided.

Von Veltheim looked doubtful. 'Until I get my remittance, I've only my Colt 45.'

Bracer glanced around them at the undisputed proof of his creditworthiness, and winked. 'I'll have a word with a friend.'

A giant bruised thunderhead obscured the moon above Rose Deep where Charlie waited with the mule cart. They finished loading just as a highveld thunderstorm was breaking. For a long terrifying moment a thread of lightning, spiky as barbed wire, slit the black rolling clouds and an ear-splitting thunderclap rent the night. Feverishly, von Veltheim struggled to help Charlie lash the canvas sail over the cart just as the curtain of rain came down.

From the shelter of a blue-gum plantation they watched the storm change pattern, the bolts of lightning coming and going like giant flares lighting up the lunar landscape. Rose Deep kept disappearing and reappearing like a magic lantern slide of a ghostly spit of beach sand. Von Veltheim watched it, transfixed, and suppressed a shudder.

Barnato had shivered like that in the Queen's Hotel carriage park. And though he was angry at himself for being so superstitious, the memory persisted.

Wernher ticked Lot 39 on his Christies' catalogue: a *fête champêtre by Watteau.* 'From here no one else sees you,' he whispered, 'but the auctioneer knows you mean business.'

'Doesn't everyone?' Beit took the vacant chair beside him at the rear of the hall.

'Don't know so much about Woolf.'

'Oh, he'll come around in the end, Erich.'

A hush fell as two clerks put the Watteau on the easel. The auctioneer, his eyes flicking left and right like a metronome, began taking brisk £500 bids from two competing buyers at opposite ends of the front row.

Wernher pulled on the white kid gloves from his old dragoon officers' dress uniform. 'Can't you just see it in the new drawing room?' he whispered. 'Overlooking the rhododendrons?'

The auctioneer's eye flashed a warning. 'The bid's against you, Lady Hawthorne, and I'm not going to dwell. Going once at £5,000. Twice . . . For the third and last time . . .'

Wernher held up seven fingers and there was a collective gasp as the auctioneer rapped out, 'A £2,000 jump, ladies and gentlemen. A new buyer – and very determined. Against you in the front row, sir?' His glance whipped to the end of the row. 'Lady Hawthorne?' Back to the other end.

Both buyers consulted their spouses in whispers.

'Going to Mr Wernher. Once? . . . *Twice*? . . . For the *third* and last time, are you all done?' The ivory hammer crashed on the lectern.

'You're right about the Watteau and the rhododendrons, Erich. Champagne's on me.'

Wernher drew off his gloves. 'And you're probably right about Woolf. Tend to forget he's still a Whitechapel boy.'

'Right now he's a Whitechapel boy nearing Table Bay.' And Beit made a mental note to lay in a decent stock of champagne.

Von Veltheim looked up at the kopje. It seemed an eternity away. It also seemed far steeper than it had on the dummy run. There was nothing for it but to unhitch the mules, load the ingots into saddlebags, and see.

The climb was backbreaking and gut-wrenching. Soon they were bathed in their own sweat, the flailing rain plastering their clothes to their bodies, their breath shuddering in great gasps. The gradient became steeper. Now they were stumbling and slipping, slithering and sliding, as stones dislodged by unwary feet twisted in the mud.

Clambering higher and higher, the mules, their coats sodden and flanks heaving like bellows, fought for footholds. Staggering, skidding, sliding, sprawling, they reached the cave threshold.

Between curses and gasps, they struggled to unload the saddlebags and stack the ingots. Now their chests were wheezing and their muscles quivering with strain. With their last reserves of strength, they wrestled rocks across the opening and while Charlie forced grass sods into the cracks, von Veltheim made a rough sketch of the terrain and pocketed it.

Then down again on legs that felt like rubber over rocky terrain running with slush. Back at the cart the mules stood mute in their misery but somehow they got them harnessed and painfully started back. A half-hour later Charlie braked outside Michael's Railway Hotel.

'That boat you promised?' Every word torn from von Veltheim was still an effort.

'Deposit's already paid.'

'And the safe house a couple of weeks from now?'

Charlie held up one thumb in the affirmative. 'Leaves you Kruger's house, then Joubert, and *then* . . .' And he cocked his head gleefully in the direction of the kopje they'd just left.

'Then we meet at the Wanderers bandstand the second Sunday in March,' von Veltheim corrected him. 'Woolf Joel's still the joker in the pack.'

'*He* won't give you any trouble, Count,' Charlie promised, as he started the mule cart down the Main Reef Road to Johannesburg.

Von Veltheim stood watching it go. It was first light and the mules seemed to be moving unsteadily but conscientiously in three-four time as Charlie whistled *The Band Played On* just a shade off key.

16

'It won't be the first election Kruger's crooked. Print that.'

'*You* print it.' Francis McDermott stabbed the air in front of Harry Caldecott. 'Ye canna deny the *Standard and Diggers' News* is Barnatos' propaganda organ?'

Von Veltheim had just joined the men over port and cigars in the smoking room. If the port at Clapham House was mild, the conversation was getting heated.

'Propaganda?' Caldecott snorted. 'As a director of Barnatos' and member of their legal arm, I assure you we're categorically apolitical.'

'What were those auction notices? Nursery rhymes?' McDermott topped up all four glasses. 'Granted, they might have been Barnato's unilateral decision. Though, personally, I think he confided matters to Woolf Joel that he kept from Solly. And this visit here now's to follow them up.'

Caldecott stiffened in annoyance, and knocked back his drink. 'Our business is to run public companies. Yours, evidently, is to sow speculation.'

'Speculation on Barnato's "suicide" flames on, nonetheless. And with nary a spark fanned in print.'

'But can there be that much smoke without fire?' Young Coenraad Juta was looking penetratingly at Caldecott.

Rattled, he pointedly ignored Juta and poured himself another port.

McDermott winked at Juta. 'It's not in Mr Caldecott's interests to comment.'

'But not against the *Johannesburg Times*'s?' Juta enquired mildly. 'You're not suggesting murder, Mr Deputy Editor?'

'Now that you mention it . . . too much at stake for change through the ballot box, laddie.' He raised a quizzical eyebrow at Caldecott. 'But even thinking that can be risky.'

Caldecott eyed him balefully. 'If you're proposing Mr Barnato would've replaced the Kruger regime illegally, you're on dangerous ground.'

'Ah, but it's him who's six feet under. And it's no secret you mining men'd support a switch to Joubert. 'Tis a question of finding the catalyst.'

Caldecott recklessly splashed another tot into his glass and turned back to Juta. 'You're from Pretoria? Let's have an informed opinion.'

'Afraid I'm neutral.'

'A neutral from Pretoria?' McDermott scoffed. 'No such animal.' He smiled apologetically at von Veltheim. 'With politics such a disease on the Rand, Count, we canna help being boring.'

'On the contrary, gentlemen. I'm here to learn . . .'

'Really? Is that all, Count?' Under McDermott's bushy ginger Scot's eyebrows his eyes were keen. 'You've had us all wondering.'

Von Veltheim threw up his hands in mock despair. 'All right, I'm one of those shady customers whose families send them here to save embarrassment in Europe. On the other hand, they're closely connected to the Kaiser, so I'm still expected to convey his respects to the President.'

'Aha! I smell a story.'

'If he receives me, I'll let you know.' Von Veltheim pointedly turned to Juta. 'And what are you doing in Johannesburg, sir?'

'Just looking around,' he said truthfully.

Caldecott cocked his head. In the next room someone was playing *Für Elise* on the piano. 'Excuse me, gentlemen. That sounds like my daughter.' He gave a courteous little bow and moved off.

'We all enjoy Miss Caldecott's playing, I think. Gentlemen?' McDermott gestured for the other two to precede him.

In the music room everyone was listening with rapt attention to the almost hesitant touch that made the simple little Beethoven piece that bit more wistful. The pianist was a tall slender creature with a cloud of golden brown hair piled high above her long curving neck. Her dark shadowed eyes met von Veltheim's briefly and moved back to the keyboard, but a moment later she lifted them again and held his gaze. He nudged McDermott. '*Miss* Caldecott?'

'Elise,' McDermott whispered. 'Care to meet her when she's finished?'

'Is that a bribe?'

'Shh!' someone hissed, and several people turned to glare. Von Veltheim drew McDermott back into the smoking room. 'Just so I've got it straight – Caldecott's a Reformist, you think Juta's a Kruger man, and where does that leave you?'

'An observer like yourself, Count. *Are* you an observer?'

'I've already told you I am.'

'Ah, but newspapermen have this wee devil curiosity about people in the know who refuse to comment.'

'You think *I'm* in the know?'

McDermott tapped his nose. 'It's standard newspaperman's equipment. You think it dinna work?'

The music ended and was followed by applause. Von Veltheim tapped McDermott's shoulder. 'Come, let's meet your Elise.'

'The Kaiser's congratulations?' Paul Kruger slid the embossed card back across the rattan table. 'But tell me, Mr von Veltheim, when was this?'

'Let's see . . . When His Majesty bagged that marvellous stag at a hunt on the family estate. We had Berlin's finest taxidermist stuff it for him for Christmas.'

'But with your skin nearly as sunburnt as mine, these congratulations must be over a year old? Before the elections?' Kruger thoughtfully filled his meerschaum pipe from a leather drawstring pouch. 'It couldn't be this last Christmas past?'

The gleaming white smile in the sun-bronzed face was engaging. 'I was in the Bechuanaland Border Police until last Christmas. My visit to you, sir, is as informal as His Majesty's was to us. But we both know those greetings would now be his warmest congratulations.'

'Is there some service I can render His Majesty?'

'I'm a soldier-diplomat, and speak several languages. He suggested I put myself at your disposal.'

'Any knowledge of field arms?'

'I know your Commandant-General's ordered thousands of Guedes rifles, Martini-Henrys and Mausers. Millions of rounds of ammunition from Creusot's and Krupp's. Maxim-Nordenfeldts. That you've field guns, siege guns, howitzers, not to mention Birmingham Small Arms . . . Do I go on?'

Kruger's bushy grey eyebrows arched in theatrical surprise. 'And you learnt all this in the Bechuanaland Police?'

'I've also a friend on the *Johannesburg Times.* With respect, Meneer die President . . .' Von Veltheim eyed the two uniformed guards at the front gate delicately. 'This's more than just protection against raids.'

'That last raid showed that one spark could set the veld on fire.' Kruger angrily tamped down his tobacco and lit up. 'How does the *Johannesburg Times* think we'll acquit ourselves next time?'

'With your terrain and snipers?' Von Veltheim flashed a broad grin.

'So now you're also an authority on my terrain and men?'

'It's my job. I once served Prince Alexander in Bulgaria. Now I'd like to serve you.'

Kruger gazed thoughtfully at the marble lions at the edge of his stoep. They were Barnato's Jameson Raid peace offering. 'Let me think about it. Where do I find you?'

'At Clapham House in Johannesburg. It's a boarding house near Joubert Park.'

'That must be the place where my son Tjaart's friend stays.'

'A man called Juta?'

Kruger tapped out his pipe on his boot. 'I don't remember the *jonge*'s name,' he said shortly.

'Didn't I notice an orchard at the back of your house . . .' Von Veltheim cocked his head, listening. '. . . And I can hear poultry. 'A man misses farmyard sounds in Johannesburg.'

'That's what's wrong with the place.' Kruger heaved his huge bulk out of the rattan chair. 'Here, we keep fowls and a cow Mevrou Kruger milked herself until a few years ago.' He walked to the threshold and beckoned to von Veltheim to follow him inside. 'You've missed the fruit, but we can see what's in the vegetable garden and the fowl hocks. Perhaps I can send the Kaiser's friend home with some fresh eggs.'

By the time von Veltheim had followed him through the house and out into his back garden, he had made a mental note of the long narrow passage with two pairs of doors leading off it on either side, and the back stoep that had no Presidential guards.

The birdsong rose like a cantata as Hendrina spread their picnic on a linen cloth beneath a willow tree on the Apies River bank. The whole of Fountains Valley bloomed like one great garden, a riot of brambles and wild gooseberries, and the yellow-flowered wild pomegranate.

'We call this *sandappeltjie*,' Hendrina crushed a leaf and gave it to von Veltheim to smell. 'And this's *stamvrugte*. I bottle them for jams and chutney.' She poured him a glass of her homemade ginger-beer.

Von Veltheim raised it in a toast. 'What do we drink to this time?'

'After those election results?' she scoffed.

'Victory's easy: it's how you take the reverses that counts. I drank to the one per cent chance; and there's far more than that going for Piet Joubert in Johannesburg. If he has the heart.'

Hendrina's eyes shone with eagerness. 'If I could be sure I'd . . .' She caught herself. 'You see, Piet's a pacifist who's got to end his days as Commandant-General. I'd call that funny, if it weren't so sad.' She looked away and von Veltheim thought she was listening to the river. But when she looked back at him he saw that her eyes were glistening. 'Every disappointment takes its toll. Always Paul Kruger's shadow's lain across his life. We thought it would move one day. The tragedy is, it never has.'

'And if it did, would he be ready?'

'When a man has waited for something all his life, how can he not be ready?' she asked angrily.

Elise Caldecott was a tall sinuous creature with the crown of her head reaching almost to von Veltheim's shoulder. With the front of her hair piled up and the back loose, she was a Rossetti painting with dark velvety eyes underscored with smudges that came and went. That was what first interested him.

But this was the third time in a week he'd found her waiting for him to walk home through the park. It had made him wary, and now he knew why. He frowned. 'A threatening letter?' he repeated, mystified. 'As in blackmail?'

'*Blackmail*? It's not to extract *money*, silly!' she laughed. It was a musical laugh – but the kind that made him wonder if she practised it with her scales. 'This man gave Papa a rotten share tip. He can keep his money: but I want to see him squirm.' She took his hand and interlaced her fingers with his. 'Trouble is, he knows my handwriting . . . So I'm asking you.'

'I'd say your father can take care of himself.'

'All right then. It's for me,' she admitted. She dropped all pretences and her voice was scarcely audible. 'He . . . Well, he . . . I mean, he made promises . . .' Her eyes had been fixed in her lap. Now she raised them and locked them on his. 'Be my typewriter, Franz? *Please?*'

When she fixed her great fawn's eyes on his, she looked defenceless. Only now he knew she wasn't. Careful, von Veltheim. 'Who's this poor idiot you want me to put the fear of God into?' he asked cagily.

So she flashed her dimples that also came and went, and told him.

Much later that evening at his desk von Veltheim reread the final draft of the letter Elise had partly dictated.

12/2/1898

Solomon B. Joel,
Sir,

You capitalists are the scourge of the world.

I have gambled in your stock and lost everything. Now unless I can have £12,000 at once as a loan, I face ruin.

But if my race is run, so is yours.

I advise you not to mistake me for a blackmailer or a harmless madman. I am actually remarkably sane with an honourable cause that could net your house a handsome profit – an opportunity Barney Barnato was the first to seize.

If you and your brother Woolf are really astute businessmen cast in his mould, put an advertisement to 'Kismet' in the personal column of 'The Star'.

Life or death, the decision is yours.

KISMET

It might have been a favour to Elise, but it also stated his own case and could draw a response from Woolf. Even an inauspicious start to negotiations was a darned sight better than no start at all. One meeting to put him in the picture as Barnato had intended, and they'd be in business.

He moved back to the bed and lay watching Elise sleep among the tumbled bedclothes He felt strangely empty, and a persistent yearning tugged at his gut. Oh, Anne-Marie . . . Did your guardian force that annulment? Couldn't you have waited? Or written?

He realised that Elise had opened her eyes and was watching him. She smiled invitingly. He'd been so long without a woman, he was again surprised at his automatic response. And again it did nothing to assuage his hunger for Anne-Marie.

Down the passage Juta listened to the tension in the creaks and silences of that night. They made his own loins distinctly uncomfortable. In the rhythmic breathing of the sleeping house, he pictured them lying together curved like spoons. *Ja, lepel lê,* he sighed sleepily. But he still could not sleep.

He got up and made an entry in the logbook. It was the official property of Detective Coenraad Jacobus Juta of the *Geheime Dienst.*

He stood at the window and looked broodingly out across the park at the sleeping houses. As he watched, an upstairs light in the Joel House winked on.

In the perimeter of the bedside light at 13 Wilhelm Street Diana Joel watched her husband thrash about among the bedclothes, half mumbling, half crying in a strangled voice, 'Murder!'

She leaned over and, crooning comforting sounds as though to a baby, gently rocked him awake. 'It's only the dream, dear. Woolf will soon be here to make it stop.'

White and shaken, Solly raised himself on one elbow. 'Some nights it feels worse and bigger than Barney,' he muttered hoarsely.

Diana slid out of bed and poured him a brandy from a decanter on the dressing table.

He swallowed it with a shudder. 'Some nights it feels as if it could swallow Woolfie too,' he whispered. He swung his legs over the side of the bed and buried his head in his hands. He was thinking, 'Hell hath no fury like a woman . . .'

He sat there brooding about the woman across the park.

'That weak link in Barnatos' Johannesburg personnel . . . I think we've got something. An ex-bank clerk incarcerated with Solly Joel over the Jameson fiasco.' The secretary handed the banker a slim dossier.

'Well done, Friedrich.' He opened it on his writing table and scanned it. 'So far, so good. What's he done that's shady?'

'A bit of dealing for his own account on the side. Includes holding up a certain gold deal with a friend of Barnato's.'

The banker read on. 'And with good reason, if he's really planning to buy into the company himself.' Halfway down the page he looked up. 'An odd name – Harold Fairbrother Strange?'

'You'll get used to it when you've seen it often enough in print.'

The banker to the bankers agreed with that. 'What counts is how Braun uses him now Joel's on the Rand.'

17

Barnatos' Johannesburg Consolidated Investment Company – popularly known as Johnnies' – stood on the corner of Fox and Harrison Streets, its gay red retractable canvas blinds half veiling its windows like so many winking eyes in the know.

A gust of cyanide dust from the mine dumps scoured Woolf's eyes and scored his throat, and a nostalgia that must have slumbered for four years suddenly awoke. From the walkway into Johnnies the mine dumps ringing the town as far as the horizon were the same giant sunlit sand castles he remembered, only bigger. And everywhere he kept catching whiffs of half-forgotten smells – sun-dried peaches and fresh corn bread, Magaliesberg tobacco and cattle dung. And at the back of his palate he could taste the draught beer he suddenly realised he'd missed.

He strode through the glazed double doors whistling, so homesick for old faces that he took the stairs to the directors' offices two at a time.

In the doorway to Solly's office the tune died on his lips. Solly was slumped behind his desk, his face twisted into that peculiar rictus he had teased him about as a child when he'd suddenly been scared. And beneath his chair spread the telltale pool where his bladder had failed.

A large, lumpy man hovered over him with a glass of water and a bottle of smelling salts. He blinked up at Woolf through gold-rimmed spectacles. 'Someone called "Kismet" has just threatened Mr Solly's life.' He said unsteadily, and passed him the letter. 'Oh, but allow me to introduce myself. I'm Harold Strange.'

Woolf had heard that he was an ex-bank clerk of good family and modest means. Now he saw that he was also a gone-to-seed athlete, and he guessed he belonged to that class of English gentry who felt it necessary to inform one that 'some of my best friends are Jews'.

He took the letter and read it through twice, but he only asked one question.

'I . . . Why, I naturally alerted Chief Detective Ferguson.' Strange nervously pushed his spectacles back up the bridge of his nose. 'Since Mr Barnato's death, advising the police on anything out of the ordinary's standard procedure.'

Woolf expelled a sharp breath in irritation. 'Well, from now on keep this between ourselves,' he said testily. He scribbled two lines on a letterhead and slid it back across the desk to Strange. 'And try to set this up for Thursday.'

Solly hugged himself with both arms and looked up at him piteously. 'This Kismet geezer, Woolfie . . . He won't do for me like he did for Barney?'

'Not a chance.' Woolf gripped his shoulder reassuringly, but he added briskly, 'I'd best get you away to the Cape.'

Strange watched Woolf support Solly down the passage. Then he picked up the telephone and set up the appointment for him to meet Kismet. But he replaced the listening tube thoughtfully. Woolf couldn't possibly know about Thursday? That he, Strange, was due to meet Alphonse Baruch at the Pretoria Club? And he *couldn't* know he'd been delaying the Lydenburg Gold deal to buy in himself via a nominee?

Because if he did . . . It meant his own hidden agenda with this Kismet bounder came first.

'Sir, this gentleman says he is here on behalf of Kismet.' Harry Calvert, Woolf's senior JCI clerk, gave von Veltheim a sharp look and withdrew.

Woolf gestured him to a seat. He took in the Jermyn Street tailoring, the Turnbull & Asser shirt and the Italian custom-made shoes; but he also noted the odd anomaly of military bearing on a man who could move like a cat. He passed the letter across the desk to von Veltheim. It sat there as accusing as a warrant for arrest.

'Don't quite know where to begin,' von Veltheim admitted wryly. 'With an apology or an assurance that you've nothing to fear.'

'Specially as, since our family bereavement, it's just easier to frighten my brother?'

Not a great start, but von Veltheim had been prepared for that, and he had made up his mind to take his medicine. 'Look, that letter was in rotten bad taste but it was a favour to a . . .' A delicate pause. '. . . a rather fetching young lady who didn't want Mr Solly Joel to recognise her handwriting.' A sheepish smile inviting Woolf to agree that boys will be boys. 'I'd already committed myself before I even knew for whom the letter was intended.'

'P'raps so. But you must see it irrevocably excludes our doing business.'

' "Irrevocably" is a harsh word, Mr Joel.' Von Veltheim presented his honorary consular card. 'You see my name. Heard it before?'

Woolf read it curiously and returned it. 'Never.'

'Not in connection with Mr Barnato's last trip to the Rand?'

Woolf shook his head, and the invisible mechanism that operated his poker player's face shifted into gear like a one-way mirror. Well, well, well. Houldsworth's foreign gentleman on the Rand? Bet you'd have less to do with funding an election than sabotaging it.

'You're not suggesting you came to meet my late uncle on confidential business? I assumed after his death any off-the-record matters would naturally have been dropped.' But his poker player's half smile was saying: calling my bluff, von Veltheim? We'll have to raise the limit and then annihilate you with a straight flush.

Von Veltheim recognised the language. You may fancy yourself as a Mississippi gambler, Joel, but I know every card in the pack. And in this fashion they moved into each other's space. 'This is one off-the-record matter it's not possible to drop,' he said gently. And he told him why.

Oh, Barney, did you think one man could stop Armageddon? 'Suppose I choose to withdraw?' Woolf slowly took his racing binoculars from the bentwood coat stand behind him and removed the repairer's label. 'That £12,000's a reasonable enough sum for your inconvenience. But dashed awkward in our books here. Now in London . . .'

But von Veltheim was shaking his head firmly. 'Here, Mr Joel. And soon.'

'Or?'

'You're going to have to compute the risk of my selling you mining men to the Krugerites against my natural disinclination for blackmail.'

They had led each other right to the edge of the precipice and stared down, and it was Woolf who backed off first. 'Trouble is, that blasted letter of yours has every detective in Johannesburg on our tails.'

Von Veltheim smiled lazily. 'That's why I know you'll find a way.'

'With Ferguson breathing down our necks?'

'One letter'll sort that out.'

'Then be a good fellow and write it. And give me a day to consult someone?' From the window Woolf focused his binoculars on the mine dumps, and grimaced. He replaced the repairer's label on the binocular case. 'Can't use the bloody things if they're still out of true.'

As von Veltheim passed through the clerks' office on his way out, Harry Calvert looked up briefly from the paper aeroplane he was finishing. He walked over to the Fox Street window and took careful aim before launching it into the air. For a long satisfying moment it glided through the sunlit corridor between the Colonnade Building and the Standard Bank.

Across the road a man who looked like a tourist with his checked cap and camera retrieved it and saluted the second-floor window. As von Veltheim emerged, Detective Van Dyk swiftly focused and took two snapshots before melting into the crowd.

Farther along the pavement, Detective von Harnach extinguished his cigarette by treading on it and, at a discreet distance, trailed him past the Rissik Street Post Office all the way home to Clapham House.

'*£12,000!*' Strange looked at Woolf in shocked disbelief.

Woolf dropped into his chair and steepled his fingers. 'Listen to me, Strange. I've just lost my uncle – the best friend I ever had. My brother's health's broken, and the firm's wellbeing's threatened. Now *you* quantify that?'

'You . . . You're asking me to find a way without any awkward book entries?'

'And without further reference to the police,' Woolf confirmed. 'Your banking experience must've taught you something?' he added casually, but his dark penetrating eyes commanded: Think!

Strange nodded. He'll have to make it worth my while. *Think*!

One floor down von Veltheim roved the empty office. Impatiently, he ground to a halt before a framed photograph.

The inevitable picnic group: bottom row seated, the second standing arms folded across their chests like a football team. Barnato seated on a carver dead centre, staff members looking studiously informal except for the two men flanking him like book ends lounging uncomfortably on the ground. Solly Joel and . . .

'Strange. Harold Fairbrother Strange.' He came through the doorway and offered a hand that felt like a discarded piece of clothing. 'I'm here to talk about that £12,000. Mr Joel told you he'd be consulting someone?'

'We're talking much more than that,' von Veltheim said drily and offered his card. 'Permit me . . .'

Strange slid into his chair and examined it, baffled. Honorary American Consul? 'I say . . . Pardon me, I just wasn't expecting anyone of your social standing.'

Von Veltheim passed him a printed pamphlet. 'And this testifies to my professional status.'

'It's in Spanish?' Strange queried, puzzled.

'It urges a party of dissidents against revolt. But here a more direct approach would avert full-scale war.'

All Strange's half-forgotten alarm signals from his Reform Committee incarceration were suddenly on full alert. 'Who *are* you?'

'A professional revolutionist contracted to remove the Transvaal's one obstacle to progress.'

Strange stared at him, his worst nightmares reawakened. 'My God, you're talking about a change of government.'

My God is right. If it's the first the bastard's heard of this, he can't have Joel's confidence. 'I also have key information that could treble Barnatos' profits,' he ad-libbed truthfully.

'Even if I didn't abhor revolutionary movements, my brief's simply to transfer £12,000 . . .'

'Without any awkward reflection in your books?' von Veltheim finished for him, chuckling.

'You find this a laughing matter?'

'A bear market at the right moment with the right information, Mr Strange, and you'd be surprised.'

'But quite beyond my scope. Now . . .' A note of reason grew in

Strange's voice as he warmed to his subject. 'Now if you could sell us a farm . . . Call it a "diamond proposition" – at say £12,000 in excess of the cost price – we could take it off you . . . You follow?'

Von Veltheim followed all right, and he didn't like it. 'Positively out of the question. I'm a stranger here.'

'Barnatos'd assist with a reputable attorney. Costs.'

'A reputable attorney like Harry Caldecott?'

'You know him?'

'From the same boarding house.'

Strange swiftly scribbled '31 Kock Street' on a piece of paper. 'It certainly dispenses with the post. The letter you promised Mr Joel hasn't arrived. It's probably still sitting on Chief Detective Ferguson's desk.'

Police! Von Veltheim felt as though his arteries had been severed and the blood was draining away.

'Morning, von Veltheim.' The voice seemed to come from a long way away, and he was surprised to see Woolf Joel standing in the doorway. 'Everything settled?'

He looked from one to the other, uncertain. Angry. Unnerved. 'How?' he demanded. 'When Mr Strange hasn't really been briefed?'

'But you have my word,' Woolf said evenly, 'when you keep yours about the letter.'

Von Veltheim's forehead creased in anxiety. 'I certainly posted it. But now it seems the police are in on the act.'

'Blast!' Woolf shot Strange a look of irritation, and turned back to von Veltheim. 'Could you get another off to me right away by hand?'

Von Veltheim nodded coldly to Woolf, and turned to go.

But while Strange was hurrying ahead to open the door, Woolf's eyes found his in a silent pact: Of course, Strange hasn't been briefed. This is between you and me.

By the time Strange turned back, Woolf's expression was as neutral as the not quite formal handshake and winding-down patter. 'Change your mind about London? . . . And it's like falling off a log. Here? . . . And we'll need to meet again. But no commitments yet?'

But to von Veltheim that flashing glance had said everything. You cover my back, and I'll cover yours? The look, the 'yet,' – and wasn't there an ever so slight pressure in that handshake? – were as good as a commitment. 'You'll have your letter by tomorrow,' he promised. 'But you've got to understand that money's now imperative.'

'Generally is,' Woolf agreed cheerfully. But as he walked von Veltheim to the door, he also made a promise. 'We'll wrap it up on Monday. Tea for two at the President Tea Rooms at eleven?'

'I found this in the morning mail at home, Mr Woolf. It looked sort of urgent.' Jan Bakoven handed Woolf the envelope as he walked through the Colonnade with Strange.

Woolf tore it open and read aloud: ' "*Woolf Joel, Sir – Some new developments have made your help redundant – but for my passage home. I take my leave of you for good. – Head of the NCR.*"

Head of the NCR?' he repeated, mystified, and then shrugged. 'Well, anyway . . .' And he waved it in the air in triumph.

'Now we can stop all these ridiculous meetings,' Strange agreed.

The Rissik Street Post Office clock striking noon echoed through Chief Detective Ferguson's office on Government Square.

He wore his hair no-nonsense short back and sides and had a bristly toothbrush moustache, but he also had a divergent cast in one eye that refused to line up with the other. Woolf handed him the letter.

Without consultation, Strange held out the page from his scratch pad. 'And here's his address to make an arrest.'

'Not yet, I'm afraid,' Ferguson demurred. 'We know he's Kismet; but I want his friend, too. If this "Chief of the NCR" business isn't subversion, it's too damned near.'

'When it comes to duty, s'rather a case of to each his own,' Woolf reasoned. 'Mine happens to be to our shareholders. And it's not to get involved in your cockeyed plot.'

'And your duty to the State, sir, is to co-operate when we're on the verge of a breakthrough.'

'Come on, Ferguson. In this town we all get information about each other we're sensible enough to ignore.' Woolf spoke rationally, but in his eyes lurked something else.

Ferguson knew what it was. A spot of illicit gold buying and these blighters smell it in London. 'We're asking you to give von

Veltheim enough rope to hang himself,' he said tightly.

'Sorry, old man. I'm here to sort things out smartly and head home.'

'Then I'm going to have to insist on a few little formalities.' Ferguson was trying to match Woolf's even manner, but it came out all stiff. 'No more tête-à-têtes with von Veltheim. I expect Mr Strange to be present, too.' He walked them to the door, and watched them move into the passage before he called after them, 'By the way . . .'

They swivelled in enquiry.

'I take it you gentlemen possess firearms?'

Strange paled, and Woolf's eyes widened. Now Ferguson was enjoying himself. 'Just a precaution,' he added.

He watched them retreat. Then he called Detectives von Harnach and Van Dyk and showed them Strange's slip of paper.

Von Harnach screwed it into a little ball and tossed it at the corner desk. 'What does our man from the *Geheime Dienst* say?'

Juta looked up from the previous day's reports on von Veltheim. 'What he's been saying all along. Those jokers at Barnatos' are playing something too close to their chests.'

'Like?'

'Like Joel probably making von Veltheim an attractive offer to get out of town.'

'Ah, but a little visit to the *Geheime Dienst* in Pretoria tomorrow, and by Monday we'll make some arrests,' was Ferguson's promise.

18

'Farmland's not the only problem, Papa says.' Elise trailed her fingers in the lily pond among the goldfish playing between the water-lily pads at Clapham House. 'He says that it takes huge cash reserves to close two back-to-back deals at such short notice . . .' She hesitated.

Von Veltheim propped up on one elbow on the lawn beside her was thinking: he's right, of course. '*And*?'

She took a deep breath. '. . . And either you're lying to them, or they to you. That it's all tied to Solly's letter. And that he's never seen so many plain-clothed men as there are right now between Johnnies and here.' Brooding, she cocked her head, listening to the Sunday church bells peal all the way from Hospital Hill to St Mary's in town. 'He's never wrong, you know. If he knew you'd involved . . .'

Von Veltheim angrily cupped her chin in his hand, forcing her to look at him. '*Who* involved *whom*?'

Her eyes filled. 'I don't know any more. It's all one hideous merry-go-round going too fast to jump off.'

'You're right. It's gone far enough.' He let her go. He didn't like himself as a bully. 'I actually posted Woolf Joel a letter to stop the whole mess.'

Elise clasped his hand in both of hers, and closed her eyes. 'Thank God.'

'Trouble is, your father's right about the police. I think the Chief Detective's intercepted it. Who knows when he'll release it. Or *if*.'

'Then write another!' Elise balled her fists against her eye sockets like a child trying to blot out a grisly image. 'Just make it *stop*!'

'All right. But this one, *you* deliver?'

She nodded vigorously, but she looked uneasy. 'Coenraad Juta keeps watching me, and Papa says he's got "secret police" written all over him.'

'Juta's just a nice Pretoria boy smitten by you.' Von Veltheim stood and drew her to her feet. 'Let's go,' he said briskly. 'You'll need that letter if you're to drop it after church.'

'Do I have to?'

''Fraid I'm meeting someone bringing some clobber I need from Rose Deep.' He consulted his pocket watch. 'And I need to hurry.'

Woolf was late for his breakfast with Baruch at Heath's Hotel. But for a solitary out-of-towner reading a newspaper, the Palm Court was empty. There was a miniature aviary of budgerigars in the centre where a green-plumaged male lustily ducked itself in the birdbath. Baruch watched his mate hesitate on the rim of its tiny trough of bird seed.

'*Nu?*' he coaxed. '*Essen?*'

He cocked an eyebrow at Woolf, as he strode in. 'So, if breakfast meetings in nonkosher hotels is the new fashion, can we at least eat?'

Woolf led the way to a corner table. 'Things like Goldfields of Lydenburg are best discussed on neutral ground.'

'I'll be frank, Woolfie. Each time Solly's ready to sign, this Strange says "no". Who *is* this *momzer* leading him by the nose?'

'An ex-bank clerk – one of the Reformers in *tronk* with him. Solly's still got to get used to taking decisions. It's scarcely nine months since poor Barney died.'

'Suicide, they called it?' Baruch shook his head angrily. 'As if he would break God's law.' His eyes brightened as a waiter passed with a plate of Kranzkuchen for the other patron, and he decided on the same.

'You were close to him, Alphonse. Do *you* think he was being followed?'

'Ever since that *schlenter* verdict, there's no doubt.' Baruch glanced meaningfully at the waiter awaiting their order.

Without consulting him, Woolf ordered two anchovy toasts with tea. 'Do *you* think he was involved in subversion?'

Baruch thought back to Barney's public threats after the Jameson Raid verdict, and thereafter to his fears of being followed. 'That's exactly what I think.' He gave a heartfelt sigh. 'And I think that's why he died.'

'Then his soul should rest easier if I make a donation to Oom Paul to help counteract Joubert support.'

Their order arrived and Baruch looked sadly at the other diner devouring his second serving of Kranzkuchen. 'You're right about Joubert. Some speak quite openly of a split among the Boers. That's why the President's own son Tjaart is now a high-ranking officer in the *Geheime Dienst*.'

'The *Geheime Dienst*'s also worrying. Solly's received some letters with revolutionary undertones, and they've been intercepted by Chief Detective Ferguson.' Woolf sliced his toast. 'Now, with his IGB record, I could handle him. But he must be working with the *Geheime Dienst*.'

'*Nu*?'

'So, I'd like to make my donation to Oom Paul personally. Can you arrange it?'

Alphonse smiled meaningfully. 'It's always a pleasure to do a favour for a friend.'

'This week if possible. And I'll sort out Goldfields of Lydenburg, Strange, or no Strange.'

'*No* Strange,' Baruch said emphatically. 'A man who could ruin a straight deal with one of your uncle's oldest friends must have something crooked up his sleeve. For a start, he's feathering his nest. And he's not to be trusted. Get rid of him, Woolfie. Or you'll rue the day.'

On their way out they passed the man eating Kranzkuchen. 'It's good?' Baruch enquired wistfully.

The man just nodded and retired behind his newspaper. Braun wanted neither Joel nor Baruch to remember him.

'Oh my dear, Woolfie won't be back before noon,' Olive Joel smiled. 'But do come in for a cup of tea.'

'Thank you, but I don't believe there's an answer,' Elise answered lightly. 'And Papa wishes us to lunch early. We're all going to the open-air concert at the Wanderers this afternoon.'

Olive Joel tapped the letter. 'I'll see he gets this just as soon as he comes in.'

A pretty girl, she thought, watching Elise move gracefully down the street. Not that one believed all those rumours about Solly's womanising.

Waiting for Elise to turn out of Wilhelm Street, Coenraad Juta also thought she moved gracefully.

She flushed when she saw him, and forced herself to speak with mock severity. 'Coenraad Juta, are you following me?'

'Oh, guilty. Guilty. Afraid if I don't, someone else will,' he explained cheerfully. 'Mind if I walk you home?' His eyes grew serious. 'A bit worried about the company you keep.'

'The Count?'

'And some of the company he keeps, you might say. I know *he's* being followed. As was Barnato.'

'The *Geheime Dienst*?'

'Not only. There's a man hanging around I once came across in German West Africa. A dangerous one.'

Elise's eyes grew large and frightened. '*How* dangerous?'

'Very. Or I wouldn't have spoken.' He lifted a hand and touched her cheek softly. 'Sometimes I wish you'd never got mixed up with your Count.'

'Me too.' Miserable, she laid her hand over his. 'Can you tell me his name?'

He put a forefinger over her lips, sealing them. 'I've already said more than I ought.'

'His name, Coenraad?' she whispered. 'What *is* it?'

19

Harold Strange fired the shot and the Wanderers' Club A and B rowing teams pulled away from Wemmer Pan's shoreline. Sixteen athletes, backs flattened and arms stretched, sliced the water with their oars, and then, torsos curved in a pelvic tilt, they leaned back and pulled. In perfect synchronisation their oars broke the water, glistening with droplets, and the twin V's of their wakes rippled the lake.

'They're good,' Strange said proudly.

'Oh, first class.'

Strange turned with surprise and pleasure. The man was tall with powerful rower's shoulders and the kind of muscle definition that reminded him of Michelangelo's David. 'You look like a man who can use a pair of oars yourself,' he beamed. 'Care to join us?'

The man grinned rakishly. 'Funny, I was about to ask you that.'

'In *what*?' Strange gave him an expansive smile.

While the team was packing up their gear and leaving, the two men strolled along the water's edge, Strange listening. He interrupted only once to the ask the question: 'Are you sure?' But by the time he had finished, Strange was no longer smiling and there was no need for him to repeat the question. The man knew too much in every sickening detail of his abuse of privileged information in the various misdemeanours he thought he'd brought off. What was worse, this stranger's grasp of his own current vulnerable position as a result exceeded his own. Strange felt his stomach turn.

'That means you're for the high jump.' Braun gave him a cosy little wink. 'Check who Woolf Joel breakfasted with at Heath's this morning, if you like.'

Strange looked at the derringer in his hand with revulsion. 'It's my wife's. It only fires one shot. I just use it to start the rowing team.'

'Good enough.'

Strange shuddered. 'I could never do anything violent.'

'No one's asked you to. That's for a professional.'

'You've got the wrong man for the job.'

'I don't think so.' Braun smiled lazily. 'No leverage, you see, like a bit of the black.'

For a moment Strange wanted to plead with him for reassurance he wouldn't go to that extreme. But the next instant he realised he'd just been given sickening proof that he'd go much, much further.

'What do you want me to do?' he asked dully.

Von Veltheim retrieved the two foaming draught beers from the counter, slid one to Foster, and raised his own gratefully. 'I'll have to let you treat me till I get my remittance. Thanks.'

'Can't let a chum go about Johannesburg half naked,' Foster smiled magnanimously, and looked around at the other customers, sizing them up. 'Still, there'd better be someone here we can thrash at dominoes. I rather fancy a suit like yours. And the trimmings.' He tapped von Veltheim's gold pocket watch with the von Veltheim crest, but his eyes continued roving the other customers for potential.

'Dinner tonight?' von Veltheim hastily headed him off, adding apologetically, 'Your treat?'

'Moss's Grillroom. And you're going to sing for your supper.'

'Dominoes?'

'No, poker.'

Von Veltheim sighed theatrically. 'A man gets nothing for nothing.'

And he slid the blue Colt 45 out of his pocket and checked it.

Ferguson sat on a vacant bench on the station platform and opened his copy of the *Rand Post.*

'Pardon me . . .' The man who'd been browsing at the newspaper kiosk took the seat beside him. 'When's the Pretoria train due?'

Ferguson consulted his pocket watch. 'In about seven minutes. You should be there for lunch.' Rattling his paper, he retired behind it with an air of finality.

'No, I don't think so.'

Ferguson pointedly ignored him.

'You, of course, will keep your appointment with Tjaart Kruger,' the stranger drawled, with an infuriating smile. 'But you won't divulge anything about a conspiracy yet.'

Ferguson lowered his paper and looked at Braun in shocked disbelief.

'Unless you're prepared to be dismissed from the force?'

'Who *are* you?' Ferguson asked hoarsely.

'Unimportant. Unlike my advice.'

The annoyance in Ferguson's eyes was rapidly becoming fear.

'I mean, how would it look,' Braun reasoned, 'if just as you were about to drop your bombshell to the President's son, he queried your susceptibility to IGB bribes?'

'You've no proof.' But the minute he'd said it, Ferguson realised he'd incriminated himself. He composed himself, and forced himself to speak lightly. 'I meant, things aren't what they seem.'

'If they were,' Braun said drily, 'you wouldn't be taking this train to Pretoria now with orders from me.'

Ferguson stared. 'My God, *you're* Kismet!'

'Let's just say, I'm the puppet master who pulls his strings. And yours,' Braun added. 'Like this.' And though his instructions were brief, they were explicit.

'You're asking me to betray my office,' Ferguson blurted out.

'You've already done that. I'm simply giving you the chance to keep your job. The pay's not up to much, but think of the perks.' He cocked his ear at the sound of the shunting train, and stood up. He shot Ferguson a penetrating look, and then smiled almost tenderly. 'Thought you'd get the point,' he said softly, and he sauntered off to the Noord Street exit just as the train steamed in.

From a distance Ferguson could better appreciate his immense height and muscular shoulders. He raised his *Rand Post* to block out the image, but behind the paper his face was white, and he kept muttering in a ragged whisper, 'Oh, my God. Oh, my *God*!'

20

A cricket ball arced through the sunlight over the Wanderers cricket pitch and the batsman hit it with a sweet thwack.

'Jolly well played!' The exclamation came from von Veltheim, and Elise joined in the desultory applause. Arm in arm, they continued on to the gingerbread lace gazebo where a uniformed brass band was joyously belting out excerpts from *HMS Pinafore* in the autumn sun. There von Veltheim exchanged pleasantries with Elise's family, and then excused himself.

Two angelic little boys in sailor suits ensconced in the front row sucked oranges with fiendish delight. The trombone and French horn developed saliva problems, hesitated, lost their places and had to catch up. Charlie was supplying the oranges, but directly he saw von Veltheim, he gave the boys the packet and joined him.

As they moved off towards Joubert Park, Charlie courteously raised his hat to Elise, and she inclined her head and flashed her dimples in response.

'Ooh! Nice smile, Count!' he remarked. 'Not a bit on the wan side for you?'

'A heart ailment. And an uncalled-for remark,' von Veltheim admonished him. 'Beggars recruiting new couriers in a strange town can't be choosers.'

Some girls were playing on the swings in the park, and a uniformed nursemaid with two small boys in knickerbockers was struggling to get a kite aloft.

Von Veltheim dropped onto a nearby bench. 'Any problems?'

'Only budget ones. You realise there's been nothing since the instalment your mystery boss sent after that newspaper article. Scarcely covered the deposit. and you don't get horse relay-stations or yachts on tick.'

'And now it seems I need to see that mystery boss myself,' von Veltheim said carefully. 'Means a delay.'

Charlie's mouth set stubbornly. 'We're already committed, Count. Joel's got to see that.'

'Joel couldn't care less. This was Barnato's scheme and Joel only wants out. He's talking of paying the £12,000 cut-off fee just to keep their name clean.' Von Veltheim watched the kite climb aloft and do a complicated dance on high. 'But he says he's got to find a way to hide it in their books. He needs time.'

'You're not considering it?'

'It's not up to *me*. Barnato meant to brief Joel after he got home. Now he's either too jumpy to take Barnato's place, or too jumpy about where it got him.' Von Veltheim noticed the kite fly out of control, and the two little boys followed it, wailing. 'If we want that £12,000, he's going to make me go to London to get it.'

'Why can't we cash some of that gold against it? Bridging finance?'

''Fraid that's strictly redeemable only after the new administration's in place.' The kite came careening within reach and von Veltheim caught it.

Charlie frowned. 'Joel didn't mention the gold?'

Von Veltheim shook his head. 'And in view of his reluctance, nor did I.' The younger boy, encouraged by his brother, shyly came to claim his kite, and von Veltheim returned it to him with a smile. 'Aside from Joel, only one man can redeem it now. But he's strictly low profile. And means to remain so.'

An image of the contents of the cave with all its problems lay between them, as tangible as Midas's gold. And just as inaccessible. Charlie thought a moment, computing the delay against its value. 'Can you get me enough for another yacht schedule?' he asked cagily.

'With change. There's just one more complication . . .' Von Veltheim gave a wry little smile. 'An admirer of Miss Caldecott's in the *Geheime Dienst* let slip that Barnato was being followed. And now he thinks I am.'

'By the *Geheime Dienst*?'

'*And* some joker he once came across in German West Africa.' Von Veltheim paused fractionally. Vigilant. 'Name of Karl Braun.'

Charlie whitened. 'Charlie Brown, like me?' he croaked.

The moment Elise told him the name a warning siren had sounded in von Veltheim's brain. And now Charlie heard it too.

'Just too much of a coincidence,' Charlie muttered distractedly. 'Who *is* this joker? And if I find him, what's next? Do I make him disappear?' The words were spoken jocularly, but his face was grey. They sat locked in uneasy silence, and it was Charlie who broke it first. 'We'd hoped this wouldn't be messy, Count. But it's like they say . . . You can't make omelettes without breaking eggs . . .' He looked to von Veltheim for confirmation.

At last von Veltheim nodded wearily.

'Then leave him to me while you get Joel to bankroll your London trip.' Charlie spoke briskly, but it sounded like the briskness of someone whistling in the dark.

They stood and started to leave, but the two little boys with the kite shyly blocked their path. Von Veltheim crouched down on his haunches to bring his face level with theirs. They watched worshipfully as he showed them how to feed the string smoothly through their fingers.

'Charm Joel like you do women and children,' Charlie advised, 'and you'll still pull something out of the hat tomorrow.'

'At eleven,' von Veltheim agreed, tousling the younger boy's hair. 'And let's hope it's not a rabbit.'

'The police know he wrote those letters, and they know where to find him.' Strange swallowed down his port. 'Let's just get it over with.'

The faint murmur of the women's discussion of the charity performance of *Charlie's Aunt* in the drawing room of 13 Wilhelm Street made it convenient for them to talk in the smoking room.

'And let the police think there was something we can be blackmailed about?' Woolf lit up a Romeo y Juliéta to give himself time to think. 'Even when an enquiry yields nothing, dirt like that sticks. Rather let it all blow over now Caldecott's daughter dropped this off.' He held out the note.

Strange scanned it. 'He's asking for a damned sight more than his passage to London. You're not considering it?'

'I'd keep him on a string till he settles for a fiver. 'Cept there's Solly.'

'But this whole business of our carrying firearms? It's unnerving. *Us?*' Strange shrilled. 'He's a professional gunman!'

'Still . . . Can't see him starting anything at Johnnies,' Woolf said mildly.

'Just so long as we only meet there.' Strange tried to subdue the tremor in his voice. 'Then if we *were* obliged to draw, the police'd know it was self-defence.'

'Won't come to that, old chap . . . Pack him off tomorrow.'

They moved to rejoin the women. Outside the drawing room they could hear peals of laughter and Olive Joel's voice exclaim, 'Of course the West End's quite a different kettle of fish.'

'Why, *Charlie's Aunt* in the West End . . .' Flora Strange broke off as the men entered. 'My, you do look seedy, dear. Is it our tummy again?'

'Afraid so. Unless I'm better in the morning . . .' – Strange gave Woolf a desperate look – 'I'd best stay home and doctor myself.'

'Some Beecham's pills and a night's sleep, and you'll be right as rain,' Woolf predicted cheerfully. But he added sympathetically: 'Just for an hour. I breakfasted with Alphonse Baruch at Heath's this morning and picked up a query I promised to iron out tomorrow.' Woolf noticed the blood drain from Strange's face. 'I won't keep you longer than it takes.'

'If you're sure it can't wait,' Strange said unsteadily.

21

Several times during the night von Veltheim kindled the candle in his room. A cockerel crowed in the distance. A dog barked nearby. Across the park a train shunted to a halt. He got up and looked at the lightening sky. The morning star. How would Joel talk with Strange out of the way?

A worm of unease twisted in his gut, and he recognised it. He opened his Gladstone bag, took out his blue Colt and cartridge case and removed the six bullets. Methodically he loaded it.

Woolf Joel closed his eyes and soaked in the claw-and-ball legged bathtub, thinking.

His passage home, the £12,000 and a bonus if he leaves on the next mail boat. But if he's *not* on it, Solly and I'd better be, because he's not taking no for an answer.

Woolf stood and soaped himself with a cake of Lifebuoy. Of course, if he messes up, Kruger'll appreciate my warning. And if he *doesn't* . . . Woolf filled the sponge with water and squeezed. He's right about the market. I'll have to cut him in for a percentage of the gross.

He stepped out of the tub and reached for the bath sheet. Participating without being seen to do so – more commonly known as sitting with one arse on two chairs.

As he massaged some bay rum into his hair, he regarded his mirrored reflection ruefully. And you were the bastard who said fence-sitting was easy?

Immaculately dressed half an hour later, he was halfway down the front steps when he realised he'd forgotten something. With a shrug of impatience, he dashed back to fetch it. He disliked the way his suit hung now with that bulge.

'Let's move, Jan,' he called to Jan Bakoven as he swung into his carriage. 'It's going to be one hell of a long day.'

Harold Strange glanced at his wife's kippers swimming in butter and felt queasy. 'He's an inconsiderate monster,' he said bitterly. 'Making me come in when he knows I'm unwell.'

'Nonsense, dear,' Flora Strange crooned. 'He just wants to finish what he came for and go home.'

Strange pushed his dry toast and black tea away. 'Excuse me, my dear. But the sooner I leave, the sooner I'll be home.'

Flora helped him on with his jacket and spotted her derringer peeping out of the inside pocket. She pouted. 'Oh Harold, I know everybody's walking about armed to the teeth on police's orders, but you *do* have your own revolver. A loan is a loan.'

'It's too cumbersome,' he said shortly. 'I'll be home before noon.'

'Woolf *promised* only an hour. Do remind him,' she called after him as he slammed out of the front door. 'You old cross-patch,' she remarked to his retreating back.

Woolf ran into Strange in the corridor returning from the toilet, and noticed that he still looked ill. 'Old stomach still playing up?'

'I should really be in bed,' Strange muttered. 'You had some query about Lydenburg Gold?'

'Not yet compared our documentation with Baruch's.' Woolf looked at him more closely. 'P'raps I ought to tell him you're poorly, and get a day's grace.'

'You're sure?'

Woolf nodded vigorously. 'Just stop in at the President Tea Rooms on your way. Von Veltheim's expecting me at eleven. Explain it's mail day and I'm hard pressed until tea.'

'Is this necessary?'

''Fraid so, old boy. You see, there's Solly. Barney'd call the blighter's passage home "cheap at the price".'

'I don't know any more,' Strange said raggedly. 'My God, I don't *know*.'

Woolf searched his face for a moment, and then nodded. 'Just get rid of him until this afternoon, and go *home*. By the time you're fit again, it'll all be over.'

Strange clasped a hand over his mouth and spun off again to the toilet.

Woolf passed and heard him still retching ten minutes later.

Another casualty, he thought soberly. I'll finalise with von Veltheim today before there are any more.

Von Veltheim looked at the shirting in the window of Kneebone's Outfitters. His own shirt cuffs were starting to fray. He had fifteen minutes to get to the President Tea Rooms. As he turned away he saw Strange.

'Mr Joel's regrets. But Mondays there's always this dickens of a rush to catch the mail boat.'

'Don't I know,' von Veltheim said feelingly.

Von Veltheim started to move past but Strange clutched at his sleeve. 'He *can't* come.'

But von Veltheim was already striding away towards the Colonnade Building. Strange hurried after him, making pleading noises. At the entrance von Veltheim looked at him, perplexed. 'Really, Mr Strange, you'd think I meant to shoot him,' he said mildly.

Together, they entered the building and walked along the corridor to his office.

'Frank?'

'Mr Strange?'

'Please take this up to Mr Woolf.'

Twice that morning Frank Hall was summoned from the clerks' office to Strange's to deliver notes for Calvert to hand to Woolf.

Woolf glanced up from the pile of outgoing mail, and scanned Strange's message: *Party is here and declines to let me see you. Please come at once.*

Declines to let *me* see *you*? The poor bastard's nerves are shot, and he just won't go home.

He scribbled his answer: *Am in the middle of my mail. If I don't get on with it I shan't get through.*

Strange showed it to von Veltheim.

'Woolf Joel suggested I go, damn it,' he snapped. 'Now I'm booked on the afternoon train to catch the mail boat.'

'I can only try.' Strange scribbled the second message and handed it to Hall.

Woolf looked up from a London letter to find Calvert at his elbow with another note. He read it. 'Damn, damn, *damn*!' He crumpled it into a ball and flung it across the desk with such vehemence it spun off the other side.

As Calvert stooped to retrieve it he read: *He says it's urgent. Do come at once.* 'Let me speak to the gentleman,' he offered. 'Perhaps *I* could get him to return later?'

'Thanks, old chap, but now my concentration's shot.'

Woolf stood up and strode out.

Strange sat at his desk, the bitter taste of nausea in his throat. 'I've told you it's no use. You might as well leave.'

'Not until Joel asks me to.' Strange had lowered his eyelids, veiling his frustration, panic, funk. And something else. It prompted von Veltheim to add, 'But any dirty tricks . . . and I shoot.'

The door opened and Woolf entered, locking the Yale catch behind him. 'Well, von Veltheim?'

'You've received your letter. Now I'm here for that loan.'

Woolf saw that Strange was watching them anxiously. 'How about an advance if your friend endorses your promissory note?' he ad-libbed.

'You know damned well he can't.'

'It's negotiable.' Woolf looked at him steadily. We need to talk alone. 'Why not call back after tea?' he suggested casually.

'You wouldn't be reneging on your word?' von Veltheim demanded. But a moment later he understood exactly what he was doing. Strange had no idea of his deal with Barnato, and Woolf obviously needed to be seen to be trying to elicit information from him for the police.

Then Strange fumbled in his pocket, and again von Veltheim knew exactly what for.

'What are you *doing*?' he whispered hoarsely.

The three men each felt the precise weight of his firearm in his inner pocket. Then the butt of one pressed into the heel of a sweaty palm, the forefinger curled around the trigger, and squeezed.

Suddenly bullets were going off everywhere. The first shot went wild, but the retaliatory fire sent the aggressor sprawling. And then there were two.

A pair of blazing eyes looked into a pair of puzzled ones, unaccountably apologetic as three bullets were pumped into him at point-blank range. They sent the body jerking in three different attitudes in a rag doll dance before it slid to the floor in a half-sitting position. For an instant he looked as if he were just sitting there thinking, 'Fancy that.'

Hall stiffened in the next office as the tattoo rang out. It sounded like Morse code – one dash and four dots? 'Heavens, that man's banging his cane on Mr Strange's desk. Ever since they've been in there he's been sending frantic notes to Mr Woolf. They need help.'

Upstairs, the moment Calvert heard the exchange of gunfire, he realised he'd been waiting for it all morning. 'My God, Strange knows Mr Woolf's querying his Lydenburg Gold deal, and he's paid that foreign bastard to get him first.'

He bolted for the stairwell, his thoughts churning, 'Leave them to me, Mr Woolf. Don't discuss any of it. Don't say another word!'

He never would. Just as the faithful Calvert would never again close his eyes without seeing Woolf Joel with a bullet through his brain.

'Great Scott, revolver shots!' Stephenson gasped. 'It must be Mr Woolf and Strange dealing with that German lunatic the detectives are watching. We'd better get there first.'

He hurtled across the clerks' office and, aiming his shoulder at the closed door, burst the Yale catch.

22

Von Harnach saw the man bolt out of the building, and yell, 'The police! Oh my God, someone! The police!'

He showed his badge and they spun and raced back. As he reached the monogrammed door, he turned and signalled wildly to the other end of the block. But Van Dyk had seen it all and was already pounding after them.

Von Harnach burst into the office and tried to make sense of what he was seeing: Woolf Joel dead from a shot through the brain. Strange, white and shaken, hauling himself up from behind his desk. And two clerks pinioning von Veltheim's arms while a third was working him over. Enraged, and with a two-fisted action, he repeatedly walloped him across the face left to right, and then right to left.

Von Harnach grabbed him and showed his badge again. 'All right, gentlemen. That'll do.' As the clerks released von Veltheim, he got his own body between them and snapped on the cuffs.

Van Dyk erupted through the doorway and looked from Woolf's corpse to the endangered von Veltheim. 'Got to get him to the Fort fast. Best get the pick-up.'

'We'll also need a doctor.' Von Harnach nodded at Woolf's body. 'And seal off the room.'

Von Veltheim frowned and shook his head as though coming out of a trance. 'He's really dead?' he asked von Harnach shakily.

'Afraid so.'

'God, I'm sorry,' he whispered to himself, and closed his eyes. When he opened them again, he focused on von Harnach. 'But those bastards shot first.'

'Just come quietly. We don't want a lynching.' Von Harnach threw a glance at the window that gave onto the street.

Then von Veltheim heard it, too. A score of voices raised in a muffled hum was steadily growing into a kind of animal baying sound. And suddenly he was scared.

Van Dyk herded everyone into the clerks' office. 'Right, everybody. Let's get some statements.'

There was a commotion as Dr Philipot arrived and began using his medical bag to cleave a path through.

'Take care of the prisoner for me?' von Harnach asked Van Dyk, and showed the doctor through Strange's open door.

Woolf still lay in that half-sitting position, the surprised look frozen on his face; and Philipot moved swiftly to close his eyes.

Von Harnach was astonished to see other people still there. Strange, in a state of near collapse behind his desk, and Frank Hall, leaning over him giving him a brandy. He looked up at von Harnach. 'Mr Strange has been proper poorly . . . I'd best see him home, if that's all right with you?'

'Just as soon as we've his statement, sir.'

Dazed and unnerved, Strange began shakily, 'I think von Veltheim fired first.' His mouth worked convulsively. 'I can't. I just *can't*,' he gulped, and then broke into great shuddering sobs.

'The brandy'll help the shock, sir. Just a few questions and you'll be on your way.'

Caldecott shouldered his way past the ZARP reinforcements trying to establish calm in the outer office. He saw the doctor working on Woolf, and fell back a pace in shock. 'Oh my God, no!'

'It was that swine, von Veltheim,' Strange spat with venom, but also with an undercurrent of cunning. 'Your daughter delivered his letter to Woolf yesterday. And now she's going to have to say why.'

'Staining an innocent girl's name won't get *you* out of that crooked land deal.'

Von Harnach looked from one to the other, and changed his mind about allowing Strange to go home. 'I'm going to *have* to insist on a full statement, sir.' He gave Strange a piercing look. 'Until I get it, *nobody* leaves.'

'All this happened this morning?'

'At about eleven o'clock.' Wernher read the ticker tape unrolling in their office. As it ended he tore the message off, and sat down opposite Beit at their partner's desk to reread it. 'But now who is this Harold Strange?'

'Joint manager of Barnatos' Johannesburg office. Holding up

the Lydenburg Gold deal with a friend of Barney's, Oscar says.'

Wernher continued reading the ticker tape. 'The press plan to publish some threatening letters von Veltheim wrote the Joels. They think he was trying to blackmail them. That's what they take him for. A *blackmailer*!' he chuckled. 'Let's hope Kruger's *Geheime Dienst* does too.'

Beit didn't chuckle. 'First Barney, and now Woolf?' Then a new thought chilled him. 'If I was the betrayer, why do I feel betrayed?'

Von Harnach removed von Veltheim's handcuffs, pulled out a chair for him, and then took his place behind his desk. He didn't know whether it was the physical beating or the anguish, but the powerful swaggering man he'd been following for a week seemed to have shrunk inside his skin.

He filled a tumbler from the water carafe and pushed it across the desk to him.

Von Veltheim looked at it dumbly.

Von Harnach's words were offhand, but his eyes were compassionate. 'Come on, drink it. It's only water.'

Von Veltheim swallowed.

Von Harnach took out a charge sheet, and dipping his pen into his inkwell, prepared to write.

'The bastards shot first,' von Veltheim burst out.

'All in good time. Let's first have your name.'

No answer.

'Your *name*?'

Von Veltheim's eyes narrowed. 'Karl Braun.'

'*Karl Braun*?'

The resolve grew in his voice. 'Yes. Karl Braun.'

Von Harnach veiled his surprise and wrote it down. He looked up at von Veltheim. In spite of his bruised face, suddenly he was no longer beaten.

In fact, quite the reverse.

The *Johannesburg Times*' half-glazed door swung open and McDermott clattered down the steps to the hansom cab rank.

'Where to, Guv'nor?'

'Jeppestown. Know a place called "The Oval"?'

'Yes, sir. But hasn't Mr Strange already had a corker of a day?'

'I expect him to kick me out, laddie. You might as well wait.'

The driver clicked his tongue at his horse. 'Giddy-up, luv. It's a scoop on the Joel murder case.'

And the cab lurched away from the kerb.

'But didn't it strike you as odd, when you arrested him?' Ferguson took the charge sheet from von Harnach's table 'We all know him as von Veltheim, and he suddenly says he's Karl Braun?'

Von Harnach shrugged. 'It struck me as a useless attempt to cover his identity.'

'Or expose someone else's?' Juta filled his pipe with Magaliesberg shag. 'Suppose the Landdrost's Court were persuaded to overlook this oversight? We've a couple of months before the Circuit Court Case sits. Who knows what we'll smoke out of the woodwork by then.'

Ferguson looked morose. 'We'll get nothing further from that Barnato bunch. I've a feeling that they were even holding something back.'

Von Harnach prodded the air in front of Juta's chest. 'Do you think this Karl Braun's a real person?'

Juta nodded, and then quickly looked away. 'If he's who I suspect he is, he's bad.'

'But was he working for or against von Veltheim?'

Juta stuffed his leather tobacco pouch into his pocket and got up to go. He turned in the doorway, an eyebrow raised quizzically. 'If von Veltheim's trying to blow the whistle on him, it must be for *something*.'

23

'My sincerest condolences, sir. The whole town's reeling.' McDermott grasped Strange's limp hand and shook it. 'I think von Veltheim'll be lucky if he doesn't get lynched.'

Behind half-drawn bedroom blinds, Strange lay on the double bed in his shirtsleeves, suit trousers and stockinged feet. His sensible, well-polished shoes lay abandoned crookedly on the floor. He swivelled to get a better look at McDermott. 'You know him?'

'As a fast-talking foreign gent. For the past six weeks we've stayed in the same boarding house.' McDermott perched cautiously on the fragile bustle-back chair Flora had arranged next to the bed and pulled out his writing materials. 'How on earth did you get mixed up with him?'

Strange subsided on his pillows, and appeared to study the pressed-iron ceiling pattern. 'A few weeks ago Mr Solly Joel received this letter signed "Kismet". It threatened his life unless he discharged a £12,000 debt.'

'Was Kismet von Veltheim?'

'It would seem so.'

'And *did* Barnatos' *owe* him that money?'

'Don't see how. He hinted at wild schemes for overthrowing the government, but he was strapped for cash. Kept talking about how he was a professional revolutionary, sent here to remove South Africa's obstacle to progress.'

'The *President*?'

'Who else? Bastard went on about how Barnatos' would profit. But after what the family's been through, his threatening Solly Joel's life had Woolf all in a state. So we met with von Veltheim – then purporting to be Kismet's friend – on the Saturday.'

'To negotiate with him?'

'Hardly. There was never any question of giving him such a sum. It was more a case of Woolf's playing along at the Chief Detective's request to lull him into disclosing some friend's identity.'

'But *something* must have provoked that shooting?'

'The man was dangerous and, on police orders, we were armed.' Strange heard the rising note of hysteria in his voice and made a conscious effort to pitch it lower. 'While he and Woolf were arguing, I stood, turned aside, and struck a match to light my cigar. I put the matchbox in my pocket that held the derringer, covering my move of cocking it ... You follow?' He closed his eyes wearily and shook his head. 'After that everything happened in a flash. Von Veltheim must have realised the game was up. He suddenly turned to Woolfie and said ...'

Abruptly, Strange swung his legs off the bed and began to pace in his stockinged feet. 'He said, "You two know too much now. You'll never leave this room alive." Then he whipped out his gun – he swung it on his forefinger like a professional gunman – and fired it point blank at Woolfie's head.'

Strange stopped his pacing to check that McDermott's racing pencil was getting all this down. 'I *had* no choice. I drew my derringer and fired at von Veltheim's head.' Strange subsided on the bed, his head in his hands. 'Tragedy is, I missed.'

McDermott looked up from his Pitman's shorthand, the eyes under his bushy eyebrows penetrating. 'Who fired first?'

'Can't say for sure, but I had the impression we both fired at once. The next thing I heard was three shots in quick succession. Only a practised gunman could have fired like *that*.' Strange looked at McDermott for confirmation. There was none. '*I've* only ever fired a gun to start the rowing team.' He gave a little giggle, inviting McDermott to laugh with him at the absurdity of his confronting von Veltheim. But the mirthless grin and the anxious eyes just made him look demented. Also sinister. McDermott looked away.

Strange was disconcerted. He got up and began to pace again with a measured tread, his voice pitched lower as though willing himself to act calmly. 'Woolfie sank to the floor. As he fell, he dropped his revolver from his hip pocket. Seeing him down, I made a grab for it.' He extended his arm, miming the movement. 'I slipped. Before I could get up, von Veltheim had come around the desk and planted his foot on Woolfie's gun.'

Strange noticed that McDermott had stopped taking notes and had resorted to diagrams. 'I had it by the butt ... You follow? But von Veltheim trod on my hand and fired at me again. That's when the clerks burst in. You must know the rest.' He looked out of the window at the blue gums. 'I'll never forgive myself for not seeing through him earlier,' he said dully.

The Johannesburg Fort crouched on Hospital Hill like a great ugly stone toad.

The floors were hewn from stone quarried from the hillside on which it was built. And on the interior cell walls, painted a bilious Public Works Department green, blossomed the culture of graffiti – a series of not quite uniform scratches chronicling a former inmate's incarceration. A legend advising that Hennie Oosthuizen was here. And another more chilling message that resembled claw marks that had been painted out. Superimposed over the persistent smell of boiled cabbage and disinfectant was the more sinister smell of ancient panic and recent fear.

Deep in its bowels in the security section von Veltheim lay on his bunk. Shadows had bloomed beneath his bloodshot eyes, and the area around the right one was misshapen by a livid purple bruise overlaid by the deeper red grid of an abrasion that was beginning to scab.

But the skin over his cheekbones was stretched tight, as though to contain the pain of a deeper wound that throbbed in his skull.

His mind ticked like a metronome. Who *was* this Karl Braun? Some kind of exterminator? First Barnato. Then Joel. And now he's neutralised me. Is this all part of a master plan? Could Charlie really make him disappear? Or would it be the other way around? Because the malevolent power stalking him, as it had the others, went beyond the casual bad luck a gambler might encounter at the throw of the dice. And if it wasn't casual, who was doing the planning? And was there a connection to Karl Braun? The more he tried to thrust the thought away, the more it stuck like a burr. He thought of the powerful forces to which Anne-Marie had alluded, and was chilled. 'Who profits?' The metronome in his head ticked on and on. 'Who profits more from war?'

He heard the two pairs of approaching footsteps echo off the cavernous walls in the corridor outside. The key grated, and the iron-bound door swung open as Governor Menton, the prison superintendent, showed McDermott in.

'Valet service, suh!'

Von Veltheim briefly raised himself on one elbow, and then sank back and replaced the cold compress over his swollen face. With each movement of his head came jolts of pain as his blood throbbed with sudden malignance through the vessels in his head. 'Valet service? Must be some mistake,' he said weakly. 'I actually asked for the wine steward to bring port.'

McDermott stooped over his bunk and peeled back the compress to inspect his shiner that was threatening to shade from purple to green like a vicious bottle fly. 'It's a good hard head,' he approved. 'Grazed a few of the enemy's knuckles and sprained a wee ligament. That's a fair tally.'

'Six against one? And I was just standing there asking someone to send for the police.'

McDermott unearthed his writing materials from his shapeless tweed jacket. 'The enemy's statements show minor discrepancies.'

'You bastards'll do anything for a story.'

''Tis the nature of the beast,' McDermott apologised, 'but you'll notice I'm the only paper prepared to tell yours.'

Von Veltheim painfully hauled his legs over the side of the bunk and spoke haltingly for about ten minutes, before McDermott interrupted, 'But you're sure you were *chatting*, Count? Not threatening?'

'I was *urging* Woolf Joel not to renege on a business transaction. I had to leave by the mail train that afternoon to catch the steamer.'

'But you *were* agitated?'

'I suppose so.' Grudgingly.

'And you had your hand in your right-hand pocket, where you also just happened to have your Colt?'

'All right, Mac. But I was just reasoning with the man when Strange stood to light his cigar. The next moment I heard the shot that damned near grazed my head, and saw Strange standing with his derringer in the air. When Woolf Joel drew his revolver, I stood between two guns, and I emptied mine into both men. Tried to, anyway.' Von Veltheim tossed the compress into the tin dixie. 'It was self-defence. You've got to believe that.'

'I'm trying, Count,' McDermott stopped writing and looked at von Veltheim levelly. 'Did you not say, "You two know too much now: you'll never leave this room alive"?'

'Is that what Strange is saying?' von Veltheim asked hoarsely.

'*Did* you?'

'*No*!'

'And *are* you a real Count?'

'Where I come from the "von" means honourable.'

'Forget the semantics. I'm asking about your kin.'

Von Veltheim's jaw knotted.

'Because, if you are a real Count . . .' McDermott continued equably, '. . . you're going to need some of that filthy lucre you foreign aristocrats are supposed to have so much of. Either from them, or from the people who sent you here. The other side has plenty of resources to fight this case. Premeditated murder, Count.'

'You know it's trumped up.'

'With a wee bit of treason thrown in. And for an advocate to convince the Circuit Court you're innocent of both, 'twill take money.' McDermott shoved his pad in his pocket, and stood. 'Or a miracle.'

24

Hal Smithers sat in his law office in the Aegis Buildings, nursing his hangover and trying to recall whether the young lady he'd taken to bed the previous evening had been worth the exorbitant sum he'd forked out. An entire bottle of British Grenadier London Dry Gin, and all one had to show for it next morning was a tongue like blotting paper, an empty wallet, and not even the foggiest notion of whether it had been fun.

His clerk came in with the coffee tray. 'Bless you, Watson. And in the nick of time,' he greeted him. 'Was ju-ust on the point of going out.'

'For a hair of the dog, sir? Tsk, tsk, tsk.' Watson clucked, and poured the coffee. 'Strong and black,' he crooned soothingly. 'And this, sir . . .' – he placed a cable beside the coffee cup – '. . . is marked *urgent*.'

Smithers groaned. 'Sweet Jesus, not today.' He was a tall, elegant man with a gaunt, ravaged face that looked a good decade older than his thirty-five years. But as he read the contents, that decade seemed to drop away. 'Watson, I'll be asking you to go to the booze shop after all.'

'Not bad news, sir?'

'Not on your Nellie. This is a celebration, dear boy. We've just been briefed to find the finest legal counsel in South Africa, and money's no object.'

'That should pay the rent,' Watson said cautiously.

'Hell with the rent. We'll be drinking champers.'

Watson looked dubious. 'Does it say who's retaining us?'

'Some Austrian bank. Quite unpronounceable – they always are.'

'For *what*?'

'The von Veltheim case, my good fellow. The von Veltheim case!'

Watson had started to leave, but turned in the doorway, aghast. 'Not that blackmailing crook who shot Mr Joel?'

'*Someone*'s got to defend the poor bugger, and attorneys in arrears with their rent can't be choosers. And do bring us back the latest editions of the *Standard and Diggers' News* and *The Star*.'

'Barnatos' just about own the *Standard and Diggers' News*,' Watson warned grimly.

'Precisely why I need it, you see.' And, whistling *The Man Who Broke the Bank at Monte Carlo*, Smithers began to study the reports of McDermott's two interviews in the *Johannesburg Times*.

A half-hour later, he'd telephoned McDermott to invite him for a beer at the Deep Level Bar.

'Down the hatch, old bean.'

'Bottoms up, laddie.'

To Smithers and McDermott, their introductory beers were but a memory. They had quickly switched to Johnny Walker, and were sizing each other up with interest.

'Astonishing!' Smithers said. 'You believe the bounder's innocent.'

'Of premeditated murder . . . Yes.'

'And you think he's a decent sort?'

'An officer and a gentleman . . . With a wee talent for trouble.'

'Fortunately, money's no object.'

'Then, if it's not a rude question . . .' McDermott fixed Smithers with a sceptical eye. 'Why you?'

'Damned if I know yet. As a student in Paris I was once madly in love with his ex-wife, Anne-Marie. Could this be reciprocation at last?'

'Could be, laddie.' McDermott thought about it. 'Could be.'

'Still, a defence attorney's job at a preliminary hearing's simply to keep mum and let the other side disclose its hand.'

'*And* find the right counsel for the Circuit Court Case. Ye realise he's going to need the finest legal talent in the country?'

'Indubitably.'

'But d'ye have anyone in mind?'

'A Cambridge man, actually. Only recently emmigrated from the Cape. Still having a lean time financially.'

'Good. Because money talks.'

'Most eloquently, old chap,' Smithers agreed feelingly. 'But not necessarily to young Smuts.'

'Jan Christiaan Smuts? Of course.' McDermott said softly, 'I once heard him lobbying for Rhodes in Kimberley. Most persuasive, he was.'

'Ah, yes. But that must have been before the Raid? He's a Kruger man now.'

'Then – to borrow a phrase – square him.'

'Oh, we'll have a shot, old bean. We most definitely shall.' Smithers signalled the barman to set up the last round and prepare his bill. 'You'll be visiting von Veltheim again?'

'Aye. With his laundry.'

'That's extremely good of you.'

'Won't you?'

'No, actually. I've a spot of work to do,' Smithers smiled winningly. 'But do tell him not to worry.'

McDermott was suddenly stone-cold sober. 'Did ye mark the preliminary hearing's tomorrow?'

'Oh, yes. Tell him that I just said we'll reserve his defence, and I'll see him soon.' Smithers raised his glass. 'Down the old red lane?'

'And mud in your eye.' But McDermott meant it.

And they both tossed back their drinks.

'The charge is murder, and the plea self-defence.' Jan Christiaan Smuts spoke in an uninflected Malmesbury *bry*. 'It's a simple case of who shot first.'

Studying him across his desk in his modest chambers in Steytler's Building, Smithers wondered about the curious blend of youthful innocence and ascetic wisdom that made him seem more than a man in his twenties. Clean-shaven and hollow-cheeked, his arresting blue eyes – said to be those of a *siener* – a seer – reflected something of the horizons he'd scanned.

'Quite simple,' Smithers agreed dolefully. 'If you ignore the conspiracy part.'

'He's got to decline to answer *any* question that could incriminate him on another charge not before the court. We must emphasise that.'

'*We*, Mr Smuts? Then may we assume you'll represent him?'

Smuts began removing his notes from his desk. 'You may assume I'll let you know directly after the hearing. In a case like this it's unfair to dwell.'

Smuts locked his chambers early that afternoon. He had no further appointments and a great deal on his mind. He walked home up Hospital Hill, but thoughts of his Riebeek West boyhood made him veer off to Nugget kopje.

He was homesick for the Zwartland. There life moved to the rhythms of the farmer – the ploughing, the sowing, the reaping, the threshing. Here, farmers had ceased to farm. All sold to the mining houses. The earth raped. There was no dearth of law-breakers. Men needed to be defended in court all the time but – so far – rarely by him.

On the summit of Nugget kopje he sat on an outcrop of *ouklip* and hauled from his pocket a dog-eared pocket-sized notebook – a once discarded, then retrieved, then recycled relic of his early university days at Stellenbosch. If the margins of all his university textbooks were annotated with the closely written comments of his ongoing dialogue with their authors, this scrappy little notebook chronicled his dialogue with himself. He flipped back the pages to an entry three years previously and began to read.

London
January 1895

England has been kind to me. Gratifyingly, Maitland writes of me as the finest law student ever examined at Cambridge, and caps it with offer of a professorship. Yet not this, nor the Middle Temple, nor the two (valuable and welcome) money prizes in honours examinations can keep me in these northern latitudes. I long for home.

Home. I thought that back among the hills of my beginning I would satisfy my hunger for the landscape. Now I know this isn't possible. The landscape creates its own appetites.

He scanned the jottings that marked his return.

Cape Town
September 1895

An advocate's practice in Cape Town seems to be the logical place to start.

But while in the Boer Republic President Kruger remains locked into same old isolationist brand of Afrikanerdom, here the charismatic Prime Minister C. J. Rhodes talks of union and world peace.

What better vocation can there be than to serve such a cause through the law?

That first. Then the next page:

Riebeek West
New Year's Day, 1896

Bouleversement. All navigational references scrambled. All direction dislocated.

His mind reeled back to his father's farm when the first reports of the Jameson Raid began to break: of Rhodes's closest friend in charge of the invasion. Of his brother sent to organise the Johannesburg Reformers. Of his orders to smuggle them arms in crates through the De Beers' Diamond Company.

At this point the neat, cramped handwriting became an uncharacteristic scrawl.

Kruger was right all the time. Evidence overwhelming. R. colluded with British Imperialists – probably even the Colonial Office – to seize the Boer Republic for their Empire.

Extraordinary. He had the tools for peace. And he has set the veld on fire.

Can no longer bring myself to live under his administration. Have applied for admission to the Transvaal Bar.

Seated now on the *ouklip* outcrop on Nugget kopje, Smuts began to write:

Johannesburg
April 1898

At last. An important case: the State versus von Veltheim. My services retained by an undisclosed European source. I can name my fee if I prove v V innocent of premeditated murder. (Technically, he is, if I confine my argument to 'Who shot first?'.) Only this is no mere murder trial . . .

His pencil raced on.

When he eventually got to his feet and trudged home to his lodgings on Hospital Hill, he seemed much older than his twenty-six years.

25

'Killer! Killer!'

The crowd had been gathering around the Landdrost's Court in Government Buildings since 8.30 that morning.

At eleven the Black Maria dropped its prisoners outside the Marshall Street entrance. The police horses – nostrils flared and eyes rolling – whinnied nervously, their shoes sounding a metallic tattoo on the street. The mounted police formed a cordon, and a human shield of armed foot constables hurried the prisoners through the passage between them and the boiling mob.

'Avenge Woolf Joel!'

'Hang von Veltheim!'

The angry chanting reached him behind the glass of the second-storey window from which he looked down on them sombrely through a half-drawn blind. 'And I thought you were exaggerating when you said a closed carriage at dawn.'

Von Harnach peered over his shoulder. 'They all knew Woolf Joel.' He glanced sidewise at von Veltheim. In his collarless shirt and with his battered face he looked like a wounded matelot. He just didn't seem the type to gun down a man in cold blood. Curious, that shoot-out. He touched von Veltheim's shoulder.

As von Veltheim moved to follow him, he could see that his whereabouts had leaked out from the way the crowd surged towards the First Criminal Court.

At the door a ZARP sergeant screening visitors to the public section was repeating, 'Only legal fraternity and the press through the landdrost's office please.'

Von Veltheim took his place with a sense of unreality, and gazed at the tapestry of alien faces. Among the press, he caught McDermott's encouraging salute. Right at the back he glimpsed Charlie in the red whiskers and spectacles he'd used for his New Orleans getaway. For a moment he believed it could turn out all right. Then he saw the Public Prosecutor – Krause with the impeccable grooming of a man always on show, the tight little smile, the watchful hunter's eyes. He knew he was the prey, and he felt his heart throb like a robin's breast.

Krause stood. 'May it please your Worship, the prosecution would like it recorded that accused volunteered the alias Karl Braun.'

The Sheriff faced von Veltheim. 'Please state your name.'

'I'd like to withdraw that statement. My real name is Franz Ludwig Kurt von Veltheim.'

Landdrost Van den Berg's large hands looked as though they were more accustomed to farming implements than law books and records. 'What's the charge?'

'Murder, your Worship.'

'How plead you?'

'Not guilty.' But von Veltheim felt the burn of hostile eyes, and had to make a conscious effort to steady his voice. 'I reserve my defence.'

The court fell silent when Strange took the stand to give much the same version McDermott had recounted to him up to the point where he said: 'The Sunday evening before the shooting, Woolf showed me a begging letter from the prisoner Miss Caldecott delivered to his house that morning.'

'Did Mr Joel treat this demand seriously?'

'He said he'd think about giving him the money against his friend's promissory note. Accused was quite open about being a professional revolutionist; and as a favour to the Chief Detective, Woolfie tried to find out who the friend was he was working with.'

'Assuming there *was* a friend.'

Von Veltheim casually turned, and caught Charlie's twinkling eye.

'What was accused's reaction?' Krause continued.

'Vicious. He said, "You two know too much now, and you'll never leave this room alive".'

'You're a liar!' von Veltheim lashed out.

Krause shot a look from von Veltheim to Strange. 'You solemnly swear the accused said those words?'

'Absolutely. I swear it.'

'Did he act on this threat?'

'Certainly. He pointed his gun at Woolf Joel's head, and shot him dead. Had I shot first, he'd have shot at me.'

Von Veltheim heatedly turned to the newsmen. 'It's a pack of lies, and he knows it!'

The murmur rustling through the courtroom rose to a sullen rumble, and Strange shrank back in his chair.

With a black look at von Veltheim, Van den Berg rapped his gavel and then nodded at Strange. 'You're excused.'

Anger and despair flooded von Veltheim like a tidal wave. Against its rising waters, he dimly registered that von Harnach was well into his testimony and was talking about him.

'. . . He seemed stunned Mr Joel was dead, and said – more to himself – "God, I'm sorry". Then, he burst out . . .' – Von Harnach looked around apologetically at the ladies present – '. . . he burst out, "But the bastards shot first".'

An indignant murmur rippled through the legal and stock-broking fraternity, and the newsmen sat forward like hounds on the scent.

Krause consulted the detectives' report. 'But Mr Strange stated directly after the shooting, "I think von Veltheim fired first"?'

'Yes, sir.'

'But he lied!' Von Veltheim glared around at all the sceptical faces. 'Where I come from a man's innocent until proven guilty. And *Freiherr* means an honourable man.' He stood like an animal at bay. 'It means *honourable*!'

Van Dyk tried to get von Veltheim back into his seat, but he angrily shook him off, and didn't even register that von Harnach had been excused.

Until Krause's voice cut through his rage. 'The Prosecution calls Miss Elise Caldecott.'

Anne-Marie looked up from the letter she was writing.

It was the first time she had ever seen Rainer with his shoulders slumped, and his movements had acquired the stiffness of a clock-work toy in need of oil. She knew what he was thinking. Even if he put all his resources at Franz's disposal, wasn't it too little too late?

Even his voice sounded drained. 'He's not a bad person; he's just done some bad things. Only who'll believe him?'

'Hardly anyone,' she agreed, 'apart from those who orchestrated it.'

'*Orchestrated* it?' He shook his head dumbly.

'Dearest Rainer, whoever's destroying the Barnato family won't think twice about Franz.'

When she stood to adjust the coverlet on the perambulator, Rainer recognised the hazy look that had come into her eyes, which usually denoted fierce concentration on something else. 'Unless?' he prompted hopefully.

But she changed the subject. 'Sir Graham Bower's been retired from the Cape because of the Raid and he needs help with his records. Be a darling and listen for little Franz while I finish writing to him I know an archivist going cheap.'

And she picked up her pen.

Elise looked frightened and vulnerable as she took the stand. Wraithlike, von Veltheim thought, with a prick of conscience.

Krause gave her an encouraging little smile. 'You heard Mr Strange tell the court you delivered a letter from the accused to Woolf Joel the day before he was killed?'

'Yes,' she whispered.

'And you've also heard accused make no bones about his being a professional revolutionary?'

'Yes.' Scarcely audible.

'Then you were a courier for a revolutionary conspiracy?'

Elise shook her head vigourously, but although she framed the word 'no' with her lips, no sound came out.

'Speak up please, Miss Caldecott. The court stenographer has to record.' Krause's gentle tone was curiously at odds with his uncompromising words and implacable eyes. 'Hadn't you the faintest idea of the contents of the letter you carried?'

Elise looked imploringly at von Veltheim. The entire courtroom followed her gaze, and caught the fractional shake of his head.

Krause struck with the speed of a mamba. 'You had *no* knowledge of the Kismet correspondence? Do you swear it?'

She bit her lip and shut her eyes for a moment. In the front row next to Coenraad Juta she could see her father gazing fixedly at the floor, his face white with shame. She had a sudden image of herself – a butterfly impaled on a pin and exhibited under glass.

'Miss Caldecott,' Krause's voice broke into her whirling thoughts.

'You were either being used by the accused, or were intimately involved. The court needs to know which.'

Her eyes sought von Veltheim's.

He felt compassion and guilt rise like water in a spring. My poor little Elise, who could have guessed it could come to this?

And assailed by her own freight of compassion and guilt, Elise could only think: but for my stupid letter to Solly, you wouldn't be fighting for your life in court. Oh, Franz!

The first sob that broke from her lips sounded like a tiny hiccough.

'*Which*, Miss Caldecott?'

Her eyes filled. 'I don't know,' she said brokenly. Confusion, betrayal, shame, all ravaged her voice and destroyed the last vestiges of her control. In plucking at her veiled toque to dash away the tears spilling down her cheeks, she accidentally pulled it off, loosening the pins that had held up her hair. It tumbled about her shoulders and onto her face as she shook her head hysterically from side to side. The court stenographer watched her, transfixed. He'd stopped counting the number of times she'd cried, 'I don't know. My God, I don't *know!*'

Krause waited patiently for a minute while great shuddering sobs racked her. Caldecott was on his feet, looking imploringly from Krause to Van den Berg. Then the landdrost nodded brusquely, and Caldecott moved to the witness stand to assist her. Almost simultaneously and unbidden, Coenraad Juta was also there supporting her by the other arm. Together they helped her to the vacant space in the front row.

Krause turned to the bench. 'Will your Worship please instruct the stenographer to let the record reflect that we adjourned today because Miss Caldecott was too unwell to conclude. And that when the case is remanded, my question stands. We need to know whether she was the accused's victim or accomplice.' Krause added reasonably. 'We sympathise with Miss Caldecott, but sooner or later it must all come out.'

Van den Berg nodded wearily to the court stenographer. 'Let the record show that the Public Prosecutor has to see that it all comes out.'

Elise lay on her bed, her hands clasped to her ribcage, and waited for her pounding heart to ease.

Her mind went back to the moment in the Landdrost's Court when she'd first noticed Franz's eye stray to the stranger.

He was tall with spectacles and a great bushy red beard. She couldn't remember having met anyone like him before, and yet something familiar teased at her memory. She smoothed the note he'd slipped into her muff as she was leaving court on her father's arm. She reread it: '*May I call on Franz's behalf? A friend.*'

The clatter of a handful of gravel tossed at her window-pane sounded like a stick drawn sharply over wooden louvered shutters. Elise opened the sash window and peered out at a tall bearded man standing in the path below.

He saw her and signalled. 'I'm Franz's friend. May I come in?'

She hesitated, doubtful. But he was already shinnying up the drainpipe, and silently vaulted inside.

With a sigh of relief, he peeled off his false beard and spectacles. 'I'm getting too old for all this.'

'You're really Franz's friend?' She looked at him searchingly. But a moment later an image stirred in her subconscious: the memory of Franz talking with the man at the Wanderers' bandstand who'd raised his hat to her. Then another came to her in a flash. 'Why, you're Charlie!' she exclaimed. 'The friend in the snapshot with Franz! The one captioned, "New Orleans – a couple of rascals"?'

'Had a feeling you'd remember me,' he said softly. 'Then you also know this isn't our first tight spot?'

'I suppose,' she admitted cautiously.

'Franz was worried that Dr Krause's ill manners might've aggravated your heart condition.'

Elise gave a wan smile and subsided back on the bed.

'So I took the liberty of bringing you my own remedy for heartache.' Charlie gallantly produced a split of Veuve Cliquot from his baggy jacket pocket, and perched on the side of the bed. 'At least, it works pretty well for me.'

A wider smile. But as soon as it faded her face looked white and pinched.

'Where's the pain?' Charlie's voice was gentle.

'Right here.' She pressed her ribcage.

'This what you take for it?' He indicated a phial next to her bed.

She nodded.

Charlie read the label and uncorked it. 'My old mother used to say, "This'll put hair on your chest". Yours actually looks very pretty just the way it is.' He held the phial out to her, and she swallowed obediently.

He worked the cork loose from the champagne bottle. 'I personally swear by the old bubbly. May I?' He removed the upended glass from the water flask. 'And I never travel without mine.' Like a conjuror, he removed a silver tot measure from behind her ear, and she giggled. 'And my old *father* used to say "Laughter is the best medicine".' He poured them each some. 'You could use a bit more of that,' he advised.

'I could certainly use an end to all those questions,' Elise sighed wearily.

'I'll drink to that.' Charlie tossed back his drink. 'No more questions.'

'No more questions,' Elise echoed, and emptied her glass.

Charlie refilled the glasses. 'Your toast now.'

'No more tears?'

'No,' Charlie agreed. 'They make your eyes all puffy and your nose red.'

Elise stumbled to the mirror. 'Lord, I'm a fright!' She was dizzy, and collapsed back on the bed.

They drank up and Charlie recharged their glasses. 'How about, no more sad thoughts?'

They clinked glasses, and recklessly, she knocked hers back. 'No more sad thoughts,' she repeated, slurring her speech. She felt woozy and out of control. Her last clear image was of Charlie moving to tuck the coverlet over her.

'No more of any of those things,' he said soothingly. 'Charlie's here to take care of you now.'

26

'Briefly, Mr von Veltheim, it'll hinge on your word against Mr Strange's.' The rolled 'r's' showed that Cambridge had done little to erase Smuts's Malmesbury burr.

The small unbarred visitor's room Governor Menton had put at his disposal was bare except for some rudimentary Public Works Department furniture, with a wire-mesh wastepaper basket. The walls were hung with the *Vierkleur* and a couple of watercolours of Fountains Valley and the Apies River. Von Veltheim wondered whether they were the handiwork of a warder's wife, as he lounged in a swivel-thread chair watching his legal team across the table taking notes.

Smuts's speech was terse and economical, as though he was reluctant to dissipate energy. 'If I'm to take your word that Mr Strange shot first – and I do – I have to ask why.'

'Inexperience? Nerves?' von Veltheim suggested cagily.

'Then why have I this feeling the whole thing was motivated?'

Von Veltheim straightened to look at him more closely. 'I've felt that too.'

'Motivated *how*?' Smithers was puzzled. 'Who would Strange have been trying to shoot? Joel or von Veltheim?'

Von Veltheim stood and began to pace. 'And why a one-bullet weapon? The man's an amateur.'

'But *you're* not, Mr von Veltheim.' Smuts fixed him with his blue *siener*'s eyes. 'Suppose he wanted you to do the killing for him?'

Von Veltheim stopped pacing, incredulous that Smuts had fielded his thoughts. 'But why?'

'If *you* can't tell me, we're going to have to wait until I've got him under cross-examination in the Circuit Court to find out. Let's leave Mr Strange there for the moment.' He looked at von Veltheim levelly. 'If I'm to protect you at your own cross-examination, I've got to put myself in the Public Prosecutor's shoes. All these aliases you use . . . *Why?*'

Von Veltheim stiffened. 'My family's highly respected in Europe. I try to protect them from unsavoury publicity.'

'Then, presumably you've had reason to do so before? Many times?'

'A few. Women are fond of scandal. I tend to get involved.'

'Ever been involved in blackmail?'

Von Veltheim turned to Smithers. 'Do I have to put up with this?'

'We're not playing tiddlywinks, old chap. If Mr Smuts is to defend you, do *let* him. He has to know what brought you here. You, in turn, have his assurance this information is privileged.'

'Client's privilege is as sacred as the confessional,' Smuts confirmed. 'And it's far better I ask this before the Public Prosecutor does.'

Von Veltheim glared at Smuts. 'I've never blackmailed anyone in my life.'

'But you realise that first letter could be construed as such?'

'That first one to Solly Joel was written to accommodate a lady.'

'Miss Caldecott?' Smuts and Smithers exchanged a glance, and Smithers shook his head. Before von Veltheim could frame his question, Smuts continued, 'And Kismet was her choice?'

'It sounded exotic. I thought it would appeal to her.'

'The others you used at random?'

'Except for Karl Braun.'

'What was the purpose of that one?'

'A *Geheime Dienst* man at our boarding house leaked it to Miss Caldecott that a certain Karl Braun who once followed Barnato had recently shown an interest in me. Placing his name on a police dossier would deactivate him.'

Smithers snapped open a silver monogrammed cigar case and selected a Havana. 'I say,' he said with boyish glee, 'you mean the fellow really exists?'

'Resourceful,' Smuts conceded. 'Have you any idea who he is? And why?'

'I suppose this brings us to this privileged information.' Von Veltheim took a deep breath and, looking into Smuts's icy blue eyes, he told him concisely his purpose in the Boer Republic. He finished: 'Now could *you* find out if the *Geheime Dienst* has a counter-subversion arm that could identify this Karl Braun?'

'Even if they have, I've no authority to subpoena him.'

Von Veltheim looked at Smuts steadily. 'But you could subpoena Juta and under oath *he'd* have to answer.'

Smuts returned his stare coldly. 'Strange's motive for shooting first – if I can prove it – and Braun's interest in you are both central to your predicament. But I would defend you solely against the murder charge, and you'd have to refuse to answer any question on conspiracy. Do you think you're equal to this after seeing Dr Krause in action? Because, if not, it might be better for you to retain someone else.'

Smithers exchanged a quick glance with von Veltheim. 'That won't be necessary.'

Von Veltheim weighed Smuts's coolness against his logic. 'If you represent me, I think I can manage Krause.'

Smuts closed his writing pad. 'A clear understanding's a good enough start.' He looked at Smithers. 'I take it you're staying?'

Smithers nodded. 'I've still a personal matter to discuss with our client.' He waited until they could hear Smuts's footsteps retreating before he said, 'It's about Miss Caldecott.'

'Let me guess. She's now sleeping with Juta?'

'I'm not much good at this, so I'll just say it straight.' He hesitated. 'Miss Caldecott was found dead this morning.'

Von Veltheim's supercilious smile faded, and his expression registered a mixture of shock and self-reproach. He turned and stood staring out of the window for a few moments before he spoke. 'She had this heart condition, you know.'

'Evidently. Dr Bertram took possession of an empty phial of chloral found near the body. And her father disposed of an empty champagne bottle. *The Star*'s calling it an accident . . .'

'Chloral with champagne!' A whisper.

'The memorial service is at St Mary's Cathedral. Probably neither of us is much of a praying man. But we could try this once for her immortal . . .'

'Except it wasn't suicide,' von Veltheim burst out. 'That champagne was administered.'

'I say! You mean someone else wanted to prevent Krause from making her talk? Reveal information she might have gleaned as your courier?'

That was precisely the thought that had insinuated itself into von Veltheim's subconscious, and the only person he could cast as the accused struck a blow at the very foundations of trust. For an instant he was caught in a conflict: appalled by all the hideous new possibilities this opened up and revulsed by his own disloyalty. But the next instant it vanished and only two thoughts now drummed in his head. If Charlie was Karl Braun, who had turned him? And for how much?

He tried to pace angrily, but the room was small and there was nowhere to go. He looked helplessly from the window to the iron door, and then slammed his fist into the wall.

Smithers's gaze was steady. 'Put it out of your mind. There's nothing you can do to help her now.' He cut the end off his Havana and lit it. 'Let her rest in peace, and *you* stay focused.' He offered the cigar case to von Veltheim. 'This case has more layers than an onion, and they keep peeling away.'

'The press is now calling him a blackmailer-cum-political conspirator.' Piet Joubert looked up from his special edition of the *Standard and Diggers' News*. 'These days a man never knows whom he's harbouring under his roof.'

Hendrina poured coffee at the window that gave onto Pretoria Street. 'We offered a stranger good old-fashioned Boer hospitality.' She glanced around the book cases at his leather-bound law books, their titles engraved in gold leaf – the works of Van Leeuwen and Van der Linden. 'And since when does a student of Roman Dutch Law hold with trial by the press?'

Joubert gave her a teasing smile. 'You told me you two went picnicking at Fountains Valley. He's a good-looking *kêrel*. A man gets jealous.'

'Curious, Piet Joubert. Flattery doesn't suit you.'

'All right. I just wondered whether your conversation that day left you with any particular impression?'

'Like, did he have other plans for Kruger?'

Joubert's expression was studiously neutral. 'He seems to have had the right credentials. He was evidently a soldier with leadership qualities. Colonel Grey writes he'd be honoured to testify to his courage under fire.'

'I understand Smuts has been inundated with similar offers from half his column,' Hendrina said drily. 'But that's hardly to his advantage now.' She looked out at the lengthening shadows in the garden. 'Van Aswegen told me he wanted to organise a chain of horse relay stations west of Pretoria to Mafeking. He actually thought von Veltheim meant to go into the transport business.' She stood and smoothed the few silver threads at her husband's temples. 'It could have worked, you know . . . But for a random shot.'

'*Bly stil, vroumens*! I forbid you to talk treason!' Joubert flared, but the yearning in her eyes softened his anger. 'Thank God, he's been charged with murder,' he said wearily, 'and Joel's blood doesn't lie on our hands.'

Hendrina enfolded his head in her arms and rocked it on her meagre bosom. 'If I'm grateful to God, it's because von Veltheim *tried*,' she defied him. 'Now I pray that this Jannie Smuts is as clever as they say.'

'*Kom, duifie* . . .' Joubert stood and, tucking Hendrina's arm through his, led her out onto the stoep. 'Are the sunsets not lovely this time of the year?'

She looked at him suspiciously. 'When you start with your sunsets, I know something's got to be wrong.'

'*Ja*, well . . . How else do I tell you Kruger's got his own plans for young Smuts?'

'A political appointment?' she whispered.

He nodded. 'Attorney General. *Staatsprocureur*.'

'*No*! He's not *allowed* to!' Hendrina argued fiercely. 'He's too young, and he's not even a Transvaal burgher.'

'But who else can debate with the English diplomats in their own language?' he asked gently.

'Then who'll defend von Veltheim?' She shook her head to try and drive out the thought. 'Smuts was acting for him. He *knows* what he was doing in Barnatos' offices.'

'That's privileged information.'

'If he's bending the law to be State Attorney he'll bend that privileged information.' She laughed harshly. 'And you thank God we don't have *Joel's* blood on our hands?'

Helplessly, he enfolded her in his arms.

'What about von *Veltheim's*?' she sobbed against his chest. 'Who'll defend *him*?'

Smuts secured the string on the last cardboard carton just as the telephone shrilled. 'Ah, Smithers? You got my messages? Apologies.'

'Heartiest congratulations, and all that,' Smithers's voice crackled over the wire. 'But now what about . . .?'

'Yes, yes. I've been thinking. Herman Coster was Krause's senior when they prosecuted the Raid offenders?'

'Ex-State Attorney? Rapped over the knuckles for treading on Oom Paul's corns?'

'Depends how you see it. Some say Coster did the rapping. Refused to draft Kruger's Undesirable Aliens Expulsion bill.'

'Hardly an advantage if this now makes the entire defence team "undesirable aliens".' Smithers sounded as though he was reaching for a drink. 'Krause'll eat us for breakfast.'

'With Coster as an opponent, he'd best remember his Eno's,' Smuts replied. And if he hadn't known better, Smithers might have thought he'd heard a chuckle.

'Legal adviser to the *Volksraad*, the Executive Council and all government departments?' The President's son, Tjaart, sat across the desk from the new *Staatsprocureur*. 'You look a bit *skraal* for all that. First we've got to fatten you up.'

'First we've got to purge Johannesburg of corruption.'

Both men were in their late twenties and beardless, but there the similarity ended. Smuts was clear-complexioned and his prominent Adam's apple vibrated against his shirt collar when he spoke.

Tjaart Kruger's heavy swarthy features inherited from his father were incompatible with the musical operetta dress uniform he had worn to an official function. His high braided collar choked him, and he loosened it. 'I heard you were a devil on corruption.'

'And nearly as bad as your *Geheime Dienst* on treason?'

'We get our man in the end. It just takes too long.' Irritably, Tjaart looked around for somewhere to put his plumed dress helmet, and then dumped it on a vacant chair. 'Von Veltheim had at least seven men on his trail, but it took the Joel murder to get an arrest.'

'If your friend weren't staying in the same boarding house, we'd still be waiting for Ferguson. And you don't smell corruption?'

'Like rotten eggs. What with Ferguson's waiting for Strange . . . Strange not wanting them compromised? It's as well we've got him.'

'It could be even better? . . .' Smuts suggested delicately.

He didn't need to spell it out further, and Tjaart considered the thought. 'Even if we could get him to, his testimony'd be questionable.'

'Why? He claims the two mining men pulled guns on him. Even in Johannesburg, that's self-defence.' Smuts gave him a sly little smile. 'Still, he might appreciate a little visit?'

'Would that not be unfitting?' Tjaart had reached for his dress helmet and was smoothing the plumes rhythmically.

'Highly. And, therefore, precisely what the circumstances demand.'

27

'Commandant Tjaart Kruger of the *Geheime Dienst*.' Tjaart extended his hand to von Veltheim, and they shook. 'Governor Menton's lent us his office . . .' Von Veltheim glanced around at the serviceable Public Works Department furniture, the portrait of the President on one wall, and beneath it the President's son with his genetically inherited features. He continued, 'He also laid on some good Boere biltong and Cape wine.'

They sat, and he poured them each a glass. 'It's bad when a man's duties keep him away from the veld,' he continued conversationally as though this were not part of the interview, but von Veltheim knew it was. 'Weren't you in the Vryburg district last year?'

'In the Bechuanaland Border Police until December.' Von Veltheim also kept his tone light. 'This an official visit?'

'Confidential, but authorised. If we reach agreement, this talk could get you off the Joel murder charge.'

'And I thought your job was to gather information?'

'Only stuff we don't already have.'

'Like Barnato knowing he was under surveillance?'

'Two years out of date. You might tell me about his London connection, though. His name, and your purpose here as his agent?'

'I'm here on a trumped-up murder charge,' von Veltheim said evenly. 'And my plea's self-defence.'

'Misfortune might be dogging the Barnato family, but to them, £5,000 per jurist's vote is cheap.' Tjaart cut some biltong and nudged the plate closer to von Veltheim. 'On the other hand, if we were dealing with an attempted coup and one of its casualties, as a state's witness you'd be out of their reach.'

A cagey look.

'Who's paying you?'

'You've miscalculated badly if you really think I'd say.'

'Before Dr Krause's finished with you you'll want to change your mind.' Tjaart swirled the wine in his glass. 'You know, Barnatos' have collected this nice fat dossier on you.' He drained his glass and pushed back his chair. 'If you'd care to talk further, my door's open – as they say. Think about it.'

Von Veltheim's chair also scraped and they stood. But as he reached the door, he turned. 'Did Smuts prompt this meeting?'

'You know, your priorities worry me.' Tjaart's tone was deceptively lazy. 'This isn't the first attempted coup here. And Dr Krause's fascinated by treason. I'd think about that, too.' With a half smile, he consulted his pocket watch. 'About eighteen hours before I see you in court?'

Von Veltheim thought of giving him the same mental advice he'd given certain schoolmasters in interviews of a similar type expressed in words of one syllable – Anglo-Saxon ones. He managed to smile back, but his stomach felt like a dark slimy pit.

Fritz Edward Traugott Krause sat in the pool of light cast by the same student lamp by which he'd written his doctoral thesis in Amsterdam, and carted with him to the Middle Temple in London. 'Just eighteen hours,' he mused.

His unremarkable good looks enhanced by super-fastidious grooming reflected the attention to detail of a man who believes in taking no chances with anything within his control.

Opposite him, the assistant Public Prosecutor, De Villiers, began packing up the paperwork. 'I wouldn't like to be in von Veltheim's shoes tonight. By now he must've heard how you handled the Jameson offenders. And the Joels are big fish.'

'Busy big fish,' Krause agreed. 'Add this . . .' – he tapped the file Barnatos' had compiled at such great expense – '. . . his Kismet letters, and public opinion baying for blood? He's as good as ours.'

'And you know how defence counsel thinks?'

'Oh, intimately.' He was thinking of Coster as he had several times in the past two years. I was your junior then, but tomorrow we meet on equal terms. 'Quite intimately,' he confirmed.

'Pity it's only a murder trial.'

Krause recognised the stirring of the predator in him. 'We'll *call* it that . . . till I get him under cross-examination,' he said. Almost dreamily.

Hal Smithers looked about the new defending counsel's office. 'We're not only taking on Smuts, Krause and Kruger's Secret Police, but God knows what dirt Barnatos've been able to dig up.' He savagely bit the end off his cigar and jammed it in the corner of his mouth. 'Where do we start?'

'Everyone's presumed innocent until proven guilty?' Coster suggested equably. 'The other side's got to prove premeditation. Gives us the edge.'

Smithers gave him a sidelong glance. Dr Hermanus Jacob Coster was thirty-three. But in some ways he looked older, and in others, younger. His fairish close-cropped hair was thinning at the temples, but his full moustache and pointed beard were darker and vigorous, and belonged with his energetic eyes. Mentally Smithers checked off his credentials. Treason trial Public Prosecutor and ex-State Attorney? And the beggar's resignation left the gap Smuts dumped us to fill.

Nervously he lit up. 'You don't think Krause'll use murder to indict for treason, with Smuts stage-managing from the wings?'

'This is the law, Mr Smithers, not a circus. Smuts's information is privileged. And von Veltheim's politics, irrelevant.'

'In this climate of subversion?' Smithers began searching for an ashtray.

'The indictment's murder,' Coster reasoned mildly. 'With two guns pulled on him, I call that self-defence.' He looked pointedly at Smithers's cigar. 'Are you going to smoke that filthy weed, or just wave it around?'

Smithers opened a sash window, distractedly ground out his cigar on the cement ledge and stared blankly at the stub. Coster deposited it in a wire-mesh wastebasket and opened a second window to create a through draft to clear the room of smoke.

'A nightcap tonight. Tomorrow? Perspective,' he promised.

Johannesburg is cold in July. And that Wednesday in 1898 in the closed carriage with the Republican coat of arms von Veltheim felt it. Outside the Circuit Court on Government Square a chill dry wind whipped the cyanide dust in pale spirals, and the crowd turned downwind to shelter their eyes.

'Oh God,' he whispered.

Von Harnach grabbed his elbow and gave it a squeeze of

encouragement as he hurried him through the mounted police cordon into the building, and then escorted him through the crowded courtroom to the defence table. Coster looked up from his papers and nodded absently, but Smithers pulled out his chair for him and briefly gripped his shoulder.

'*Stilte*!' the Sheriff demanded. 'Silence in court!'

The expectant buzz died. Slight of build, and with a skull naked but for a fringe of dark wispy hair, Judge Morice took the rostrum and adjusted his reading glasses. In a gravelly voice, that still carried in it the smell of Highland peat fires, he asked for the indictment to be read.

Listening to it, von Veltheim could make out some of the official Dutch, but Smithers had told him the interpreter would repeat it in English. Trying to still his thudding heart, he forced himself to concentrate on the configuration of the court.

Krause sat with De Villiers, at the prosecution table, out of earshot of the defence table and equidistant to the judge's rostrum. Von Veltheim noticed that he'd arranged three files before him, and he wondered which was the dossier Tjaart Kruger had meant.

Among the press corps in front of the public section he saw McDermott hold up two crossed fingers, and he smiled back. The room grew quiet, and the court interpreter began to read the indictment in English:

'The State versus Franz Ludwig Kurt von Veltheim, alias Karl Braun, alias von Veltheim, alias Kurt.

J.C. Smuts, State Attorney of the South African Republic who prosecutes in the name of the State, informs us as follows:

That Franz Ludwig Kurt von Veltheim, alias Karl Braun, alias Baron von Veltheim, alias Kurt, at present in prison at Johannesburg, Witwatersrand Goldfields, South African Republic, is guilty of the crime of murder: whereas on or about the 14th day of March 1898, at Johannesburg, aforesaid, he, the said Franz Ludwig Kurt von Veltheim, alias Karl Braun, alias Baron von Veltheim, alias Kurt, unlawfully, illegally and with premeditation killed and murdered Woolf Joel, by then and there aiming and firing at him with a revolver loaded with powder and balls, thereby causing him to receive three bullet wounds in the head, in consequence of which he died.

Wherefore, the State Attorney, after proper proof thereof, asks for the verdict of the State against Franz Ludwig Kurt von Veltheim, alias Karl Braun, alias Baron von Veltheim, alias Kurt.

J.C. SMUTS,
State Attorney.'

The side door opened, and the jury filed in and took their places. Von Veltheim guessed they were mostly older than the Johannesburgers he'd met, and all of them, Boers.

Judge Morice rapped his gavel and announced: 'The Court will come to order.' He studied von Veltheim over his spectacles. 'Franz Ludwig Kurt von Veltheim, alias Karl Braun, alias Baron von Veltheim, alias Kurt, how plead you?'

Von Veltheim's voice carried in the silent room. 'I am innocent.'

'*Mon Dieu*! He's a trained killer!'

'There's a difference between battle and assassination, Erich. It could've been self-defence.'

Wernher watched his partner work his way around the tiny perfect rose garden at 26 Park Lane, his secateurs clipping rhythmically. It was laid out as if it had been landscaped with a protractor and compass. Wedges of Rosa Mundi and Louise Odier glowed amid their shiny dark green foliage virtuously free of blight or pests.

'Next thing Wernher Beit'll be footing the bill to help him prove it.' Wernher gave him a shrewd look.

Click, click. Beit disbudded another Rosa Gallica Versicolor.

'In fact, *someone*'s already doing so?'

Studiously impassive, Beit busied himself with a minute spot of dieback he'd just detected on a Fantin Latour he was considering entering for the local flower show.

'*Zut*! Woolf never handled anything more lethal than his racing binoculars. *He* didn't lure von Veltheim into that office to kill *him*.'

'A spot of Epsom Salts should do the trick,' Beit murmured to himself. He caught Wernher's blank look, and hastily explained. 'Woolf was disturbed by Barney's death. That's why he went.'

'Quite. In fact, I'd say he met von Veltheim to pay him off.' Wernher stroked his beard thoughtfully. 'Still, one wonders what happened to start this gunfight?'

Beit cut a Blanc Double de Coubert just beginning to unfurl. 'One wonders, all right. There were three armed men in that office, and for me . . .' – he adjusted the rosebud in his partner's buttonhole – '. . . the only unknown quantity is Strange.'

28

Harold Fairbrother Strange lowered his right hand, and von Veltheim watched him telling a better rehearsed version of the same story he'd told at the preliminary hearing until Krause prompted, 'You say accused threatened you?'

Strange shifted position. 'I'd anticipated something like this. So I stood up to light my cigar, and replaced the matches in the pocket with my derringer in order to cock it.'

Krause gave him an encouraging smile. 'And then?'

'When accused shot Woolfie, I pulled it out and fired at him. There were several shots. I turned. Woolfie was falling, and his revolver dropped to the floor beside my desk. As I reached out for it . . .' – Strange mimed the movement – '. . . accused stepped on my hand. That was when the clerks burst in.'

Morice leafed back through his notes 'Who fired first?'

'Accused, I think. And I returned his fire.'

'But you're not absolutely certain?'

Krause held up some papers. 'If you please, my lord . . . Might I refer to Mr Strange's statement in the landdrost's minutes?' He read rapidly, "*Had I shot first, he would have shot at me.*" He looked at Strange. 'You said that?'

'Oh, yes.'

Morice nodded for Krause to continue, and so the day proceeded with the pattern of question and answer, building Strange's case until Krause asked, 'When you met with accused did you try to find out who the friend was who was conspiring against the government?'

'Objection!' Coster stood. 'My lord, my learned friend's not only leading the witness, he's putting the answers in his mouth.'

Morice nodded. 'Sustained.'

Krause turned back to Strange. 'Let me rephrase the question. The object of those meetings . . .'

'*Objection!*' Coster was on his feet again.

'To *what*?'

'Dr Krause's trying to elicit answers prejudicial to my client on patriotic grounds. I'd like to remind the court that the charge is murder . . . That there were three armed men in the office that day, and the only one who didn't fire his gun is dead! Accused must be presumed innocent until proven guilty. In fact, it could be argued that you're trying the wrong man.'

A shocked murmur rustled through the courtroom, and Morice arched his eyebrows. 'I must caution you, Dr Coster. I believe you're in contempt.'

'Perhaps so, my lord. But I trust my objection stands?'

Morice nodded crisply, and then to Krause to continue.

Krause was white and tight-lipped. 'I conclude my examination of Mr Strange.'

Morice eyed Coster. 'Does Counsel for the Defence wish to examine the witness?'

'Yes, my lord.' Coster consulted his pocket watch. 'But may I suggest a postponement until morning? There's a mass of contradictory information to work through.'

Krause gave an impatient sigh. 'Dr Coster exaggerates, but if my lord wishes to indulge him . . .'

Morice looked from one to the other. 'This case does seem to be developing certain complexities. Until tomorrow morning, we're adjourned.'

One day in the witness box: Strange polished his spectacles with an unsteady hand and then folded his handkerchief into diminishing squares.

As Coster prowled to and fro before the witness stand, von Veltheim realised that the frame he'd considered slight was, in fact, very wiry – a conduit of energy he was getting ready to release. He'd begun his warm-up questions using a self-effacing style, as though he were unsure of his subject and genuinely wished to be better informed.

'The Chief Detective asked you to meet von Veltheim with all three of you present. Yet you met with him alone?'

'Because Woolfie was unavailable, he sent me to tell him,' Strange explained.

'Was your *first* meeting to discuss how a large sum could be paid him without its appearing in their books?'

The self-effacing manner had gone and Strange moved back slightly in his chair. 'Yes. I mean, no. There can be no question of such a transaction without half a dozen people in our office knowing about it. To buy a farm, we must have the title deed. Shares? The scrip. Numbers must be entered in a book and accounted for.'

'Does all this really deter middle management from making a little on the side?' Coster enquired with interest.

Strange whitened, and Krause opened his mouth to object, but Morice's crashing gavel was faster. 'Dr Coster, if you please!' he roared.

'Nothing personal, m'lord.' Coster managed to look suitably bewildered as he turned back to Strange. 'Why haven't you told us about all these safety measures before?'

Strange polished his spectacles distractedly. 'One can't remember everything that happened in a conversation three months ago.'

'Especially if one's nervous. You were, I take it, a little nervous?'

'I was sent on a message I disapproved of to meet a man I disliked, and I didn't know what to say to him,' Strange replied testily. 'Yes, I might have been a little nervous.'

Coster suddenly swivelled his head. 'Will your lordship minute that reply please?' He turned back to Strange. 'On Monday morning Mr Joel instructed you to meet von Veltheim at the President Tea Rooms. Although he'd suggested you give him the money, you refused?'

'Yes. On Saturday Woolfie made it clear to the Chief Detective he didn't want us involved in any trumped-up plots.'

'You told accused you abhorred revolutionary movements?'

'Yes.'

'Yet you were indicted for treason in the Jameson . . .'

Krause stood. 'My lord, I protest. Mr Strange is not on trial.'

'And I protest, perhaps he ought to be,' Coster snapped. 'His record as a dissident exceeds the accused's. The true account of Joel's murder is still under investigation here. And the evidence that places von Veltheim in the dock instead of Strange is circumstantial.'

The buzz among the spectators threatened to become an uproar.

Morice rapped his gavel. 'That will do, Dr Coster, I believe you've made your point.'

'I'm pleased to hear it, my lord, because now we come to the crux.' He turned to Strange. 'You told my learned friend that you used the action of getting a cigar and matches out of your pocket to cock your derringer?'

'Correct.'

'Then you prepared for mortal combat?'

'No. If I had, I'd have used a proper weapon.'

Coster's eyebrows arched in disbelief. 'Accused's shots – were they at long intervals or in rapid succession?'

'In rapid succession.'

'Will your lordship please minute that, too?' Coster asked, and turned back to the witness box. 'You say that the first shot was fired at you as you stood at your desk. And then?'

'I shot at the accused. When I saw Woolfie sink to the ground and drop his revolver, I reached out to get it.'

'And slipped?'

'Yes.'

'Weren't you *already* on the floor? You said you had to *reach out* to snatch Mr Joel's revolver.'

'I . . . I don't know.' Strange's glance darted to Morice. 'In my haste, I must've slipped on the linoleum.'

'*I* can't even glide over linoleum.' Coster's clumsy demonstration provoked a ripple of nervous laughter from the gallery. '*Slipped*, Mr Strange?'

'Yes.'

'Before or after von Veltheim fired at you first?'

'Objection!' Krause snapped. 'Defence is trying to confuse the witness.'

'Overruled.' Morice frowned. 'More decorum, Dr Coster?'

Coster adjusted his tone. 'While you were on the floor did accused fire at you again?'

'I . . . I don't know.'

'You told the *Johannesburg Times* he shot like a professional gunman, yet you were untouched?'

'Ye-es.'

'Because when accused fired his first shot you were already hidden under the desk. Well *did* you?'

'What?'

'Hide under the desk before von Veltheim fired at you?'

'I . . . I don't know. I mean, I don't know whether he fired at me or not.'

Morice looked at Coster with a touch of impatience. 'Witness has already said he didn't know.'

'Yes, three times, my lord. To the arresting officer, in the *Johannesburg Times*, and in the Landdrost's Court. And three different versions. No more questions.'

'Court is adjourned until this afternoon at three,' Morice hastily announced.

Von Harnach escorted von Veltheim to the closed cab. 'Coster's good.' He reached into his pocket for his cheroots and matches and offered them.

'*Really* good.' Von Veltheim took one gratefully. And his hand shook only slightly as he lit up.

'One match is all it would take to set the veld on fire.' Sombrely, Smuts surveyed the hoar-bleached grassland west of Pretoria.

He plucked a handful of grass for Tjaart Kruger. '*A child said, "What is grass?" fetching it to me with both hands./ And now it seems to me the beautiful uncut grass of graves.*'

'*Uitlander* words?'

'Walt Whitman - American frontier poet.'

They hiked on through the shallow Broederstroom hills until they came to the confluence of the Crocodile and the Jukskei Rivers. And when they subsided on a grassy knoll to rest, the water in their canvas water bottles tasted sweet.

A flame-tipped candelabra aloe sprang from the rock cleft and Smuts unearthed the fork and trowel from his haversack to capture it for his collection. 'You know, Saturdays used to be the beginning of my weekends in the veld,' he grumbled. 'Lately they've become more an extension of the trial.'

Tjaart craned to look up at the bowl of Highveld winter sky – brilliant blue airbrushed with cirrus clouds. 'I suppose it's all wrong for me to bring you out here, and then ask you how you found yesterday's proceedings?'

'With the JCI clerks so unanimous on the pattern of the shots?' Smuts smiled crookedly.

'You know, until yesterday I never thought we had the wrong man in the dock.'

'Oh, we've the right man, all right,' Smuts said, grimly wrestling with a refractory root. 'Perhaps for the wrong crime . . . But he's the tip of an ugly iceberg we're still going to expose.'

Tjaart squatted to hold the thorny succulent leaves out of Smuts's way while he reached for his pocket-knife. 'And if Coster get's him off?'

'There now . . .' Smuts said, finally prising the aloe loose from its purchase and shaking it clean. 'Before that, I've a wild card or two.'

Only Tjaart didn't know whether the look of triumph was for the aloe or his secret agenda. And he didn't ask.

29

Four days: and von Veltheim felt his shirt collar was too loose.

Krause had taken von Harnach over the same ground he'd covered in the preliminary hearing, and yielded the floor to defence. Now Coster was into his cross-examination.

'Officer von Harnach, how would you say a derringer shot differs from a six-chambered Colt's?'

'The derringer's grain is closer and the calibre greater, so its report would have been louder.'

Coster riffled back through his notes. 'The JCI clerks agreed that the first shot was the loudest. That there was a distinct pause between that one and those that followed. How would you reconstruct this?'

'The first shot would have come from the derringer, sir. Even with a brisk reflex, there'd've been a pause before the retaliatory fire.'

'Detective von Harnach, I want your professional opinion on who fired first.'

Von Harnach raised his voice a couple of decibels and enunciated clearly. 'The first shot could only have been fired by Mr Strange.'

There was a collective gasp. And a sombre murmur rumbled through the room as von Harnach stepped down.

Krause quickly adapted his frown to a look of concentration and shuffled his papers. He stood up. 'The prosecution calls Robert Ferguson, Chief Detective of Johannesburg.'

Von Veltheim thought that Ferguson looked ill at ease as Krause took him through his account of the Kismet letters until he asked, 'Why do you think Mr Joel pursued the matter?'

'To identify Kismet's friend for Solly Joel.'

Krause gave him a sharp look. 'But do you think they were acting in the state's interest?'

'Yes.' He added hastily, 'To my knowledge.'

'Your witness.' Krause jerked his head at Coster and returned to the prosecution table.

Coster sauntered past him to the witness stand. 'You've just told my learned friend the Joels and Strange were working with the Detective Department?'

'As far as I'm aware.'

'But didn't you also once say you felt they were keeping something back?'

Ferguson fixed his gaze somewhere above Coster's head. 'No, never.'

'Are you *sure* you didn't say so in the presence of someone sitting in this courtroom now?'

Ferguson darted a look at von Harnach and swallowed. 'I might've *wondered* if they could be keeping something back. But it was idle speculation.'

'Could this "something" have been that Mr Joel was willing to pay accused to get him out of town?'

'No. I mean, certainly not.'

Coster turned to the rostrum. 'If it pleases the bench, this is a court of law, and the witness is an officer of law under oath. I'd like to record my surprise that he can be *allowed* to pursue this story of complete confidence between the ZARP and Barnatos' when it's a barefaced lie.'

Krause stood. 'My lord, I wish to record my surprise at counsel for the defence's impertinence for daring to question your judgement.'

Coster smiled, 'And yours, Fritz. The last I heard, this was still Judge Morice's courtroom.'

Morice slammed the rostrum with the flat of his hand and there was an instant hush at the unaccustomed sound. 'You're *both* out of order. Dr Coster, could you refrain from these allegations and proceed in a manner compatible with your office?'

'I was trying, my lord,' Coster said cheerfully, and then added, 'I believe this witness is finished.'

'The prosecution calls Frederick Boswell Foster,' Krause snapped.

The smile died on von Veltheim's face as Foster took the stand. Foster, a witness for the prosecution? Foster, turned out in an expensive Donegal tweed suit, a gold pocket watch ostentatiously draped across the waistcoat? Nervous? Evading his eyes? 'Something doesn't fit,' he muttered.

Coster studied him. 'And any second now, we'll know what.'

'What with longer sessions, Dr Coster's requested this office be put at our disposal during adjournments.' Smithers put his attaché case on the tiny deal table and sat down.

'*Office*?' Von Veltheim glanced gloomily about the small dun-coloured room. 'I thought it was a cupboard with a window.'

'Steady on.' Smithers unpacked a linen napkin and a wad of beef on rye. 'Sandwich?'

'I'm not hungry.'

Coster took one and began picking out the caraway seeds. 'Don't fret. All those prosecution witnesses scored points for you. Strange and Ferguson were both unreliable on the stand. Von Harnach told the truth. And as for Foster . . . Even if he did say you never met with Barnato at the Cape, everyone could see he was lying.'

Von Veltheim gnawed the quick of his thumbnail. 'Could everyone see why?'

Smithers took a delicate bite. 'Absolutely, old chap. And you'd rather it weren't money?'

'If they bought him, who's next?' von Veltheim demanded. 'The *jury*?'

Coster had finished his sandwich and was nibbling at the little pyramid of caraway seed he'd saved. 'Not even Barnatos' would risk jury tampering in a case like this.'

'We've our witness for the defence after lunch.' Smithers firmly put down a sandwich in front of von Veltheim. 'Now do stop arsing around, and keep up your strength.'

'A witness for the *defence*?' Von Veltheim gave a hollow laugh. 'Try offering me a brandy.'

Smithers gave him a look of deep reproach and removed his half-jack from his attaché case. 'I've been accused of ugly things in my time. But temperance? Never.'

McDermott took the stand and shot von Veltheim an almost imperceptible wink.

Coster asked, 'Shortly after the shooting you interviewed Mr Strange?'

'Yes. For the *Johannesburg Times.*'

Coster handed him a copy. 'Would you read his words to the court?'

McDermott began: *"Whether or not I fired first, I cannot say, but it seemed to me von Veltheim and I fired simultaneously."*

'That's what Mr Strange said?'

'Correct.'

Morice leaned towards the witness box. 'When did you write that down?'

'At the interview, my lord. 'Twas important to have his exact words.'

'You declare those were Mr Strange's exact words?'

'I declare it.'

Coster bowed to the bench, and turned to the prosecution table. 'Your witness?'

Krause strode straight to the witness stand and snapped, 'Mr Strange says your report's incorrect.'

'It *is* correct, nonetheless.'

'After you saw Mr Strange, you interviewed accused in prison?'

'Yes, sir.'

'And their interviews, no doubt, were substantially different?'

'They were substantially the same – up to the point where they were arguing about a business negotiation.'

'Go on.'

'Von Veltheim claims he was urging Joel to reconsider when he heard a shot and turned to see Strange with a discharged pistol in his hand. He looked at Joel and saw himself covered by another revolver. He thought it was his life or theirs, so he drew and emptied his gun at them. Both men fell – Woolf Joel dead, Strange not even wounded.'

'We're aware of the outcome,' Krause said testily. 'It's the sequence we're examining. No more questions.' He turned back to the bench. 'My lord, since this closes the case for the defence, may I request we adjourn to be fresh for accused's examination tomorrow?'

Coster stood. 'My lord, it's in everyone's interest to be fresh for tomorrow. But while we have Mr McDermott in the box, I'd like to re-examine him on mitigating circumstances.'

Morice nodded wearily. 'That's your prerogative, Dr Coster.'

Krause briefly stood his ground as though unwilling to yield.

Coster walked unhurriedly past him to the witness stand and

asked, 'You know von Veltheim well?'

'Very.'

'Did you ever notice how he stands and talks to people?'

'Generally with his hands in his pockets.'

'Did he ever take his hands out of his pockets to gesticulate?'

'Invariably, in the course of an argument.'

'Objection!' Krause was on his feet.

Morice turned to Krause with the impatient look of a man who has been interrupted while trying to concentrate on something intricate. 'To what?'

'Irrelevancy, my lord. I've been listening patiently for anything mitigating.'

'Dr Coster?' Morice prompted.

'My lord, testimony offered in mitigation often simply establishes conditions that prevailed at the time. Context. The accused's intentions. I assure you this evidence *is* pertinent, and the court will recognise this. If I'm permitted to continue?'

Morice thought a moment. 'Will both counsels please approach the bench?'

They stepped up to the rostrum and Morice lowered his voice. 'Dr Krause, Dr Coster's trying to establish mitigating circumstances. Now *let* him. Because until it's been proved accused fired the first shot with the wilful intention of killing Woolf Joel, he has the benefit of the doubt. Do I make myself clear?'

Krause flushed. 'Yes, my lord.'

Morice turned to Coster. 'If your questions are pertinent, Dr Coster, you may continue, providing you don't engage in obfuscating tactics.'

Coster inclined his head frostily.

Krause retreated to the prosecution table, and Coster turned back to the witness box. 'What was von Veltheim's reputation in the boarding house?'

'Popular. Everybody liked him.'

Krause was on his feet again. 'My learned friend has asked about accused's reputation. If *this* is relevant, *I* shall also be asking questions about his reputation. In *depth*!'

Von Veltheim tried to control a tremor in his hand. 'I refuse to be questioned on my reputation.' He thumped the desk with his clenched fist. 'I *refuse*.'

Walt Whitman. Smuts added a subtitle to the manuscript he was revising: *A Study in the Evolution of a Personality.*

His study had started out as spacious enough, but over the months it had filled and filled with much-thumbed German textbooks and notes on philosophy, economics and sociology. His Cambridge papers and essays – and not only on law. It had filled and filled with his own published articles and unpublished manuscripts – and all filed in a mysterious order known only to himself. Now bursting at the seams also with his collection of succulents and grass specimens, he saw it rather as their domain and himself as their custodian. Much more than a place of work, it was journey and harbour, departure point and womb.

But this day the work wasn't going that well. He laid it aside, and thoughtfully reached for the old journal he hadn't opened since that afternoon on Nugget Hill. One of its covers was coming adrift, and he had to open it carefully to reread his last entry:

... this is no mere murder trial, but a treason trial masquerading as one.

Yet if I ignore conspiracy, I obfuscate this. But how do I defend v V, and then attack England for sending her warships against us?

He dated it July and added:

And how do I live with my conscience if he's acquitted?

30

Von Veltheim stood in the dock. When he'd shaved that morning a gaunt stranger with bruised eye sockets had stared out of the mirror at him, and because of the tremor in his hand he'd given himself an unsightly nick.

He stared at the sea of faces. This is all wrong. What a foolish way to fight for one's life. Dumbly, he focused on Coster. His eyes were an energy source, and he willed himself to tap into it.

'You are the accused?'

'Yes.'

'Why did you come to South Africa?'

'To meet with Mr Barnato.'

Steadily. 'Now, I know this is a question whereby you could incriminate yourself, but did you come to kill the President?'

'*No*! I'm not an assassin!'

Coster had deliberately caught him off guard and he waited for him to compose himself. 'Then can you tell us in your own words how that shoot-out occurred?'

Von Veltheim took a deep breath and began shakily. 'There was a shot. I felt a blow in the face, and saw Strange dimly, his hand held out like this . . .' He struck a pose, his mimicry so evocative of Strange that a few jurors smiled and he began to relax. 'I turned to Joel. He was drawing his revolver. Taking aim. I suddenly realised they meant to kill me, so I drew and fired.'

'At whom?'

'At Strange, of course. He disappeared under his desk. I actually thought I'd shot him, but he must've dropped before I fired.'

'Why?'

'I'd never have missed him. He'd have been dead.' A little giggle escaped from the spectators – a release of tension quickly suppressed. 'I wheeled and fired three shots at Joel. At the time I could've sworn he returned my fire. I was wrong.'

'Mr Strange says you warned them: "You know too much now.

You'll never leave this room alive." *Did* you?'
'How could I with two revolvers drawn on me? There wasn't time.'
Coster bowed to the bench and then turned to Krause. 'Your witness.'
Von Veltheim looked at Krause. But in his mind's eye he saw Elise. Tear-stained. Out of control.
Krause sauntered up to the dock, and flashed von Veltheim a dazzling smile. 'Your name is Franz Ludwig Kurt von Veltheim?'
'Yes.'
'On the *Ionic* and in the Bechuanaland Police you used the name Kurt?'
'Yes, I often did that.'
'At the preliminary hearing you said you were Karl Braun?'
'No. When I was arrested.'
Krause shared his bewilderment with the gallery, and then refocused. 'I understand, Mr von Veltheim that you're not really von Veltheim?'
'For family reasons, I prefer to leave the matter in doubt.'
'But I don't want it left in doubt. Is your name Franz Friedrich Moritze Ludwig Kurtze?'
'I don't know.'
Among the spectators, speculation simmered like so many pots.
Morice looked at him over his spectacles. 'It is a matter of your credibility against that of Mr Strange.'
'Thank you, my lord, I've a duty to perform,' Krause said crisply, and then turned back to von Veltheim. 'Have you ever heard the name Franz Friedrich Moritze Ludwig Kurtze?'
'Perhaps I heard it as a boy at college.' Grudgingly.
'At college where?'
'I've forgotten. Why can't you leave my boyhood alone?' von Veltheim demanded. 'Ask me about my manhood, and I'll answer you like a man.'
'Were you born on 4 December 1857?'
'I prefer to leave the matter in doubt.'
'But you were born in Germany?'
'I don't know.'
Coster looked up from the defence table. 'That's hearsay, my

lord. How is the man to know?'

The court erupted with laughter, and Krause shot him a scorching look. All right! He turned back to von Veltheim. 'After your service in the German Marine you went home to Bohemia. To which relative does this home belong?'

'I have forgotten the exact relationship.'

'What is his name?'

'I don't know. I haven't' seen him for a long time.'

Krause glared at him in exasperation and disbelief. 'You've continually to *see* people to remember their names?'

'I forget my own name, let alone other people's,' von Veltheim reminded him cheerfully.

There were smothered chuckles. A comely redhead who had somehow wangled a place in the front row dimpled at von Veltheim, and he grinned back.

'You forget your name!' Krause exploded. 'You forget your family's! Where you were educated! We'll have to jog your memory.' With a little smile, Krause handed up a photograph. 'Please take a look, and tell us if this is you?'

Von Veltheim made a show of impassively examining an old snapshot of himself with Willi at Kiel, but a treacherous nerve made his gunshot scar twitch. 'I wish it were. I know the man you're confusing me with, though. We're the same height.'

'Then read us the inscription on the back.'

He turned it over and read, '*Zur guten Erinnerung – Kurtze.*' Rattled, he looked up at Krause. 'I can explain. He was an acquaintance serving in the navy with my relative, Willi von Veltheim. I got a discharge sheet from him when I left the Marine.'

'Did you know that Kurtze deserted with stolen property?'

Stolen property? Von Veltheim had an image of Willi's watch and ring lying fathoms deep a hemisphere away, and himself in the Johannesburg Circuit Court and no place to run.

'I've an affidavit signed "Willi von Veltheim",' Krause pressed.

Ah, Willi, this too? Von Veltheim closed his eyes wearily to blot out the thought.

A hush hung over the court. The kind athletes remember before a match.

Krause moved round to the other side of the dock. 'Ever heard of Kurtze's guardian? Kaufmann Thomas?'

'You want to prove I'm Kurtze, and I tell you I've used the von Veltheim name for the past fifteen years. And never disgraced it.'

'But it's not your real name?'

'It's certainly not for the purpose of this case.' Ah, Rainer . . . If only I could have kept your name out of this muck altogether. 'Have you *no* consideration for my family?' he thundered.

'Did you show the dead man's any?'

'I was fighting for my life. I'd a right to protect myself.'

'Ah, fighting.' Krause sounded as though his memory had just been jogged. 'Didn't you do some fighting in Bulgaria?'

Morice raised his eyebrows with interest. 'What happened there?'

'War broke out in 1885, my lord. I offered my sword to Prince Alexander, and served on his confidential staff.'

'Then give us the the names of some of your generals,' Krause snapped.

'I decline.'

Morice frowned. 'It's your word against Mr Strange's.'

Von Veltheim thought a moment. 'You can put down Prince Josef of Battenberg. I was with him before I was wounded and sent to Bucharest.'

'Wounded where?'

Von Veltheim glanced apologetically at the redhead. 'I shouldn't like to say where.'

'But you *were* wounded? How many times?'

'Twice. One of which was very nasty,' he told the redhead frankly.

'Mr von Veltheim, may I please have your attention?' Krause demanded testily. 'At what battle?'

'At Tirnova on 24 November, and Pirot on the 29th.'

Coster inclined his head to Krause. He'd just made von Veltheim a hero.

Morice consulted his pocket watch. 'We've gone so far beyond lunch recess, we'd best adjourn.' He glanced up at the wall clock behind him and saw that his timepiece had stopped. 'Until tomorrow,' he added hastily.

Krause turned to protest. He didn't want to adjourn on that note, but Morice was already leaving his rostrum, the defence table had packed up, and the ZARP were manning the exits as the crowd began to disperse.

Coster snapped open his attaché case on the cramped deal table and glared at von Veltheim. 'Mind filling me in on this Kurtze? It makes me uncomfortable when the other side knows more than me.'

'Consult your notes.' Von Veltheim jerked his head at Coster's pad. 'I said it all in court.'

'It'll take a miracle to justify four aliases,' Coster said patiently. 'More scores points for the other side.'

Von Veltheim's jaw set obstinately. 'I've nothing to add.'

'Bloody hell, von Veltheim! You were lucky on the battlefield and today. But the way Krause's honing in on this Kurtze business, you could just run out of it.'

'Damn Kurtze!' Von Veltheim stood ready to pace before he realised that the confined space prevented him. Angrily, he thrust his hands into his pockets. 'I can decline to answer.'

'Certainly. If you want to play Russian roulette over your family tree? But *you're* on trial here. The *charge* might be murder, but before Krause's finished, he'll have you on conspiracy. It'll take a bloody miracle to get you off that one, and I'm not even going to try.' Coster snapped his attaché case shut and stood. 'Let me know if you change your mind.'

Von Veltheim glowered at him. 'I'll think about it.'

Coster strode to the door and turned. 'Do that, Franz Ludwig whatever-the-hell it is . . . It's your neck!'

31

A sleepless night had etched livid shadows about von Veltheim's eyes. He slumped down beside Smithers at the defence table. 'My counsel resigned yet?'

'Still might, dear boy. The day is but a pup.'

They looked up. Neither could tell how long Tjaart Kruger had been standing there. Straight-faced, he extended his hand and said, 'Commandant Kruger of the *Geheime Dienst*.'

Von Veltheim stood and they shook hands as though this was their first encounter.

'Morning, gentlemen.' Coster thudded his attaché case on the defence table, and gave Tjaart a curious look. 'Joining *us* today, Commandant?' Two constables escorted von Veltheim to the dock, and Coster pulled out the vacant chair for him.

Polishing his gold pince-nez with a silk handkerchief, Krause walked to the dock at a leisurely pace. 'You say you never disgraced the von Veltheim name? What did you do in Australia?'

'Bought some horses and a wagon. Went from Java to Sumatra to Australia and through the Never-Never country to Port Darwin – something only one other man managed. And he died.'

'Meet anyone special there?'

'My agent's name was Beitman.'

'What about Molly Yearsley?'

Ah Molly, with her freight of bitterness, like a debt collector demanding her pound of flesh. Von Veltheim gave a twisted little smile. 'She's written to you. Of course.'

'Written to me!' Krause pretended to share his mock alarm with the crowd. 'I don't correspond with other men's sweethearts. 'S too dangerous.'

He was rewarded by a polite ripple of laughter, but von Veltheim's voice was like a bucket of cold water. 'I'd have preferred not to discuss women . . .' A laconic shrug. 'But Molly Yearsley and I became fond of each other, and when two ladies of the house found her in my room one evening, I offered to settle the matter.'

'But *how* did you settle it?'

'I bought her a ring and arranged for a mock marriage. To cover the girl, I made some false statements. I gave the wrong Christian names, but I kept the von Veltheim.'

'That was probably false already. Did you make these false statements under oath?'

'Certainly not. In English law, you simply declare, "I'm so and so, and I am so and so", and finished. It was only intended to stop a scandal.' He turned to the redhead in confidence. 'You know how women are in a small town?'

Krause cut through the laughter like a whiplash. 'Then where did you go?'

'New Orleans for the English and West Indian Pacific Steamship Company until they sent me to Santa Marta.'

'Didn't a revolution break out while you were Honorary Consul there?'

'Yes. But about the same time rain also swept away several miles of railway, and the company sent me home.'

'In London you stayed at 55 Gower Street. Who else lived there?'

'Lots of people.'

'Just give us a couple of names.'

'Please don't. You know all about the young lady.'

'Was it Anne-Marie Mavrogordato?' Implacable.

'Yes.' Scarcely audible.

'Do tell us what happened?'

Von Veltheim kept his tone even. 'We were close. She knew I was going away, and there was a clause in a will preventing her touching her inheritance. So I proposed, or she proposed. I don't remember exactly.' If only he could stop remembering. 'We got a piece of paper and went before a registrar . . .'

'So that was your *second* mock marriage?' Krause feigned admiration, and was disconcerted at the absence of laughter.

'Yes, this young lady needed her inheritance and I tried to help.'

'But she still instituted divorce proceedings against you?'

'If she did, it was the trustees. They must have put her under a cross-examination like this.'

Krause was aware of a developing chemistry. Women were intrigued by him, and men were fraternal. 'Then you fled to South Africa?'

'No, I left to meet Mr Barnato at the Cape on business.'

'What business?'

'I refuse to incriminate myself.'

Krause looked from von Veltheim to Coster in theatrical bewilderment. 'But you've just assured my learned friend you didn't come to kill the President?'

'No, damn it, I did not come to kill the President!'

'Then what special qualifications did you, Franz Ludwig Kurt von Veltheim, alias Kurt, alias Kurtze, claim that Barney Barnato would seek you out to bring about a change of government?'

Silence. But his heart thumped in his ribcage with the resonance of a pagan drum.

'Why do you refuse to answer?'

'I refuse for political reasons . . . I refuse . . . I . . .' Von Veltheim stopped in mid-sentence with the hunted look of an animal in the dark trapped in a beam of light. Scores of eyes were trained on him in fascination and dread.

Krause turned to the bench. 'My lord, the question is crucial, and I submit accused is compelled to answer it.'

Coster stood. 'Objection, my lord! He is *not*! Accused is not obliged to answer that question or any other question that might lay him open to prosecution on any charge on which he has not yet been prosecuted. My learned friend is trying to get accused to make certain admissions, so that if he's found innocent of this charge – as I hope he will be – he could immediately arrest him on another.'

'And I submit accused is bound to answer,' Krause began evenly. 'He told Woolf Joel he's not an assassin. And I want to find out if that's true. If he declines to answer, you can commit him for contempt of court, draw a pen through the whole of his evidence and direct the jury to ignore it. That's already been ruled by the Chief Justice.'

Morice frowned. 'Wouldn't that be an artificial way of disposing of the case?'

'It certainly would not. We have the chief witness in the box, but it doesn't help if I can't cross-examine him on the whole quintessence of the case.'

Morice looked from one to the other, and then turned to von Veltheim and said gently, 'You're not obliged to answer. And you're certainly not obliged to protect the Barnatos.'

There was a stir as a man Smith had once pointed out to von Veltheim as QC Leonard stood up from the barristers' table. He said: 'If you please, my lord, I represent Barnato Brothers here today; and it is our most earnest wish that everything should come out.'

'But this actually doesn't concern Barnatos',' von Veltheim remarked drily. 'I'm refusing to answer questions that would compromise someone else with no bearing on this case.'

Morice's forehead knitted, and he referred to his notes. 'That's your prerogative, Mr von Veltheim, but if you plead self-defence you *do* need to prove that the two mining men had reason to shoot first.'

'And if I do, I incriminate myself.'

Morice peered at him over his spectacles. 'How? You weren't in the Transvaal: you were in the Cape. If you don't answer, I must conclude that no conspiracy existed.'

'That's what the judge thinks.' Beit sketched the banker's *Andernacht* terrace in a blank corner of *Der Spiegel* with his gold pencil. 'It's out of our hands now.'

'Oh, I wouldn't say that. I've found that for the right price verdicts can be swung either way.' The banker leaned forward to inspect Beit's pencil. 'Most elegant,' he pronounced.

'Crafted from Rose Deep gold.' Beit offered it to him to examine more closely.

'Rose Deep, eh?' he approved. 'Of course you know Erich's just about persuaded me to diversify?'

'Really?' Beit gave Wernher a sharp look.

'Actually, it didn't take much. Gold's so attractive. South Africa's one great Pandora's box. All that mineral wealth. It brings its problems, of course, but that's part of the fun. All the money men scrambling for shares, and all the colonial offices for territory. But who's going to win? Britain? Germany? France?'

Wernher shifted his chair closer to the banker's. 'That's what's worrying, Alfred. We do enormous business with Rothschilds', and Leo was very clear about it. Rothschilds' are for peace.'

'Rothschilds' are for Rothschilds'...' The banker's words took on the soothing cadences of a lullaby in time with his rhythmic stroking of his one-eyed alley cat purring noisily in his lap. 'These days one offsets one's mineral interests against industrials.' Beit was fascinated by the caressing hands. They wore two gold bands on the ring and middle fingers of his left hand and another together with a gold signet ring on the pinky of his right. 'You know in the American Civil War the North was financed through Rothschilds' American agent Auguste Belmont, and the South through Erlangers', Rothschild relatives? Government debt's useful.'

'And nothing drives a country into debt like war,' Wernher agreed.

'You know, Alfred, you could control Westminster instead of the other way around?' The attentive inclination of the banker's head and the reptilian focus of his hooded sleepy eyes made his listening far more than a receptive act.

Beit watched the water-borne traffic moving down the Rhine. It looked like a flotilla of toy boats in a furrow. Yet how many billions of Deutschmarks were flowing past at this moment? How innocent things can look, and so deceptive.

'Whoever controls a nation's credit, *mon vieux*, controls the nation.' Wernher put his hand on his shoulder. 'It's time for Wernher Beit & Co to be for Wernher Beit & Co? As Rothschilds' are for Rothschilds'?'

The banker to the banker's voice was silky. 'Europe's less than twenty years away from world war. You could do worse than invest in an interim crisis.' And in his patience Beit divined a predatory quality that could draw answers to questions he hadn't yet framed.

Beit thought of von Veltheim fighting for his life. He passed his hand back and forth across his forehead. It was a gesture of futility. 'I don't know,' he said. 'The rules keep changing, and now there are people getting hurt.'

'The rules were always changing. And you've only just grasped how.' The banker's cat deserted him. 'That's why it's better others think no conspiracy existed.'

'I put it to you, no conspiracy existed.' Krause took a step nearer the dock. 'I put it to you, it's all fabrication.'

'I wish you'd give me six months to do what I decline to tell you.'

Von Veltheim suddenly swivelled to face Coster. 'Shall I tell?'

Coster frowned at him.

'Never mind your advocate,' Krause snapped. 'Mr Strange has said you're a professional revolutionary. *Are* you?'

'Well, perhaps an amateur revolutionary,' von Veltheim said modestly.

'You speak several languages?'

'Correct.'

'Any Romany?'

'Afraid not.'

'But you must know the letters NCR aren't simply the initials of "National Committee of Reform", they also stand for "*nolte ciesta regaiti*"? – the Romany motto of a secret revolutionary society?'

Von Veltheim shook his head, mystified.

'And it means . . .' Krause rattled notes and pitched his voice as though for a drum roll. '. . . No peace for the *rich*?'

'Fancy!' Von Veltheim looked pleasantly surprised, as though he'd just been given a clue that had been eluding him in a crossword puzzle. 'And I took it for "Northern Cape Rifles".'

Krause frowned at the smothered chuckles, and drove on. 'Did you ever seek work at Rose Deep?'

'Not really. I just needed an excuse for going in and out. So my friend Foster suggested I ask the mine manager.'

'You're saying Foster was your *friend*?'

'Till the Barnato millions came into it. Did you know they pay better for perjury than they do for options?'

'Order!' Morice thundered.

'Did you go in and out as an amateur revolutionary?' Krause snapped.

'Objection!' Coster was on his feet.

'Sustained!' Morice banged his gavel sharply, and frowned at Krause. 'May we recess for lunch, Doctor? Before *everybody's* peckish?'

Krause smiled tightly.

The gavel rapped. 'We're adjourned.'

Von Veltheim saw that although Krause's smile was still firmly in place, for a split second he stood rooted to the floor, fists clenched. Then he flexed his fingers. By the time he'd moved back to the prosecution table, the court was emptying.

Smithers stood. 'Excuse me, gentlemen. I'd best see that von Veltheim gets lunch.'

He left by the side door, but although Kruger and Coster pushed their seats back, neither seemed anxious to follow. The last ZARP waited expectantly at the exit for almost a minute before it occurred to him this was one of the few places the President's son could meet defence counsel in private. Poker-faced, he locked the door and stood guard to see they were not disturbed.

Tjaart looked around the empty courtroom that was strangely full of meaningful resonances. He shifted his chair forward and leaned his arms on the defence table. 'You realise the Joel case is incidental, and it's still Krause's intention to expose him?'

'And mine's to defend him on the murder charge. And prevent him incriminating himself on any others.'

'Whose side are you really on?'

Coster indicated his robe.

'And if you were still State Attorney?'

'I certainly wouldn't try to destroy von Veltheim like Smuts.'

Kruger cupped his chin in one large hand and studied him. 'Two such extremes. What's it like at night?'

'They're a bugger,' Coster admitted unexpectedly. 'I sometimes try a glass of port or two. Doesn't help, of course.' He shook his head wearily as though trying to clear it. 'I s'pose I ask myself: do I defend the man with designs on the country? Or the country from him? But in the morning a shower and a strong black coffee fixes that. Then they can all start saying their prayers – those prosecution witnesses obscuring the truth . . . And any perjuring bastards Barnatos' can buy.'

Coster stood and began removing his robes. 'He *is* innocent, you know. And any law man who thinks otherwise has no right to wear this.' He shook the black silk he was folding.

Tjaart leaned over and fingered the material, then nodded at the *Vierkleur* behind the judge's rostrum. 'And which piece of cloth weighs more by day?'

'If it weren't the law, I'd still be State Attorney, Smuts'd be defending von Veltheim, and *you* wouldn't be using his privileged information to offer him a deal.'

32

An unseasonable rain had begun falling during the lunch hour, and from the tiny office von Veltheim had watched the scurrying people caught unprepared. When the court reconvened some were still shivering, and huddled together as if for collective warmth. Dispirited, he envied them their wet shoes and damp clothing.

Krause was dry and groomed, and he looked as if he'd lunched well and was refreshed. He dabbed at his chin with a silk handkerchief, ceremoniously refolding it, fold for fold, and this time he made a point of addressing von Veltheim ultracourteously.

'At the office that Monday morning did you say, "Any dirty tricks, I shoot"?'

'Yes. Strange had a curious look in his eye, and I was uncomfortable there.'

'Afraid of the police?'

'The police least of all.'

'Of Joel?'

'*Joel*? He *certainly* didn't want me arrested. If I were to turn state's evidence . . .' Von Veltheim's eyes flicked to the defence table and locked with Tjaart Kruger's. '. . . he was frightened I'd say something about Barnato.'

'But on Sunday you wrote . . .' Krause drew a letter from a sheaf and read rapidly: "*Some new developments have made your help redundant - but for my passage home and £2,000 to see me through. Disaster is averted, etc.*" Your business was finished then?'

'No, sir. That letter was a front. I was going to London to get a great deal of money from him.'

'But when Joel said he didn't want any such thing traced in the books, you must have thought this a false reason?'

'On the contrary, it was a very wise reason.'

'D'you think a rich man like Joel was afraid to give you £12,000: but unafraid to join you in a revolution?'

'He wasn't afraid of the sum. Of its being traced back to him.'

Krause positioned himself in front of von Veltheim. 'You're an expert shot?'

'In battle, certainly.'

'Then you know the difference between a pistol shot and a smack in the face?'

'Usually. But I was quite dazed when Strange suddenly fired his revolver. And then I saw the glint of Joel's.'

'And you fired at Strange?'

'I fired at the nearest man, and he disappeared under the desk.'

'And then?'

'I fired three shots in succession at Joel's head. I could just see Strange's back. I wouldn't shoot him while he was down, so I fired at the wall to keep him there.'

'Wasn't it impossible for him to reach Joel's revolver?'

Von Veltheim gave a twisted smile. 'From where he was hiding, he couldn't even see it. As I walked to the door, the clerks burst in . . .'

'One last question, Mr von Veltheim . . .' Krause's voice sliced through the the courtroom. 'I want your friend's name.'

'*No*! It's enough I didn't come to kill the President.'

'And I'd like a little more.'

Von Veltheim looked desperately from Krause to Coster, and then to the bench.

'The state may not charge you with conspiracy if I direct you to reply,' Morice pointed out.

For von Veltheim his equable gaze was an oasis. A refuge. And he longed to rest. He took a shuddering breath. 'Then, my lord . . .'

But Krause cut him short. 'And if you do, I shall want the rest. Particulars about your whole family. *All* your connections with the von Veltheims and who *they* are!'

A taut silence engulfed the courtroom. When von Veltheim finally broke it, he spoke hoarsely. '*No*! I decline to drag in my family or my friend. They've nothing to do with with this case.'

Morice steepled his fingertips. 'But Joel has. What was your business with him?'

'My lord, it involved a change of government.' The words were all ragged.

Every witness has his breaking point and Krause recognised it. Von Veltheim was a runaway vehicle from which he'd removed the brake. 'How?' he snapped.

'My lord, I've answered your questions. I'm fighting for my life. You can't ask more.'

Morice's nod above his steepled fingertips was implacable.

'A change of government in what way?' Krause's voice was like velvet.

It came out choked. 'By giving another power control.'

'Which power?'

'I decline to say.'

'*Which*?'

'I decline to *say!*' Desperation rent von Veltheim's voice. In despair, he pounded the dock with his fist. Thump, thump, thump. 'I *decline*!'

Krause bowed to the bench, and tossed a triumphant glance at Coster: I've got him for much more than manslaughter.

Tjaart Kruger stowed his notes away for a quick getaway. The redhead had been twisting her handkerchief, and tore the fabric. Policemen manned the exits and suddenly the room was reverberating with pent-up emotion. It was several minutes before anyone realised that Morice had been banging his gavel at regular intervals demanding, 'Order! Order!' Finally he jerked his robe straight. 'Court is adjourned.'

As Krause moved back to the prosecution table, he made eye contact with Coster. It's been a long wait, Hermanus, but *now* we're even.

Coster stared him down. It's not over yet, Fritz. We'll see.

33

'But by then it's too late.'

Von Veltheim looked at Tjaart Kruger soberly. Even without biltong or wine Governor Menton's office had overtones of persuasion. Trade-offs. Deals.

Tjaart shook his head in disbelief. 'Think they'd do it for you?'

They? He wished he hadn't thought of Elise. Now, the thoughts kept buzzing in his head like a swarm of gnats.

'. . . you respected a confidence . . .'

'A damned sight more than Smuts did.' Von Veltheim stood at the window looking out on the cement yard, brooding.

'What counts is that we appreciate it and we can show it.' Tjaart joined him at the window and leaned against the sill. 'Know how things really work? Jameson's on his way back to help Rhodes build his Cape to Cairo line, and his officers've all had their commissions restored. It's outside the system it's unhealthy.' He smiled his lazy smile. 'Like with Barnato.'

Von Veltheim watched a warder's wife sprinkle breadcrumbs for some mossies. He wondered why they hadn't migrated. Do they really have freedom of choice? Even freedom? He gave Tjaart a weary smile.

Tjaart's heavy features split in a broad grin, and he stuck out his hand to shake von Veltheim's.

Only the words were wrong.

'You *decline*?' Tjaart dropped his hand and managed a loud laugh that sounded like a bark. 'Strange alleges that you said, "You know too much now." This time *they*'ll be saying it.' And suddenly he wasn't smiling at all.

And this time when thoughts of Elise swarmed in von Veltheim's head, a clamminess swam in his gut.

Moments later von Harnach escorted him back to his cell. They walked in step, their footsteps bouncing mournfully off the corridor walls like the tread of a chain gang. They? They? *They*?

Von Veltheim lowered himself carefully into the chair between Smithers and Coster, and looked at the wall clock. Five to ten.

Coster stood and bowed to the bench. 'I close my case, my lord.'

There was a flurry of whispers among the legal fraternity and a discreet scrambling of documents.

Krause seemed taken aback by the unexpected, but only momentarily.

He tugged his robe straight, walked to the jury stand, and bowed to the bench. 'My lord . . . Gentlemen of the jury . . . We are here to try Franz Ludwig Kurt von Veltheim for the killing of Woolf Joel. In a three-way shoot-out in a locked Johannesburg office one man is dead, and the other two proclaim innocence.'

Von Veltheim watched some of the jurors prepare to take notes while others settled into more comfortable positions. This could be a marathon.

'Naturally, the defence seeks to weaken Mr Strange's credibility. Yet what of the accused's? He solemnly swore to tell "the truth, the whole truth and nothing but the truth", yet his first words in the witness box were perjury. First he said his name was Franz Ludwig Kurt von Veltheim. Later he would neither confirm nor deny it . . . For family reasons. Was he the black sheep of a noble family, trying to shield it from dishonour?' Krause arched a sardonic eyebrow. 'I leave the jury to decide.'

'When the photograph was shown of him in the German Marine, at first he confused him with another man of the same height.

'Then he suddenly remembered it was Willi von Veltheim's curious friend Kurtze – the one with a fancy for Willi's watch and crest – who also obligingly gave him his own naval discharge sheet to go to sea as an able seaman. Was Kurtze as casual an acquaintance as accused would have us believe? I suspect he'd rather leave that in doubt.'

Only, Krause was delivering this catalogue of misdemeanours with the almost fraternal indulgence of an affectionate older brother embarrassed by a high-spirited younger one, and von Veltheim noticed his growing rapport with the jury with a sick slide of unease.

'But it has been proven beyond doubt that accused has more

than once entered into irregular marriages. In Australia with a minor, Molly Yearsley, and thereafter with a Miss Anne-Marie Mavrogordato, potentially of comfortable means.' Krause cocked a cosy eyebrow at the comely redhead. 'The second a bigamous marriage, but both, he claims, in the *ladies'* interests.'

She had been trying unsuccessfully to attract von Veltheim's attention. Now she had it, she flashed him a wicked grin, and a rustle of levity bubbled through the courtroom.

Krause's good-humoured expression wavered fractionally, and was instantly reinstated. 'Accused claims it was at Mr *Barnato*'s special request they met at the Queen's Hotel. Yet, a fellow guest, von Veltheim's friend, Foster, never saw them together!' Preposterous?

'And after Mr Barnato's death when his means was exhausted, did he go to Barnatos'? Or his mysterious friends? No, he joined the British Bechuanaland Border Police!' Another regretful look inviting ridicule.

On through the BBP period. The Thames Murder Mystery exposé to . . . 'But when his superior officer demanded the precise connection between Trooper Kurt and von Veltheim, he refused him an explanation. Why? What could a distinguished soldier dread divulging so badly that he was ready to forfeit his career?

'Next we find him at Rose Deep Mine. He needed to assess the miners' temperament for friends in England. Why? Barnato was dead and so was his conspiracy.

'Now for a *new* crime . . . He wrote threatening letters to Solly Joel, a sick man from whom he wished to extort money.'

Von Veltheim noticed Coster dart a look at Solly and then make a swift note.

'One loses track of all the tall stories that follow.' Krause crossed to the prosecution table and picked up a wad of letters. Using them as props, he flourished a fresh one for each tall story. 'That Woolf Joel simply forgave him for the threatening letters. They were meant for his brother Solly, anyhow. The real motive was politics. Then politics were abandoned for business. Business, backed by powerful friends.' He shook his head as though pitying von Veltheim for having such a flimsy case.

Pacing back and forth before the jury in the hypnotic rhythm of a caged tiger, Krause worked through to the Saturday morning in the JCI offices. 'He expects us to believe that when Joel came in *he* gave *von Veltheim* a wink, warning him not to speak politics. That the only thing that stopped Joel giving him the money was fear of allowing the sum to . . .' He paused mid-stride, focusing the jury's attention. '. . . to *appear in their books*.'

He resumed his rhythmic path, repeating the same three steps this way, and the same three that way, and using the tempo to emphasise his words.

'Accused expects us to believe the money was to be paid him in London. That Joel requested a letter to put the *detectives* off the track. That Joel and Strange were keeping something from the police is as absurd as von Veltheim and Joel keeping something from Strange!'

Krause scanned the jury, inviting them to scoff with him at this preposterous proposal. He stopped at the foreman. Burgher Viljoen was concentrating on von Veltheim, oblivious to his stare.

'On Sunday he writes another letter asking Joel's aid to avert a disaster. What disaster? *Political*? He's been in the Johannesburg Fort three months, and *I* see no disaster.' Krause's look challenged Viljoen. 'None!'

'Monday in the office Strange was told not to admit him. Yet he expects us to believe Joel was ready to see him . . . With*out* Strange!

'Strange sends Joel a note. He replies: "*Am right in the middle of my mail. If I don't get on with it, I'll never get through.*"' Krause jabbed the air in front of him with his forefinger. 'Joel never got through.'

The gathering caught its collective breath at this grim reminder that there'd be no more Woolfie swapping yarns 'between the Stock Exchange chains'.

Krause played the silence like a virtuoso and drove on. '"Mr Strange" – accused states – "had a curious look in his eye." Even if he thought so, does this justify his saying, "Any dirty tricks, and I shoot"?

'Then Strange drew his derringer. This, by the way, was justified. If a man uses threats and then flourishes a revolver, Mr Strange, by law, would've been perfectly justified in shooting.

'On the other hand, accused has told us *he* is an excellent shot. Experienced soldier. Survivor of several battles. Yet he asks us to believe that *he* felt a stinging blow. *He* was dazed and saw Mr

Strange's revolver pointed at *him*. That whole rigmarole that Strange shot first . . . That seeing Joel raise his revolver, he stood between two guns and fired in self-defence is ludicrous.

'Was it likely that Mr Joel, the millionaire, and Mr Strange, the businessman, would've enticed him into their offices to kill *him*? One man with his wife's toy pistol and the other with a revolver he wasn't used to – when they could've hired a dozen professionals? Was this likely?

'Most unlikely of all, he expects us to believe that Strange fired the first shot. And seeing a revolver also in Joel's hand, he shot in self-defence. After this?' He rattled the Kismet correspondence, and then looked at von Veltheim almost with regret at this insult to their intelligence.

He took his stance in front of the jury stand and, clutching his lapels, made eye contact with the jurors one by one. 'On this evidence you must decide as to accused's innocence or guilt. This is about the murder of one of our most respected citizens. And I'm convinced you can come to but one conclusion. Accused planned it, and he carried it out.'

He touched his handkerchief to the gleam of perspiration on his forehead. 'I've done my duty. I ask you to do yours.'

He inclined his head to the jury stand, and bowed to the bench.

Krause's address had taken the better part of the morning, but it seemed to have aged him ten years. As he walked back to the prosecution table, he favoured one leg. It was an old sporting injury, but he gave the impression of a wounded veteran returning from a bloody war.

There were a few handclaps, hesitant and involuntary at first. Hisses of '*stilte*!' from the ZARP. A few people were embarrassed, but soon their whispers were drowned by growing applause that gained momentum like a veld fire. The court room and eventually the whole floor resounded with a storm of ovation accorded only to heroes.

Coster's lunch was untouched. He sat in his chambers staring at the framed photograph in his hand. Two years back Krause had scrawled across the bottom, '*The Jameson trial team – invincible*!'

Krause's summing up had shown a fair mix of sympathy for the victim and outrage against the perpetrator. Humour had never been his strong point, but he could throw a look around the jury as neatly as a lasso. Coster knew he'd been the first to recognise Krause's skills. He had moulded and refined them, and invincible they had been.

Only, after the Raid Kruger had insisted on his right to expel undesirable aliens. He could understand the president's need for that law. He just couldn't administer it.

Bleakly, he'd contemplated the anticlimax of returning to the bar. What opportunities could it offer after the Raid treason trial? Probably none.

In the shaft of sunlight that slanted onto his overflowing desk that day, he'd written his letter of resignation.

He'd glanced around his office at his own unorthodox filing system, and then considered his successor briefly. By the time he'd removed the various categories of paperwork from the furniture and floor and assigned them to their rightful cabinets, the office looked strangely vacant. Dispossessed. But he knew that its neatness would appeal to an obsessively tidy man with the skills of the Acting State Attorney-to-be. Funny how easy it had been while Krause had deferred to him as his mentor. Now he'd have to get used to thinking of him as his successor.

Von Veltheim studied Coster in front of the jury, and was struck by the contradictions. The bow tie beneath his wing collar was usually skew, and his jacket and waistcoat each had their own lapels which kept catching in his robe. But the gaze he levelled at the jury was true as a plumb line.

'Gentlemen, I never knew the late Woolf Joel,' he began steadily. 'But I know most of you did. So, I'm going to ask those of you harbouring a special sympathy for him to try to consider him as you would any other man. And for those with an antipathy towards the accused – and this is a problem – I ask you equally earnestly to strike it out. For only without preconceived prejudice can he receive a fair and reasonable trial.

'When I say that this is a difficult case for me to deal with, I touch my own heart.' Indeed. 'Accused acknowledges having conspired against the sovereignty of our country. But to love our land means to serve it with honour. We have always dealt fairly and impartially with our enemies, but can you do so today? Because without your pledge, I cannot defend him.

'My learned friend . . .' Coster's gaze locked with Krause's and the old Jameson Raid treason trial team surveyed each other, polarised. 'My learned friend has spoken for over three hours; yet to the crux – the scene in Strange's office that Monday morning – he gave only ten minutes. But remember . . . We're here not to judge the man, but the deed. Did he kill in self-defence? The whole quintessence of this case is: "Who shot first?"'

Deftly he catalogued Strange's trio of mutually exclusive statements – to the press, the police and the Landdrost's Court. 'How can we believe a man who for one event gives three different versions?' he challenged. 'I submit that on this point Mr Strange's evidence is inadmissible.'

A few journalists looked at Strange, and then from von Harnach to McDermott, and their reporters' notebooks rustled as they hurriedly made fresh notes.

'The JCI clerks were unanimous: the first shot was the loudest. We all know now that a derringer packs more powder than the usual kind, and its report is more powerful. And, by consensus, the time difference between the first and second shots was also greater than those that followed.

'I submit that after receiving a shot in the face von Veltheim was stunned and took a second to draw. By the time he fired, the pause the clerks noticed had elapsed. Therefore, I submit that it wasn't he who fired the first shot, but Strange.'

A subdued murmur rose from the public. Coster looked across at them and they fell silent.

'Now for the most important aspect of the case. We're told von Veltheim caused Woolf Joel's death. Of that there is no doubt. But in what circumstances?' He took a moment to shuffle his notes, and then looked up at the jury again. 'Strange had shot at him and now Joel stood with a revolver in his hand. When a man stands between two armed men, by law he's entitled to kill both. And so, von Veltheim killed Woolf Joel . . . – the compelling eyes flashed round the jury – ' . . . but in self-defence.'

He looked at Strange levelly. 'This puts Mr Strange in quite a predicament. Because if it's been proved that von Veltheim didn't fire first, who is the moral perpetrator of this crime, if not Strange himself?'

A murmur broke from the spectators, and Morice rapped his gavel.

'Gentlemen, be careful of this evidence . . . If two men are in a room and each accuses the other of murder, which will you believe?' Coster paused, focusing the jury's attention. 'Mr Strange fired the first shot and when he said he fell grabbing the revolver, he lied. He would have been putting the rope around his own neck if he said otherwise.

'To understand what really happened in that locked office that day, you need to grasp Strange's mental attitude. We all know that in war the inexperienced man shoots either too soon or too late. It takes practice to get it right. I submit that Strange, frantic with fear, fired before any necessity arose.'

Coster threw a careless look at the dossier on the prosecution table. 'The prosecution reasons that because accused committed fraud, had two wives and wrote threatening letters, he shot first. No, gentlemen, and on this the judge'll also direct you. Had accused every crime possible on his conscience, this does not make him guilty of the one with which he is charged. Being a bigamist or a blackmailer does not make him a murderer.

'The prosecution wants to make out that because he *threatened* murder in the Kismet correspondence, he *committed* it. And I'd like to point out once Woolf Joel began receiving these letters, whatever threats may originally have been levelled at Solly Joel, the entire tone of the correspondence changed.

'Is it really the absurd nonsense my learned friend tries to make out that von Veltheim met Woolf Joel to discuss a political plot?' He fixed the jury with his blowtorch eyes. 'Do you truly believe that these gentlemen, these financiers, are so absolutely against a little revolution?' He glanced at Tjaart.

Tjaart looked back impassively, but the pencil he'd been twirling was arrested in mid-arc.

'Mr Strange says he abhorred revolutions.' Coster looked across at Krause. 'But my learned friend knows he was one of the Johannesburg Reformers we prosecuted in the Jameson case. And couldn't Woolf Joel's reluctance to become involved in this new conspiracy account for his excluding Strange from his own embarrassing knowledge of it?'

Coster planted himself in front of the jury. 'Some of you gentlemen may still give Mr Strange the benefit of the doubt. That's your prerogative. But only beyond reasonable doubt can you send a man to the gallows. Without the proof to commit von Veltheim, you must acquit him. I leave his life in your hands.'

Coster bowed quickly to the jury and then to the bench. He was halfway back to the defence table before the courtroom reacted. Handclapping, which had started hesitantly, soon took on the measured cadence of a slow march past. From other parts of the crowd came an equally insistent hissing. Together the clapping and hissing drowned the ZARP's helpless appeals for '*stilte*'. Both sets of sympathisers were recording their support with the solidarity of football fans without a cheerleader.

Von Veltheim's heart thudded dully as he watched Morice gather his notes and adjust his robe.

'Gentlemen of the jury,' he began in his rich Scots burred bass, 'the accused before you, Franz Ludwig Kurt von Veltheim, alias Kurt, alias Baron von Veltheim, alias Kurtze, is charged here with the crime of murder. Namely on 14 March 1898 he premeditatedly fired on Woolf Joel with a revolver, inflicting three wounds, in consequence of which he died.

'I never knew Woolf Joel.' He glanced at the JCI contingent. 'But I know most of you did. After nine days of testimony in South Africa's most sensational murder case I ask you to forget that the victim was a man of substance and the accused an outsider in our society who has several times fallen foul of the law. He must be considered innocent until proven guilty.

'This case has been complicated by talk of some political plot. Inconclusive talk. But were it not, I ask you to remember that any incriminating statements accused made were at *my* behest. I so directed him to clarify pivotal issues in the only case we are here to try.'

Von Veltheim saw Tjaart Kruger trying to catch Coster's eye, but it was steadfastly fixed on his boot as if he could listen better that way.

Morice changed tonality for his wrap-up. 'Therefore I ask you to regard only the murder indictment and accused's plea of self-defence. If you accept this, your judgement will be culpable homicide. Unless you're convinced otherwise, he has the benefit of the doubt, for the burden of proof lies with the state.'

He removed his reading glasses and announced: 'Court will remain in session as usual until six this evening. If by that time you've not reached conclusion, you'll return to your lodgings in the Grand National Hotel and resume tomorrow. You may retire to consider your verdict.'

Coster consulted his gold pocket watch as the jury filed out. 'Two counsels and one judge covering nine days of testimony in just over six hours. That should be enough to keep any jury busy a while.'

Von Veltheim looked at him bleakly. 'So, why've I this feeling it hasn't all been said?'

34

The Rissik Street Post Office clock chimed five, and von Veltheim stared at the door that had just closed behind the jury. There was the low buzz of conversation as the spectators relaxed, but he noticed that Krause was far from relaxed. He was putting his papers in order with deliberate obsessive movements in what would be his own idiosyncratic way of winding down. Coster, on the other hand, looked tired but at ease, as though relieved of a heavy burden.

Von Veltheim was uncomfortably aware of dozens of pairs of eyes surreptitiously observing him. He shifted irritably in his seat. 'What do we do until six? Play poker?'

Smithers gave him a sympathetic look. 'The jury foreman'll probably send word there'll be no verdict today, and we'll adjourn.'

Von Veltheim tried a smile that failed to come off.

'Each man has to satisfy his conscience beyond reasonable doubt, old cock. And they've got to be unanimous.'

Coster locked his attaché case. 'Time is on your side. You wouldn't have it otherwise.'

The side door opened and a messenger of the court delivered a note to the rostrum. Morice adjusted his spectacles to read it, but before he could make his announcement, the jury began to file in.

Coster hauled out his pocket watch again. 'I've overestimated before, but five minutes is ridiculous.'

Von Veltheim felt someone touch his shoulder. He turned to find von Harnach and Gaoler Witzel flanking his rear, and his heart leapt in his ribcage. With his back ramrod straight, he stood and walked to the dock.

The foreman of the jury stood. Burgher Viljoen had a rough texture to him, but when he spoke it was with a beautifully modulated voice that made everybody sit forward straining their ears. And the words he spoke seemed to rest on the silence.

Then, dimly, he could hear the spectators roaring and cheering.

They seemed to belong to a world he'd already forsaken. Only when the crowd began to swarm towards the dock to shake his hand did it penetrate. Suddenly Smithers was wedged into the box at his side, thumping his back and crowing, 'Not guilty!'

Not guilty. Von Veltheim clasped his hands over his face and whispered, '*Not* guilty!' When he removed them his eyes were full.

The women were jostling each other to reach him. The redhead tried to dab at his cheek with her lace handkerchief and left it behind as a memento as she was swept away, and a blonde in a veiled toque pressed a posy of wilted sweet peas into his hand.

Von Veltheim searched the defence table for Coster and caught his eye just as he had finished stowing away the last of his documents. In gratitude and elation, he raised his clasped hands above his head like a victorious boxer and mouthed his congratulations. Coster acknowledged the gesture with a little bow, and then turned and swiftly left the courtroom.

Von Veltheim felt oddly deflated. He noticed Ferguson waiting patiently just below the dock. He seemed to be trying to hide his embarrassment. Von Veltheim seized his hand and gave it a hearty shake.

Ferguson managed to dislodge it. He came around to the entrance to the dock and murmured something. Von Veltheim missed the first part and leaned closer to catch his words. 'It's my solemn duty to serve on you a warrant ...'

It took a few moments for the rest to sink in.

'*Blackmail! Barnatos' charge von Veltheim with blackmail*!'

Braun slammed the sash window shut on the news vendors' shouts. First he eludes the rope, and now this! He felt that his athletically primed body and his finely focused instincts were all flung out of true as if he had been in a collision. Dislocated.

He picked up his Indian clubs and swung them with the ferocity of all his frustrated drive in a state of arrest. All climax and no resolution, damn it!

There was a vast difference between a man's being detained by the law, and being eliminated. Elimination was provided for. Barnato. Joel. Then von Veltheim. And while he was about it, he'd taken the precaution of seeing that the unfortunate Miss Caldecott would now never connect him to von Veltheim in a witness box. In so neatly discharging his brief, he had not only scuttled von Veltheim's coup, but exposed it.

Problem is, hadn't this also created his most pressing problem? No matter how generous his pay, he could not ignore the gold bars in the cave which only one man could redeem. But who was he?

Forward. Then reverse. Figure eights. Then combinations. This unfinished business left him with a wild agony of sensation – the screaming nerve syndrome an amputee feels in the empty space once occupied by a severed limb. Who *was* he? He needed the name. *Who*?

Like a fault in the earth, the sinkhole of his dilemma yawned wider and deeper. He also needed von Veltheim permanently out of the way. For so long as he was detained for a minor offence without knowing when he'd be at large again, those gold bars might as well still be in the vault at Rose Deep.

The litany in his head changed. Round and round arced his clubs. Out of the way. Permanently. Permanently out of the way . . .

After fifteen minutes his forehead had filmed with sweat, but his thinking was crystal clear.

First he shaved his moustache. Then his head. The transformation was stunning. His naked face and skull were less a disguise than a revelation – the peeling back of a wrapper to expose a truer identity.

By the bedside light in his Jeppe boarding house, he worked carefully but professionally to substitute his new passport photograph for the old one. And a name as fictitious as Charles Brown had been.

35

'It's not over yet.'

The President didn't answer Smuts.

'At Rose Deep, they say he wasn't working alone.'

'*Ja.*' Brooding, Tjaart stared out of the *staatprocureur's* office window at the Johannesburg road. 'Juta says he was being followed – and he doesn't mean by ours.'

'There's still someone out there.' Smuts's *siener* eyes seemed to look beyond the veld rolling away from the town.

Tjaart cracked his knuckles again and again. 'But for Barnatos' charge . . .'

The President tamped down the tobacco in his pipe with a calloused thumb. 'We're not here to please them. That law . . .' He struck a match and lit up. 'I've been criticised for it often enough.' And one grizzled grey eyebrow rose like a circumflex.

'Of course.' A slow smile lit Smuts's ascetic face, and with scarcely a reference to the statute book, he began to write.

The August wind howled around the Johannesburg Fort. Inside all sound was muted. The sound of a prison listening.

'. . . *Whereas it appears from your own evidence that you, Franz Ludwig Kurt von Veltheim, alias Kurt, alias Baron von Veltheim, alias Kurtze, had the intention of bringing about the intervention of a foreign power in the affairs of this state . . .*'

'*Therefore now, I, Stephanus Johannes Paulus Kruger, State President of the South African Republic, order and command that you, Franz Ludwig Kurt von Veltheim . . . shall be sent over the borders of the Republic . . .*'

That pool of fear oozed in his gut again and made him lose the thread. 'Forty-eight hours?' he repeated stupidly.

'That's when you leave for Lourenço Marques,' Tjaart confirmed.

Von Veltheim balled his fists, the panic rising in his veins and viscera like some perverse sap in spring. He managed a twisted smile. 'Probably a lot healthier there.'

'Wouldn't bet on that – with Braun? . . . His boss? . . . Barnatos'? . . . Best way to hush something up is . . .' – Tjaart playfully made a gun with forefinger and fist and a popping sound with his tongue – 'course, we'll be watching, but Mozambique is, well . . .' He spread his hands in exaggerated helplessness.

Von Veltheim had schooled himself to take his chances in some of the most alien unchartered landscapes of the globe or – man to man, steel to steel – on the frozen frontiers of Bulgaria or the steamy jungles of South America. But a sense of impending doom now came in waves from the dark places of his soul. And it sprang from the knowledge that those implacable forces that had frustrated his purpose at every turn, and had shattered irrevocably the dream that had – rightly or wrongly – fuelled his life these past months, would finally destroy him.

He had fought down the panic, but he was left with a terrible despondency and weariness. Exhausted, he lowered himself onto his bunk. He sank his head into his cupped hands, and felt the dark waters of this new empty fear close over his head.

'Why not negotiate?' Beit asked, appraising the banker's parlour. Its rich Biedermeier pieces. Its chess and backgammon tables. Its globes – celestial and terrestrial. Its maps.

Their owner's eyebrows rose in disbelief. 'And have the Rand elude us indefinitely? Far neater to have the ultimatum come from them. And simple, now that Milner's High Commissioner.' The plump hands moved lightly as butterflies over the chessboard setting up his problem. 'Incidentally, he's full of your contribution to the war effort.'

'*If* there's war,' Beit said shortly. He shot a sharp look from him to Wernher.

'Once it's inevitable,' Wernher apologised, 'with the might of the empire behind Britain, it'll be over by Christmas and we can all relax.'

'Once we're in and we've a decent testing ground for new weaponry, it'll take as long as it has to,' the banker corrected him mildly. 'Diamonds and gold might have dragged the Boers kicking and screaming into the nineteenth century, but I hear they're stubborn fighters. Kitchener says he's prepared for a four to one fight. Two imperial soldiers to fall to the Boer's superior marksmanship, one to dysentery, and the fourth to even the score. That all takes time.'

And what manpower, Beit thought. Was it really only eighteen months since von Veltheim had convinced him that his solution made the soundest sense?

The banker held out his fist with the two pawns for Wernher to pick. White.

Beit shifted impatiently in his deep easy chair. 'If all this is such a foregone conclusion, what about von Veltheim?'

'What about him?'

'Someone must have a stake in his welfare to have forked out for his legal costs.' Beit's fish eyes were fixed unblinkingly on the banker to the bankers. 'The question is, who?'

'If *you're* asking, then it's probably those fancy family connections he's so worried about.'

But Beit had a nagging presentiment that he wasn't quite disclosing his hand, and his fish eyes remained fixed on him until he spoke again.

'You don't play chess, Alfred?'

'Afraid snooker's my game.'

'Pity.' The banker picked up two opposing pawns. 'Teaches you that exchanging a couple of pieces is common practice.'

Wernher studied the chess board. 'You just axe two?'

'Opens up the game.' The beringed hand hovered over the board a moment. Then the black knight leapfrogged a white pawn and swept away its bishop. 'You know, after the Raid we had two options. And the second just made better financial sense.'

Beit passed a hand over his forehead and his voice came out as a croak. 'Before Barney's death?'

He gave an apologetic shrug, but he only said, 'Check and checkmate.'

Were they all just parts of an equation? Barney? Woolfie? And now? Beit looked at the banker's chess exercise, and his heart felt like a stone. And now, von Veltheim? A voice at the edge of his mind tolled like a bell.

Lourenço Marques reminded him of Santa Marta. The way it sprawled at the confluence of two sluggish rivers. The languorous heat, the houses with their *azuléjo* tiles and cast-iron balustrades. Its sibilant Portuguese.

The weeks of shellfish diving on the western shore of Delagoa Bay had tightened his belly and defined his shoulder muscles. Regular practice with Dirk Fish's sjambok had made his reflexes needle sharp; and as he took a vacant table on the Cardosa Hotel patio his smile flashed like a beacon in his sun-bronzed face. 'I'm celebrating,' he announced.

'Aha!' The white-robed waiter beamed at the mail he was waving. 'And not one, but two!'

Von Veltheim propped both letters in front of the luncheon menu. 'What's the speciality of the day?'

The Zanzibari tilted his red fez. 'The bwana must have half a dozen queen . . .' He hesitated and, taking in his size and smile, amended: 'if it's a *big* celebration, rather a dozen king prawns on a bed of rice with a bottle of our green Avelida.' And the white-skirted kanzu swirled about his ankles as he hurried away.

Von Veltheim considered Anne-Marie's outsize envelope and then the smaller one. The writing was equally familiar. The hell with it. Pleasure before business.

He drew out the single page and a tissue-wrapped cardboard rectangle. Carefully he removed the wrapper and stared with wonder at a picture of his son. Anne-Marie had been snapped exhorting him to smile for the camera. A sturdy boy of a little under a year gazed out at him. He's like Rainer. No. A strange new feeling caught at his throat. He's like me.

He traced the inscription on the back. *To Franz, with love from . . .*' For signature Anne-Marie had made an impression of the child's handprint in blue pastel chalk. It was labelled *Franz's hand at ten months.*

He didn't know he'd spoken until he saw the smiling faces of the Portuguese couple at the next table. But now he had their attention, he said it again exultantly. 'This is my son!'

The *padrone* had the air of a father of several sons and a connoisseur. He got up for a closer look. 'Aha! Strong like his father, eh?'

Von Veltheim covered the bottom half of the face, and appealed to the woman, 'But they're his mother's eyes. Extraordinary. Right?'

She clapped her hands in empathy. 'Si . . . si.'

He turned back to the picture, a wistful smile tugging at the corners of his mouth. His arms felt empty, and his fingers longed to touch. To caress. To tease. He needed to see the pulse flutter at his throat, and smell his hair. The hunger aching in his heart and his mind and his gut, he turned to Anne-Marie's letter:

Bielorat
September

Dearest Franz,

I write you with both tremendous relief at your acquittal, and anxiety for your safety. In the three unnatural deaths – Barnato's, Woolf Joel's and Miss Caldecott's – I see a dreadful singleness of purpose, and pray God, 'Please, not you.'

I beg you to ask asylum in the Transvaal, and think we can arrange it. You may remember that Sir Graham Bower was Secretary to the High Commissioner at the Cape during the Raid? I recently filed his archives, and believe we could be his agent in making his record of that infamous act available to Smuts. I urge you to trade this for protection.

The newspapers here libelled you so dreadfully that people were taking bets on your life. That was when I made my bargain with God. If you were acquitted, I'd make it up to Rainer and Willi. What I'm trying to say – only it doesn't want to come out – is that Willi and I are now man and wife.

I pray for us all.

Always and always,
Anne-Marie

Pray for us all? He crushed the pages in his fist. Couldn't you have *waited*?

In anger and despair, he ripped open the second letter.

It was the last thing he remembered before the explosion rocked the hotel. It lifted him like flotsam in a high wind, and flung him across the patio.

'Bwana, are you all right?' From the edge of his consciousness the waiter's face swam into focus. 'Who did this thing to you, bwana?'

'I thought . . .' Von Veltheim tried to sit up, but a wave of nausea washed over him, dragging him back. 'I thought . . . I don't know.'

It was almost dusk before the doctor pronounced him steady enough for the Zanzibari to escort him the few blocks to the Hotel Continental. And so he didn't notice the solitary diner at a sidewalk café lower his newspaper. And it was just as well he didn't look back as the man settled his bill and, keeping to the shadows, started after him.

At the rear of the Continental, Braun watched the upstairs bedroom light flare and von Veltheim's shadow flicker in silhouette on the roller blind. Then, whistling softly, he turned back to the task in hand.

The distant wail of a fado singer mixed with *The Band Played On.* Just a shade off key.

The pen scratched across the page:

Lourenço Marques.

Anne-Marie Dearest,

My thanks for the photograph. Forgive my confusion re your marriage. Thought I was still the groom.

Your premonition was spot on. So far, have dodged a letter bomb. (Ironically, I used to think the writer my friend.)

Will lie low on Inhaca Island till I can get that message to Smuts . . .

Hands steady on the fuse, Braun smelled the fuel soak the straw.

It fed thirstily, and exploded in a sheet of flame that roared and hissed and crackled and snapped. In an instant the wood-framed building was an inferno, its flames licking at the night sky as though to slake an unholy thirst.

Von Veltheim darted to the window. Framed in the smouldering curtains, he stared down at the pyre of straw blazing directly beneath.

He spun and, snatching up his *sjambok*, wrenched the door open. The corridor was solid with panicky Portuguese elbowing and shoving, as the billowing smoke pall drove them back. A toddler, eyes wide with fright, clutched his teddy bear and stared down into the stairwell. Von Veltheim swept him up in his arms and, shielding the child's body with his own, clambered onto the first-floor banisters. With the piteous cries of the trapped in his ears, he jumped.

From the first-aid station von Veltheim took in the devastation and chaos. The wounded, weeping guests . . . The soft, soothing voices of the doctor and nurse. Two police officers worked their way through the crowd, asking questions about the remains of the incendiary device they'd found.

He stared at it for a moment and, recognising the unmistakable hallmark of handiwork he knew well, turned away quickly, the taste of the bile of betrayal in his throat. Around him were the casualties who'd simply been in the way of a hunter closing in on his prey, and he felt revulsion for the callous disregard of their fate flood his being as fear never had.

He realised that the boy was looking at him with large solemn eyes. 'How are you called?' he asked gently.

The child hiccoughed. 'Françesco.'

'I'm Françesco, too.' And he gathered him against his chest.

The white-robed Zanzibari shouldered his way to their side. He looked from the child's tear-streaked face to von Veltheim's, blackened and filmed with sweat. '*Who* did this thing, bwana?'

Von Veltheim shook his head dully. 'You wouldn't know him.' Karl Braun: Charlie Brown?

The Zanzibari eyed him shrewdly, and then nodded. 'Then do likewise unto him. But first let him feel how this . . .' – he tapped the *sjambok* meaningfully – '. . . can sting.'

'I want to go home,' Françesco whimpered.

Me too. He set the boy on his feet. 'Oopla! Come, let's find your papa.' But saying that didn't make him feel any better. He felt betrayed. Cuckolded. As homeless as the child whose hand he held.

Then on the edge of the crowd he saw the man in the slouch hat and, almost gladly, he recognised the broad farmer's face.

Twice daily the tides at the Costa de Sol river mouth yielded its bounty of tasty pink crab and plump silver sardines. Rodgrigues harvested them and lovingly wove them into gastronomic poems with the marjoram and oreganum he grew from seed, and the fat cloves of garlic he kept on long plaited strings.

Tjaart Kruger poured the garlic butter over his crab, speared a morsel and listened to the end of von Veltheim's story. 'Unhealthy's one thing, but that's ridiculous.'

'Amen,' von Veltheim agreed fervently. 'And you?'

'Just a good Samaritan to our Portuguese neighbours,' Tjaart said vaguely.

'You once quizzed *me* about border campaigns?' von Veltheim suggested hopefully.

'Uh-uh. You wanted to talk, now *talk*. We know you controlled someone.'

'That's what I thought . . . Till the letter bomb.'

'Still, he's got to be working for someone.'

'I'm still working that one out.'

'Who sent you?'

Von Veltheim parodied Tjaart's infuriating smile, hands spread in a gesture of helplessness.

'*You* wanted to trade. Now *what?*'

So von Veltheim told him.

Tjaart's indolent manner vanished. 'British troops are already on the Natal border, so you'd better cross at Komatipoort into a police trap. Now.'

'Or I . . .'

'*Now* you want to talk?' Tjaart shook his head and stood. 'Now you wait and tell it to Smuts.'

Von Veltheim looked about the *staatprocureur*'s office. The book shelves were lined with scuffed leather-bound volumes of Roman-Dutch law. But crammed onto the lower shelves, handy to the touch were a second-hand edition of the *The Complete Works of Walt Whitman* and an ancient botanical dictionary. Next to them, dried tufts of grass were fading and powdering. The smell of fresh coffee filled the air.

Smuts put down a mug in front of him. 'Still on the run, von Veltheim? Who's it this time?'

'Who bought my jury? Paid for my trial?'

Smuts nodded and the keen eyes, now webbed with fine lines, narrowed. 'I've often wondered if they didn't also pay my fees?'

'Once I didn't get the rope, they wanted me out in the open. Like Barnato . . . Elise Caldecott . . . And don't forget Woolf Joel. You were the first to suggest I was manipulated to do the killing for Strange even if you couldn't bring yourself to go all the way and help get the *Geheime Dienst* to identify my tail.'

'You knew this Karl Braun?'

'I thought so. Until they turned him.'

'*They*?'

Von Veltheim shrugged. 'The other money men. The ones with a stake in my failure.'

Smuts raised an enquiring eyebrow.

Von Veltheim shrugged. 'Just ask yourself who profits more from wars. Armaments manufacturers. And the men who finance them must do so for gain.'

'A third force?' Again Smuts nodded slowly as if in confirmation of a truth he'd known all along. 'As if the kill weren't ugly enough without the vultures.' His look was accusing and at the same time deeply sad as if he were thinking, What chance could either of us have stood against them?

He moved stiffly to the window, all resilience of movement gone, and stood staring out at where the veld encroached. A crystal sharp image sprang to mind of himself on his father's farm in the Zwartland the day news of the Jameson Raid broke. Of how he had climbed Riebeek Kasteel with his betrayal and his shame, and had stooped to pick up a handful of earth. Almost red it had been, but from a distance it seemed nearly black. It was the finest wheat land in South Africa. Forever embedded in the minuscule complex whorled patterns of his fingertips was the memory of soil kneaded between his fingers that day. And he remembered the feel of it as it trickled away.

'We Boers grew up with such killing,' he murmured. 'Now with British troops on our borders, there'll be more; and we're just simple farmers.'

'And the Widow Oosthuizen had a simple farm until a prospector stumbled on that gold seam. But ever since, the battle lines have been drawn.' Von Veltheim's voice fell like an axe. 'The first shot fired in Jameson's Raid.'

He joined Smuts at the window. And so the adventurer and the statesman – *sieners* both – gazed out at the veld. Above its precious metals were its aloes and thorn trees.

Had there been a kill? In the distance the vultures were circling.

THE SUMMARISING YEARS

Between 1902, shortly before the Anglo-Boer war ended, and 1929, shortly before *von Veltheim's* life did, he defied his expulsion order four times, returning to the Rand through various routes in attempts (all unsuccessful) to retrieve his cache of gold bars. He would probably have defied it even more frequently had he not been prosecuted in a second trial. In 1908 at the Old Bailey in London he was sentenced to twenty years' imprisonment in Parkhurst Prison on the Isle of Wight. For the charge: 'trying to obtain £12,000 from Solly Joel with menaces', it was an extraordinarily severe sentence.

That was what Winston Churchill thought. As Home Secretary, Churchill examined von Veltheim's case but, for 'political reasons', was unable to get his sentence remitted. *Reynolds Newspaper* fought a battle on his behalf for several years and got up a petition of 75 000 signatures in his favour. It was fruitless. Von Veltheim was finally released on licence in 1920 for his courageous conduct in defending a warder during a prison revolt. He had served twelve years.

He died in 1930 in a lonely hotel room in Hamburg, leaving the manuscript of his memoirs to be published 'for cultural reasons' by Ledig Rowohlt Verlag.

Alfred Beit settled his account with von Veltheim – £10,000 in cash – over lunch at the Savoy Hotel in December 1900, but not until von Veltheim's memoir was posthumously published and translated was it ever suspected that Beit could have played a vital role in the conspiracy to seize the President.

Unable to avert the armed struggle for the richest gold deposits in the world, Beit would, through Wernher Beit & Co, render Great Britain crucial financial assistance during the Boer War. It was consistent with his elitist philosophy. In fact, when he died in 1906 some of his obituaries suggested that Beit was the real soul of the diamond monopoly and Rhodes merely an instrument in his hands.

Cecil John Rhodes, that apostle of Anglo-Saxonism, convinced he was serving God's purpose, strove all his life to make the continent of Africa British from Cape to Cairo, and then to extend this dominion across all continents where there were English-speaking people. A martyr to his own messianic dream, he died in 1902 still trying to force the times to fit his vision.

President Paul Kruger was too old to die, as he would have wished, fighting at the head of the last commando. After the British forces occupied Pretoria, he left South African soil to plead the Boer cause in Europe where he died in exile.

Of the legal talent who had virtually fought two treason trials in the courtroom, and who would continue to fight for their country in the hostilities they had been unable to deflect:

Public Prosecutor Fritz Edward Traugott Krause was appointed Commandant of the Witwatersrand by President Kruger. He played an important part in saving the gold mines threatened with destruction by those Boer extremists who believed that the mining magnates were behind the war, and should not be allowed to retain the spoils intact.

Defending Counsel Hermanus Jacob Coster was sworn in as a lieutenant of the ex-Hollander volunteer corps on 11 October 1899, and was killed in action ten days later.

State Attorney Jan Christiaan Smuts fought as a general in the field, was a major architect of the peace that followed and twice Prime Minister of the Union of South Africa he helped to forge. After World War I he was a major force behind the establishment of the League of Nations, intended to weld together so great a power as to render all future war impossible – a philosophy still compatible with that of the messianic Rhodes. When it failed to avert World War II Smuts was appointed Field Marshall in the Allied Forces. He is remembered by the world as one of the great statesmen of his day.

In 1931, thirty-six years after Jameson's Raid, Sir Graham Bower, the British Colonial Secretary at the Cape at the time of the Raid, simultaneously wrote to Smuts and the Colonial Office placing on record the true events of the Imperial conspiracy. To Smuts, he entrusted a box of top-secret correspondence to be deposited with the trustees of the South African State Library, not to be opened until 1946 (fifty years after the event), thereby making the imperial factor's complicity one of history's best kept secrets.

The documents which became public domain in 1946 related the story of the intimate participants and posed the question: Did the Radical inquisitor, Sir William Harcourt Q.C., stop the British parliamentary enquiry only because such high-ranking people as the Prince of Wales and Queen Victoria were implicated?

The Secret Service files memos 395 and 401 of 1898 record how shortly after the von Veltheim trial State Attorney Smuts brought the police service directly under his personal control, summarily dismissed *Chief Detective Bob Ferguson* and refused him recourse. He believed him to be a clever detective who made curiously few arrests.

The trigger-happy *Harold Fairbrother Strange*, whose close-grained high-calibre bullet resounded through the JCI offices in 1898 never to quite die away – accidentaly or not – aborted what Kruger believed to be the second attempted coup.

Contrary to a Randlord's advice to Woolf Joel, documented in a Rand to London letterbook, folio 309, Strange was never sacked from Barnato Brothers'. He rose through the hierarchy to become General Manager in 1909, having been President of the Chamber of Mines in 1904-5. His collection of Africana books formed the basis of the Strange Library of South African history in the Johannesburg Public Library, where the Strange scrapbooks of the von Veltheim case are presently lodged.

The launching pad of Strange's meteoric rise is located somewhere between the parentheses of two company reports.

1. At the JCI meeting convened for shareholders on 13 October 1897 the Directors' Report stated: *It is with great and sincere regret that the Directors had to report to the shareholders the sad and untimely death of the Chairman and founder of the Company, Mr B.I. Barnato. Mr Woolf Joel, the nephew of Mr Barnato and a partner in the firm of Messrs Barnato Bros, has been elected Chairman of the Company and will devote most of his time and interest to the management of its affairs. Mr S.B. Joel will continue as the Chairman of the Company in Johannesburg.*

2. At a similar meeting in November 1898 the Directors' Report stated: *With feelings of regret, I refer to the loss of our late Chairman Mr Woolf Joel. Your Chairman, Mr S.B. Joel, has taken up residence in London for the present, where he devotes himself to the affairs and interests of the Company.*

For Alphonse Baruch, present on both occasions, Solly lacked Woolf's magic and he felt that there was something tenacious in his patience. The patience of the survivor.

All the characters are based on fact. The reconstruction of events is culled from the documents of men long dead: and yet they breathe life that tells us much of the motives and morality of their times.

At the request of *Alphonse Baruch's* family I have substituted his maternal name. Baruch did not become a Randlord; but in 1906 he was appointed Chairman of the Johannesburg Stock Exchange and on the 1st Sivan 5691 (1933) he laid the cornerstone of the Beth Hamedrash Hagodel (synagogue and large study house) in Saratoga Avenue, Johannesburg.

THE RESEARCH

The Von Veltheim File began as documentary research into the violent deaths of two Randlords – Barney Barnato, drowned at sea in highly suspect circumstances, and that of his nephew, Woolf Joel, gunned down by an assassin's bullet in Barnatos' Johannesburg offices nine months later.

When I filled in the standard form for material on the Joel murder case in the Africana section of the Johannesburg Public Library, I was brought two scrapbooks of news cuttings covering the incident and a volume hand-printed in German Gothic script, its pages hand-cut and hand-sewn, titled *Alias von Veltheim.*

I was interested to learn that Harold Strange – after whom the library is named – was the third member in the three-way shoot-out that claimed Joel's life, and these were his personal collection of news cuttings and the posthumously published memoir of Joel's slayer. More interesting were the two diametrically opposed perspectives of that unexplained bullet in his locked office that day.

I did not know it then, but I had begun a twenty-three-year exploration in a time capsule located somewhere between history and memory where my focus shifted to the von Veltheim case and the story that was never meant to be told.

When the Bower Papers became public domain in 1946, they exposed the fifty-year-old secret of the imperial factor's collusion in the mining magnates' first attempted coup. Their second one they succeeded in covering up until now.

They devised an elaborate web of disinformation to destroy incriminating evidence. Documents were removed from archives and spurious substitutes planted. In negotiating these camouflaged minefields and other archives still in private domain I noted whilst internal directors were scrupulously protected, it was fine to blow the whistle on the other chaps; and if accumulation of information was often by default it was, on that account, more piquant.

Item: In 1907 the official court record of von Veltheim's trial in the Johannesburg Circuit Court for the murder of Woolf Joel in

1898 was removed from the Transvaal archives by Barnatos' agent, Lourens Juta, Assistant Registrar, for the sum of £100 and never returned.

I quote a letter in private domain from Barnatos' Johannesburg office to Barnatos', London: *Re the state versus von Veltheim: Under separate registered letter I have forwarded you a certified copy of the full record of the above case as kept by the Master together with a translation thereof.*

Why the necessity for a translation when the proceedings took place in English? And if 'the full records as kept by the Master' had been available for this 'translation', why was it never returned? Moreover, in no Transvaal law library have I thus far been able to trace any court report for 1898.

Item: In three different decades von Veltheim was indicted for three different crimes in three different countries.

1. In Johannesburg's Circuit Court for the murder of Woolf Joel.
2. At the Old Bailey in London in 1907/8 for attempting to get money from Solly Joel with menaces.
3. In Ravensberg, Germany, circa 1921-2 for trying to raise money under false pretences to search for the Kruger millions (possibly his gold bars in the veld?).

In each case the court record is missing from the official archive. Professor Ellison Kahn of the University of the Witwatersrand's Law Department believes that this exceeds the law of averages.

It is ironic that the first leak should have come from Harold Strange. In so obsessively preserving his press cuttings, his Russian roulette finally exposed the whole affair. Whether perversely or unknowingly, he provided the outline for the jigsaw puzzle. The additional pieces were supplied long after his death in 1911 and not that long after von Veltheim's by the posthumous publication of the von Veltheim memoir in 1934.

Fahrten und Frauen – Alias von Veltheim, translated for me from German Gothic by Rosanna Frasson, checked surprisingly accurately with obscure detailed information confirmed by Carol Leigh who, together with other members of the Strange Library staff, must have confirmed hundreds of such facts during the twenty-three years it has taken me to research and write this book.

Given the paper chase of disappearing documents, and the blatantly slanted one compiled nine years after the event purporting to be a translation of the 1898 court proceedings, I chose to reconstruct my story from the daily newspaper reports. They had the advantage of being independent of hindsight and prior to the disinformation campaign to discredit von Veltheim.

James Winters actually assigned me a wire-mesh underground cell in the Johannesburg Public Library known as 'the cage' where, with a Heath Robinson invention of Dr Fourie – then of the Department of History at the Rand Afrikaans University – I copied and reconstructed the *Standard and Diggers' News* – in which Barnatos' owned shares – and for good measure, the accounts published in *The Star*, the *Johannesburg Times*, the *Rand Post* and the *Cape Times*, in which they did not.

These dovetailed with further research in the archives of the Johannesburg Consolidated Investment Company (supervised by Edgar Pryce of the remarkable memory) and those of Barlow Rand, the South African State Library, Cape Town, the Kimberley Library and De Beers', Kimberley and the State Archives, Pretoria.

In 1978 the National English Literary Museum and Documentation Centre, Grahamstown, gave me limited access to the Fitzpatrick Papers. Very limited. Despite prior permission from Percy Fitzpatrick's daughter, Cecily Niven, to read the von Veltheim files, these were removed two days before my arrival, and up to the time of publication have never been made available to me.

Thomas Pakenham confirmed first in his book, *The Boer War*, and later at a meeting in London that Alfred Beit was a far more powerful figure than history had thus far given him credit for – a conclusion we had each arrived at independently.

More pieces of the mosaic came from members of the academic and legal fraternity, namely: Professor G.N. van den Bergh of the University of Potchefstroom gave me access to his thesis on Kruger's Secret Police, the late Jos de Wahl to his histories of the Stellaland and Goshen Republics, Dr Jean van der Poel to her work on *The Jameson Raid* based on the Bower Papers. And there were the consultations with UNISA's Professors Jan Barnard and Marinus Wiechers, Pretoria's late F.A. (Floors) van Jaarsveld, and Johannesburg's Professor Ellison Kahn and Judge Cecil Margo.

Through Lufthansa, Vivienne Goodall arranged a German news

network radio and press appeal for information on von Veltheim. And through Joan and Gerry Shaper I made contact with the Caldecott family, permitting me to research the true circumstances of Elise Caldecott's death, then suppressed in the press.

Over the far too many years it has taken me to write this book my sounding boards have been my son Jonny, my granddaughter Georgia Black, and my colleagues and friends, the late Gordon Vorster, Carl Jeppe, Sue Cooper, Shirley Milne, Dee Stafford, B.P.J. Erasmus, the ever-professional and tireless Lee Marcus, and the publisher's readers, Cecily van Gend, Alta Oosthuizen and editor Jill Martin.

My husband, Gerald, contributed his recollections of Alphonse Baruch, Dr F.E.T. Krause and his overview of big business in relation to that part of our history we can still touch.

Most of all, he gave me space and encouraged my need to record it.

Text and historical research registered with Dramatic, Artistic and Literary Rights Organisation (Pty) Limited (DALRO)

Copyright © 1997 by Valerie Rosenberg

The cover illustration of von Veltheim is a detail from a photograph from the archives of *The Star*, Johannesburg, and is reprinted with their permission
First published in 1997 by Human & Rousseau (Pty) Ltd
State House, 3-9 Rose Street, Cape Town
Cover design and typography by Robert Meas
Set in 11 on 13pt Worchester
Printed and bound by National Book Printers,
Drukkery Street, Goodwood, Western Cape

ISBN 0 7981 3671 5

No part of this book may be reproduced or transmitted in any form or by any means, electronic or mechanical, or by photocopying, recording or microfilming, or stored in any retrieval system, without the written permission of the publisher